PAPHOS

AF096275

Nick Burnette

PAPHOS

HISTRIA
SciFi&Fantasy

Histria SciFi & Fantasy

Las Vegas ◊ London ◊ New York ◊ Palm Beach

Published in the United States of America by
Histria Books
7181 N. Hualapai Way, Ste. 130-86
Las Vegas, NV 89166 USA
HistriaBooks.com

Histria SciFi & Fantasy is an imprint of Histria Books encompassing outstanding, innovative works in the genres of science fiction and fantasy. Titles published under the imprints of Histria Books are distributed in the United States and Canada by Simon & Schuster and worldwide through Unified Book Distribution. We appreciate your support of copyright by purchasing an authorized edition of this book and for respecting intellectual property laws by not reproducing, scanning, or otherwise distributing any part of it by any means without permission. You are supporting authors and enabling Histria Books to continue publishing books for everyone.

All rights reserved. No part of this book may be reprinted or reproduced or utilized in any form or by any electronic, mechanical or other means, now known or hereafter invented, including photocopying and recording, or in any information storage or retrieval system, without the permission in writing from the Publisher. No part of this book may be used or reproduced in any manner for the purpose of training artificial intelligence technologies or systems.

This is a work of fiction. Names, characters, places, and incidents either are the product of the author's imagination or are used fictitiously, and any resemblance to actual persons, living or dead, business establishments, events, or locales is entirely coincidental.

First Edition

Library of Congress Control Number: 2025944107

ISBN 978-1-59211-683-6 (softbound)
ISBN 978-1-59211-703-1 (eBook)

Copyright © 2026 by Nick Burnette

I dedicate this book to Jules, who taught me about the girl in this book, Carolina.

A special mention to my wife, Taylor, for her ability to inspire me, and another special mention to Walt Boyes for reigniting the fire in me.

CHAPTER 1

Austin hated this. "Don't be nervous," he told her. This part of the voyage was his least favorite, but he'd keep that to himself.

His twelve-year-old daughter, Carolina, glared at the bulkhead next to him.

"It's not so bad, landing is really easy, almost fun," he said, trying to sound convincing. No getting around it, she was nervous and being difficult because of it. He hated guessing what to do about all of her moods. Eventually, Austin chose water, so he filled a cup from the spout and brought it to her, sloshing the tiniest bit. They both needed a break, and that wouldn't happen until touching down on the unexplored planet, Paphos. This was cabin fever, that's all.

"Here, you should drink this. Planet entry takes a while, might get thirsty."

Carolina ignored him. He exhaled, a long and deliberate move that kept him from getting upset. Her mother would know what to say. "We only have a minute before the ship starts. Don't princesses like water?"

"Ugh," Carolina rolled her eyes. Frustration swelled. Didn't she like princesses? She used to, he knew that much, when she was four. Twelve-year-olds didn't like princesses? Probably not, he guessed. He rubbed his head. This would only be for a few months; he could handle it. He had to handle it. At the end of the calendar summer, he and his research team would pack up and head home, and her mother would be well enough to take her back. And as soon as he thought it, he regretted it. He wanted this time with her; he wasn't as involved as he should be, and this was his chance to make up for it. He swallowed the water and stowed the cup.

"Everyone, finish strapping in, this one's choppy, lots of stratospheric winds," their pilot and team leader, Dmitry, said over the intercom. The cruiser about to shuttle them planet-side was much smaller than the Orbiter that brought them here, a deep space rig that waited in a geosynchronous pattern for their return. Carolina was getting visibly nervous now, not just moody. Personally, he hated re-entry too. But for her sake, he wouldn't let that show.

"Okay, we'd better get buckled now," he said, fussing with her belts and latches. Once she was locked to the chair, he carefully slipped the helmet on over her head and secured it, being certain not to yank her long chocolate hair. As soon as he was done with her, he strapped himself in and struggled with the first wave of nervousness.

"I'm thirsty now."

Austin gripped the armrests. "It's a little too late for that, kiddo."

"My throat is really dry," she pleaded.

"Wait until we land."

"I won't make it," she cried.

"I said no!"

He regretted it the moment it happened. He regretted it every time it happened. Did she do it on purpose? This wasn't how he had pictured bonding with his daughter.

Now the cabin was too quiet, as if his crewmates silently cursed him for bringing young Carolina along. When he stole a look from the corner of his eye, she had her helmet angled down. The face he pictured was likely worse than the one she actually wore, but that didn't make it any better. Okay, maybe he had enough time to get her water. *Again.*

With a grunt, he unlatched himself. Artificial gravity hadn't kicked off yet; he could do this. He filled another cup of water and grabbed a straw.

He slid her visor open, as taking the helmet off was a real pain. He thrust the straw in the cup and handed it to her.

She wouldn't touch it.

"What?"

"There's a floaty."

"Won't kill you. Drink it anyway."

"That's disgusting," she said as she crossed her arms.

Out of the six researchers here, one of them might be willing to babysit for the next three months. It would involve a bribe. *Don't even think it.*

Austin slapped her visor shut and plopped into his seat with more force than he wanted, trying not to fling buckles or yank belts as he secured himself for planet entry. The last latch snapped in place just in time as the rockets engaged. They lurched with a drop in speed, and the ship angled slowly over its end for a standard reverse entry, guided by sporadic dazzles of popping thrusters. With that, his stomach yelled *objection*! Upside down and around, he was in it now. This was just how you entered a planet's atmosphere.

He watched as the cup he forgot to stow floated in the air, the water dancing in a globule. Damn it… he ignored the glares from his team. Its contents fell upwards, and the cup rolled into the air.

There, natural gravity. The water and the cup felt it too. Something jarring about natural gravity when the faux-grav was all you knew for months. That first sensation didn't always register smoothly. He prayed it did this time, especially for his girl. It wasn't the worst, but he held his stomach just in case.

Breathing out was the trick as the cruiser started to shake. Shaking meant they were passing through layer after layer of atmosphere at speeds that sounded make-believe. Every time his hands jumped, he exhaled long and slow, tightening his abdomen. Somehow, that made turbulence feel better. He looked over and found Carolina had gone pale, but her face was determined. Brave kid.

The vessel shook fiercely until it finally passed through the atmosphere. As the air thinned, the turbulence eased, and they coasted pleasantly after that. Austin knew where they would set down; he helped pick it out from the planetary photos. Despite his earlier frustrations, which stemmed from his guilt over his daughter, his thoughts now began swimming with some excitement. This would be his fourth planet to jot down in the books. They would explore and document another untouched planet for the archives back home, adding new plantae to their databases. No teams had yet logged animalia, those vicious alien lifeforms, or even non-vicious ones, just plants. But the plantae were exciting enough. Exciting enough for the archives and explorers anyway. Life was not uncommon, but the Kingdom Animalia of Earth remained an anomaly.

The shaking had subsided, and he gazed eagerly out the porthole. The horizon was blue and purple, and he could easily see the outer lines of Paphos' rings. As they descended through cloud cover, rich green forests protected everything in all directions, changed only by mountains and brightly colored riverbeds that snaked like slain leviathans. Paphos was smaller than Earth, but it was similar in critical ways. Paphos was part of a single star system, and like Earth, it had neighboring planets in its system, most of them gas giants, all of them barren. Paphos' tilt yielded tropical weather almost everywhere, and the air was a breathable cocktail of oxygen and nitrogen thanks to that lush forest.

Of course, they all carried personal air devices, just in case.

Paphos wasn't the first of its kind, but it was still something to behold as the team took in the view. He hoped Carolina shared at least some of the excitement, as this was the particular moment he had been looking forward to with her. But when he gazed in her direction, her head was just down at her lap.

Dmitry was their pilot, a skilled pilot who could maneuver in any weather, but even a rookie could handle the *Landers* their company provided. Austin raised his hands out and then let them drop, feeling the effect. He couldn't say how natural gravity was any different, but it just was. He had argued with Helena over it, as the popular vote seemed unable to distinguish between faux-grav and the real thing. The real stuff hadn't jarred his equilibrium, thank God.

He looked out the porthole again to take in the view as planetary details became increasingly visible. Orange, purple, and green swirled in ponds dotting the forests below. He'd seen preliminary photos, but those weren't the same. They'd be nearing the quadrohuts soon, their base of operations, which had been sent and constructed ahead of time via drones and automated robots. He spotted them a minute later. The lights were on, which meant they had electricity. Always a miracle to find the quadrohuts fully functional. Usually, the robots get stuck on the littlest things.

The vessel docked easily with popping stability boosters before gently settling down on flat ground. Carolina released a sigh of anxiety and eagerly rocked back and forth. She unlatched her helmet, her face red and sweating.

"It's going to be a few minutes, kiddo, you need to put that back on," Austin said when she started clawing at her buckles. Before he knew it, she was out of her seat and trying to open the emergency-release door.

"Carolina!" She didn't hear him without her helmet. He flipped his visor open and yelled her name again, but she wasn't listening.

He unlatched himself as quickly as he could. He knew what the crew must be thinking; *yet another example of why family, friends, and kids shouldn't come on expeditions*. He set his helmet aside and fiddled with his latches.

"Calm down, we can't open that yet."

"I need out!" she cried, the telltale signs of panic as she tugged against the emergency release. Then the door hissed open and slid out, forming a ramp. Pollen-rich air filled their cabin, earthy and strong, warm, abrasive.

"Damn it!" Austin yelled above the protests of crew members.

Carolina was fleeing down the ramp. He wasn't supposed to breathe this air yet; none of them were. There were safety procedures first. Officially, the air on Paphos was *determined* to be breathable, but this was a hell of a way to find out for sure. She disappeared down the ramp, her hair trailing behind. He sent the last latch flying and chased after her, raising his hand to block the intense light. So much for protocol, so much for safety tests. He almost fell down the ramp when the blinding light met him outside the ship. He wasn't about to run, not with his balance still adjusting. This was going to get them both in trouble.

"Carolina!"

It was about as useful as the last time he said it.

"What happened?" called Dimitry. The other crew members groaned, not that Austin could hear them. But he felt them, felt their judgment. He rushed after Carolina, his equilibrium struggling. The protocol didn't exist anymore.

For a twelve-year-old, Carolina was fast. The green and pink bushes were taller than she was, and she was getting far enough away that he could barely hear the rustling of her body weaving through them. If he lost her on this planet, her mom would never forgive him. He bolted into a sprint and almost toppled over a gnarled root. Between the foliage and his equilibrium needing to settle, it was tough to run. Cursing, he took a breath and tried again, willing his feet to get steady. Fresh, yet-to-be-named giant foliage parted as he ripped through them, but the sudden intake of pollen-heavy air was a little much. Foreign pollen and gravity, those things took time.

How Carolina was managing it, he could only wonder. He realized then that this was her panic mode. His eyes were sharp and focused now, having adjusted to solar lighting. He sped around a U-shaped tree, his legs feeling like clay. The ground was steady enough in this part, even if his legs weren't. He'd never trampled on alien vegetation that he hadn't studied yet.

Kids.

He found Carolina doubled over, hands pulling at her throat, gasping and choking. Foreign pollen danced in the air around them, kicked up by her commotion.

"Hey, it's okay," he said, scooping her into his arms. She gripped him with a strength he didn't know she possessed. He hadn't held her like that since, well, not since she was three and had woken up from a thunderstorm.

"Breathe and relax, you're okay, calm, *calm*," he soothed. The anger, the frustration, it wasn't there anymore. When he saw her in need, everything else faded away.

Beams of sunlight pummeled through his sweat-matted hair; they needed shade sooner rather than later.

"Are you okay?" he finally asked.

She answered with a nod, standing upright with stiff shoulders. He'd been ready to throttle her a minute ago. Now, like an idiot, he realized he should have coached her on some first-time fears. He should have made it easier on her. Here she was, far from home, on an alien planet, with her dad, whom she barely knew, and she was just a kid. She was twelve, sure, but she was always going to be a kid to him. She took a few more deep breaths, each one slower than the last, as color returned to her face.

"I'm okay," she said.

He put his hand on her shoulder, which suddenly seemed cold. "We need to head back, then."

She replied with a nod. He scruffed her chocolate hair, but her mood didn't improve the entire hike back.

It took him a moment to figure out where 'back' was, and he usually had a strong sense of direction. The trail of matted plants helped.

When he returned, he found the rest of the crew had disembarked, and he wondered how long he had before Dmitry yelled at him about this. He looked at Carolina.

"Seems you've inspired them. They usually take hours to get off the ship." His smile didn't seem to do much for her.

"I'm sorry, I just…" Carolina began before losing the words. She didn't need to finish; he knew what she was trying to say. He didn't know what to say either, and they both lingered in the silence.

"Do you smell that?" he asked, and then an unnecessarily loud inhale through his nose. "Rich and fresh, completely un-modified pollen," he said with a champion smile. She raised an eyebrow.

"Not a single genetic modification or pollutant. You try."

"Pollen?"

"It's amazing, I swear. Nothing like it," he said, drawing in another over-sized nose-inhale. One of the crew members shook their head as they walked by.

Carolina closed her eyes and pulled in half the inhale through her nose before gagging and coughing in small fits.

"Nope, you gotta go deep, get the full effect. Open those nostrils," he said, showing off once more.

"Stop doing that."

"Not until you try it."

She closed her eyes and tried the most obnoxious nose-inhale she could. It gave him a chance to notice the dried tears on her face, cracked under a sudden smile. They both laughed then. He couldn't remember the last time they laughed together.

"Come on, we may as well check out our headquarters."

Ironically, after being cooped up for months, the first thing they all wanted to do was get inside. He stopped Carolina with a serious hand in the air. "No more running off. Deal?"

She nodded, brown eyes sincere. "Dad, it feels funny here."

Austin gave a tiny smile. "That's normal... because it's not Earth, and it's not the faux-grav we've endured for six weeks. But our bodies will feel normal in a day or two. We will adjust."

Dmitry and the rest of the crew—who were Dublin, Orlean, Helena, and Athen—then mustered outside the door of the quadrohuts, waiting for the pilot to disable the security door.

Drop stations like this were standard and made nice dwellings. All manned expeditions used them, and they were auto-assembled by the drones that preceded them. The drones were still there, mostly gardening and performing basic maintenance for the remainder. Athen and Dublin, with whom Austin worked with last summer, were the team's engineers and took care of the equipment. Analysis and documentation were handled by Orlean and Helena, the tedious but necessary side of this job. Every crew needed a specialized programmer, and Austin was the lucky one to get that role. Dmitry was in charge, serving as both the company representative, their medic, and pilot. They were a seven-person crew, counting his daughter.

Any family member was allowed to accompany a company assignment, provided their sponsor covered the expense. It was a seldom-used policy. Considering the time an expedition took, it wasn't practical to bring family, but it made a great face for the company to offer it nonetheless. Most crew members never took advantage of it, because deep down it was viewed to be in poor taste, not to mention the cost involved. But Austin wasn't as concerned with his career of late, and Carolina's mother helped with half the cost. And while Austin was second in command, he knew he'd never have his own ship. He didn't play the company game well enough, and more than that, he didn't care. When Mom got sick, bringing Carolina made the most sense.

Carolina stayed by his side as they huddled outside the *quadrohuts*, taking in the alien vegetation of their surroundings, waiting for Dmitry to open the doors. He seemed to be having a hard time with the security password.

"We're locked out…" he finally said. "I've never had that happen before."

"Tis' there a problem?" Dublin asked. He would gladly use a wrench to fix this.

Dmitry gave a frustrated grunt and tried the security code one more time. "It's the right code, I don't know why it won't open."

"So now what?" Helena asked.

"We all fly back," Orlean smirked.

"Bloody hell! Let me at it," Dublin cursed, digging into his tool bag. He pulled up something large.

"Stand down. We want the door to work."

"I only break a wee-bit!" Dublin's accent thickened when he got excited.

"Dublin…" Dmitry said, shaking his head. "One thing at a time."

"That's one," Orlean whispered with a little smile.

"I guess I'll have to reset the codes from the Orbiter; it will take me a minute. We're off to a great start so far." Dmitry removed a personal transmitter and began his interface with the Orbiter, entering override codes and finally resetting the door. The team waited, passing a few nervous smiles. This far from home, it didn't take much to make you feel doomed.

The technical issue has been resolved, and the door is finally open. They all went inside and dropped off their gear with rehearsed precision, except for Carolina. Dmitry planted himself at the *quadrohut's* internal computer and logged in for a diagnostic. Aside from the security issue moments ago, everything appeared in order.

Austin lay on his bunk, smelling the new foam of his mattress. He could close his eyes and get a little nap, somehow feeling zapped.

"What do we do now?" his little girl asked.

"We settle in and begin our documentations. A thorough study takes a few weeks, and then we fly back home."

"So… what do I do?"

And that was the question for days.

Despite her initial excitement, Carolina grew bored after the first hour, and this feeling persisted for several days.

Now, a week after landing and settling in, she was still confined to the *quadrohuts* and the area immediately surrounding. There were a few trinkets to pass the time, but they soon grew old. She was only able to bring a little bit of luggage with her. She had clothing, a digital camera, a marker pen, and her camera lens. Mom wanted pictures, so Carolina took pictures. Lots and lots of pictures. It kept her sane while waiting for permission to explore the forest, which she still wasn't allowed to do yet. She couldn't go beyond the perimeter, at least not until dying of boredom first. Seriously, how many tests were they conducting?

She couldn't get sick, or at least her dad said so. She had so many shots and vaccines put in her that it was supposedly impossible. There hadn't been an outbreak since the first expeditions began; inoculations were good now. *Genoscience*, it was called, grown-up things always had names like that. And she didn't have to worry about wild animals; her dad also said that. Things like that didn't exist, just plants and microscopic stuff. No one ever found anything more than that. Nothing with a face, she was told. Dad always went on and on about how these unexplored planets had amazing plants and bacteria. Who cared about that?

Austin cared, of course. He had dreamed of such things ever since he was a boy. As more planets were explored, they continued to prove that Earth was an anomaly. Each expedition discovered amazing, exotic, and wonderful forms of plant life, but intelligence was still the missing factor. With solace, he knew he would never make such a find; his life was one without destiny.

When the crew was finally and completely ready, they began to explore beyond the initial perimeter. A month went by, and all Austin ever saw of his little Carolina was the back of her bouncing head as she traipsed off into the bush. She ventured at her leisure. It was the best way to keep from hating each other, and they all had their personal radios in case Austin needed her for something or if she got lost. She refused to acknowledge him, and he stopped trying to keep an eye on her because she just tried harder to lose him. How close was he supposed to watch her? She was eleven, after all, and her mother hadn't left him any instructions. No, twelve. She was twelve. Pretty sure. In dealing with Carolina, he realized he knew much less about her than he thought he did. They used to have a lot of fun together… when she was entertained by puppets and spooky voices.

Carolina felt the same way, more or less. She found her afternoon adventures to be the only thing that caused the day to turn, and she had many more days to turn until she could get home. Mom was supposed to be better by then. And while the planet was a lush garden with a breathtaking skyline, and while the night sky shimmered like a cavern of gems, she was homesick. Completely and utterly homesick. Her digi-pad had long ago become a paperweight; she could only play so many puzzle games and read so many books. Without messaging and streaming, she hardly had any use for the device. She found herself drawing with the marker pen more than anything else; she mostly drew pictures of home. But she usually erased whatever she drew because it never looked right.

And so out of boredom, if not desperation, one afternoon she traveled far beyond the secondary perimeter. It wasn't the first time. But it was the first time she saw something.

Deep into the hillside, behind a growth of brush and bramble, she found an obsidian, perfectly flat wall that stretched the length of a building.

CHAPTER 2

Carolina blinked. Not jungle, not earth, not rock.

This was definitely a wall.

If there was a building too, then it was buried in the hillside. Or the hillside was swallowing it.

Had she found an abandoned bunker or something? It looked old. Something other than bushes and trees was a welcome addition, but then her face rightfully changed. If they were the first ones on this planet, and no one had been here before, which she was certain they said, then who built this?

Carolina blinked again, trying to remember what the grownups had talked about. She was certain they said something like that. She went to scratch her head, but her hand froze when she saw something move, small and quick. She jumped, frightened by the suddenness of it. Waiting in stillness, she stared ahead, arms clutched to her chest. After a minute, she had to doubt whether she had really seen something move or not. It was probably a vine or a spindly bush guided by the often rambunctious wind.

She took a moment and tried to gather her composure, something her mom had taught her. She was always quick to panic, and her mom spent a lot of time getting her to slow down and just breathe. She was just a kid, and she knew there must be a logical reason for what she found. Obviously, someone had been here before, or the wall wouldn't be there. She would just have to ask her dad, assuming she wasn't in trouble for going past the second perimeter.

When her fear subsided, she followed the long stretch of black edge, which was hard and cold enough to be steel, to see where it went. The hillside lay over it like a blanket, and there wasn't a window or door. She climbed around gnarled tendrils of foliage, thicker than her, and they reminded her of Earth's ancient ruins. She didn't understand how no one had seen this before landing; she thought they had different satellites that could read building materials and other things. She would ask her dad about it, and he would know. He always knew. He was the scientist.

The longer she walked along the wall, the more it felt like trespassing, as if she were being watched. She continued down the ominous wall another thirty meters, wondering when it ended. It would be easy to miss this, since the hill went over it and didn't stop, like any other tiny mountain. Finally, the wall disappeared into the hill, and it didn't resurface. She backtracked and stopped to analyze her reflection in the smooth, reflective black, surprised at the state of her messy hair. This was much farther beyond the second perimeter than she was allowed. "Time to head back, before I get in even more trouble."

The hike back, a few kilometers long, offered no relief from the feeling of being watched. She walked with a jitter that would become an outright sprint should anything else move. She was thoroughly spooked; she had to admit.

Finally, the forest was recognizable, and another minute later, she approached the quadrohuts. Upon entering, she found the crew inside, all looking ill as they listened to Dmitry speak. Muster, they called it. Apparently, Dmitry wasn't happy with their progress; they were running out of time to make good on key initiatives that the company had commissioned them for. So many big words, being an adult didn't seem very fun. Carolina didn't understand why they couldn't just stay until the job was done, although she didn't want to be here forever. Daddy mentioned something about a schedule, something about a launch window, gravity, alignment… he was never good at explaining simple questions.

Carolina paced; they would want to hear this immediately, but Daddy glared, so she waited. Dmitry was long-winded tonight. She sat down and, out of boredom, began to draw little circles and shapes on the wall next to her. Then, realizing what she was doing, she quickly put her marker pen away. She didn't need to be in trouble for graffiti, too. All she could think about was what she had found, and when she'd go back. It wouldn't be tonight; it was already getting dark. But she'd definitely go back tomorrow with her photolense and take some pictures this time. She wondered if she might not tell them about the wall… At least not yet?

It was hers, but telling them would make it theirs.

Dmitry's voice droned on. It was exciting, knowing something that the others didn't know, wondering what else was up there. When the meeting was over, Dublin and Athen sat in the tiny room called a *mess hall* and ate, while dad and the others took their meals to their dorms. Carolina followed him, first grabbing a package of ham slices and a juice. They ate in silence on the bottom bunk bed.

She had a feeling he was in a bad mood. He had a faraway gaze that broke when he finally said something.

"Did you get enough to eat?" asked Austin.

"Yeah," she said. He smiled. Carolina had forgotten that she had been giving him the silent treatment for two days now, although he hadn't noticed.

"What have you been up to? Any new pictures?"

"No, I forgot to bring my camera today," she replied, gnawing on her tongue. Should she tell him about it?

"We get to leave soon," he added with a scoot to get closer. He smelled like lab equipment, like that sterile chemical smell, and his eyes were sunken under dark circles. He hadn't been sleeping, staying up late to work. He had to redo some experiment because of organic contamination or something.

She heard about it yesterday, and out of pity, she considered ending the silent treatment then. She managed to stay firm, though, at least until today, when she forgot.

"That's great, I can't wait to see my mom. Uhm… want to guess what I found today?"

"An elephant."

"No, duh."

"A drive-thru? I could go for some burgers. I'm sick of space meals."

"Daa-aaaad…"

"Okay, what did you find?"

"I found a wall! I think…"

"Oooh, that's neat," he said, stifling a yawn. Austin closed his eyes and leaned his head back.

"Yeah," she said, her excitement gone. Perhaps it wasn't actually important. "It's just, you said no one was here before us."

"Yep, that's true, it's just us, we are the first."

"Then who made the wall?"

Austin blinked his eyes open. "Well, no one, it's just a rock formation or something." Another yawn.

"It's steel, or another metal. It's just past the second perimeter…"

Now his eyes were open. She bit her lip shut.

"You went past the second perimeter?"

"…yes, and I found a wall!" Didn't finding a wall excuse breaking the perimeter rule? The silent treatment might be back on.

Austin stared quietly for a few moments. He was mad, but the little father skills he possessed said this was important to Carolina. "It can't be a wall, it's a natural formation, I've seen some strange things on other planets."

"I'm not stupid! Let me just show you tomorrow?"

"I can't go running around in the bush, honey. I'm way behind on my projects." He gave her a nudge, trying to garner some understanding from her. "And besides, you're grounded to the first perimeter from now on." He didn't like upsetting her, but she needed to learn.

She squealed in frustration. The silent treatment was definitely back on! Austin stared at the back of her head. She was going to be angry until he said something; she was stubborn enough to go for days.

"Listen…" he said, not sure what to say. He chose to say nothing and climbed up to his own bunk. It wasn't lights out, but it was late enough, and they were all tired enough.

When morning came, she was out of bed and dressed faster than anyone else. She bounded down the hallway and suddenly stopped because Dmitry blocked her way.

She didn't like him. He wasn't mean, but he wasn't nice either. He was always serious, and he was even more so lately. She guessed he was that way because he was the boss, and bosses were mean.

"Good morning," he said, nursing the rim of his coffee.

Carolina didn't reply.

"You're awake early." It felt like a question. Dmitry smiled, holding his mug, still blocking the hallway.

"Excuse me," she said, forcing past him and down the corridor past the equipment lockers. She took a moment to double-check the latches on her boots and verify the contents of her water pouch. She felt ready, standing in the vestibule, patiently waiting for the doors to open outside. She turned her gaze and saw him staring as the hydraulics shushed and a breeze swelled.

He didn't need to know what she was up to.

Early light meant the forest would be shadowy. With a determined look she began her hike. The journey took less time than yesterday; she gauged it to be about two kilometers. There were no trails, but the terrain had easy-to-remember markers: a small river, some unique finger-branched trees, and a large mossy rock. Unfortunately, it was mostly uphill, and definitely beyond her groundation.

She approached her wall and slowed her walk. "Hello again."

She wished it could talk back to her; she'd been waiting all night to see it again. Somehow it looked different today, perhaps because of the lingering shadows. She pulled out her photolense and took a picture. She took several pictures, in fact, before deciding whether there had to be a door or a window to this wall. Nothing yet, though there were occasional grooves.

Striking out and bored with her photos, she picked up a stick and pretended to be a wizard protecting her castle. Lunchtime came and went when she heard her name on a very crackly radio. Dad, calling for her. She was starving, hadn't eaten breakfast out of excitement, and she had just now realized it. Carolina sped back to camp, dragging her photolens with her. Dad waited at the door to the quadrohuts.

"Where were you?"

She wouldn't answer.

"I asked you a question."

"I went to the wall again."

His head tilted in disbelief. "But I told you to stay in the perimeter."

She wielded her photolense. "Don't you want to see it? I'm not lying!"

Austin snatched the photolens from her. "Nothing changes the fact that you did not listen to me, miss, and for the last time…"

He gazed at the picture on the screen. After a moment he looked at her again. "You altered this."

"Daaaad."

"Did you alter this?" he demanded.

"Just let me show you!"

Dmitry walked by. "Show what?"

Austin went stiff. "Just some phony picture," he said.

"Phony?!" she cried.

Dmitry took the photolens and looked at the photo. "Take me there."

"What about our workload?" Austin asked.

"It can wait," Dmitry added.

"Here," Austin said, handing Carolina the rest of his oat and peanut butter bar.

This time, the walk took forever, this time there was pressure. Maybe it was a natural rock formation. Maybe she made it all up. No, she had photos. She thought of mom's breathing exercises and tried to practice them. It wasn't working.

Her dad offered several excuses about why this was a waste of time. Maybe he was afraid of being embarrassed.

She ate her snack on the way and finished the water pouch, wishing there was more to drink. Her dad noticed and handed her his hydropouch, which was nice, but didn't stop her from being mad at him. Why was the walk so hard this time? Her dad noticed that too, and hoisted her up on his shoulders. That made her giggle; she was definitely too big for that. Which made her miss the days she used to do this all the time. Maybe she wouldn't give him the silent treatment after all.

"Where did you say this was?" Dmitry asked. He stopped to rest, a look of doubt prevalent.

"Uhm..." she looked around. "Maybe we passed it."

Austin exhaled. "There's nothing to look into..."

Now she wanted down off his shoulders. He sighed and lowered her. The three of them continued around the corner of a hill, stepping carefully around an orange root that crumbled under her weight. When they cleared the bend, they saw that Carolina was right. There was a wall, just like she said.

"*Now* do you believe me?"

"I..." paused Dmitry. "...I believe you."

Austin stood still.

Dmitry approached the wall, but he said nothing. Austin followed, fixated.

"Is this a good thing, daddy?" She didn't understand why they seemed upset. Dad looked at her, then again at the wall.

"Well, I found it first, so I get to name it," she said, crossing her arms. She watched Dmitry reach forward and touch it, as if needing to prove it was really there.

"Dmitry…?" Austin asked.

"Yes?"

"We need to call the others."

Dmitry nodded and activated his radio, sending a muster order through the team's headsets.

Dad looked down at her and smiled, but she had learned to recognize mom's troubled smile. Dad's smile looked exactly the same.

CHAPTER 3

They arrived together, the five other team members all interrupted from their tasks, jabbering and wondering what was so important. They all carried locators, and it wasn't difficult to hone in on any one of their locations.

A collective gasp followed by silence. Then the questions came.

"Ah grand… what is this?" Dublin asked.

"Is this…real?" from Athen. Dublin scoffed.

"It's real," Orlean answered. Two seconds of silence followed.

"Made by us?" from Helena. The others looked at her. Everyone knew what she meant by 'us.'

"Nay. Bloody can't be."

"It's definitely not," Orlean said, reading the screen on his prosthetic arm. He carried a lab with him at all times. It required good handwashing, as many of the sensors were his fingertips.

More silence followed. Dublin walked up to the wall and gave it a hearty tap with his knuckles.

Carolina felt herself shrinking. They were too serious; it was all making her upset. She turned away and took those deep breaths, staring into the forest, trying to calm down the way she was taught. It at least kept the tears from swelling.

Austin noticed, and he squared his shoulders.

"This is a good thing, honey, it's a good thing. You did a real good job," he said. It took a few moments for her breathing to steady, but when she looked up at him, she smiled.

Austin addressed the team. "We had better get back and radio this in. Hand it off to a team, one properly equipped to study this."

"No."

Eyes fell on Dmitry. "Not until we know what we are reporting."

"Aye, we don' need to get the corpo in a tizzy by jumping the gun. We'd be the laughing crew for all time, sure and begorra."

Dmitry and Dublin seemed to agree, though Austin couldn't believe his ears.

Dmitry addressed the others. "Listen, this may be exactly what we think it is. And it also may be something entirely different."

"Like what?" Austin asked. They needed to report this immediately.

Dmitry was unfazed. "Like a government project. Or a corporate experiment. This planet has been in the queue for a while, at least a year before our arrival. Either way, if we say we found proof of intelligent life and it washes out, we all get fired."

He forgot to add *'or we keep it to ourselves and get filthy rich'*. The pit in Austin's stomach grew.

"But… we are under contract." That was Orlean, in the loudest way he would dare to protest. Under contract, any discoveries of value made during a financed expedition became the property of the sponsoring company.

"Aye, Orlean," Dublin cut him off. "But jus' think for a moment about what Dmitry is sayin'."

Austin gave a look to his daughter before speaking. He could sense where this was going, and someone had to be the voice of reason. "Guys, we *are* under contract. An agreement is in place, we must report the find."

Dmitry pursed his lips. "Absolutely. *After* we know what it is."

"But the protocol states--" Austin began.

"*--and* my orders are that we research it first. Then, once we've made sure this isn't a classified outpost, we can report what we know," Dmitry smiled.

"Won't take long to confirm. The material is unlike anything we would use," Orlean whistled. The digital displays on his prosthetic struggled to compare chart after chart of known and unknown compositions.

Athen didn't know where she would side. She was Dublin's assistant engineer, so it wasn't a stretch to see her leaning towards him.

"Is that understood?" Dmitry asked. He addressed the team, but his gaze remained fixed on Austin.

"Tis."

"Sure, we can report it after we study it a bit," Orlean chimed in. Athen nodded, as did Helena.

"Austin?"

What else could he say? "I got it."

He didn't have an issue taking orders, never did. And he didn't need to make a fuss; everyone was just too excited to think straight. When Dmitry and the crew came to their senses, they would follow protocol. He had nothing to worry about.

"Good. Engineers—find me a door," Dmitry ordered.

"Aye aye!"

"Researchers, get your files ready. This is a worksite now. No place for kids."

At least Austin could agree on that. "Honey, head on back to the huts. I'll see you in a few hours."

"But daa-aad, by myself?"

"You didn't have a problem going by yourself before; you won't have a problem now."

Carolina huffed, crossing her arms as she walked back to the quadrohuts. This wasn't fair. She was the one who found the place, not them, and now they were kicking her out! She never should have told him!

She glowered all the way until the quadrohut door zipped. The details of her journey were lost in her tangent, but when she walked inside, she saw a blinking green light and smiled. *Mom!*

It was the weekly drop from the company, which also carried messages from home. She logged into the part she had access to and found her drop, a video message from her mom. Carolina watched eagerly as the video played. Her mother's face sent pangs of homesickness, and she had to watch it twice. Mom looked better, not as sick. She transferred it to her dataPad, next to the other files, full of videos and pictures from home. It made her sad sometimes, because while she looked forward to these video packages, they also made her realize how badly she needed to go home.

She really missed her mom, but they wouldn't be here for much longer. Another week or two. But then she wondered, what if they decided to stay now? No, they couldn't, Daddy explained the whole launch window thingy. Finding the wall didn't mean they'd stay longer; they weren't allowed to.

"It's *my* stupid wall anyways!" Carolina huffed. She decided then and there that she would go back; she could wait in the bushes or something. She had a legal right to it since she found it. Carolina grabbed a pouch of fruit slices and took her locator bracelet off. She could at least *appear* to be at the huts. She wouldn't want her dad checking on her and not be where she was supposed to be.

This time, Carolina worked up a sweat. She was hiking as fast as she could, and parts of her were beginning to hurt. She stopped at a large mossy rock and held her side, waiting for the pain to go away. For a slight moment, she considered against this, but the thought of them finding something boiled her blood. Ten minutes later, she heard Dublin's booming voice.

She took refuge behind a thick, sparse growth of heavy bush, slowly and quietly, if she could keep the leaves from rustling. As long as they kept talking, they probably wouldn't hear as she found the best hiding spot.

Crouching behind a pineapple-shaped plant, Carolina sneaked over to a tree with shedding bark. The pale green trunk was wide enough for her to peek around without being seen. This was a good hiding spot. Peering through a web of branches, she found a window with the outline of her daddy and his boss. Dmitry was talking, her dad was just listening with a patient look on his face. She poked closer to hear what Dmitry was saying.

"…performance on the last mission was unsatisfactory. My report decides your future with this company."

"I understand," her dad said.

"Besides, you have your daughter to think about."

Dad's face twisted.

"What do you mean by that?"

Please don't get in trouble again dad, please just do what he says, Carolina wished.

Dmitry smiled. "You need employment to support a family, don't you?"

Dublin hollered, accent so thick she barely understood what he was saying, but she gathered that he still couldn't find the door. Dmitry walked away, but Dad stood there for a while.

Carolina crouched to her left to peek over at Helena and Orlean. Moments later, Daddy joined them, or from what Carolina saw, pretended to join them. He simply stood next to them, occasionally taking a deep breath, every now and then glancing over at Dmitry. She hoped he wasn't in trouble; she didn't like it when her dad was in trouble.

Half an hour passed, and her dad still wasn't focused on work. She could always tell when something bothered him. Orlean analyzed the same plot of wall now as earlier. Dublin and Athen were just banging with their wrenches, hoping. Dmitry stood with his arms folded, watching everything like a hawk. That was how she thought of him; like a hawk, always watching the mice.

Carolina blinked, staring at a jellyfish with eyes, perched in front of her. So close she could kick it.

She fell back, and it came after her on spider legs. She crashed into a bush, clamoring to her feet, terrified and shrieking. *Where did it go?! She couldn't see it anywhere!*

Carolina's chest pounded, but the jellyfish with eyes had vanished.

Something fell on her shoulder.

"AAAHHH!" Her shriek split the forest. Austin flew through the bushes after her, the others chased behind him. Then a shortened blood-curdling scream.

"Carolina!"

Austin ripped through the bushes, plowing through them and snapping branches out of his way. He found her with her hands at her side, unmoving and wearing a blank expression.

"What are you doing here? What's the matter?"

"Tha' did give me a heart attack! Thought she was at the quads!"

Austin put his hand on her shoulder. "Hey, honey, you okay?"

She wouldn't move. Austin shook her by the shoulders.

"What?" Carolina said, blinking into the now.

"Why were you screaming?"

"Was I?"

"Did you see something?" Dmitry asked, pulling up.

Carolina looked around.

"Hey… you okay?"

"I am sorry. I am better now. I forgot to tell you, I found the door," Carolina said.

CHAPTER 4

Aust shook his head. "There is no door, honey. Why were you screaming?"

"Follow me..." she said, following her own outstretched arm. Whatever had happened, she now appeared calm. He plopped a hand to his forehead before following her. Kids were so hard to understand sometimes. And now a door?

Carolina regarded the faces staring at her. "Sorry for screaming. I thought there was a bug on me. I was wrong. The door is right over here."

"G'wan, you be the one to find it, and I'll make you chief engineer!" Dublin laughed. If the head engineer couldn't find the door but a twelve-year-old could, he might as well.

Austin put a fatherly hand on her shoulder, unsure of what to say, trying not to doubt her. "It may not be a door, kid, don't get your hopes up."

Carolina stopped in front of an inconspicuous piece of the wall, looking as unremarkable as the rest. There was a collective holding of breath until nothing happened. After a minute, Austin shrugged, and the others resumed conversation.

Except Dmitry, who continued watching this one mouse. It may have been a minute later when Carolina closed her eyes. A steady beam of light shot straight out from the ground. The blue light spread into thousands of beams, small and pinpoint, like a thin sheet that studied her from head to toe.

"Watch out!" Austin ran to her, but the blue light slipped away.

"It's okay, Daddy, I *wanted* it to do that."

"To do... what?"

As if to answer him, the wall rumbled. Austin grabbed her and retreated. All eyes watched as a section of the wall regressed inward and slid to one side. Dmitry's icy gaze fell on Carolina.

"Whoa..." Orlean said, looking into the hallway that appeared. "How did she do that?"

Dmitry lowered his chin. "Report."

Orlean raised his sensor-laden fingertips and started gathering his readings. The data on his forearm danced with charts and graphs. "I'm getting strange readings, strange energy patterns, unknown compounds."

Helena was Orlean's backup, reading the same graphs on her separate device. "But look at those levels, they're off the charts. This has to be a power reactor for these numbers."

Austin put his little girl down, wondering how she did that. He rested a hand on her shoulder and found heat coming through her jacket. He touched her forehead, then her glowing red cheeks. "Are you feeling okay?"

She was feverish, but that was not possible, not with the kind of vaccine cocktails they all had. She shouldn't even come close to getting sick. Maybe it was time for a booster shot. "Let's get some water in you. I think you might be dehydrated."

"I am fine." Carolina brushed his hand away and stepped towards the entrance that appeared.

Behind the entry, soft lights flickered. A stream of stale, aged air escaped.

"Jus' let us take this one, miss, ye can't get all the fun."

"We have to be good for something around here. Whoa, you're really burning up." It was Athen who noticed this time. "Austin?"

"She's just dehydrated," he said, offering his water. Carolina ignored it.

"Nothing radioactive, oxygen remains breathable, we can advance," Orlean said with a look towards Dmitry.

"We can?"

Dmitry gave Helena a smug little grin. "Helena, if you aren't comfortable with this, I could use help standing watch at the quadrohuts."

"N-no, I'm right behind you."

"Talk to me," Dmitry ordered to no one in particular.

Carolina moved as if to speak, but she stayed quiet. The lights were now fully powered, revealing a massive tunnel that stretched at least forty meters into the earth before disappearing downward. It was no mining cave; the floor and walls were not made of dirt and rock. As a group, they remained outside, staring.

"Suppose we do now?"

They looked at each other, waiting for Dmitry to give the command.

"We go in."

The entryway angled down almost too steeply to travel on foot. Steady warm air flowed past them, evaporating up into the forest as if freed from confinement. Austin took the first step in, doing so carefully. The floor was incredibly smooth, to the point of being slippery. The boots they all wore were made for more natural surfaces and gave little friction.

"Not much grip on this," Austin warned.

"I can see that," Athen agreed, her hands out for balance. "We should get ropes."

"Carolina, stay at the entry." Austin glanced up to make sure his daughter listened when he heard a yelp. Athen had fallen and threatened to slide downhill.

"Athen!"

She flailed to stop herself, grabbing Orlean's outstretched hand, but the momentum yanked him down too. Dublin leaned over and gripped Orlean by the scruff of his shirt, his thick forearm bulging. "Where ye' think you're goin?"

"Do you have them Dublin?"

"Aye, but I could use a little help," Dublin said softly and controlled, his arm unwavering. Austin leaned against the slope, rooting himself to help steady Orlean on the other side of him.

"Athen, take your gloves off, and your boots," Dmitry ordered. "Your skin will have more friction on that smooth floor."

Athen, dangling from holding onto Orlean, tugged a glove off with her teeth. How Dmitry thought she was going to get her boots off was another thing. But her hand carried enough friction to hold herself from sliding. She spat the glove free and managed to get back to her hands and knees, lending a thank-you smile to Orlean for catching her. Or at least for falling with her when trying.

"Anytime," Orlean smiled.

A sharp pop of electricity stole their attention.

"What was that?" Dmitry asked.

"I don't know, but... where's my glove?" A snaking line of white ash hovered where the slope leveled a meter below them. Athen's glove was gone. "Where's my glove?"

Everyone studied the area where the popping and snapping white ash was located.

"Could've been you, love," Dublin said, suddenly reinforcing his grip and his stance.

"Okay… everyone get back to the top, carefully," Dmitry ordered.

"That's why we need to get another team here, guys," Austin urged. Somehow, his words still fell flat.

"Whoa whoa whoa… I see it now," Orlean cooed, scanning with his prosthetic hand. "There's an intense field of energy down there. A security measure, I'm assuming. But we almost lost Athen just now. That field could annihilate us as easily as that glove."

"Get me up!"

"Just relax, you can walk back up with the friction of your palms, just go slow and steady," Austin said to calm her. It wasn't that steep, but certain death added some fear.

"Get me up! Now!" she cried again. Athen clung to the slope like a cat.

"Just don't move, we're coming," Austin tried calming her again.

Carolina stirred at the top of the walkway, dying to come down.

"Stay up there!" Austin ordered. No acknowledgement, just a determined face.

"Okay… okay… just hurry…" Athen quivered, gaining some control of herself.

Orlean had to climb out first, and his foot slipped an inch, causing a wave of gasps.

"Dublin?"

"Jus' holding on from here, don't want to go sliding myself," Dublin added, calm but tense. The singed air served as quite a warning.

Orlean had climbed up, but Dublin was deadlocked, keeping Athen from sliding. Austin removed his boots, socks, and gloves. On all fours, he steadily went backwards down towards Athen.

"Can I come down now, daddy?" Carolina asked.

"Absolutely not." *What has gotten into her?*

Austin moved slowly to ensure he didn't go sliding down into the invisible field. Judging from the floating ash, his vaporization would be painless. He slowly went past Dublin and took hold of Athen's hand. The floor was warm.

"I've got you."

Athen smiled sheepishly. "I know I won't slip, I'm just not ready to move yet. It was just those boots, right?"

Austin stood with caution and then slowly helped Athen to stand. She remained terrified, not that he blamed her. When her glove vanished, it seemed everyone could taste their sudden mortality. Austin kept his fear from getting to him this time.

Helping her to the top was easier than coming down, but by the time Athen could stand without worry, she crumpled to the floor in a sweaty mess. Carolina stood over her, expressionless. Kids handled stress in the oddest of ways. Dublin came back easily now that he wasn't anyone's anchor. Soon they gaggled at the top, but this time with some apprehension.

"It's no wonder I didn't see it at first. My scanners can barely process the energy output of the facility. I'm just now honing in on this room. I'm sorry," Orlean apologized. Helena's tablet copied everything Orlean's prosthetic arm picked up; the two analyzed the same readings separately.

"If it's trapped, then they didn't want visitors," Austin reminded everyone. He hoped this would be enough to drive some sense home; it was past time to go back and report this. They were barely a few meters in; who knew what other security traps were down there? Hopefully, everyone saw that now.

Carolina stepped away for a moment and came back, her hands full of dirt. She flung the dirt and watched as the field zapped and obliterated it. For the briefest moment, they saw the energy beams and discovered a gap leading towards what was basically a panel. The key panel disappeared when the commotion of dirt being annihilated finally settled, explaining why they didn't see it until now. Austin considered it a key panel, but nothing certified that it was. It didn't have the box exterior, buttons, and cables that he was familiar with, but it was definitely a panel for something. That observation aside, how did Carolina know to do that? Maybe she had explored more than she let on. He was going to have a long talk with her about this.

"Guys, enough is enough. We need to report this," Austin pleaded as the group put their boots and gloves back on. Helena likely agreed with him; she looked downright green, but Austin didn't see anyone else nodding. "Guys?"

"Our safety is of the utmost importance, naturally, but I'm confident Orlean can help us find a way in," Dmitry said. Austin could have punched him. Had everyone lost their senses? Athen almost died just now, and still, they only saw treasure. If nearly losing Athen wasn't enough to convince them, what would it take?

CHAPTER 5

The sun was setting on this planet, and it would soon be too dark to see in the forest. The team was still perched in the entryway as they had for over an hour, ever since Athen almost slid to her atomized death. They argued over the safest way to access the key panel. Carolina's dirt cloud showed them a great deal, but they were far more cautious than before.

"Carolina, it's getting late. Let me take you back to the huts."

"No, daddy, I'm fine," she answered, though her eyes were drooping and she wavered on her feet. Her cheeks were still flushed.

"Just do the dirt thing again," Athen groaned, throwing her hands in the air. Orlean and Helena chuckled together. Engineers had no patience. But a researcher could analyze this data until next week.

"If you insist," Orlean gave in. "I don't know how capable our instruments will be in there; there's just so much bombardment on these sensors. I have a feeling our radios will be even worse in there."

"One more reason to go back and call it in, guys."

"We stick together for safety. Staying in groups," Dmitry crossed his arms.

Austin groaned. An empty mess hall waited for them back at the huts, and it would soon be time to hit the rack. "I'm heading back to the quadrohuts, it's dinnertime, no one's eaten, Carolina has had a long day."

"Me too!" Helena chimed.

"Save me a pint. We be stayin' awhile, catch up later," Dublin added, studying the entry like a chess grandmaster.

"I will head back with you," Dmitry said. "When I get back, we go on shift rotations. Everyone sleeps tonight, but we stagger it."

"I'd like to stay." It was Carolina.

Austin looked at her for a moment before wrapping his arm around her. "Sorry, kid, you're coming with me."

"Please?"

"Not a chance."

She turned away from him.

The walk back was already dark, and Austin could barely see his own feet. Their suits came with a utility non-directional light, a glowing lime green, and without it, they would never find their way home. He held Carolina's hand the whole time; it was still overly warm. He kept looking up at the speckled night sky. Paphos' heavens were full of marbles, diamonds, and its glowing rings. He would think of this view long after leaving, which was only a few weeks away. But somehow that glow wouldn't reach the ground, as if the inescapable forest around them prevented it. Carolina let go of his hand and walked in front, and Dmitry took the opportunity to walk shoulder to shoulder.

"We made an incredible find today, I'm sure you agree…"

"Incredible is an understatement." Austin also wanted to say, *'but now we need to report it'*.

Dmitry had a way of controlling a conversation and getting what he wanted, which were some of the reasons he was the boss—always in control. That got him thinking; perhaps Dmitry wasn't just accompanying him back to the huts, maybe this was more like an escort. He was babysitting. Austin gritted his teeth in silence. That was it. He was there to make certain Austin didn't contact the company on his own. He just realized it.

"Everyone else thinks so. I've never seen a crew work through dinner without threatening to file a grievance. Probably the only meal Dublin's ever missed?"

"Yes, probably," Austin replied, choosing his words and his reactions. Carolina kept her pace as they followed close behind.

"You know, we never got to finish our conversation from before. I was hoping we could come to an agreement on what's best here."

"And what's best?"

Dmitry smiled. "I've always thought you were a real smart guy, Austin, someone who saw the gray between the black and the white."

He didn't have a reply to that.

"Dublin sees what I was trying to explain earlier. He's even going to use his cutter on our boots, something about scouring them for added grip on those smooth surfaces, so no one slips again. See, he's looking for solutions, and the rest of the team is too," Dmitry added.

Peer pressure. Austin nodded. "Yeah, but there's no getting around it; violating the contract will only muddle how great a discovery this is. We'd face criminal penalties, not to mention the fact that we signed away any claims of discovery."

"Exactly. That's why the whole team is counting on you to make sure that if we do bring something back, it's ours. We are the ones on this expedition, risking our lives, giving up precious years. We earned it; they didn't. The company only cares about profit, but we have the opportunity to change people's lives. And besides, if anyone should profit from this, it should be the crew that traveled across the galaxy to find it."

Austin bit his tongue. No matter what he said, it wouldn't be good.

"Naturally, we are going to report the find, but we just want to know what's down there first. We can't do that without you." Dmitry's voice had lowered some by the end.

"It's fine. I may not agree, but I wouldn't cross the others. It's not like I'm going to contact headquarters by myself."

"I know you won't. You have too much to lose."

The way Dmitry said that, and the way he was staring at the back of Carolina's head, brought an icy chill that stopped him mid-walk.

"Exactly what do you mean by that?"

Dmitry planted a finger against Austin's forehead. *You'd better get that off my head.*

"You won't say a single word. I'll make absolutely certain of it."

A hundred thoughts ran through Austin's mind, all of them ending badly. He slapped the finger away and barely withheld the punch that wanted to follow.

Carolina was looking at them.

This close to Dmitry, and with this sudden confrontation, Austin calculated all variations of punching him square in the jaw. Dmitry was bigger than him; a fight may not go well. Not to mention they were a long way from home, and with everyone impregnated by greed over this discovery… What's to stop them from killing him and Carolina both? A day ago, they were a friendly crew doing a job. Greed changed all that, he saw it now. Now, Dmitry made open threats. Hate it for certain, but he needed to be more careful.

"I already said I won't. I may disagree, but I'm a team player. You have nothing to worry about from me."

He grabbed Carolina by the hand and stayed well ahead of the rest of the way. The anger was strong, but being out here, being vulnerable, and needing to protect his kid were realities that kept him from doing something about it. Would the crew really go along with Dmitry? Yeah, he feared they might. With a discovery like this, all bets were off. The important thing was getting his kid home. He never would have held that punch otherwise.

He tried to calm down, sensing doom and paranoia. *I'm overreacting; he's just warning me not to intervene. I already let him know—I'm not a threat, I won't stop them.*

When they returned to the quadrohuts, Austin practically had to drag Carolina to her room. She refused dinner. After a while, she lay her head down on the pillow.

"Daddy, I don't feel good."

Austin stopped fuming and looked at his little girl, her cheeks red and hair matted. "Here, water. Take it. It's been a long day, and with some sleep, you'll feel better in the morning. Are you sure you don't want a bite? You haven't eaten since lunch."

She turned away and seemed to drift off to sleep.

He scratched his head, walking to the mess area. She looked sick, but that was impossible on this trip. The inoculations were 100% efficient; getting sick just didn't happen. And if she was somehow actually sick, Dmitry was the only medic.

He sat down with his instant coffee and a slice of toast and powdered eggs, all fresh out of the wrapper. It was breakfast food, but he couldn't stomach the dinner menu right now. As he pretended to review whatever data was on the table, he ignored his toast and eggs, thoughtfully sipping his black coffee. Dmitry sat down at the table across from him. The coffee almost didn't survive.

"I've been thinking, we still need our core assignments done on time," Dmitry said.

"Why?"

God, he wanted to punch him.

"Isn't it obvious? I have to make the weekly report, and they'll wonder why research is stalled. And it's what we came to do. Our discovery doesn't automatically negate that."

Of course, Austin thought. Dmitry would give him busy work, keep him out of the way so that he wouldn't be a problem. Fine, he didn't care, as long as he stayed far away from him. He had nothing to gain and everything to lose by arguing. To top it off, his girl might be sick. He hated needing anything from this man, but his daughter came first. "As long as Carolina is alright, I don't care. I think she's sick. I need you to take a look at her."

"She's just exerted, you know, we don't get sick on these expeditions. She'll be fine by morning." Dmitry stood up and clapped a hand on Austin's shoulder before leaving the mess area.

Alone now.

The cup crumpled in his hand, burning.

He remained in the mess hall another hour, staring at the shoe-sized drone methodically cleaning instant coffee. He forced himself to finish the egg and toast. Carolina's moaning was audible down the hallway. Maybe a stomachache from anxiety, hopefully, some good sleep would fix her up. He needed sleep too, but he couldn't leave the table yet. Not until he knew for certain that Dmitry wasn't his target.

Carolina slept in the women's dorm, but it was otherwise vacant without Athen and Helena, so finally he picked a bunk across from her. He lay there for some time, wandering in thought, feeling like he had to be close by in case she needed something. He was outraged, but he also didn't care; actually, he would report all of this, or he would do nothing, back and forth, on and on. The team just wanted to make themselves rich, be the ones to make history.

Let them. He didn't care. With that, he slept.

He thought he heard birds chirping, but realized he was dreaming. He roused enough from his sleep to find Helena and Athen there, undressing and getting into their racks. The five hours must be up. Austin rubbed his eyes and sat upright, feeling like his head just touched the pillow minutes ago. He still wanted to punch Dmitry, but he felt in control of that.

"Hey," he said to Athen, rubbing his face.

"Are you lost? Men are across the hall," Athen whispered with a smile.

"Sorry, I was just keeping Carolina company," he said, motioning to her rack. Helena was lying down in the rack that Carolina had previously been in. "She must be awake already," he said, smoothing his hair back.

"I didn't see her," Helena said guiltily.

"She's around somewhere." Austin rubbed his eyes until they opened. He rose and went across to the men's dorm. The bunks were all empty there, too.

He'd get some coffee and find her.

"Dmitry around?"

"He's been at the site for hours," Athen answered.

Austin looked out the porthole, noticing the earliest light coming over the horizon. It was about an hour before they usually woke up. "Want help finding her?" Athen inquired with a betrayal in her voice. She was tired.

"No, I'll radio her, I'm sure she's around."

"Radios have been borderline useless since yesterday. The site has too much energy output. At least it's not radioactive," Helena yawned.

"Great."

She had to be around somewhere. Maybe Dmitry took her back to the site. He really wouldn't have a reason to do that, though, and Austin would have a hard time controlling himself if he did.

He donned his suit and activated the radio in it. "Carolina, where are you, kiddo?"

Her return signal was a wall of static.

"Carolina?"

Nothing. The radios hadn't been great since day one, but now they really were useless, just like Helena warned him: technology, every time. Austin went back to the bunks and checked both rooms, then the comm station, the mess hall, the head, and the supply room. Carolina was not inside any part of the quadrohuts. *She went back?* He buttoned up his expedition coat and stepped outside. He walked all the way around the *huts*, but she wasn't there. He looked over at their *Lander* perched in a field, the eventual return craft. She wouldn't have been able to get inside, and he didn't see her over there. With a grunt, he accepted the truth. He was going to have to instill some discipline in her.

The walk to the site, just a couple of kilometers, took almost twice as long on Austin's patience as the day before. When he approached, he found Dmitry at the entryway with his hands on his hips and vowed not to jump to any conclusions.

"Have you seen Carolina?"

"Why would I?"

"Have you seen her!"

Dmitry's face changed, but he didn't look at him yet. "No," he said, his eyes still fixed down the ramp.

It took a moment, but Austin realized why Dmitry hadn't looked at him.

Are you kidding me? The door at the bottom was open, the one at the end of the decline. It was very much closed last night. The area beyond the energy field now beckoned.

His heart sank. *No, no, no, no. She wouldn't have. Would she?*

"Did Orlean get this open?"

"No. I've got here to help with the first rotation. Is your comm working?" Dmitry asked.

"Just static." Austin scanned the bushes for his little girl. *Anywhere but down there...* He kept eyeing the entry below. If she were inside...

"It's strange how the comms quit working. Dublin blames this place's energy output," Dmitry mused.

"Yeah, maybe," he answered a little curtly. Carolina was not anywhere to be found, and he was worried. "Why didn't you wake me?"

"I assumed you were sleeping."

"Was Carolina with me?"

"I didn't look."

"Carolina!" Austin begged the forest, hoping to hear her voice, needing her to just lope out from behind a bush. He peered down the ramp and into the waiting room far below, refusing to entertain the fear that she'd gone inside. How would she have even deactivated the energy field?

She had to be anywhere else.

But where?

A clatter of dirt fell, and Dmitry shook his hands clean. No pops, no light dazzles. "The energy field is down."

"Carolina! This isn't funny, come out now!" His voice cracked with worry.

"You don't think she's in there, do you?"

If Dmitry smiled right now…

"No. Not a chance," Austin closed his eyes.

"But there is a chance. She found the building, she found the entrance, and she spotted the energy fields."

"Luck."

"She's missing, and there's an open door."

"Stop. Just stop it."

"Someone opened that door, and it wasn't the engineers or research team."

"Shut up!"

His shout echoed off into the silent distance. Dmitry had a gaze that recalculated their little showdown last night. Or he was just realizing that Carolina was his weak point, as if he didn't know it long before now. Eventually, Dmitry retreated.

A minute later, Austin slid down the ramp. That open door begged him.

CHAPTER 6

Inside, he stood where the energy beams had once been, ignoring any possibility of them coming back on. From here, he could gaze into the first underground room. The floor was seemingly beige, with dark blue walls. The ceiling was twice as tall as you needed, and a tennis court would fit in here.

This was the last place Austin wanted to be.

He loosened the zipper on his expedition jacket at the neck to cool down. It was warm and echoed brightly over the slightest sound. A screen illuminated on the far wall. He couldn't identify the symbols, but he recognized data-charts in any language. He stepped around an oval table; it could be for eating or for dissecting. This room was full of them.

He didn't see her at first. She was so still that she blended in.

"Carolina!"

Her back was to him, hunched over another key panel, a different one than before. She did not turn when he called her. He raced over, dodging shelves and oval tables.

A second interior door gasped open just as he reached her, splashing them with stale air. He grabbed her and almost recoiled from her internal heat.

"Honey? Hey, hey, kiddo!" He spun her by the shoulders. Her cheeks were bright red, her eyes distant.

"Uhnnn..."

Her legs collapsed from under her, all of her weight falling into his arms.

"Medic!"

She convulsed and squirmed to her hands and knees. Her hair fell in front of her face as she vomited.

"There there, baby girl, it's okay, honey," he said, rubbing her shoulders and feeling her face. The force of her stomach contents splattered in ricochets. He had never seen someone throw up like this; every muscle in her back was tight and strained. "Dmitry!" he screamed into the radio. *He can't hear me!*

She managed to stop but remained doubled over, holding her stomach. Her back and neck tensed, veins bulged under her skin, and then she vomited again. This time, Austin heard something plop to the ground, an odd sound. He found a large and round globule, covered in murky liquid. Maybe the size of a basketball.

It had come out of her.

"What the—" he shrieked and yanked Carolina lifelessly away from it.

It squirmed on the ground in front of them, extruding long spider legs to get oriented. It was round and fleshy, transparent like a jellyfish, with deep yellow eyes.

"Oh my God..."

Spider legs extended from it, over a meter in length, and the jellyfish creature stood about chest-height. One eye blinked independently of the other, and it chased them. He backed up with Carolina in one arm and tried yanking an oval table in the way. It climbed over, moving in rapid bursts, gaining distance. He pinned Carolina to his chest, throwing something foreign at it, trying to shoo the spindly jellyfish away.

"Help me!"

He wouldn't turn his back and run, he decided instinctually. He yelled and waved while the jellyfish stalked him, cornering him against the far wall. Carolina had this thing *inside* her!

It's trapping me...

One of the oval tables skittered across the floor. Dmitry appeared, running towards them, waving his arms as if you would a wild animal. The creature considered the three of them with wisdom unbecoming of something feral and then scurried low for the second interior door. The one Carolina had opened. *It wasn't Carolina doing that, it was that thing!*

The door was on the far side of the massive room, but that creature made it in a handful of seconds, *thwap thwap thwap* as its spider-legs beat the path away.

Vanished.

Austin gasped; if not for the wall behind him, he might have collapsed.

"You're squishing me, Daddy..."

"Carolina?" he loosened his grip. Sweat beaded down his face. "Can you stand?"

"I think so," she said, feeling her forehead with her fingertips.

Dmitry approached, an expression of disbelief. "What was that thing?"

She collapsed to the floor.

"Carolina!"

"Get her topside, before that thing comes back," Dmitry ordered.

Austin raced out of the large room and up the forty-meter incline with Carolina in his arms. Long strides that he'd feel later carried them up until the forest air found them. It took Dmitry another five seconds to catch up.

"Lay her down," he ordered. Austin fell to a knee and set her down as gently as he could. Dmitry lowered his ear to her chest and checked her pulse. "She's breathing. Her pulse is weak… her body temperature is too hot. We need to cool her down."

Austin shut his eyes briefly to keep everything from trying to dawn on him. He could worry later; right now, his little girl was hurt.

He tried to help as Dmitry unzipped her coat, removed her boots, and poured water on her chest. Austin felt helpless, so he grabbed a decent rock and stood over the ramp, just in case.

"We need to get her back to the *huts*; there's medical equipment there."

"I got her," Austin jumped, dropping the rock and scooping her up. Damn, she was so warm. He bound down the forest trail; they'd taken it enough times that he could anticipate the path without twisting an ankle. His arms ached after the first kilometer, but he pushed his pace. Dmitry struggled to keep up. Adrenaline had faded, but sheer determination guided him onward. He ran with her in his arms, virtually unaware of everything else, until the moment he collapsed her onto the med table at the huts.

Dmitry opened a few cabinets looking for something. "I need the medical kit from the shuttle. Hurry."

His legs protested, but he ignored them, sprinting outside across the field about fifty meters away. A thought flittered by that some of the crew had just gotten to sleep. They would have questions.

He entered the security code to gain access to the shuttle and waited agonizingly for it to open. When it did, he spotted the water cup that he'd forgotten on planet entry. The vessel wasn't terribly large, but it felt like forever to traverse it to the locked supply closet. He smashed the cabinet open with his boot and retrieved the medical kit. His legs were going to give out if he didn't stop soon.

When he returned, he found Carolina covered with sensors and a screen that monitored her vitals.

"Set the kit over there," Dmitry ordered, motioning with a dry hypodermic needle. He reached into the med kit and shuffled through some liquids until he found a particular blue one.

"She's responding to my efforts, which is a good sign," Dmitry said, filling the hypodermic needle. "Austin… was that thing inside of her?"

I never should have brought her here! Austin buried his face in his hands. "Is she going to be okay?"

"We will both know in a moment."

Dmitry raised the hypodermic injector to ensure it had filled correctly, and then he applied it to Carolina's arm. It made an airless *puff*, leaving not even a bruise.

Carolina's color returned to her cheeks. Austin placed his hand against her forehead. She remained feverish, but not as severely as before. He fell to his knees beside her table and wept.

"Her body is responding perfectly to the injection. The synthetic antibodies were out of control, trying to cope with that…*parasite*," Dmitry said.

Austin's breathing steadied with a few tries.

"Her body defended itself with a classic fever; the parasite couldn't tolerate the high temperatures. Had this gone on any longer, she could have suffered brain damage," Dmitry reported, studying the diagnostics above Carolina. "…but we got to her in time. Her neural signs are excellent."

Watching Carolina rest, so peacefully now, he felt what he'd done to his legs. Her chocolate hair rested innocently on the table, but he was exhausted. A thought wouldn't go away; he feared he couldn't protect her.

That shriek in the forest… That's when it started. How many are there?

Dmitry handed him a glucose cocktail with optimized electrolytes and nano-proteins. Austin drank it, letting the compounds do their work.

"We need to capture that thing."

Austin tensed.

"Relax," Dmitry smiled, realizing how he sounded just now. He set the injector down and gave Austin his full attention. "That was terrifying, but without a doubt, your little girl is making a full recovery. I'll still watch her closely, just to make sure, but she's going to be fine," Dmitry said. It was a stark difference from the night before. "But it goes without saying that the creature holds significant importance."

"You can study it post-mortem," Austin replied before leaving the room. If he didn't excuse himself now, he'd regret it later. He walked to the only place he knew he could be alone in—the bathroom. He gripped the plastic sink so hard it bent against the bulkhead. Tears threatened to roll down his face, but he smothered them. *'Come on, come on, come on, come on,'* he chanted, still squeezing the sink. He had never seen her in danger before.

The mirror wouldn't give him any advice, nor would the beginnings of wrinkles on his young-enough face. When did that happen, the wrinkles? *That's life, man. And I'd give mine to keep her safe.*

He stood upright and gave one last look in the mirror. *Nothing else happens to her. Nothing.*

He attempted to wash his hands in the misshapen sink, which sputtered water to the side. Eventually, he returned to check on his little girl.

Dmitry was still there. Med Bay was rarely used and typically stored more jackets than supplies halfway through an expedition. Soothing beeps displayed holographically above Carolina.

"How is she?"

"Great. She has continual improvement in her vitals. She's just sleeping now."

"Is there anything… left behind?" Austin struggled to ask.

"Like something with spider legs?"

He grimaced.

Dmitry re-examined her chart on the screen. "There's irritation in her esophagus and her spinal column, I imagine it's attached to her there," Dmitry said. Watching Austin's face, he softened his tone some. "… and that's all. There are no eggs, or larvae, or anything that isn't completely human. I gave her a soft-tissue cocktail to repair cellular damage. She's responding just fine."

"Thank God."

Dmitry set his hands on the table. "Austin, we need to study that creature."

He nodded, rubbing his forehead with thick fingers. "Yes, I know. We also need to know if there are more of them, and why it's trying to get inside that building."

Dmitry's face brightened. "It really was trying to get inside…"

Somehow, he had yet failed to consider that the creature consciously wanted something. But of course it was possible, how could he not have thought of it earlier?

"Carolina hasn't been herself. She knew things about this place that she shouldn't know. I think it was using her…" Austin said.

Dmitry nodded. "I suspect you are correct. In hindsight, it's perfectly obvious. Listen, if there are more, I can at least confirm they aren't indigenous to Paphos. The flora here operates strictly without animal assistance. That creature is as foreign as we are."

Austin contemplated this, hoping Dmitry was right. "Pretty freakin' unreal."

"If it was already here and if it wanted inside all this time, then it needed our help to do it. Which means the building was designed to prevent that." Dmitry was connecting this in real time, his voice steady and deliberate.

"I'm still going to kill it."

"You must be joking," Dmitry laughed.

"I'm not. If it can take one of us as a host, it's too dangerous to keep alive."

Dmitry took a long breath before leveling an icy gaze. "I know you're upset, but we do not kill the first alien life that we find."

Dublin entered the medical field, rubbing his head like sanding a tree. "Jus' what's this nonsense you're keeping me awake with?"

"The population of Paphos is greater than we thought," Dmitry said. Dublin knew what he meant.

Austin's jaw clenched. "Something attacked Carolina."

"Bloody hell," Dublin said. "Is she alright?"

"Yes."

"There's more than just a building? Feck the barn! When?"

"Moments ago, it used Carolina to open a new interior door and disappeared inside," Dmitry said. Dublin leaned against the wall, rubbing his head.

"An'other door is open?"

"Yes."

Austin wetted a cloth and gently washed Carolina's forehead and cheeks. She wasn't hot to the touch like before, which removed about a thousand pounds from his chest. He rested his hands against the table. He had a duty as a scientist, and he would respect that, as long as Carolina was not in any danger. If it came down to one or the other, Dmitry would have to bring pieces of his precious discovery home. But already he saw Dublin scheming visions of fortune and fame. He also remembered the night before with Dmitry. He wouldn't underestimate their greed.

"It could be as intelligent as us. Problem solving, anticipating outcomes," Austin said.

"Alright, I'm awake too," Athen yawned, her usually hidden curves on display in thin pajamas. Hanging with engineers day after day, sometimes Austin often forgot how womanly she was.

"Yeah, me too," Helena said, wielding a coffee packet.

"You guys suck," Orlean moaned from down the hallway. He roused himself and grabbed his prosthetic arm from the desk, attaching it before joining them.

"What happened to her?" Athen asked.

Dmitry informed them of what he and Austin had already discussed. The crew took turns listening and responding to Dmitry, whose version of the story was far less dangerous. They responded with excitement, hope, and optimism. They didn't see what Austin saw. They didn't fear it like he did.

With the story before them, the questions bloomed. They wanted to know more: how smart it was, how it used Carolina, how it controlled her. Neurologically? Austin wondered, perhaps, if they really had lost Athen, would they be a little less giddy about all of this?

Carolina stirred.

"Guys, let's take this somewhere else," he interrupted.

Helena agreed, suddenly whispering. "Right, she needs her sleep."

They went outside into the morning rays and continued.

"Every question is important, but let's start with the most important: why does it want to get inside that building?"

CHAPTER 7

"Understanding that would lend significant insight into our parasite," Orlean replied. "I mean, logically." He'd begun referring to it as a parasite based on Carolina being its host.

"Booky's right," Dublin replied while checking the stubble of his face. He remembered shaving yesterday morning. "What are they protecting? Why'd they need security?"

"Security?" Helena begged.

"Aye, whoever built that facility didn't want anyone accessing it, parasites included. It's underground, for starters. So that means there's something worth hiding in it."

"Makes sense," Athen agreed.

Orlean removed and adjusted his prosthetic arm. "I concur."

Dmitry addressed them as a group. "We'll head back soon. We stay in groups for protection. Be honest with yourselves, who needs to sleep?"

"Like any of us could," Athen huffed. Dublin chuckled.

"Daddy?"

Carolina appeared at the entrance of the quadrohuts. Her face was tired.

"I'm here, honey, I'm right here," he said, rushing to her.

"I called, but you weren't there."

"I'm sorry, kidlet, I was just outside. How are you feeling?" Austin asked, checking her forehead. Her heat and colors were perfectly normal. "You look like you're feeling better."

"A little."

"Good. Thirsty?"

She shook her head no.

"What do I always say?"

"...drink lots of water."

He smiled and disappeared into the mess hall to fetch some water for both of them. They sipped under nervous silence. He studied her, wondering how to manage what would come. A thought compelled him, watching her. Now she was awake, so now they'd bombard her with questions. Obviously, she didn't need that.

It was important to give the team some answers; they'd demand it anyway. But he didn't trust them anymore. And the discovery of this parasite only made things worse. It already attacked them once, but they weren't deterred in the slightest.

They weren't thinking. Let a team with some firepower come back later. Austin recognized greed, and this was just the tip of the iceberg. Money changed people. He shut his eyes and gathered the resolve he needed to go and buy his insurance. If the people in command at least knew something, that might be enough. He just had to break the promise he made to Dmitry first. They needed to leave this planet. Staring at his little girl, sipping water with her in silence, he didn't know how else to keep her safe except to leave. She wasn't safe here.

"Wait here, honey," he said, handing her the cup. He checked that they were still conversing outside and then acted.

He walked down to the comm room beyond the lab. He was alone, though he turned his head to look just in case. With everyone still outside, he sat at the keyboard and launched a quick message. Something simple. Something permanent.

FROM PAPHOS CREW: WE HAVE ENCOUNTERED AN OFF-WORLD ELEMENT. PLEASE ADVISE.

It would be enough. Questions and orders would come down, the crew would be angry, but now they'd be on their best behavior. It wasn't an accusation; he was just doing his job. Now he and Carolina were safe because any disappearance after would cast too much suspicion. He promised Dmitry he would not do this... but that was before the parasite attacked his little girl.

Austin clicked 'send'. The dye was cast, as they say.

He stood, and with his back to the comm, he prepared himself for when they found out.

A bleep from behind. *A response, already?*

ERROR: UNABLE TO SEND

"What?"

He sat down, typing again. The computer thought for a moment.

Error: unable to send

"You've got to be kidding me," he cursed, running a diagnostic.

Cable problem?

He blindly reached behind the equipment for loose connections when something poked his finger. "Ouch!" He yanked his hand back, and a red dot formed on the end of his pointer finger. He climbed under the desk to get a better look and found frayed wires dangling. Not unplugged but seemingly torn. It was as if something just ripped them apart.

He felt the blood leave his face. He couldn't send a message. He couldn't even receive one. They couldn't even connect to the *Orbiter*.

They were trapped.

He stormed out of the comm room. "How could you do it?!"

"Excuse me?" Dmitry asked.

"You bastard!" Austin lunged at Dmitry. Dublin and Athen caught him, forcing him away. Dmitry didn't even take a step back.

"Explain yourself, before I cite you for attempted assault."

"I saw the radio!"

"What's that now?" Dublin asked.

Austin shook them loose but stood in place.

"Is something wrong with the radio?"

"No, there's nothing wrong with the radio. Austin, what are you talking about?"

"Don't play dumb, you know exactly what I'm talking about!"

"Athen, check the comm room," Dmitry ordered.

Orlean raised his hand. "Uhm, why were you in the com room?"

Austin did not answer.

"Yes, Austin, why were you in the com room?" Dmitry repeated.

Austin glared.

"Even if something is wrong with the radio, there's nothing Dublin and Athen can't fix," Dmitry said. "And you should be careful with your accusations."

Austin remained quiet, but he could do little to change the look on his face.

"Aye, well, this is exciting," Dublin said. Helena looked as if she were naked at school.

Athen returned from the comm room. "It's true, we're radio silent right now. Someone damaged the cables."

"Who was last in the comm room?" Orlean asked.

"I sent my weekly report two days ago, before the discovery," Dmitry said.

"And I checked mail yesterday," Orlean said.

"I saw someone…" Helena added, almost too soft to be heard. Everyone looked at her. "I saw Carolina in there when we swapped shifts…"

"Oh, come on!" Austin cried.

Dmitry raised his hand. "Think about it. Carolina had that thing in her; she wasn't herself. She was being controlled. Besides, why would I sabotage the radio?"

Austin opened his mouth, but only silence followed. As much as he hated to admit it, he may have just made a mistake. And against his best efforts, now his girl was in even more danger. "I'm sorry, I just thought…"

"An' we better get to fixing that radio, come on, Athen, grab our tools." Dublin and Athen ducked away. Orlean slouched while Dmitry glared.

"It's time to see what Carolina has to say," Dmitry said.

"She needs to rest."

Orlean pretended to observe the ground.

Dmitry smiled. "She's been resting. Why don't you check on her, see if she's ready?"

Austin excused himself. He wasn't thinking straight, but this was supposed to have gone much differently. Part of him wished he were as clever as Dmitry. Dmitry always had an answer.

He found Carolina asleep again. He rubbed the side of his face, a stress response of his. In guilt, he realized if she weren't here, then all of this would be different. He'd be just as giddy and irresponsible as the rest of them, just a scientist excited by discovery.

After watching her rest, Austin walked down the hall. "Wait until she wakes up," he told Dmitry and Orlean. He continued down and poked his head in the comm room to find Dublin and Athen soldering cables. The way they were ripped, Carolina wasn't strong enough to do that.

The message Austin had composed was still glaring on the screen. He realized he had stormed off without deleting it. Dublin glanced over his shoulder, giving an undecided look.

"Dublin, we need to send that message. Someone needs to know what we are dealing with. Athen almost died, the parasite attacked Carolina… we could all be in trouble."

Athen watched Dublin, waiting to see how he would respond.

"I'm not the captain, Austin, an' neither are you."

"Athen, what about you?"

Athen checked Dublin before answering. "It's not our call to make."

Austin sank. He just couldn't get them to listen to reason. "Can it at least be fixed?"

"Not sure, let you know."

Sure. The guy who regularly boasted his fix-it skills suddenly gave a flaccid answer. It was clear—Dublin would follow Dmitry's lead, and Athen, would follow Dublin's.

"An' I think I'm going to delete that message, Austin. Jus' between us."

"Thanks. But I'd rather you sent it."

Defeated, Austin returned to the women's dorm and found Carolina awake. She smiled, which took about a thousand pounds of stress away.

"Daddy?"

"Yes, miss?"

She brushed her hair from her face. "I'm thirsty again."

Austin brought her some water with a little glucose and a vitamin cocktail, similar to the one he had earlier. Sometimes water just needed a boost. She drank it down and smiled through sleepy eyes.

"How are you feeling?"

"Better. I think I'm awake now."

"Do you remember anything?" Austin asked. He figured it prudent to know before the others.

"No," Carolina said. But it was a lie. Her eyes gave it away. He wished he hadn't asked.

She was quiet; they both were. Sometimes, well, a lot lately, he didn't know the first thing about being a parent, too often, he just didn't know what to say. So, he sat next to her and put his arm around her shoulders.

She started to sob, quietly at first. He continued holding her, saying nothing, letting the tide of sobs come. The placative *'there there, it'll all be alright'* just didn't feel appropriate. Her mom would know what to say. Another wave of guilt passed as soon as he thought it. He should also know how to handle these things. He should be around more.

"It's okay, honey, you don't *ever* have to say anything. If you don't remember, that's just fine," he said.

He thought back on his childhood experiences, wondering what he could do to help Carolina right now. He remembered when he was a kid, and when things were the hardest, his dad had a way of making things better with breakfast. "Want some toast?"

"Huh?"

"I've got some world-famous toast I can whip up," he said. She looked confused. Austin gulped. "*And*, if you want, I'll let you drink coffee."

"Gross."

"*Instant* doesn't always mean gross."

"I don't drink coffee," she said. There was no smile. But there was no malice, either.

Austin returned moments later with toast and instant coffee.

"I'm going to pretend I didn't hear that last part. I want them to let you back on Earth when we return. They won't admit coffee haters."

Carolina crossed her arms. "You call *that* world-famous toast?"

"Best on planet," he said, handing her some.

"It looks like cardboard."

Still no smile.

"That's the secret ingredient!"

Carolina laughed, short and brief, like she'd tried not to.

"And the coffee has mud in it, helps the cardboard go down," he said.

"*Eww!*"

Austin took the first bite and pretended to enjoy it, so Carolina took a bite too, trying not to spit it out. He looked at her and tried not to cry himself. This was the first time she'd laughed this summer. He'd been so busy, and then everything with the underground bunker, why did it happen now? It was so simple and relaxed, enjoying the world's worst toast together. Why couldn't everything be like this?

How do you get the time back?

You don't, he realized.

CHAPTER 8

The next hour gave Austin a chance to regain his thoughts. He still had a chance to convince them to do the right thing.

The others gathered supplies to return to the site, but no one gave thought to weapons, despite what had happened. Not that they ever traveled with firearms, but it showed they weren't regarding the creature as a threat. He certainly did; he'd seen its eyes. He'd been chased by it.

He surveyed the crew and found Athen. Dublin had shut him down, but maybe Athen would be more amenable without her boss around. He pulled her aside and tried to engage without nearby listeners. "Athen, maybe we should be thinking about how to protect ourselves, instead of heading back down there."

She shook her head. "Maybe you should be thinking about a once-in-a-lifetime, history-making moment of first contact. Everything we do here goes in the history books, you know. You want us to chase it with pitchforks? We aren't the old Americas anymore," she said. She wasn't rude about it, just blunt. Ignorant. Austin watched her stuff a backpack with rope and sensors. She had a point, but she hadn't seen this thing yet. It wasn't friendly.

She hadn't even listened to him; his hope of convincing any of them faded. They were mad at him for trying to send that message. However, they knew to repair the damaged radio because of it. *Silver lining, baby, silver lining.*

He needed to show that he was part of the team, to let them know he was a friend, not an enemy. He needed their help to keep Carolina safe, and that meant he couldn't afford to be the outcast anymore.

The door outside hissed open. With a shield of commitment, he stepped out to join the others. The sun was pink and hot, pushing against the cloud-speckled horizon, the pollen thick. Behind those clouds were Paphos' rings, like brown and fuchsia brushstrokes in the sky. His radio crackled; proof that the Engineers had failed to restore functionality. The frayed wires had caused a programming malfunction, they reasoned, although the software was designed to prevent it. Austin had the software background; he could fix it… But they wouldn't let him near it.

He found Dmitry and the research team outside and approached them. Now he was the one avoiding eye contact.

"Austin, we're having a private meeting," Orlean said.

"Yeah, I know... but I have something to say. Listen, I was worried about Carolina, and I was worried about that creature. But Athen reminded me, there's more at stake here than me and my fears. This is history, and I won't miss being a part of it. Count me in, all the way, whatever you guys need." He felt wrong saying it. He hoped Orlean didn't see the blatant pandering. He just couldn't let him and his daughter remain outcasts.

"That's great, Austin. We all hoped, me especially, that you would come to your senses," Dmitry said. "Let's call a meeting, get everyone together."

"A meeting?"

"Yes, Austin, a meeting. Because, despite what you just said, we still need to clear the air about that message you tried to send," Dmitry replied.

Jus' between us, eh, Dublin? Figures.

"Sure, if you think it'll help. Sounds great," Austin agreed and led the way back inside. This was his chance to convince them all, and to convince himself, because so far it didn't feel right. He was surprised to see Dublin and Athen already waiting in the mess hall, the Irishman had his big arms crossed.

"So, Austin, about that message... You convinced us something needs to be done," Orlean said. Helena would not take her eyes off the floor. Dmitry usually led these speeches, so why was Orlean leading it?

"About contacting corporate?" Austin asked. He got the feeling they'd already had a meeting without him.

"Not what we were thinking, lad," Dublin replied, uncrossing his arms. Dmitry gave a nod, Dublin nodded back.

He approached Austin with a prong and dropped him to the floor with a zap of electricity. Austin collapsed, half-aware he was being guided into a chair. Dazed, he found his wrists bound and struggled to break loose.

"You see, Austin, I need to protect my team, and what you did put all of us at risk," Dmitry said.

Dublin prepared a gag.

"Oh, hell, guys, come on, do we really need to gag him?" Athen pleaded. "His daughter is right down the hallway."

Dmitry considered her. "Lose the gag. We just want you to listen, Austin."

He fought against the restraints, but his limbs hadn't coordinated from the shock yet.

"We all proceed together, or we all lose together. Corporate isn't here, we are," Dmitry continued.

"You… you can trust me. I swear…," Austin struggled to speak. The effects of the stun lasted about a minute, and his words came slowly.

"I appreciate you saying that. But despite your assurances, we don't trust you yet. You'll need to earn that back."

Dmitry was so pleased with himself, making this unfold with the help of the others—his little power grab. Austin resisted casting a thousand terrible threats; they wouldn't help him. This was exactly what he feared, but he could still convince them. That was how to keep Carolina safe. Speaking of his little girl, she was standing in the hallway.

"Why is my dad tied up?"

The shame given by a twelve-year-old girl was too much for Athen.

"Enough is enough, guys," Athen said with red cheeks. "This is insane." She quickly removed the plastic ties from Austin's wrists. Dmitry looked about to stop her, but didn't.

"It's nothing, kiddo, nothing at all," Austin said, standing up. *This is how I keep her safe. Just play along. It's the only way I keep her safe.* "Thank you," he told Athen.

Austin looked at Dmitry, hoping the hate was well hidden.

"I meant it, it won't happen again," Austin said, his wrists burning as much as his anger. He prayed none of that surfaced to his eyes.

Dmitry smiled. "Intense situations cause people to react poorly. I trust you've learned from this." He turned to address the group next. "I know everyone is without sleep, but we need to deal with our guest crawling around first."

"It won't come back here," Carolina said.

All eyes fell on her. Her tiny voice had stopped them mid-breath. "It has what it wants now."

An invisible weight pressed down on Austin's chest. *Oh God no, please no.*

"What did she just say?" Orlean asked.

Carolina shook her head as if coming from a daze.

"It's nothing, she's just tired," Austin said, grabbing her by the shoulders. "Hey kid, it's still early. You might want to sleep a while longer," he said.

Dmitry crossed his arms, silent in his thoughts.

"I'm not a kid," she argued.

"Go. I'll be with you in a bit."

Carolina looked half-asleep as she turned and walked, drooping her shoulders all the way to her bunk.

Orlean raised his hand again. "Did she say what I think she said?"

"She doesn't remember anything," Austin stopped him. His stomach twisted in knots. He wished Dmitry would just say what was on his mind and get it over with. Instead, he remained silent, calculating.

"Are there more of them?" Athen asked.

Helena cringed. "There could be hundreds!"

"No," Orlean argued. "We've been here for months, and our satellites have found no trace of any ecosystem."

"Aye, well, our satellites missed the wall and everything inside it," Dublin replied.

"That's a good question for later. For now, this is from surveillance we set up in the lobby of our site," Dmitry said. The change of focus felt abrupt, and the word lobby was strange to use. Dmitry turned to a monitor. Was that it? Did everyone forget about Austin then? Was Dmitry switching attention away from Carolina, too?

Orlean studied the screen. "These look like signs, words even." Orlean pointed to shapes painted on the walls over entryways. There were also some on doors. They were looking at the first evidence of alien script. Austin caught a sideways glance from Dmitry. He wanted them to go back in; he knew it.

"Buy me a pint, this looks just like a security checkpoint."

"That fits, the building is very complex. There's much more than this top level. A checkpoint would be a natural start," Dmitry agreed.

"Complex?" Athen asked.

Orlean answered. "I couldn't get all the readings I wanted, but I scanned enough to see that the facility extends well into the mountain, and probably deep underground as well. I gathered evidence of multiple floors, but the radio interference makes getting a better reading almost impossible."

A silent agreement, then, they weren't going to teach him any more lessons today. They'd switched the focus to this. Austin stood up and walked next to the monitor, squinting at it. He made sure his back wasn't to Dublin. "Those markings appear soft, almost inviting. At least to me," he said.

"It does, right? This entire room has a certain flow to it," Athen said, pointing at parts of the screen.

"Maybe it's a hotel, like a vacation resort," Helena wondered. Maybe. Secluded, far away, some feel of interior design... except the lobby was a bit too stale for a hotel.

"Team, let's face facts. We can only learn so much from the outside. If we choose to continue our research, we must explore the interior. And something else... if Carolina is right, then the creature is after something. Are we going to ignore that?" Dmitry asked.

Austin wished he hadn't brought her up again, but so far, no one seemed eager to push her for more. At least he had that.

"Dat' wouldn't be in our best interest."

"Are you suggesting we hunt this thing?" Helena asked.

"If there's a weapon inside that building, and that creature wants it... Consider the implications," Dmitry replied.

Orlean sat in his chair and rocked back. Helena's face had gone pale.

"We find what it wants first, or we capture it along the way," Dmitry said.

"Austin should stay here. Someone should watch Carolina," Athen suggested.

"I disagree. She'd better come with us. She appears to have... *unique insight*," Dmitry said. Austin swallowed hard. "But it is up to Austin, of course. He is her father, after all."

He hoped he did not growl out loud. Here it was, his first test. This would tell them if they could trust him or not. Though Dmitry gave Austin the courtesy of deciding, he knew it wasn't really a choice. His wrists still had marks from the plastic restraints.

"If things get crazy, we'll just come back here."

Dmitry nodded.

Austin tried to focus on preparation as the team stocked up on snacks and water. Dublin and Athen grabbed cutters and multi-purpose tools until every cargo pocket bulged. Orlean resisted the urge to load Helena up with heavy lab equipment. Austin was going to travel light. Being quick would come in handy, they'd see. And the moment things did get crazy, he'd scoop Carolina out of there. He wouldn't wait one second to do it.

They embarked on the hike, keeping mostly to themselves. Austin took note of each crew member, gauging them, unable to file what had happened. He knew one thing: they wouldn't get the advantage like that again.

He nurtured his vow until they arrived. The crew wasted no time. Dmitry went down the ramp with Helena close behind. Dublin was just behind her, and then the others. The ramp was easily passable now that Dublin had scoured their boots with his cutter. Austin was surprised how well it worked.

He examined Carolina before following. Even though the parasite was out of her, she didn't seem to be herself. He considered going back right now, except he wouldn't have an explanation for it, and he'd probably end up tied to a chair again. She looked at the obsidian wall and then down the ramp leading inside.

"Come on, father," Carolina said, holding his hand. *Father?*

"I wonder what's powering these lights?" Orlean asked.

"Solar power?" Helena suggested.

"We didn't find solar panels, but there's definitely a power source," Athen said.

The lights were recessed in inverted domes in the ceiling, providing a soft, pleasant glow. Austin looked closer at the signs over the doors, trying to make sense of them, as if he could. He stood near a desk with stacks of sheets or files, perhaps marked with symbols similar to those over the doorways.

Austin blinked twice when he found Carolina doodling on the table with her markerpen.

Watching Carolina's scribbling triggered a visual of sorts. She looked like a patient in a waiting room, passing the time until the doctor called her back. He studied the room, looking from corner to corner, as puzzle pieces wanted to fit together. "Guys," Austin said loudly. He waited until everyone looked at him. "I think it's a hospital."

CHAPTER 9

Carolina doodled on her notepad, eyes innocent as she drew. "They came here for safety."

She realized everyone was staring at her and set her marker pen down. She went from casually doodling to head down and shoulders slouched.

"What do you mean?" Dmitry asked.

Carolina looked at her drawing and crumpled up the paper, tossing it and glaring at the empty desk. Dublin and Dmitry shared a look.

Austin put a hand on her shoulder. This was a mistake. But being at the quadrohuts was a worse mistake; he had to believe that he was making the best of the bad choices.

"Do you know where the parasite went?" Orlean asked her. She pursed her lips and hid behind her hair. Austin was ready to interrupt, but surprisingly, Dmitry did it for him.

"Orlean, how far do your sensors reach? I see three pathways in this room."

Inside this room was a hallway to the left, to the right, and a path across. Dmitry and Dublin judged each one without much to go on. The hallway in the middle was glowing with red lights; the hallways to the left and right were dark.

"My readings aren't clear."

"Follow the light?" Dublin suggested.

"I'm thinking so."

They went ahead as a group, entering the domed hallway, which was filled with a soft, red light that saturated their suits. Austin followed Carolina in front of him. He wouldn't let her be further than arm's reach away, hating every moment of going this way. There was excitement buried somewhere, but he was otherwise just worried about Carolina. A few meters in, he noticed square-shaped patterns on the wall, which were decorative. There were also ventilation slits about every ten meters.

The red glowing light stuttered and flicked off, bathing them in darkness as the ever-persistent hum of electricity died.

"Power's out."

"Thanks, Captain Obvious."

"Quiet. Stay calm, we all have personal flashlights," Dmitry said. Before Austin got his activation, the hum returned, and the red lights came back on. Faces in the passageway proved they all still existed, grateful to see each other again.

"The power is unstable," Orlean sighed. "That's exactly what we need."

After a moment, they continued. The hallway wound down and around, sending their silhouettes in different directions. The floor lowered a half step, abruptly and seemingly for no reason. Then Austin noticed water damage along the floorboard, rising about three centimeters. At some point, this hallway had flooded. He supposed that wasn't totally unexpected, being underground and all. The floors were still polished and smooth, except that they now encountered debris piles, decades old, with no indication of what had caused them.

Dmitry slowed as they came upon a smooth, round crate in the hallway. Empty, but they stopped and studied it anyway. Then, traveling further down the hallway, which was approximately fifty meters long, and passing over an odd step in the floor, they discovered two more crates. They took less time examining them and continued deeper inside.

It reminded him of a mining tunnel as they reached the end and found a gaping chute.

They stood in front of it. There was a frame over two meters tall and wide enough for all seven of them, with a drop on the other side that went further than they could see. Dmitry traded a glance with Dublin. Being the Engineer Element, it was Dublin or Athen who had the official opinion on safety, even if they were on another world. "I bet there's a lift."

"I bet it only goes down. Thinkin' we should backtrack, try the other hallways," Dublin said.

Dmitry poked his head down the chute, satisfied with what he saw. "We came all this way, let's find out." He pressed a hand-sized panel and stood back as a guttural *whirr* brought something to them. A large, doorless elevator climbed up the chute and stopped at their level. It was not pulled by any cables they could see. It was empty, too, Austin remarked gratefully.

When the elevator arrived, a light came on in the domed cabin, and a key panel was glowing blue.

Dmitry looked expectantly at Dublin.

"It climbed up here smoothly, no stuttering or whining of parts. This elevator is functional," Dmitry said. He stepped on and turned to the crew. "We're here for a reason, guys."

Austin prayed this was the moment they all came to their senses, but instead, he watched each of them muster their courage and step onto the elevator.

"It's okay, father," Carolina said, leading him by the hand.

"When did I stop being dad?"

She only smiled. She'd never called him father before today. That was twice now.

Dublin examined the foreign symbols that illuminated after the elevator arrived. "G'wan then, why not?" With a hopeful smile, he pressed a button. A near-gasp among them as the elevator smoothly descended, the floor rising up to seal them in.

Austin's stomach twisted. His knuckles were squeezed white, but it wasn't Carolina squeezing; it was him. He looked down at her, realizing he was far more anxious than she. In fact, she wasn't the slightest bit nervous. He gave her a smile and a wink, a timid effort to reassure her, and suddenly the elevator came to a halt and opened its doors. They hadn't traveled much at all. *Thank goodness.*

It was warmer here, at least ten degrees. There was also steam drifting up through the floor vents. Dmitry stepped off, studying their surroundings. The elevator had stopped at a cave-like room, all carved from stone. A hallway stemmed away from them, walled and floored, full of lighting and ventilation. Green lights turned on, sensing their presence. Most of the facility was fully constructed, but spots like the elevator chute and this landing pad were strangely just carved out of rock.

A sharp *snap* of electricity shot out from the ceiling, sending a dazzle of sparks. Damage or decay had loosened electrical wires in the ceiling of the hallway. He found something comforting about the use of electricity and cables, though he wasn't sure why. They shared the same laws of physics; it felt familiar in this strange environment.

"Jus' look how much dust is down here, plus it's hotter than hell," Dublin hacked.

"How is the electricity still running? The motion sensors, lights, elevators, what's maintaining it?" Athen asked. No one voiced speculation yet.

Austin detected mechanical struggles in the ceiling, like metal fans chipping at water. A similar sound would come from a clogged coolant system. "Whatever it is, it hasn't been maintained. Orlean, you're watching for death traps, right?"

"Way ahead of you. I'm calibrated to their energy signature now; it won't happen again."

Orlean approached a terminal sticking out of the wall. It had several slots in it, he guessed, for connecting other devices, but they were shaped in unfamiliar ways. "I wonder if they rely on binary computing like we did, or if they've gone full quantum. I suppose it could be something totally different, too."

"You don't usually share your thoughts out loud this much," Athen kicked his boot with hers.

"Yeah," he chuckled. "Well, I'm not usually staring at something like this."

Helena studied her sidepiece, reading the charts from the prosthetic mini-lab. "There is a lot of energy being used on this floor, a thousand times more than needed for lights and ventilation. There's something big we haven't found yet."

"Radioactive?" Dmitry asked.

"No, not radioactive," Orlean said, looking at the screen on his forearm. He studied for a few moments, making small "*tsk*" sounds with the end of his tongue. "It's not an energy leak, not like a faulty reactor. This is stable and deliberate. My best guess is some kind of active system that needs a lot of power. Like, a lot."

"Like vaporizing beams of electricity?" Austin said, wishing he'd kept his mouth shut. He was trying not to be the voice of reason, dammit.

"Could be a security system like on the top floor," a pause as they collectively remembered Athen's glove becoming white-hot ash. "Or it's interference, because my sensors just stopped working."

Athen stared at the data-ports with Orlean. "Give it a moment. It's alien technology, maybe they are using something completely unknown to us," she said. "This and everything we've seen so far needs to be documented and studied."

"Let's continue on."

Dmitry led them down the hallway, which turned a few meters later. Then the hallway opened up, displaying a barracks-style room. Double doors lined both sides of the vast chamber, dozens of them in sets. They were oval in shape and clear for viewing. Orlean approached one, scanning with his prosthetic arm.

"It's a type of clear plastic, basically," he said as if having read Austin's mind. They squinted at what appeared to be specimen cages on the other side. Whatever this floor was used for, it did not match the décor from the hospital lobby above.

Austin didn't like it and wanted to go back, but he needed someone else to suggest it. He needed someone else to become the voice of reason so they could forget about hating him. He saw something in one of the rooms, something organic. He looked through the window, shining his light inside. On a table in this room were murky beakers and vials full of liquid, and inside them were specimens—dead specimens, of unknown origins.

"Guys…"

Dublin peered over his shoulder, making Austin step out of the way with a little more aggression than called for. "I've got fish in this room," he said.

"Alive?" Dmitry asked. He was looking through the other doorway across from them.

"Dead. What have you got?"

"I've got fish too, and mine are alive," Dmitry confirmed.

They huddled around Dmitry, peering past him at a table lined end to end with specimen jars. One of the jars, round and squat, contained an aquatic organism with triangular gills and long antennae emanating from its head and belly. It looked like something from the deep ocean. It floated lethargically through the grey, murky water until Dmitry shone his light on it, then it reacted in tight bursts.

"Okay, wow, this is amazing," Athen almost cried. As scientists, it was an easy feeling to get caught up in. "How long has it been down here? This place has been abandoned for decades, at least, right?" Athen asked.

"At minimum… ten years based on the age of the debris. Possibly as much as fifty."

"Dublin?" he motioned to the oval door. The Irishman took one of his tools and pried it open so they could all enter.

"They did experiments here, obviously, look at all the equipment and the way the specimens are laid out on the table," Dmitry said. "Quite a smell, though." He looked around and found Carolina still in the main hall. She was apparently uninterested in alien fish.

A fact dawned on Dmitry. "Orlean, document everything you can in sixty seconds. We need to move ahead if we are going to catch that parasite, but we'll definitely come back to this."

"Let's go, Orlean," Athen said, sixty seconds later, pulling him and Helena away. It was like dragging a bear from its nest, but they reluctantly came.

And it was just as well that they moved on; the experiments in each room continued to astound. Orlean took copious pictures and scans. Some lived, while most did not, and thankfully, the ventilation was partially working, as the smell of the dead fish was putrid. So far, all were aquatic organisms. Austin watched Dmitry's impatience grow specimen by specimen. He was worried about letting the parasite get away.

They stopped at a giant hole in the wall.

"I could park my bulldozer in there," Dublin whistled. Orlean snapped a photo and scanned the hole. It did not appear to be a deliberate part of the building, not in the slightest.

"What could have done *this*? These walls are very thick," Athen asked.

Carolina tugged at Austin's hand. "Daddy, it's time to go back."

He looked at her. "Why? What is it, what happened?"

Her eyes went to the floor.

He waited, but didn't get more from her. If he thought for a moment that he wouldn't be the outcast again, he would have marched her the hell out of there. But he tasted their greed once already. She was still safest with him, and he was still safest in the group.

Dublin straddled rubble that had spilled on the floor near the giant hole.

"Something exploded here," Orlean finally said. "I've got warps and scorches, not to mention this giant hole. But I swear… these are claw marks on the ceiling."

They all looked up. Helena audibly gulped.

"Maybe a gas-pipe burst, or something of a similar nature?" Dmitry wondered. "Come on, we need to keep moving. We reached the end, let's go back to the elevator. Orlean?"

"I'm reading a floor beneath this one," Orlean said, scanning his fingers over the floor tiles.

"Great then. We'll go there next."

"Daddy?"

Austin looked down; she was terrified. He nodded. "Alright, kid, let's get the hell out of here," he said. The chips were going to fall where they may; he was getting her topside. "Guys, I'm calling it, gonna' take her back to the huts."

"Nay. You'll reside where'n I see you," Dublin said.

"Relax," Dmitry said calmly, which made him seem more threatening. "Don't be paranoid. Everybody is safe right now."

Austin wasn't going to wait for their permission; he'd seen enough. He grabbed her by the hand and took a step down the hallway anyway.

Dmitry walked with him. "This was a dead-end; we're headed back anyway. So just keep your cool," he added. Austin led the way with his daughter as the team trailed behind through the specimen hall. Dublin made certain to linger within arm's reach of him at any time. When they made it to the elevator, Austin realized it'd been silent the entire way. No one had made any small talk. He was doing it again, and they were sidestepping away from him again. They stepped onto the elevator. He needed to get Carolina to safety *and* smooth things out with the crew.

"Just take us up first, we'll wait in the lobby room, and we won't leave until you guys are there too. We won't go to the huts without you," Austin said.

Dmitry hit a button to take them lower. "Soon, but not yet," he said.

The elevator slid a few inches down when a sharp popping erupted beneath them, flashing light and arcing.

"Get off the bloody elevator!"

The elevator tilted to one side. A wave of shrieks flew. Orlean tried to get off just as the elevator fell, trapping his prosthetic arm. The ground disappeared, taking his limb with it.

A weightless terror filled them as the elevator fell, scraping and rocking down the chute. Shrieks evaporated as the air rushed, and for a moment, Austin thought this was it. He held Carolina to his chest and whispered, "It's okay, it's okay, it's okay...".

Another pop of electricity and a powerful gushing of servos slowed the elevator to an uneven halt. Cries of relief and a flood of thoughts to decipher what saved them. Emergency brakes of alien design, taking their blessed time to engage.

"Damn it!" Orlean cursed, holding the stump of his left arm. "It's up there! I've got to get it back... There has to be another elevator!" Orlean looked up as if he could see through the ceiling.

"Jus' give me a minute to accept I'm still alive, would you!" Dublin roared, holding his chest to keep his heart from falling on the floor.

"Oww..." Helena groaned. Dmitry examined her scalp and found it was bleeding.

"You hit your head pretty hard," Dmitry said. "Is anyone else hurt?"

"Guys," Athen said quietly. "I might have a problem."

She sat on the floor of the elevator with her legs out. A narrow steel rod was poking out of her thigh, with blood pooling from top and bottom.

"Just stay put, Athen," Dmitry said calmly. She looked down and stared at her leg in frustration.

"I'm so sorry. It's not real bad, is it?"

"Not bad at all," Dmitry said, removing his belt. He wrapped it around her upper left thigh and applied a tourniquet. He motioned at Dublin, who scrambled through the medical bag until he displayed a small syringe.

"I'm giving you a little something for the pain," Dmitry said.

"I don't feel any pain, weird right?"

"This will ensure you don't feel anything later." He sank the injection into her arm. She looked away from him and tried not to cry. It wasn't the pain causing her tears.

"Oh no, Athen," Helena gaped.

"Easy now, lass, we'll get you patched up. This is just a minor issue," Dublin tried to calm her. They were close as coworkers, being part of the Engineering Element. They had been teammates long enough to know each other's habits and read each other's thoughts. A gesture with a tool or a shrug was often all the dialogue they needed.

Dmitry whispered in Dublin's ear. "It's a little close to the artery. We have to cut her free without removing it, or she could bleed out. We'll remove it later at the quadrohuts."

"You failed whispering class, boss," Athen said, her words happy from the effects of the painkillers.

"I need my arm back!" Orlean cried again.

Dublin went to work cutting the steel rod loose. Athen looked away as the sparks flew. "Alright, lass, the good doc says the rod is safer inside your leg right now. We can remove it at the huts."

Dmitry gazed out at their surroundings and wiped a layer of sweat from his brow. It was even warmer down here. Where he was looked like the inside of a shoebox with stairs on the left leading down. The noise on this floor was ambient and silent, like a giant, empty warehouse.

"How are we going to get back up?" Orlean demanded.

"Somehow," Dmitry said. "But it won't be the elevator. Also, someone has to stay here with Athen," he said. "Not you, Dublin, this place is falling apart, and I may need your tools. Austin, I'll need you too. We don't have a way to scan for traps. I'll need a third pair of hands in case one of us gets hurt."

"We just need my arm!" Orlean vexed, rubbing his stump.

"I'll stay," Helena volunteered.

Orlean kicked the wall. "I'll stay too, with that thing running around; they may need my help."

Austin swallowed. The worst thing to do in a bad situation was to panic, but what was the best thing to do? They couldn't have fallen more than a couple of floors, but the commotion was so loud that anything with ears would have heard it.

"How are you doing, kiddo?" he asked his daughter.

"I'm okay. We should go down those stairs."

"I'm sorry this happened. I'll still get you out of here."

"It's okay. We should go down those stairs."

Austin winced, though he didn't mean to. Just now, she didn't sound like herself. He'd best see down those stairs first. "Carolina, you'd better stay here, too," he said.

CHAPTER 10

"I want to come with you," she said, her voice monotone.

Austin winced again. This was eerily similar to the moment before she was vomiting a parasite out of her, and she'd been under constant watch since then. "We are just going to take a look. I'll be right back."

She would usually cross her arms when he put his foot down. Instead, she just nodded. No pouting, no pursing lips, no furrowing her brow; he wished she would do some of those things. Maybe she just wasn't acting like herself because of the medicine she had earlier. He really, really needed that to be it.

"Come on," Dmitry said. Dublin checked his tool belt and stood, waiting for him to join. He gazed down the long hallway, ribbed with piping, wondering why it seemed even less friendly than the last one. At the end, there were stairs.

"We'll be right back. Just scouting it out first."

They took a few steps ahead as he gave one more look at Carolina, who gazed through him. He would be right back, and then he'd make Dmitry take another look at her just to make sure there was nothing wrong.

They traveled a dozen meters, the sound of Orlean's curses fading. The hallway opened to the left, revealing a narrow set of stairs leading down. They descended to discover an arena, some thirty meters beneath them. Dmitry continued as their walkway devolved from a stairway into floating, grated platforms suspended from the ceiling. Like walkways at a construction site, the arena rested under the umbrella of these temporary platforms. Austin did not like the way they swayed under his weight as he stepped onto one.

Beneath them, the walls had little rooms carved out, like open dorms.

"An' what you suppose is down in there?" Dublin asked, pointing to the floor beneath them, right in the middle, where something like a shipping container waited. He noticed it had barred windows.

Austin really didn't want to know. "Over there! Another elevator," he pointed to a section on the other side. How they would get over there, or especially how they would get Athen there, was a riddle yet to be solved. These platforms didn't go in a straight shot that he could see.

"What is the bloody purpose of this?" Dublin wondered, referring either to the suspended walkways or the arena below them. He walked carefully across the floating platforms as they began to sway more. To think, all of this had been hidden beneath them, under the planet's surface, all this time.

Austin looked down and fought the dizzying sensation of the floor. Dmitry continued undeterred, albeit slowly. The platform swayed lazily. One didn't need to fear heights to be uncomfortable up here, but Dmitry continued on, leading the way. After what felt like forever, he made it to the elevator across from them. The sooner Austin was on solid ground, the better.

"That wasn't so bad," Dmitry said, giving a smooth grin to Dublin as he arrived. A round-floor design waited in front of the new elevator, which they studied. They found another key panel recessing into the frame, with faint lights that flickered as Dublin pressed them. "Lookin', I'll need to wedge the door open; these damn buttons aren't working," he cursed, selecting a tool from his cargo pocket. He retrieved his cherished pneumatic wrench, about the length of his forearm. There was a story behind that particular wrench, though Austin never heard the complete version.

"Problems?"

Dublin kept searching but couldn't find a gap to wedge into. This door was different. As he searched, they heard a faint motor behind the wall, stuttering as if wanting to work.

"Maybe it needs more power, notice how the lights dim each time that motor spurs," Austin said. Dublin grimaced.

"Dublin, I want you to stay very still, and don't move," Dmitry ordered in a slow, deliberate way.

"What's that?"

"Dublin…" Dmitry said again. The engineer stopped and gave an irritated *'What now'* over his shoulder.

Dmitry motioned softly with his head, down and to the left. Austin looked as something zipped by. Dublin saw it too. *Oh damn…* It moved again, and he knew for certain it was the parasite, scaling underneath the rafters.

"Act natural," Dmitry said with a soft voice. Austin kept his eyes forward, observing out of the corner of his eye. Thinking itself undetected, the parasite scrambled its way across the hanging platforms. "We need to follow it; this may be our only chance," he added. Austin just held his tongue.

They followed carefully and quietly in slow pursuit, like hunters sneaking up on their prey. They crept towards the center and followed a descending ramp, all the while keeping a keen eye on the jellyfish parasite and trying not to rock the platforms. The creature scurried to the far end of the room and disappeared into one of the carved-out spots. Austin noticed its haphazard path was taking them closer to the container in the middle of the arena. As the heat continued to build, his chest soaked with sweat. He wiped his forehead as they crossed another lazily swaying platform. The parasite should be visible from this angle, but he couldn't see it.

They were closer to the ground, and he was able to make out a dozen old scorches on the floor, like ricocheted bullets. He found another sizable hole in the wall, which wasn't visible from their earlier positions. Dmitry and Dublin stared at it too, just as the parasite scurried up and over into the hole.

Dmitry smiled. "It cornered itself in there."

"We told the others we'd be right back," Austin argued. "Do you even know how you are going to catch it? Come on, guys, we can't just tackle it."

Dmitry removed something from his inner pocket, a folded-up durasack. It was a woven poly-fiber material that weighed nothing but was so durable you'd need a tool to cut it. "Satisfied?"

Dmitry went down the ramp, along a wall that stopped just above the floor of the arena, followed by his trusty engineer. Austin had no choice but to climb down with them, though he would make certain he could backtrack. He had sworn to Carolina he'd be right back, and this was threatening that promise. Although catching it might mean they could focus on getting out of here.

They lurked outside the gaping hole in the wall. Dmitry motioned for Austin to enter. *Figures.* He looked over the lip of the hole, reevaluating its size. The cavernous path began in the wall and then angled quickly downward. He flashed his light, praying not to see a jellyfish staring at him as the light swung to the side, uncovering rubble and dust. The hole was deep enough that it led to the floor beneath, like a hastily made shortcut. The parasite wasn't as trapped as they'd hoped; there was an entire floor down there to hide in. And at this point, Austin figured it had to know they were stalking it.

"Something did this, and it goes down to the next floor. We'll need rope if we're climbing in there," he said. He pushed aside thoughts of heading back to the others, where Carolina, Athen, and Orlean still waited at the broken elevator. They could manage another five minutes or so to get this over with. Dublin secured a rope to one of the thicker pipes and flung the spool down. So much for a clandestine approach. Austin gripped a piece of rubble and transferred his weight to the rope as he climbed in, slowly rappelling down. The rubble kicked up penetrating dust, and he found himself holding his breath. Towards the end, his feet dangled uncontrollably. Slowly twirling until touching down, he was grateful to get his feet on solid ground. It'd been reasonably stealthy, all things considered.

"I'm in," he called up. He'd be in pitch black without his flashlight, which did a decent job in his immediate vicinity, but left gaping mysteries beyond that. He did not like being alone down here, with a careless rope as his only lifeline. He closed his eyes. *I can only deal with one thing at a time...*

The best he could tell was that the hallway went in both directions. Something either tore through the ceiling to make that hole or tore through the floor to get down here. Either looked impossible without machinery. When the others joined him, he felt a little relief, and they picked directions to get moving again. He looked at the rope to ensure he could reach it, because he damn sure wasn't going to get stuck down here. He had a promise to keep.

The flooring and wall materials on this floor were identical to what he'd seen above. Too bad none of the lights had come on yet. Their flashlights led them to the first room, where a door was bent and lying on the ground. A thick, heavy door was casually ripped off the wall and left there. *What could have done that?* Inside the room, they found a long table covered with jars and liquids. Another lab? He wiped continuous sweat from his face; the heat just wouldn't let up. This lab had one noticeable difference; instead of aquatic organisms floating in small vases, there was a table. On it were a series of restraints, thick but torn. Ripped in half, to be accurate.

"What do you make of this?" Dmitry asked.

"I think they were studying bigger specimens here. Straps that thick should be impossible to break," Austin said.

"Should be..." Dublin said, holding up the frayed end of one. "Let's hope we don't run into *this* thing."

Austin shone his light down to the far side of the wall. The parasite may as well have vanished at this point. They backtracked down the hallway and found four more rooms, all similar to the first one. The first was sealed shut, but they could see inside through the window.

Something moved as the flashlight came back to the hallway, so fast it may have been nothing more than a shadow playing tricks on him. He flashed his light again, but didn't see anything.

"You okay?" Dmitry asked.

"I thought I saw it down there."

"Are you sure?" Dmitry shone his light down the hallway.

"No, not really."

"Where?"

Austin aimed his flashlight through the window of the next door.

"Austin, head in that direction, Dublin and I will make sure it can't double back."

"Great..." he replied. This must be a form of payback for trying to send that message. He crept forward, flashlight scanning slowly. He checked another exam room and gave an all clear to Dmitry, who waved him forward. Austin crept to the next sealed door. He flashed his light through the window and fell backwards in a panic, the light skittered across the floor.

"What? Is it in there?"

"No, it's something else, I wasn't expecting it," Austin said stupidly. He gathered himself and retrieved his flashlight.

"The parasite?"

"Just take a look while I put my heart back in my chest."

The door remained sealed, but through the window, they found something larger than either of them strapped to the exam room table, something that would need those thick straps to hold it down.

"Aye, very dead, a good thing too," Dublin whispered.

The creature in the room was huge. It had a thick, squat head the size of Dublin's chest. Its face was comprised of empty eye sockets and a mouth full of jagged teeth. The exam table was raised, making the beast seem upright, which was part of what gave Austin a heart attack moments ago. It also had six arms, thick as tree branches, each individually restrained. It didn't have hands; instead, the arms ended like suction cups, folding off into lips of flesh. Its feet were trunks, attached to lanky and disjointed legs. It was about twice the size of a man, seemingly bipedal.

Dmitry began snapping pictures. "Well, I don't have Orlean's prosthetic to get a multi-layered shot, but these will do for now."

Austin took a moment to gather himself and then looked inside the room again. "Why hasn't it decomposed?"

"Bloody good question for later. Where'd he see the parasite?" Dublin asked, rubbing his chin.

"Austin wasn't certain, but he thought he saw it over here."

He craned his head down the hallway, wondering if the other rooms had similar specimens, wondering if the parasite was about to jump them, or if he'd actually really seen it a moment ago. It had to be down here, unless it somehow doubled back on them.

In the next room, there was a similar specimen, though smaller and at the early stages of shriveling. "I got another one in here," Austin said. The muscles were more pronounced as the flesh had sunk in. "Geez."

They approached the last room. The door was sealed shut like the others, but he detected the electrical hum. Through the window was another one of those six-armed beasts, but this one was the biggest.

"Found the big-papa," Austin said. Dublin and Dmitry appeared behind him.

"It hasn't decayed one bit," Dmitry remarked.

"Aye, he looks fresh. Maybe that's what they studied here, cell aging and such," Dublin proposed.

"Plausible, considering what we've seen so far."

"Guys, look at its chest."

They were collectively silent at noticing the slow, rhythmic rise and fall of its chest.

"It's breathing."

Dmitry moved closer to the window.

"We need a live sample of this," Dmitry said. He grabbed the door handle and tugged, turning it until the locks fell into place. With a thud, the remaining locks clicked home, and the hum of energy stopped. The door whined and opened, all three of them frozen in the doorway.

"This is a bad idea. What if it wakes up?" Austin warned.

"If this thing could wake up, it would have years ago."

Just as he started to argue, a hissing screech spun him. Austin covered his face when something sticky shot him in the eyes, blinding him. Dmitry cried out too.

"My eyes!"

"Shut the door!" Austin cried, fumbling for the control handle. He couldn't see, but he felt something brush by him before he found the door.

"It waited for you to open it!"

"Curdled maggots!" Dublin cursed. "I've got it, hand me the sack!"

Dmitry blindly held the durasack up, and Dublin snatched it from him. They heard his movement as Dublin stalked into the room, whispering taunts, holding the durasack open in both hands. The *thwop* sound of its spider legs was frantic as Dublin bolted at it, though it avoided him easily. With agony and a lot of blurring, Austin was starting to see shapes again.

The jellyfish hid behind a chair. Dublin adjusted his grip, feeling the lightness of the durasack. He readied himself to pounce again when several glass beakers fell, smashing on the floor. The commotion distracted Dublin, just long enough for the parasite to take advantage and dart towards him. He lunged in an attempt to catch it. It jumped, its spidery legs grasping Dublin's hands, keeping the length of the durasack. It wrestled onto his back. Dublin shrieked and spun, but the parasite hopped off of him just as quickly.

"Where did it go?" Dmitry cried, regaining his vision.

"Not good," Dublin panted. The jellyfish stood on the monstrosity's chest, glaring at them. It didn't have a mouth, but Austin's vision was somewhat restored, and he swore it was glaring. It stuck a spider leg in the beast's mouth and disappeared into it with grotesque speed.

"Very not good," Dublin said again.

"Dublin! Get out of there!" Austin begged.

The creature, still bound to the table, slowly began to move, starting with deeper breaths. Then it flexed each of its six arms.

"Dublin!"

"Change of plan," Dmitry ordered, squinting through the pain in his eyes. He twisted the door lever and slammed it shut, trapping Dublin inside.

CHAPTER 11

"Austin!"

Dublin screamed and pounded on the door. Through the window, he saw Austin holding the doorknob, locking him in. That coward trapped him in as payback! That bloody worm would pay when he made it out of here! Dublin pounded again. "Damn you, Austin!"

He slammed against the door, cursing and ignoring the bruising on his fist. He heard a long, slow exhale behind him, which made the hair on the back of his neck stand up. Dublin turned as the monstrosity on the table stirred, lifting its head. A dozen eyes blinked on its face.

One arm ripped free of its restraint, triggering an alarm. Red lights beamed from the ceiling, swirling *bweep bweep bweep.*

"Ya' coward! You'll pay for this!" Dublin swore. Looking through the window, he didn't see Austin or Dmitry anymore. They'd left him. *G'wan now, get it together, you lil' orphan lamb,* he focused. Dublin gathered a blast torch from the toolkit and gave it a slap. Ten thousand degrees of pure cutting ripped out of the torch. He shot it into the doorknob, hoping to cut himself free in time.

"Cut real fast now, you son of a whore!" he shouted, willing the torch through materials unknown.

Sparks flew off the door, spraying in all directions, singeing hair on the back of his hands. Another snap came from behind him, so he stole a glance over his shoulder and saw it trying to sit up, still staring at him. Its dozen eyes blinked independently. He pulled the blast torch away to inspect his progress and cursed. It'd take about another hour to get through the door like this.

"Damn you, Austin!" It looked like Dmitry had tried to get the door back open. Austin must have found a way to lock it, and Dmitry was looking for a tool or something to help. But he didn't have time to wait for that.

The monstrosity ripped apart the last restraints with ease. All sound in the room was deadened except the torch in Dublin's hand. This was a bad thing. The behemoth exhaled a low, steady growl. It stood until its head pushed against the ceiling, being too tall for the room. Dublin circled, looking for an angle, searing torch in hand, realizing he had nowhere to run. A flittering thought of hiding under the table was dismissed. He considered his torch, wondering how much flesh he could ruin before dying. Or maybe he could just keep it at bay until Dmitry returned with help, which he also dismissed. He found a socket near him full of wires. Oh, what the hell. He sank his torch into it and embraced all the consequences.

An immediate surge of energy erupted, followed by a thick cloud of smoke. The torch shot out of his hand like a rocket, and the alarm howl slowed to a stop. The secured door across the room jolted with indecision, sputtering. He went to his hands and knees and crawled as the room filled with toxic fumes, already threatening to close his lungs. A smash above him rocked the walls. The creature had tried to crush him. Crawling in the smoke had saved his life.

The doors wouldn't open more than an inch, though they jerked as if wanting to. Smoke blanketed and billowed. His vision was now blurred, and he couldn't see the creature's feet, barely his own hands. He crawled in a daze, wondering which way he was headed; it felt like the smoke was moving as he held his breath. He climbed to his feet and leaned against the wall, only for it to give way under him. A sobering piece of rubble pushed jagged edges into his side. He'd fallen through the wall, which was now connected to the adjoining exam room. The creature didn't need doors; it made them.

Dublin could no longer hold his breath. His blood vibrated with the oxygen and the nano-inoculations, fighting to purify his red blood cells. He collapsed on the other side of the hole in the wall and crawled away from the smoke, which drained up into vents along the ceiling.

He couldn't stop coughing long enough to stand, so he remained immobilized on the floor next to an exam table. Fans swirled. He ripped his jacket open to let his chest cool off, followed by fits of coughing and spitting. He didn't see the creature, but he saw where it had decided to go, walls being nothing more than a suggestion to it.

An altogether different sound beamed through the hallways, a voice in a language unknown, monotone and penetrating, creating a kind of warped stereophonic echo. It sounded pre-recorded, like the kind his ship gave when there was a malfunction. He listened, but didn't understand.

Standing wasn't easy, but he could do it. He stepped out into the hallway feeling like a bee in a hive.

"Aye, Dublin, still alive. So what'cha think of this fine mess?" He didn't usually talk to himself, but there wasn't anyone around to punch.

Dublin rested his weight against a line of service pipes. The pipes were marked with faded, alien writings. Too bad he couldn't just walk out of here.

"Jus' make it easy for me to find you, Austin, you son of a whore."

**

Dublin pounded on the door. Austin pushed Dmitry out of the way and tried to get the door back open, wrestling for the handle. He didn't have any love for Dublin, but he sure as hell wouldn't leave him trapped in there. How could Dmitry do that? The beast inside was moving, coming to life when a flood of alarms triggered. The door stayed sealed, possibly part of the security protocol, but he wouldn't give up. He wouldn't leave Dublin there. Still, no matter how he pulled, the door wouldn't budge.

Dmitry slammed into him, tackling him from the door. "Leave him! Don't let that thing out!" he yelled. "That's an order!"

"Dublin is trapped in there!" Austin scrambled to his feet and reached again for the lever, pulling on it with all his might. This time, he felt it move an inch, but Dmitry's arm wrapped tightly around his neck. He let go of the handle and clutched at the arm. Dmitry was stronger than he would have expected. With a twist, he flung Austin to the floor.

The alarm triggered activity down the halls. The hallway lights shone with stark illumination, as if a master control had been activated. A half-dozen ceiling panels shifted and inhaled as warning lights spun.

"We're going back," Dmitry ordered.

"Not without Dublin!"

"Look around—it's too late for him!"

Austin tried to step beside him, but Dmitry blocked his path. "I said it's too late!" he roared. Gone was his cool demeanor.

Austin shoved Dmitry into the wall. Their fists were clenched for only a moment when an electric field blazed to life down the corridor, and then another, and then another.

Dmitry saw it and fled in the opposite direction.

Austin saw the electric fields as well. He briefly pictured Carolina at the elevator, waiting for them to come back, oblivious to all this. His feet were light with adrenaline. Dmitry was faster, but survival rocketed them both. Reflections of electric death shone in the walls ahead, chasing them. He sent a fleeting prayer for Dublin as his own fate was about to be decided. Dmitry found an open room and they both dove into it.

The glowing energy zapped by as the two of them caught their breath. Austin sat on the ground where he'd landed. The imminent death was gone and this was just a room, one he shared with Dmitry. He let himself take a moment there, waiting to see what happened next.

"We should focus on getting out of here," Dmitry proposed. He'd also waited to see if the building was going to throw something else at them.

Austin glared. His fearless leader was clearly the sort of person to leave any of them if it meant saving himself. Without answering, Austin drew his gaze over to the fractures in the wall. Ignoring Dmitry, he moved across from him and inspected it, placing his hands against the material. With a gentle push, he found it willing to budge. He'd deal with Dmitry's survival flaws later.

"This might be a way out; the wall is falling apart," Austin said.

"Well?"

The facility was alive with all kinds of sounds, too muffled to make out clearly. Whatever was happening to Dublin right now, he wished him the best and tried not to think of it. At this point, there was nothing he could do, and he had his own problems to deal with. He gave a decent shove, and the wall collapsed, spilling large chunks on either side.

"Perfect. We're back near that arena," he said, looking around. "I'll go first," Dmitry added, climbing through the hole in the wall.

The arena looked the same. It was Austin's turn now. He managed to climb halfway through until his belt wouldn't fit. His head and arms dangled, looking out from the ground floor.

"Dmitry, pull me through!"

A burst of smoke ruptured about fifty meters away, echoing across the arena. The monstrosity, the one the parasite had crawled into, the one they abandoned Dublin for, it was there.

Austin's toolbelt was still wedged in the wall, with him fully stuck.

He didn't see Dmitry anymore.

CHAPTER 12

Accompanied by the walls of their defunct elevator, Athen was able to stand with help. Keeping her leg straight was the plan, and her pain meds were helping. The narrow metal rod in her leg, which Dublin was kind enough to cut proportionately, was snugly in place. They couldn't remove it until they returned to the quadrohuts, where Dmitry had access to proper equipment. At least he numbed the pain, well, most of it. Athen was quickly learning how to walk differently.

She wasn't lonely; Orlean and Helena were her human crutches. She wanted to try to stand without them, but they insisted. Carolina, of course, had wandered to the end of the hallway, watching expectantly for her father to return. And to be truthful, those guys should have been back by now.

Then a shake in the walls, hollow and distant. Fans kicked on and the lights beamed. She was so accustomed to the dimness that she was forced to shield her eyes.

"Something just happened," Helena jumped.

"Maybe the guys flipped a power switch. I'd know more if I had my arm."

"He needs our help," Carolina said. She peered down the stairs where her father and the others had disappeared. "Right now."

"I'm sure everything is fine, sweetie," Athen responded, just before something crashed. The inhuman moans of metal and debris flew up the hallway.

"What was that?"

"He needs us right now," Carolina repeated.

This time, Athen didn't argue. She slung an arm over Orlean and Helena as they dragged her down the hallway. Whirring motors and sensors buzzed around them.

The hallway descended downstairs, leading to a huge, open warehouse, or perhaps an arena, circular in shape and with spectator viewing areas. Carolina was fast, leaving the others no time to dwell. Their path ended directly into a web of suspended platforms. Athen's stomach sank. She was unstable on stable ground, so this did not look promising.

"I'm not going across those!" Helena cried.

A pyre of flames shot from beneath them, followed by an explosion several floors beneath them.

"We need to stay together and find the others!" Orlean urged.

Carolina bounded across, sending the platforms swaying.

"Wait!" Athen struggled to follow, hobbling with Orlean for support. The chains shook, and she clutched Orlean for support. Helena was on her hands and knees, frozen, not able to follow.

Carolina was now ahead of them, bounding towards an elevator just on the other side of the platforms. A working elevator would be a blessing right now.

"Slow down!" Orlean shouted. He tried not to look down as the platform started to move.

"Carolina! Wait!" Athen ordered.

Helena was still on the first platform, immobile, stuck in a crawl. "I can't do it," she whispered. "I just can't…" She turned around.

"Helena!" Orlean called. "Carolina! Damnit!" he groaned. He wouldn't leave Helena, but Carolina wouldn't wait for them. What the hell was that kid's problem? More importantly, where the hell was Dmitry?

The platforms jumped all at once, like a ship tossed by a wave. Athen's feet hovered in the air, and she watched the chain railing fly under her. Out of reflex, she grabbed onto anything she could.

Orlean's good arm held her as Athen dangled over the side, her momentum almost taking him with her.

"Orlean!" she shrieked.

Orlean's grip was slipping fast. He might not be able to hold on; the best he could hope for would be to drop her on a platform below, if it stayed still long enough.

Athen had another idea. "Stay still!" she ordered, her forearms bulging. As an engineer, she had stronger arms than most men. She climbed up Orlean's limb, gripping his sleeve and the skin beneath it, making him wince. It was all grip strength as she ascended over Orlean's shoulders, with one good leg to help her step. Then she dug into his back, and together they fell safely to the suspended platform.

"I'm so glad you work out," Orlean panted.

"I'm glad I grabbed your good arm," Athen exhaled.

"Oh, God," he laughed. His gaze lowered to the ground. "What… what the hell is that?"

A creature taller than a man and with six arms went across the floor of the arena, an unusual-looking creature, like a monster he would have drawn as a kid. It looked up at them.

"Shit!"

It reached up and snagged the bottom platform dangling nearest the floor, sending a ripple up the chain system. It was far below them; it seemed impossible, but one of its arms just extended out to twice its length and grabbed. The creature climbed up towards them, causing the platforms to swing.

A chain snapped; the added weight was too much for this dilapidated system. A platform gave way and smashed to the floor, though the creature was able to swap with ease and continue climbing.

They rose to their feet, silent and in terror. She draped her arm around Orlean's neck and gulped as they practically sprinted.

Pain ripped through her leg where the steel rod was embedded. "I… I can't go this fast," Athen cried, her leg unwilling to cooperate.

"Yes, you can." Orlean flinched as another chain snapped from the weight, felt the lurch as the platforms tilted. They moved with all the speed she could muster.

"Over there!" he yelled, pointing to an opening in the wall. Again, the platform they were on shook, forcing Athen down to her good knee. Orlean grabbed her and stifled a gasp. Gripped underneath the platform just below Athen's knee was one of the creature's wet, cup-shaped hands. The chains moaned from their combined weight. It was at least another fifteen paces to get to safety. With Athen's leg, it may as well be a mile.

"Orlean…" Athen whispered.

"I see it."

"What do we do?"

A long, probing black worm extended from the cup-hand, wriggling through the grated platform, sensing the air.

Orlean tugged Athen to her feet, and they evaded the probing worm. A chain snapped, but they ran, each step a question mark as to whether they were about to fall or worse. They exited into a hallway not far from the elevator, and a door slammed behind them, sealing them in. The echoes of other doors slamming down rippled around them.

"The building is locking us down!" Orlean gasped.

Athen gazed at her surroundings. "What the hell was that?"

"I… I don't know," Orlean said between breaths.

"Now it's just us?"

He shook his head.

"Carolina?"

"I don't… I… I'm sure she's okay. They're all okay," he said, leaning his one arm against the wall. "How's the leg?"

"Hurts." She watched him gather his calm.

Orlean walked over to the security door, his inner shirt freely soaked from the warmth and running. The door that had shut on them had no windows or door handles, just a slab. Another security wall had shut not twenty paces away, closing the hallway off in both directions. They were trapped inside the hallway and rooms.

"This isn't good," Orlean said, going to the other end of the hallway to check the other slab. Athen used the doorway of one room to slide down and sit, resting her leg as blood seeped through the liquid stitches. She looked out at the room, which could have been an office. There were shelves full of strange containers, closed cabinets, and dead screens on the wall. There were no chairs, so she sat on the floor with her leg out.

"Oh, dammit, this is just great," Orlean cursed at the security wall.

"You left the keys in your other pants, didn't you?"

"What?"

"Sorry… I joke when I'm trapped underground," she said, wiping away her smile. With a cough, she adopted a straight face. "It's the painkillers, sorry. Serious. I'm serious now. I'm Athen, but I'm serious too," she covered her mouth to stop.

Orlean rolled his eyes. "What's the maximum burning temp of a plasma torch?"

"One thousand, two hundred and seventy-three kelvins."

"Good, the drugs are only affecting your personality, I can deal with that. What tools do we have?"

"Pneumatic wrench, electron scanner, small laser cutter, and my multi-tool."

"That's it?"

"And these guns," Athen flexed her arms. The joke fell silent. "Dublin carries all the good ones, sorry."

"Well…" Orlean said, studying the wall. He traced the surface with his right hand as far as he could reach. "It's alien technology, but logical reasoning would suggest there's a system here. Something tripped the slab down, so something has to pull it back up. There's got to be a service panel or a switch."

"Maybe we can reverse it, override it, sudden pressure drop… I wish we had bubblegum," Athen said, chewing on the end of her fingernail.

"There's a tiny groove in the ceiling," Orlean observed without optimism. The ceiling was easily a meter higher than he could reach with his good arm, and reaching up with his stump left him feeling a little self-conscious.

"There's furniture in the room," Athen replied.

"Great! Go grab it, oh, sorry. You sit there. How's your leg again?"

"Still hurts."

Orlean chuckled and shook his head. At least Athen was in a good mood; he hoped it stayed that way because he was doing everything he could to keep from freaking out. He spotted a cabinet of sorts and gave it a tug. Even with one arm, he should be able to move it, but the thing wasn't budging. He wedged himself between the wall and the cabinet and pushed with his legs. It seemed bolted in place. If he dislodged it, he'd still have to drag it back, which wasn't looking fun. He needed something smaller but wasn't seeing anything. "Don't these aliens sit down? Where are all the chairs?"

"I know! I asked the same thing!"

Orlean walked over and snatched the laser cutter from her outstretched hand. She sat there chewing her nails and then watched the cabinet inch across the floor, leaving scratches. Each of Orlean's tugs moved the cabinet an inch.

"You're very manly."

Orlean looked down, holding his stump self-consciously with his good arm. Of all the ways he imagined having alone time with Athen, it was never like this. Her gruff engineering side only added to her beauty and pure feminine qualities.

But in thirteen months, he hadn't made a move. And this certainly wasn't the time.

A voice boomed ominously, everywhere. They looked up instinctively like primitive man. The language was unrecognizable; he had no idea what any of it meant. Whatever happened in the big room must have triggered these responses. Not sure why his thoughts turned to a self-destruct feature. Too many fiction stories. If he heard a self-destruct timer, he'd kiss Athen and wait for the end.

"Any ideas what *that* means?" Athen asked.

"I don't want to know."

CHAPTER 13

Carolina raced down the ramps, ignoring Orlean's demands to stop, her feet barely touching the platforms. She was not headed to the elevator; she was looking for her dad as she wound her way down.

A long descending walkway finally became solid ground, and she stayed against the wide, round wall of the testing facility… Carolina shook her head. She didn't know why she thought it was a testing facility, and she was tired of knowing things she shouldn't.

An explosion ruptured across the facility from her. The bio-suit continued its rampage, piloted by the parasite. Carolina held her head this time and leaned against the wall, shaking her thoughts clear. She didn't even know what a bio-suit was.

Pushing its way through the rubble, the creature toppled through easily. It crawled on its six arms through the smoke, looking something like a scorpion, and then stood on its two legs. When the bio-suit stood, it sent Dmitry scrambling; she only saw him because of the movement.

The creature took in its surroundings, focusing on its gaze after Dmitry for a moment, but then it turned to look exactly at her.

She felt one of those foggy memories coming on and shut her eyes. The *thing* saw her, but she couldn't run. She couldn't even open her eyes. The fog subsided, and she was able to open her eyes.

The bio-suit was gone. She spotted it above her, near Orlean and Athen. She wasn't sure if those two would get away in time, but she wasn't worried about them. She was looking for her father, who should have been with Dmitry. She shielded her mouth from the dust that was kicked up and walked over to where Dmitry had last been. She continued moving closer, aware of the security protocols engaging. At least they were filtering the air. The announcement boomed its pre-recorded message, ordering everyone inside to remain calm until the authorities had controlled the situation, praising their leader, and trying to reassure everyone that there was nothing to worry about. Obviously not.

"Carolina!"

That was her father's voice. She found him stuck in the wall.

"You shouldn't be here, baby girl."

"I had to find you," she said, oblivious to the flames engulfing the wall on the far side of the room. Dmitry had abandoned him, a mistake he would pay for dearly. She shook her head; those were not her thoughts.

"You need to get out of here and stay hidden; it isn't safe. I'll find a way out."

"I'm not leaving without you," she said, covering her mouth. The smoke was thickening.

"Carolina…"

She grabbed his arms and planted her feet on the wall, giving all the leverage and muscle her body had. Between their efforts, the wall started to crackle loose, and Austin wriggled his belt free.

"Damn, that was close. What are you doing?" Austin asked.

Carolina ignored him. She was crawling on hands and knees, her fingers tracing the floor in patterns, looking for something.

"Carolina? Hey!"

The floor had an indent, a marker, to help you orient yourself in a directionless room.

"This way," she said and pulled his hand.

"But we came down through—"

"Can't go back."

He thought she was walking to a dead end until she pressed her hand into a key panel, one he hadn't seen until she touched it, and the wall recessed. On the other side was a new path, perfectly hidden unless you knew it was there.

"How did you…" His words trailed off. Neither of them wanted to address how she knew things. A platform shattered to the ground, reminding them to make haste. They needed to get out of there. He angled his light down the hidden path before they cautiously entered.

"By the way, I think you saved us both," he said.

"Dad, your ear is bleeding."

Austin reached up and winced. "Ahh, it's nothing. Hey, where are the others? You shouldn't be alone."

"I left without them. You were in trouble."

He wanted to scold her for leaving the others, but saw little point. As long as she survived, he just wanted to get her home. Austin activated his suit radio, listening to the static as it scanned frequencies, trying to locate the others. "Too much interference. These radios are useless," he groaned, taking a moment to soak in the stream of cooler air.

Carolina hugged him from the side, briefly. He moved to hug her back, but she already disengaged. She wasn't being herself, which he felt stupid for stating. A wave of guilt for bringing her on this trip hit him again. *All I can do is get her home.*

"Well, do we know where this will take us?" he asked.

Carolina didn't answer.

"What do you think, kiddo?"

She closed her eyes, not wanting to think.

In this quiet moment, he decided to keep the silence and let the cool air hit his face. A near-death experience, and now it was just the two of them, and they still weren't out of danger. After a while, he felt ready, regrouped, and made the suggestion to get moving.

She nodded.

The hallway became shorter, and he had to hunch down. Service hatches above them came periodically; he could see light through them. This hidden pathway had been added late; why else make it so short? Carolina followed behind him without needing to crouch; twelve-year-olds were so lucky. As he crouched, they heard another muffled voice high above them, loud and automated. Austin shook his head. "I still don't understand what happened. Everything changed so fast. We went from sneaking up on the parasite, to running from some creature the parasite crawled into, to the building trying to seal us inside."

"It tricked you."

He turned his head but stopped short of eye contact. That may be a normal guess, or it was more of her unnatural insight, and she didn't want to talk about that. "I suppose it did... it needed inside that door. We're such idiots."

This time, they made eye contact.

"Just a lucky guess," she said, looking away.

Austin remembered the face she had just made; he had seen it when she was a kid, caught in a lie.

CHAPTER 14

Helena was not brave, nor was she outgoing. She was a girl who protected herself, which was pretty logical in her opinion. Staying alive was as basic as the need to eat or sleep. She even chose the safe career of being an analyst, and look where that got her. She may as well have chosen Arctic Miner.

Helena nursed her hand and consoled herself while waiting in the spot where their elevator had first crashed, the location where they were last together before Dmitry and they split up. That was the plan; she'd stay put and wait until help came. She eventually realized she was holding her knees to her chest, rocking forward and back, like a nervous kid.

She was scared, had every reason to be. She needed the others to show up, but was also ashamed of abandoning them. It was rational, she was just being smart. For one thing, Carolina shouldn't even be on this planet, and it was not her responsibility. It wasn't her job to keep someone else's kid safe. Orlean threw himself in harm's way for Athen, but that was his choice, a male thing to do for an attractive female. Not Helena, she was far more practical. Everything was wrong about that situation, and any logical person would have done the same thing. She was not brave, but bravery was for fools.

"You're a real piece of work, Helena," she scolded herself. It was several minutes before she stood, long after the voice and the lights did their thing, long after she couldn't hear that monster thrashing. The image of that creature would haunt her.

She wiped her hands on her pants, smearing blood. She had lacerated her left hand trying to climb up the elevator shaft. She gave it a try, fearful that thing was coming for her… but it didn't, and now she had a wound to treat. She adjusted the hair tie, keeping her skinfolds in place.

No one was coming back. They'd all scattered and separated, and she'd probably have to find them.

She did not like that idea at all.

It would be safe to do a little info gathering. She walked down the hallway and then down the steps, listening to the sputtering flames and the hollow ambiance ahead. Blood dripped from her hand; she tried to tighten her hair-tie again. No matter how she fiddled with her hand, she couldn't get the wound shut. Stupid hair-tie was a gift from her cousin, '*for luck*'. She returned to her crashed elevator.

No one would come back for her. If they were going to, they would have by now.

Still, she waited another five minutes, just in case.

"Ugh!" she groaned, wondering why she was still sitting there. She started to brush her hair back, spending another minute straightening it. Then she smoothed out her pants and pockets, checking the fastenings on the belt. It hurt her hand, which would need to be looked at better when Dmitry had the chance.

She couldn't stall any longer.

Another grunt, high-pitched and not sure what sound she'd made before she walked down the hallway and turned the corner down the steps.

Things looked different in the big room this time. A bed of smoke hovered beneath the suspended platforms, the ones she was unwilling to cross. A tired ventilation system worked slowly to channel the haze away. Some of the platforms had snapped and dangled inverted, or were just gone. She didn't see a way across them now. If Orlean was crippled at the bottom waiting to die, it was his own damn fault.

She could reach one inverted platform, which had come to rest against the wall like a ladder. Down was all she had, just great.

Helena huffed. She didn't want to climb down. But there was no climbing up, and she'd die waiting. All she had was down. She retreated up the stairs before forcing herself to stop.

"No one is coming, idiot," she cursed.

She got ready to climb down, sticking a leg over the end, and she panicked as her foot searched for the platform.

Hovering blindly, she finally found a spot to rest her weight on. One down, she could do this. She gripped the dangling chain with her hands and let her other foot join. The make-shift ladder felt sturdy against the side of the wall. She committed herself fully at the end of the stairs and is now suspended on the side of the wall. Her hand oozed, threatening her grip. She resorted to wrapping the inside of her elbow around the side. It was a slow descent, one she pictured Dublin doing with ease, his rippling muscles barely sweating. But Helena was content to take all day if it meant not falling.

The smoke invaded her lungs, but the ventilation system was at least giving some relief. Her mock ladder ended about five feet from the floor. Double-checking there was nothing to twist an ankle on, she hopped down to stable ground. From there, she crawled under one of the security doors that had only shut part of the way. She didn't see Orlean anywhere, which was good. Though it would have served him right to be suffering after leaving her alone.

Was this the right way? This was the only one so far. All she needed was another elevator or a stairway going up. Surely a place like this would have them; several paths, multiple emergency exits.

A dozen lights flickered to life, and she jumped before realizing it was probably her own presence turning them on. She took in the humid air and exhaled with a groan. It was hotter down here than up by those stairs, and she was dripping with sweat. Minutes passed, and the hallway gave way to a couple more specimen rooms. She would not be looking in them. She continued until stopping at another security door.

"Great," she mumbled. How many of these cursed things were there? She wasn't about to walk all the way back for nothing.

"Helena?"

Helena shrieked. "Dmitry? Oh, thank God!"

"You are alone?" he asked, taking a step towards her and placing his hand on her shoulder. "Now, how did you do that to yourself?" he asked, scooping up her hand.

"I… I was trying to climb up the elevator shaft."

Dmitry examined the cut. "Where are the others?"

"I don't know."

He looked at her in a way that prompted her to continue. "They ran off, and before I could catch up, that thing came out of nowhere and…" she trailed off.

"Have you seen Austin?"

"I thought he was with you?" she replied.

"He was," Dmitry said, smiling and looking at her. "But… we were split up, too. I'm glad you're here. You can help me get this door open."

He had an intensity that evaporated.

"Open it? How?"

He smirked. "We'll have to use our brains," he said, digging into a panel. A glut of sagging, thick wires flopped out of the wall. "Electricity is a natural phenomenon with consistent laws, though I've never seen it used like this."

Helena took a step back, even though Dmitry's gloves shielded him from electrocution. He tugged a glowing tube aside and pushed it to the corner. "*That's* not electricity, not sure what it is." He clipped two prongs into a wire and measured the readings on his pocket device before removing the prongs and trying another. He tested several wires this way, waiting for one to do something.

"How are we going to find the others?"

"Well, I imagine they are trying to find a way out too, so we'll either bump into them here or when we all make it topside," Dmitry said.

"We aren't going to look for them?"

"We'll look for them while we look for a way out."

The security door jolted. "Ah, there you are." Dmitry twisted a dial on his kit and fiddled with the buttons, watching the door's reaction as it stuttered. "Hmm. It doesn't want to be overridden," he said, applying more focus to his efforts. "You didn't tell me how you got separated from Orlean."

"Well… He ran…"

With a hydraulic gasp, the security door vanished into the ceiling, along with what sounded like other doors further away. Dmitry held a satisfied smile. "Shall we?"

Helena nodded.

He led her down the new hallway, and she traveled uncomfortably close to him.

"Do you think there's an elevator this way?" she asked.

He replied with silence.

"I'm sorry, I'm just nervous." Helena seemed compelled to make conversation. "But I bet there is one, an elevator, maybe. I'm sorry." She stuffed her hands into her pockets to keep from talking.

Eventually, they came to an intersecting hallway, branching to the left and right, with an ominous red door in front of them. She agonized over the thought of further exploration. She didn't want anything new; she just wanted out of here.

"This looks important. Check that side for a switch or a panel. I'll check this side."

She was quick to do what he asked. "Dmitry?"

"Helena, it isn't complicated, just look for a button."

"I heard something," she said.

Dmitry stopped to listen, taking a good ten seconds to do so. "This place makes noise sometimes. What's that?" he asked, pointing to a button on her si de of the door.

Helena smiled sheepishly.

Dmitry feigned a return smile.

Helena nodded and pushed the button. The door regressed into the wall, and stale air flooded the hallway. Inside was an ornate pathway, long and curved, with doors lining the interior.

It didn't feel like a way out.

CHAPTER 15

For a man with two degrees in experimental technology, Orlean should not be struggling this hard. All he wanted to do was remove the ceiling tile above him, and it was doing everything in its power to resist him. And Athen was watching him fail.

Dublin would have removed the ceiling tile by now. Big, strong, dumb Dublin, with two arms. He wished Athen had something to look at other than him.

"Open, damn you!" Orlean cursed, yanking the wrench with one arm until it slipped and clattered to the floor. The skin of his palm throbbed. He climbed down for the fourth, no fifth time now, and retrieved the wrench. When he climbed back up, he noticed a slight adjustment had been made in the ceiling tile.

"Hahaa!" Orlean cheered.

"You made a dent!" Athen clapped on his behalf.

"Pftt," Orlean huffed. He buried the tip of the wrench in the space he made and turned. Finally, the ceiling tile dropped to the floor.

"I never doubted you," she smiled.

Her personality wavered between sleepy and drunk, which would be fine if he could stop staring at her chest. Her sweat-matted hair and bloody leg just made her more exotic and vulnerable. *Focus, man.* "Sure you didn't," he smiled, hoisting the small cutter.

The intestine of wires and tubes he had exposed offered a new glimpse inside alien technology. He saw two cables that conspicuously looked like the hydraulics needed to operate the doors. "Here goes nothing."

A slice through the cable sent high-pressured gook spraying at him. He staggered and fell gracelessly. Athen slid up next to him.

"Oh, Orlean, you aren't supposed to hurt yourself," she said. He was surprised to feel her fingers run through his hair. He must have jumped a little; Athen recoiled her hand.

"You don't have to stop," he said.

Athen limped over to where Orlean had dropped the wrench. He wiped the hydraulic fluid from his face. "Try the door now," she said.

Orlean stood. He had her hands running through his hair, and he totally blew it. He thought about falling down again, to see if it'd work twice. Instead, he walked over to the door, catching the wrench she tossed to him with a smile, wearing the rest of the black gook that had sprayed him. He angled the wrench at the base of the door and lifted; a gurgling backflow of pressure leaked as the door regressed. "Oh no," he said, casually falling right next to her.

She took his head in her lap and brushed his hair again. This time, he just closed his eyes and let her.

"You are so strong getting that door open," she encouraged.

"It was nothing, just principles of leverage… and your idea with the hydraulics… uhm, but I did have to lift that, it was heavy…"

"Shall we get going?" she asked.

He opened his eyes and looked up at her, but then nervously rolled up to seating. He stood and reached a hand out for her. "Right this way, miss," he said.

"Then get us above ground, research guy."

"I'm your guy, for getting above ground, I mean," Orlean stammered.

They went down a dozen meters or so to the next wall. It regressed with help, proving the hydraulic lines were linked. A gush of smoke slipped in as he opened the way.

"Ugh," Athen said, covering her mouth.

"It's clearing, slowly," Orlean tried to reassure her. They were back in the large room with the platforms, along one of the middle tiers, looking over. The structure down below smoldered, pumping out more smoke. Between Athen's bad leg and his one arm, walking those platforms again was not going to be easy.

"Well, I see the elevator," Athen winced, leaning on Orlean for support. He tried not to think about her body weight on him. "Let me just grab my anti-gravity boots and I'll surf on over there."

He smiled. "Wouldn't that be nice?" Orlean looked out across the massive room, studying the walls. If he were a rock climber, there were enough grooves to shimmy your way across. There was a nice, thick pipe for support that covered half the distance. Even a non-rock climber might be able to do it, but not a girl with a steel rod in her thigh. "I don't see a way across."

Athen stepped in front of Orlean and examined the view for herself. "Bit of a drop," she giggled. She considered the same thick pipe going across and selected her laser cutter from her belt. She removed a piece of pipe from the wall, pulling out the wires inside it. Using the pipe, she made another cut, wrapped some wires, and Orlean watched in curiosity as she constructed… something. "Stand back," she told Orlean, hoisting her design. She pulled out a small compressor.

"I'm dying to see what you are thinking here," Orlean admitted, totally at a loss.

She sent a burst of air from the compressor into her design, launching it in a parabola. He covered his ears out of reflex. In no time at all, a heavy cable went from Athen to the end of the wall.

"I made a potato gun!"

Orlean gawked. She'd made a rappel line out of junk and wires in like a minute.

"But we'd better hurry, my leg's really starting to hurt." She wound the end of the rappel line snugly around a support beam. Orlean gulped and watched as she undid part of her pants. "Like this," she said, removing her belt. In a moment, she made a belt harness on the rappel line and went head-first. "See?"

She made it look easy until she struggled to get her wounded leg above the cable. Orlean helped get her heel over, trying not to make her wince.

"I liked your anti-grav idea better," Orlean joked. Athen pulled herself across without a second thought, repeating hand over hand. Her feet looped over to keep herself from dangling as Orlean fumbled with his belt, trying to do what he just saw Athen do. When she made it safely across, he figured it was his turn.

His design wasn't quite as graceful as Athen's, and he dangled, fumbling to steady himself with his hands and feet. He felt the line stretch under his thrashing.

"Try to steady yourself!" she called.

"Sure thing… I just… can't…stop…swinging," Orlean said. Finally, he had a hold of the line until he stopped twirling. He swung his legs up, wondering how only one arm would slow him down. He pushed with his feet and pulled with his good hand, moving about half as quickly as she had. She wore a sympathetic smile when he made it halfway.

"Doing great!" she called.

When Orlean finally reached her, his hand was shaking, and he was dripping sweat like a faucet. He would need a moment before he could move again. She waited against the wall, her eyes closed. At least they'd made it across.

"Meds starting to fade?"

"Mm-hmm," she answered.

"Well then, let's test this elevator," Orlean said.

"What about Carolina and the others?"

Orlean looked out across the open quarters. Most of the doors were sealed shut with those cursed security walls, but not all. "I don't see them anywhere."

"What about that... *thing*?" Athen asked.

"If we see it, we run like hell."

"Uhm, Orlean?" she said, pointing to her leg.

"Right, you fight it off and I'll run like hell," he said, offering a smile.

"Probably the way it would happen."

"I wouldn't leave you," he said, suddenly serious.

She looked him in the eye in a way that she had never done before. "I know." She cleared her throat. "It's getting harder to walk."

"Here," Orlean said, hoisting her arm around his shoulders.

They entered the elevator and stared wide-eyed at the massive array of buttons. The other elevator had only a fraction of them. "Which one?" she asked.

Orlean planted his hand against his forehead. "We don't even know if this goes to the top."

"What if it's as brittle as the last elevator?"

Orlean really didn't like the thought of that. "You need medical attention; we at least have to try."

Athen did an impressed-girl look, the only word Orlean had for it.

"Just press the top button, see where it takes us," Orlean said, trying not to blush.

She reached out and pressed the top button; its symbol looked like a crane without legs. The elevator whirred to life, and the door closed. It moved up smoothly, which was good, but not for very long. The doors opened to a hallway of dancing lights and crackling flames. Orlean grabbed Athen by the back of her shirt and pulled her back.

"Watch it," she said. Orlean cupped a hand over her mouth. Something was up. Athen's pulse quickened.

Orlean frantically pressed another button to close the elevator doors when several long, probing tentacles felt their way into the elevator. Athen would have shrieked if not for Orlean's hand. One of the tentacles wrapped itself around her waist and picked her up, squeezing. Another tentacle picked up Orlean, effortlessly holding them both in the air.

They beheld the creature from before, its tentacles extending like hoses from its arms. It was too tall for the hallway, head hunched against the ceiling. It dropped Athen.

"Agh!" she cried as she fell to the floor. Orlean still dangled in the air, held in its grasp. The monster raised a third arm, and dozens of needle-thin veins shot into Orlean's face and chest.

"No!"

The monster set Orlean down carefully on his own two feet, those long red lines sticking in him like the wires of a puppet. Orlean walked unnaturally out of the elevator, jolting and convulsing.

"Orlean!" Athen screamed. She couldn't get to her feet. "Wait! No!" She reached out to grab him, but missed.

He kept walking away from the elevator, passing by the monster as it watched him, controlled by those long, organic veins.

The elevator door shut. She couldn't see him anymore.

CHAPTER 16

Austin fought his anxiety as they continued to go through the hidden service tunnel, practically crawling. It was longer than he thought it would be, and shorter than he was comfortable with. More than once, he considered going back to the last hatch they had passed.

"Dad, I'm getting thirsty again," Carolina said.

He stopped and felt his canteen, which was all but empty. He was thirsty too, but she didn't need to know that. He looked ahead and back again. Another hatch had to be coming soon, he hoped.

"Here," he said, removing his water pouch. Back at the quadrohuts, he could have topped it up. He could have brought two canteens, just in case, but no one planned for this. "Help yourself."

Carolina nodded and began to drink; her cheeks were glowing red. She drank until the canteen ran dry and then wiped her mouth. "I'm still thirsty."

He took the empty canteen. "We'll have to find some more." He hated being tormented by something as simple as water, something that he had access to everywhere else, everywhere except here.

He scanned ahead. It was dark except for the meter of light coming from his suit, and after a little while, he realized the air smelled worse. "I think we are getting somewhere." He reached the end of the tunnel and found a ladder going up. *What kind of service tunnel was this?* Looking up, it seemed to go on forever. His little flashlight just couldn't penetrate far enough to lessen his anxiety. Just a little bit more would make him feel so much better. "Good thing I'm up for a climb. You'd better go first," he said, picturing catching her.

She climbed up, and he followed, hand over hand, with limited visibility above or below. Eventually, she reached the top, sealed by another service hatch. He reached past Carolina and firmly grabbed the release lever. He double-checked his balance and grip; slipping here would be a long and excruciating fall. With one hand on a rung for stability, it was hard to apply the needed pressure. Carolina added her free hand as he pushed, giving just enough help to get the lever turning. The air gasped, and the hatch slid smoothly to the side. Unfortunately, the air that followed was terribly foul.

"Eww, what is that?" Carolina asked.

"Come on," he said, gesturing her up and out. They climbed out of the ladder and took in their new surroundings. It seemed they had emerged into a new room.

"It's another exam room or something," he decided, covering his nose from the stench. The foulness cried of fish decomposition, thick and concentrated. He examined one of the specimen jars nearby, with unspeakably murky water no one should drink. These specimens were in far worse shape than the ones they'd found earlier.

"These must be the failures," Austin said. "I wonder what the experiment was?"

Carolina didn't reply, but she looked contemplative. "Can we get out of here?"

"Definitely, from now on, I'm trusting my nose, and it says let's go," Austin vowed, sliding the double doors open.

He took in the area outside the exam room, which was noticeably different from the others. There'd been a battle. The walls were singed black, and deep gashes marred everything, from the floor to the walls to the ceiling. He ran his finger along one of the gouges, wondering what could have made it. He tapped his knuckle on the wall; it resonated with a thickness. He would need a laser torch to leave indents like this.

"Whatever did this was strong," he said, thinking of the creature from before. *Maybe, possibly.* Heaven forbid something even worse.

"You admire it?"

"No, not really. Though it is quite the scientific discovery," he replied.

Carolina looked at the wall. "I've been hearing that a lot lately."

"I suppose you have." He noticed a tension that wasn't there until now. Was this a parental moment, one that he was failing? "Hey, maybe when we get home, I'll take you to that bakery you like by mom's house, what's it called?"

She glared. "You can't promise me anything! We aren't getting out of here!"

"Hey, *hey*... look at me," he demanded, kneeling down and turning her shoulders to face him. She wouldn't look him in the eye. "You will get out of here, I promise. Have I ever lied to you?"

Carolina sniffed, clearing her throat. If any tears were ready, she pushed them away and crossed her arms.

"I'm not a little kid."

"I know." He sat with her for a few moments. "I'm scared. I admit it. It's okay if you are, too. But I'm doing my best to get us out of here."

Carolina held her wrist. "Sometimes… I remember stuff."

He let a long silence follow. For the first time, it looked like Carolina wanted to open up to him. "Well, you can tell me anything, if you want to, but you also don't have to."

She studied the back of her hand, picking at her fingernails. "I'm still thirsty."

He reached for his canteen before remembering. He nearly crumpled it in frustration, but he maintained his patience. He could tolerate being in danger, but he couldn't withstand her being in danger too.

"Every life form needs water, lesson number one in biology. There has to be a source around here," he said, going to one of the rooms across from them. The door was closed, so he wedged his fingers in and forced it open.

"I'm not drinking anything from this place!"

His fingers slipped, and the doors snapped shut. "Ouch! Damn it, Carolina!"

She turned away. "I want Mom!" she cried and ran, stopping at the end of the hallway.

You and me both, kid. Austin dropped his head and punched the door in front of him. Why did he act that way? It was just one more example to prove he wasn't cut out for parenting.

"Honey, I'm sorry," he said. He looked down the scorched hallway and suddenly realized he didn't see her anymore. "Carolina?" he called. "Hey!" She couldn't leave his sight, not down here.

Now his frustration really boiled, more at himself than at her, realizing he still didn't have his temper back. He didn't see her, but he heard little sobs and knew she was close by, close enough to let her be for just a moment. It might be better to keep a little distance until he calmed down.

"I'm sorry… It's okay. Everything's going to be okay. Take your time." He slouched against the wall and stared out.

After a minute, he didn't hear the sobs. "Carolina?" He took a few steps, waiting to see her appear. He looked through the window of an exam room, thinking maybe she had gone inside. "Kiddo, this is serious now. Where are you?" he said, a little loud and stern. He walked quietly, turning his ear down the hallway, hoping to hear something. He only heard himself. The hallway was getting darker. She couldn't have disappeared, could she?

He poked his head into an exam room, staring at the silhouettes of jars. She could easily hide in a dozen places down here. "Get out here right now!" He again bit his tongue. Yelling at her is what started this; he had to keep his temper. None of this was her fault. When he found her, he was going to make it up to her.

Austin let himself sag to the ground, his boots marred with soot. "Okay, kiddo, I'm going to sit right here," he said loud enough to make sure his voice carried. "I'm going to sit here until you are ready to go." He pulled his feet into a cross-legged position. He pulled out his canteen and managed to get a drop of water out of it. He needed water too, and soon. He removed an energy bar from his other pocket, wondering if he should eat it or if it would just make him thirstier. Carolina's mother would know what to do. Or maybe she wouldn't, maybe she struggled just like him. If she did, it never showed.

CHAPTER 17

Dmitry tried not to cross his arms, but his face could only hide so much. "Are you ready to go yet?"

Helena's face remained pale.

They were inside one of the countless exam rooms, having taken refuge there.

Helena had thought she heard something, and it was enough to make her panic. Maybe if she were any less terrified, he wouldn't have run too. Following her, of all people.

He rolled his eyes. She turned sheepish, ready to apologize when something made a noise. This time, he heard it too. At least they were already hidden. He'd forgive Helena this time.

Coming from down the hallway, whatever it was seemed to be getting closer. Heavy footsteps and labored breathing, it could be a member of his own team, but he doubted it. Dmitry crouched down and was well hidden. What he wouldn't give for a way to bring that monster back to Earth. And while the planetary vessel wasn't designed for additional weight… There were ways around that. Helena, for example.

Helena stayed quiet and hidden, which was a good thing for her sake. The shuffling footsteps came closer. Then the sound stopped. Why would it stop? Silence, and he waited. A sickening fear crept in that the creature detected them. Why else would it stop? He needed to get a look for himself, so he angled his view around the door. He'd kill for a tiny mirror, but this would have to do. He squinted, not sure what he was looking at, but then his jaw dropped.

He saw Orlean across the hallway, engaging with a hologram, operating menus he shouldn't understand. That wasn't all. There were a dozen thick veins, coming right out of him, oozing at points of penetration. Following the veins, they trailed to the creature's hand, standing about two meters away from Orlean. It seemed to be in control of him.

The door opened, and as soon as it did, the creature hurled him inside. Dmitry winced as he heard Orlean's body collide with the floor. The creature ducked its head and entered, and then the big door slammed shut.

"What was that?" Helena asked. She hadn't seen any of it, curled up in the corner as far away as she could get.

Dmitry sat there a minute, breathing. Something about seeing Orlean turned into a fleshy pincushion gave him pause. If he were going to capture that thing, he'd need to be aware of its capabilities. Seeing this was actually quite fortunate for him, because now he had new information.

He knew the creature still needed help opening some doors, it still wanted something, and it had the ability to control people. What kind of value beheld whatever the creature was looking for, he wondered?

The hallway was clear, so he grabbed Helena by the wrists and yanked her to her feet. He dragged her across despite her protests.

"You're hurting me," she begged. Dmitry didn't stop until they were in front of the interface where Orlean had been just a moment ago.

"Put your hand there," he said to her.

"What? Why?"

"Just do it."

If Helena refused, he would almost congratulate her on having a spine. But instead, she predictably nodded and placed a shaky hand on the pad. As her skin touched it, it blipped green, sensors activated and swarmed around her, scanning her. The hologram appeared, but it didn't ask for any selections like it had with Orlean. From what Dmitry had seen, the creature could make doors wherever it wanted to, so why go through the menu? There had to be a reason to use this door instead of ripping it off the wall, maybe to keep from triggering security protocols, like preserving certain failsafe measures. After a quick scan, the big doors slid open. He pushed Helena in and then carefully followed. He didn't intend to let the creature know it was being tracked.

The room was spacious, with polished black walls, the middle of which tiered up a step, surrounded by dozens of terminals. A broken set of doors waited on the far side, the creature presumably having gone that way. Orlean, however, was crumpled on the floor like a dirty shirt. And he was alive, despite the contorted way his neck looked. There was something else wrong with him, too—something under his skin.

"Orlean!" Helena screamed. Dmitry spun and slapped her in the mouth. An outburst like that might give away their presence, although he admitted he hadn't told her to be quiet, and she didn't know he was following the creature. Still, she probably knew better now as she held her jaw in disbelief.

A glare, that was all, it was the most she would ever dare to challenge him.

Orlean, poor Orlean. He had managed to lift his head, and he had the faintest bit of hope when he saw them. Dmitry took a better look at his colleague, at the worms still dangling in his body, watching as they slithered into him. He took a step back and grabbed Helena by the collar.

"Wait…" Orlean gasped. They toyed with his flesh, climbing in and out of him.

Dmitry pulled Helena further away. "We can't help him."

"Please…" he managed to say through bubbles coming out of his throat.

"Don't get close."

"But, Dmitry?" she protested, unable to grasp reality.

"Leave him."

Orlean's eyes were soft steel as he realized he'd been abandoned. If Dmitry feared curses, he'd fear one now. But he hadn't been the one to condemn Orlean, and there was nothing he could do to help. It was best to move on and appreciate that he didn't have to cut as much weight before takeoff now. Dmitry stepped around, well away from the hand Orlean reached after him.

The room they were in did not concern Dmitry; it was some kind of control room, and he had given up the constant interest in alien architecture. He had to prioritize his goals, and the creature was goal number one. That said, this room felt out of place, at least compared to the stale exam rooms and drab hallways. He crossed over to where those two doors waited, beckoning Helena to follow. Instead, she collapsed.

Right in the middle of the room, on her hands and knees, he quickly diagnosed her as having a panic attack of all things. He didn't have time for this… but he might need Helena. She was the only bait he had. He looked down at her, sobbing on the ground like a child, gasping for breath, and hyperventilating at the same time. The right motivation would make her snap out of this…

"I think I hear something."

She sobered quickly to her feet, grabbing onto his arm. He gave a pretend look around and then pointed down the hallway. "We'd better go this way."

"But..."

"Come on."

"But the door is smashed... what if the monster did it?"

Dmitry walked over to the doors. They were obviously smashed by the *monster*, as Helena called it. "Hmm... no. This doesn't look recent." Helena was intelligent; she'd see right through it, but she was also spineless. She would capitulate, and did, to avoid further confrontation. "It's safe, I promise."

Helena really wanted to disagree with him; he could feel it. But instead she took a step forward, and he couldn't help but smile. He followed her because if the beast suddenly came back, she would be a barrier of protection.

The hallway was well-lit compared to the others, the walls were bright yellow with decorative tiles and the occasional panel. The path split into several possible directions, and the first one they tried was a dead end, or rather just incomplete. They backtracked, and the second hallway forked off into more branches. The left path went to a room vibrating with the hum of generators. He sensed movement, hadn't seen it yet, but out of reflex, he ducked down. He grabbed Helena by the wrist, pulling her around the corner of an empty room. At least she didn't ask 'what is it?' this time. He waited until he saw it. Bless his instincts, he was right. The creature came out of the generator room and turned down the hallway away from them. Helena covered her mouth and hid.

Dmitry felt for the tranquilizer he had in his left cargo pocket. He had grabbed it to assist him with the parasite. Had he known about this creature instead, he would have grabbed five more. He stole a glance around the corner, spotting the creature at a panel outside the generator room. If he had to guess, he would say the creature was studying a blueprint.

Just how intelligent was this thing? Fully sentient, like him? As his answer, he watched the creature lumber back into the generator room and power up a specific switch. The electricity in the hallway dipped as heavy currents of electrical power redistributed to whatever the creature had in mind. Monstrous, but no animal. It was smart. He'd seen enough to know that now.

He ducked down as the creature turned, not wanting to be spotted. Even using Helena as a shield, it was different when the beast was right there. After an extended period of silence, he again poked his head around the corner and down the hallway.

What the hell? He wondered. *Where did it go? So much for testing the tranquilizer.* He stood and again dragged Helena by the wrist. He stopped at the intersection outside the generator room, but the creature was nowhere to be found.

He went into the generator room, wondering what he had witnessed. If it gave him some clue to the creature's plan, he'd be better for it. The room was vibrating with an ungodly sound, with about half of the units illuminated while the other half were not. Heavy cables adorned the ceiling and floors, pumping energy throughout the facility.

"What is this place?" Helena asked.

"This is the power room, or one of them," Dmitry practically had to shout. *Obviously*, he said to himself. Dmitry gazed about, hands over his ears. It wasn't exactly deafening, but he didn't want to lose any temporary hearing with that thing wandering around. Dmitry examined the octagonal shape of each generator, layered in rows three by three. He went to the one he believed the creature had activated, without certainty, since his view wasn't the best at the time. "I think the creature activated this one. Any ideas why?" he asked. He did not expect any sort of useful response from her.

"Probably an exit or an elevator, or something like that."

He almost choked. She'd composed an intelligent idea, but he had dismissed that possibility a while ago. Once the surprise wore off, Dmitry had to ask himself what he intended to do. "I have an idea."

He grabbed the lever and pulled it shut, effectively undoing what the *monster* had done. He felt it exhale and quit vibrating.

"What are you doing? That thing will come back!"

"Quiet, I'm still thinking this through," he said, studying the cables, looking at the distance from the generator to the door. The creature would presumably be forced to return, double-check why its pathway wasn't powered. It'd have to come in through there.

"It's going to be here!" Helena cried, terrified.

"I'm counting on it," he said with a smile before punching her square in the nose. Helena toppled to the ground in an unconscious heap. He had work to do before that thing came back.

CHAPTER 18

Athen had known despair before, the kind that dragged you into unreachable places, and from there you either kept going or you died. She had broken her ankle once on a hike through Kazakhstan Prefecture during the Global Trekkathon at the ignorant age of seventeen; she had broken it twenty kilometers away from the next checkpoint, where she could get any kind of help. One grapefruit-sized rock had twisted her ankle just right and ruined everything. She'd looked up at the clouds first, instinctively, she supposed. Then she'd looked at the mountains which were forever on the horizon, wondering when help would come. And with no one and no thing around for kilometers, she looked at her ankle and realized she was in trouble. That part of the trek was a pure and untouched place, and you could go days without seeing anyone else on that race. It took so much to stand, and even more to hike twenty kilometers with a broken ankle. Yet as dark as that moment was, she'd made it through. Athen discovered at age seventeen that she was mentally strong. What she just saw was enough to make most people sit and cry until someone came to save them. But Athen, wounded leg and all, was not going to abandon Orlean so easily.

The elevator had briefly gone to another floor, but she found the button that took her back to where she'd last seen him. The door slid open at counter angles, a slick architectural nod to alien technology. She leaned against the wall, her weight resting on her good leg, hands clenched. Maybe it was the painkillers making her feel so bold. She staggered out of the elevator using the wall for support.

The crackling fires and smoke were subdued, though charred walls and acrid smells remained.

It wouldn't be hard to find him. Orlean had left a trail of blood. Even in this dim light, it was easy to follow.

The hallway was a little more industrial than the previous areas, with long metal pipes lining the walls and crisscrossing overhead, occasionally emitting gushes of steam. Athen shielded herself with her hand as she crossed beneath a geyser. The facility clearly spanned far more terrain than any of them had expected. And here she'd thought it was just another boring little planet. She closed her eyes and took a few more steps, still holding the wall. Her leg was angry, but not as angry as she was.

Athen wiped her forehead and pulled her hair into a ponytail. Her good leg wobbled; she was running out of stamina. She couldn't see far down this hallway as it arched, and it was taking her too long to make any distance. The trail continued. Frustrated, she propped an arm against the wall. She pictured Orlean dangling like a worm for that thing.

The pain swam through her, fueling her. She used it, forcing herself onwards. She navigated a pipe that threatened to obstruct her path, one that stuck above the otherwise beveled ground. She continued on, mumbling to herself about what a great day she was having, until stopping at a secured doorway, different than the simple ones at each room. Large recessed lights focused on a rectangular set of steel doors. The trail of blood also disappeared inside.

"Orlean, you waiting for me on the other side?"

Massive hinges held the door on both sides, and adjacent to them waited a chest-high panel that blinked red. Athen paused as a hologram appeared, backing away instinctively.

The hologram came to life with exotic symbols, then a small picture of a round and gangly creature. Athen blinked, recognizing a warning even if she didn't recognize the language. The hologram then flashed. It was a short warning that disappeared after playing, and Athen didn't really understand it. The only part she recognized was the part where the creature in the video was zapped to death by a probe coming out of the wall. Athen looked at the wall, noticing fine grooves where similar death-probes might be hiding.

"Are you kidding me?"

She stared at the door, then looked up and down both directions, searching for another solution. "Damn you, Orlean," she whined. "You owe me a drink." It was a door, and doors were meant to be used. So from that logic and the little video, she figured the wrong species got zapped, while the right species got in. And the blood trail went on in, so it must have let Orlean through. Cross-multiply and solve for x. Maybe that meant it'd let her in, too?

Big maybe.

Before she had a chance to think better of it, she placed her hand on the security panel and watched as a dozen sensors swarmed her. She shut her eyes, too spent to care if she was disintegrated. Something turned green, and she felt the locks behind the wall click open. Strange how, even here, green was the *GO* color. Some things really were universal, she supposed. The big doors opened, and she let out the breath she'd been holding.

Lunar Central Station… that was her first thought. Her schema of experiences reminded her of Lunar Central Station, which everyone who traveled off-planet had been to, or *LuCent*, as most called it. Space travel, leaving Earth, stopped at the moon as the big orbiters preferred the weaker gravity. Eight million people a year flowed through *LuCent*, she had heard. What Athen saw inside looked like a travel hub to her. Big, gaping entrances and exits, an oval control center in the middle of one giant room, smaller station cubicles for some kind of business, huge billboards hanging from the ceiling, black walls. The ceilings vaulted almost beyond sight, and dozens of control stations and monitors were housed around her. She walked inside.

"Athen…"

She jumped at the sound of Orlean's groan, finding him on the floor, barely able to hold his head up. "Oh god."

Orlean suddenly stood to his feet. She had started towards him but then stopped. Something about the way he moved wasn't right, nor was his head at an angle on his neck.

Orlean walked towards her, slowly. "Athen…" he moaned.

He wasn't walking; he was being carried, held upright by dozens of wormy veins. She covered her mouth in terror as they slithered him towards her. She grabbed a pry-bar from her toolbag. Wieldy and heavy, it was her first instinct. Somehow, he was still alive, calling her name, but she didn't know what that meant. She'd imagined no fate like this, and she stayed her distance as the worms clumsily bounced him into the wall. It almost made her throw up.

"Help me… please help me…"

"How?!" she begged, frozen. He was in there, crying for help. But this? Her stomach turned when she watched one of the worms pulsating out of his stomach to help carry him.

A worm slithered closer to Athen, and she smacked it. The hit resonated through the mass of wriggling; they recoiled in agony, and so did Orlean.

"Ahh!!" he cried, as hurt as if she had struck him instead. Orlean fell back, and the worms wriggled excitedly.

"I came to get you, and I'm not leaving until I do!"

Those things, those parasitic worms, appeared to be as vulnerable as one could hope. She could cause pain, though it caused Orlean pain too. But he must have known that, and he'd still asked for help. There was only one way to help that she could see. Athen dropped the pry-bar and grabbed her laser cutter instead. She unscrewed some wires from the battery and made a little device she'd concocted in college once. She'd stunned herself by accident years ago doing this, but she knew how to circumvent a few safety features to get a nice jolt out of a laser cutter. She calculated her time, quickly twisting wires loose and wrapping them in places they didn't belong. Then she steadied herself against the wall and let the worms get closer to her. One bold little vein came towards her stomach; she swiped it into the wall, pinning the end of the laser against it and holding it in place. She pressed the button.

Laser cutters had very concentrated battery power. An electric arc zapped from the thin wires, searing the parasite and causing it to flex uncontrollably. The current ran up into Orlean.

He screamed as those *things* lost their balance. The parasites flopped and folded, looking for something to wrap around, while others wriggled out of Orlean's body with sounds she would not soon forget. She released her grip and backed away, the scent of scorched flesh in the air.

Orlean was on hands and knees, with the remaining parasites trying to re-enter his body or attack hers. She marched towards him. One darted at her like a snake, which she blocked with the flat end of her laser cutter. It fell, and she stomped on it, with pain in her leg warning her not to do that again. The parasite coiled around itself, dying, but there were at least a dozen more. And Orlean still needed her help.

Swallowing her fear, she stepped in and swung, zapping the laser cutter into squishy worms she painfully reached. It would be much easier if she could properly crouch. The electricity stopped; her battery was depleted. Still, she'd caused enough carnage; the worms fled. When they were all gone, Athen threw up.

She leaned against one of the alien terminals, which had a monitor in sleep mode. She was spent, and the pain was no longer dulled. Orlean was trying to breathe, still on his hands and knees.

"Damn you, Orlean," she said, catching her breath from the adrenaline dump. She limped over to him, and when he looked up at her, she looked away. She wasn't ready to see what was in his eyes. She gathered her bearings and smiled at him.

"I should… be dead," he managed to say, blood bubbling air through tiny holes in his throat. His body was a pin-cushion of entrances, and he should have bled out by now.

"No. You definitely should *not* be," she smiled. She reached into her pocket. "Here, take this," she handed him a liquid vial. "Dmitry gave this to me, it's for the pain."

He touched his chest, still slouched over his knees. "There's… not much blood," he continued, clumsily trying to examine his fingers after probing a hole in his chest.

"They must…" she almost choked trying to say it. "…must carry a natural coagulant, or something, just… let's just get out of here," she said. "Drink that, we'll leave together, and a few months from now you buy the drinks," she ordered.

Orlean brought the vial to his lips and drank. He dropped the empty vial and slouched over himself again. "I didn't think… You were real… I had hallucinated before seeing you," he said. The medicine worked quickly, Orlean took an almost comfortable breath, and looked up at her. "You should have seen yourself just now," he said, wiping blood from his mouth.

She found herself staring at the holes in his neck. "Can you stand?"

CHAPTER 19

Carolina emerged from the hallway several doors down, a look on her face that told Austin not to say a word. He met up with her and they walked a ways down. Passing the room she'd been hiding in, he found she'd consoled herself by drawing on the walls with that markerpen of hers. She'd done that on the top floor, too, he remembered. That little pen is what kept her sane, even if she ended up vandalizing alien buildings with it. He didn't look much at the design; the kids needed a crutch, and hers was doodling.

The hallway continued in both directions, with a curve that limited their view.

"I've got a surprise for you," he said.

"What is it?"

"Tada!"

She smiled instantly. "Stairs!"

He'd spotted them when she wouldn't come out, a little recon while he had a moment waiting on her. He didn't know where they led yet, but that didn't matter. Up was good.

"Come on!" she hopped and grabbed him by the hand. He struggled to keep up and noticed how hard it was to navigate stairs without handrails. At the top of the stairs, they came to a spacious area, well-developed with glossy walls, a polished floor, and impressive doors. A meter-tall wall of glass decorated the middle, curving like a stream, trickling light.

"I feel like I'm in the 'show' room," he said.

Carolina approached the glass wall, which gave off soft blue and stretched across the room. It turned out to be an aquarium of sorts, with tiny bubbles and everything. Purple leaves rippled along the bottom of the aquarium, dancing slightly. A creature with short fins floated upside down… He looked over at Carolina, wondering where she had gone.

He found her standing at the end of the room where a wide cargo door was. "There you are." He resisted the urge to scold her for wandering off again; instead, he had to wonder why she stood at this particular door. Was it another one of her *memories*? "Nice door."

"Hmm," she said, pondering. Suddenly, Carolina turned her head, listening intently. She had a look of worry on her face that raised his adrenaline.

"We need to hide," she urged.

He saw nothing, but he'd learned to follow her instincts on Paphos. The only way in or out was through those stairs, unless they tried a door... He heard it too.

"Father..." she warned.

"There, we can hide by those crates," he pointed near a door looking like a cargo elevator.

"Not there!"

He considered her briefly. "What about up there?" he said, pointing above the aquarium wall. An air vent was up there, one she could crawl into. It was too tall for him to reach; he could already tell, but she could get up there, and it looked like a good hiding spot. He went beneath it and anchored himself against the wall, like prepping for a gymnastic cheerleader launch. He motioned for her to step into his cupped hands. She put a foot in, and he hoisted her all the way up. Her little feet scrambled out of view. A split moment later, she poked her head over the side and reached out with both hands. The look on her face was so beautiful.

He looked away. *If only you could pull me up, kiddo.*

She realized what he was thinking. "You have to come up here, too!"

"You hide up there, I'll find another spot... I promise."

"I'll help you up! Please, Daddy!"

"Just stay hidden, little miss," he ordered and went for the crates. He wiped his eyes and quickly looked for a way to crawl in one. He tugged on one of the lids, but it was sealed shut. The sound of long, heavy steps resonated up the stairs. His heart stopped in mid-beat. He was crouched behind a crate; it was the best hiding spot he could get.

The monstrosity loomed at the top of the stairs.

He couldn't get lower, scanning to ensure his arms or legs weren't jutting in view. His hand rested on the cool steel crate, which drained the heat from him. Its breathing got louder. He had a view of Carolina, her large eyes wide and frozen. Whatever was about to happen, he could not die in front of her. He would have to at least run far enough that she couldn't see whatever was about to happen.

Lumbered feet shook the ground, the behemoth approached the elevator where Austin hid, tiny crates his only shield. He quietly and steadily reached down his shirt and pulled out his medical tag. The small piece of metal was reflective, and he inched around to see the other side like a mirror. The thumb-sized reflection showed a dark, muddled view of the hallway. He angled it lower, trying to decipher the murky image. He held it steady and struggled to get a better angle without exposing his position.

The creature huffed, dark and throaty like a horse. It almost sent him running. He scooted to the left as the creature moved a step forward. It was a deadly game of symmetry.

His hands were shaking and he couldn't stop them. He calculated his distance to the stairs, which at best were forty meters away. A hand plopped across the top of the crate. He looked straight up, seeing the pod hand dangling over the lid. The creature seemed to be resting its weight against the crate while pressing the buttons on the elevator panel, not unlike a person.

The buttons were pressed, but nothing was happening. Then a smash as the creature slammed the door. The bang ricocheted through the entire room. The creature huffed. This time, Austin would have run, but his legs wouldn't move.

The beast slammed the wall again, and the residual jolt traveled through the floor. Footsteps again, and after an icy minute, he realized they were retreating. He refused to believe it until those footsteps echoed down the stairs and disappeared.

He stood, admiring the crater impacts on the elevator door. That creature had expected this elevator to work, and when it didn't, it left. Perhaps it aimed to find an alternative route, or maybe it was going to return and try again. But now, it was just him and Carolina and stark ambience. He waited until it was long gone before he allowed himself to breathe. He jumped when tiny arms wrapped around his neck. He hadn't noticed Carolina climbing down and coming towards him. He returned the hug and gathered his wits. Poor Dublin, being locked in a room with that thing...

"Daddy, we should go now."

"Yeah," Austin agreed. "The elevators?"

Carolina looked around. She ran up to the first elevator and tapped the panel in front of it. Nothing happened; no lights came on. "No power." She looked at the other elevators. "None of them have power…" she said. He wasn't going to challenge what she said, and he wasn't going to ask himself how she knew these things. He just wanted to get her off this planet.

She examined the hallway, and a worried face returned. "In a moment, this door will be activated."

"What?"

Carolina shook her head. The next thing he knew, power surged beneath the floor, and the elevator panels began to glow. Hydraulics whispered simultaneously as the elevator's doors gained power.

"I hate it when you're right."

Carolina gave him a look, angry and confused, and scared. Whatever she knew, she didn't like knowing it. He realized he was making a fist.

"You know, you're a smart girl, you could have deduced that. The creature left so it could power up these doors. Not psychic, just deductive reasoning." He hoped that was comforting.

Carolina didn't move. A current of air pulled at loose strings of hair across her face.

"Little miss, is this where we want to go? The creature wants to go this way, we might want to steer clear?"

She looked like she was trying to remember something, but just couldn't grasp it.

Austin kept his eyes on the stairs, gnawing his lip.

CHAPTER 20

Helena came to, but her look of confusion proved her memory was coming slowly. She didn't know what was happening.

"What... what are you doing?" she asked.

Dmitry said nothing as he finished binding her wrists with a cord, bound behind her back. Then he readied a length of gauze and gripped it tightly before covering her mouth, wrapping it around her head in a loop. He didn't need to hear her speaking.

With Helena bound, he went about his plan for the creature. There were several power cables available, allowing him to position the trap precisely. He went about stripping a cable that ran along the ceiling until its inner wires were bare. He began stripping a red cable but found that murky substance inside and moved on. He wasn't going to deal with what he didn't understand. The results could be bad.

He found a few more electrical cables and stripped them bare, then devised a way for them to collapse. He couldn't say exactly how many volts would course through these wires, but the cables were so thick he couldn't imagine them being anything less than fatal. They should be at least enough to incapacitate his beast. A dead beast was the most practical, though a live beast was the best reward. He'd settle for dead. Dmitry paused as he accidentally made eye contact with her.

"What? Don't look at me like that. This was a difficult decision, you know," he said.

Helena sobbed, muffled by the gauze wrapped around her head. He'd bound her right in front of the generator. The same one the beast had used.

"History will remember you as sacrificing yourself to save me. You'll be a legend, a hero. A museum will be named after you, probably in your hometown, a posthumous award for bravery given by the Governor in front of a thousand teary-eyed..."

He surveyed his trap. A simple net of exposed wires hung from the ceiling, triggered by a pull cord where Dmitry would be hiding. The monster would walk in, see Helena, kill her, flip its power switch back on, thereby reactivating the switch, and leave. Rather, it would try to leave. The switch would cause the wires to go hot, and Dmitry would spring the trap. The beast would get an electric death, and so would Helena in the event she was still alive. He didn't need her convoluting his version of the story.

Dragging it back to the ship would be a considerable problem, especially without the rest of his team. But he'd figure it out. He'd chop it into pieces and take it in duffel bags if necessary, because he wasn't going home empty-handed, just to let another team come back and claim all of *his* glory. The parasite inside would likely be dead, but he'd be ready with a durasack should it try to jump out of the mouth again. He had it all figured out, more or less.

He retreated to his position, hiding and readying the pull cord in both hands. He reviewed the layout of his trap one last time to make sure the pull cord was unobstructed and out of view. There were so many cables snaking around the room that concealment wasn't too difficult. Not bad for quick work, and he didn't have time to do more. At any moment, the creature would return and check on its power problem.

Helena was trying to wriggle free. Hmph, good luck.

Dmitry smirked and looked at his watch, it took Helena five minutes to gather the resolve to try and save herself. Given enough time, anyone could escape, he supposed. Too bad he needed live bait. He smirked... did he? No, he supposed not. He just wanted to see what would happen to her.

Somehow, she got a hand free. Damn, he'd have to fix this. He groaned and rested the pull-cord where he was hiding, then he pulled out his flashlight. He would have to hit her in a way that left her immobilized...

Dmitry looked around, quickly checking the hallway to make certain they were alone. Helena must have sensed what he was about to do, because to his surprise, she sprang loose of her bindings. The next thing he knew, she was free and running.

"Damn it!" He chased after her, scolding himself for letting this happen. *Why didn't I just drug her?* Carelessness. He had never tied someone up before; he was overconfident and lacked experience. As busy as he was planning the trap, he hadn't properly handled her first. But still, he was better than that. Furious, Dmitry bolted after her, gripping the flashlight. He pushed away thoughts of killing her with it.

Helena made it ten steps towards the hallway before he snatched her by the belt. He used his momentum and tackled her into the wall. Her legs gave way, and she collapsed to the ground. Dmitry was on top of her, pinning his knee into her face, while his free hand removed a tranquilizer from his pouch. He tore the protective sleeve off with his teeth and impaled the needle into her neck. Yes, he stabbed her in the neck when the arm would do. She deserved it after trying to run.

After a few defiant breaths, her muscles relaxed, the effects of the drug visibly taking over. He quickly stowed the needle and began dragging her back. It was his fault; no use cursing at her for having survival instincts. She was doing what any living thing would do. It was his fault; he should have done better.

But her timing couldn't have been worse. The sound of a door slamming shook the hallway. Helena felt very heavy as he dragged her by the collar. "Come on, stupid girl," Dmitry pleaded as he pulled her limp across the floor, back to the generator. As soon as he saw its shadow graze the wall, he let go of Helena and hid. She was almost in place, but not quite. Dmitry was out of time, though, and this would just have to do.

She lay in a daze just in front of the generator, stirring, willing herself to stay awake. The pounding footsteps stopped outside the doorway, but he could see its suction-cup hands. He choked as a gaggle of veins protruded from them. They tested the air around before entering. He approached Helena on the floor, and then, to his surprise, the creature stepped past her. Helena, despite the tranquilizer, was trying to prop herself up on her hands. The creature's huge frame filled the room, shielding everything behind it. The creature lifted another arm. He couldn't see very well from his hiding position, but the wet sound of veins protruding was unmistakable.

The creature exhaled, throaty and deep. Then it grabbed the lever and switched the generator back on. Energy swelled around them. It wasn't standing directly under the net, but his window of opportunity wasn't going to improve.

Helena was just outside of the net's reach. He had one shot, and if he missed, he would be helpless before this creature. It was better to abort if he had any doubts. Either way, finishing Helena would have to happen.

As he weighed his risks, Helena rose to her feet like a phantom. Or rather, something lifted her to her feet. Dmitry covered his mouth without realizing as he watched the worm tentacles extending from the beast and crawling into her body. It was standing her up like a puppet, just like he'd seen it do to Orlean.

Helena's head drooped like a soulless corpse. He marveled at the exotic science behind this and readied the pull cord. Enough wires would land on the creature that it would still work.

Suddenly, her head rose and she looked at him. She smiled, and a dark thought moved through him. Could Helena and this creature be sharing their consciousness, just like it had with Carolina? Was she was telling it everything?

He pulled the line in a panic.

The cable was snagged, and the trap didn't come down; he'd pulled too hard.

The creature turned its head and rested a dozen eyes on Dmitry; the same smile rested beneath those eyes that Helena had.

He screamed and pulled the cord again.

The creature's arm came free as the trap fell from the ceiling.

A burst of energy popped. The cables fired and sizzled, flickering lights washed across the room. Dmitry's nostrils were overcome with burnt flesh. He'd hit it; he had to have hit it. Adrenaline sent his heart racing. The creature wasn't moving. Maybe he killed it after all…

He looked, and he saw the creature and its bold smile, and then Dmitry ran. He bolted from the generator room and down the hallway and kept going.

He ignored the sounds that he could not name, sounds of flesh separating. If he was lucky, it was too busy killing Helena to come after him. See? She was an important part of his plan after all.

CHAPTER 21

Forgiveness had never come easily for Dublin, not an ounce of it. He blamed it on how he was raised, the way every single one of his elders kept the bar impossibly high. He'd learned to avoid disappointing them instead of how to gain forgiveness. It felt like the right way to be raised.

He chewed open a food wrapper, spat out the corner, and munched on the soupy contents. He rested his hands and took in the nutrients. His forearms ached from free-climbing two floors of an elevator shaft. He had the soft glow of his suit for light, but a climb like that he could do blindfolded.

He'd taken the time and effort to pry one set of doors open, which revealed a comical dead end. Nothing more than ten meters of hallway, no doors, no paths. A simple dead end, as if it were a movie set instead of a facility. The effort to discover this took time and stamina from his hands.

Now, by the second door he forced open, there were some blisters forming on his fingers. It was only after forcing the door open that he saw a safety latch. Flipping it from the inside allowed him to open the door smoothly and effortlessly. Well, that'd sure come in handy if he went up to the third floor. And never mind the gallons of sweat he poured, or the blisters. There was a release in his exhaustion that kept his spirits high. Like a good workout, and he'd been craving one. It felt good to hurt, and it felt good to sweat, especially because his motivation was still out there.

He'd had time to think while scaling the inside of the elevator shaft.

Dublin knew he could be impulsive, hot-headed, and other words his girlfriends named him. It was a personal struggle of his; he could admit that. As he climbed, he was able to relieve some of the anger boiling inside. It wasn't Austin's fault for being afraid; anyone would be dumping in their pants in that situation. The man was just trying to save his own skin; it was despicable, but also understandable. Add to that, the situation with the lesson they all gave him might have painted his response; in hindsight, he wished Dmitry hadn't proposed it. To top it all off, he had a kid, and the kid deserved a dad.

To advocate for the devil, however, some things were unforgiveable. It was a cycle for Dublin; when the hate subsided, he would drum it all up again on principle. Hard not to when your teammates left you to die. A therapist had taught him to feel the feelings or something like that, actually. Well, Austin better hope he was forgiven by the time he was found. Otherwise, he was a dead man.

The hallway lights flickered out; the sudden deprivation of noise made his ears ring. Deep underground and in total black, it wasn't Dublin's happy place. Other sounds from far ends of the facility crept in. He heard footsteps, but couldn't tell much more than that.

When the lights returned, he felt some relief, though he wasn't exactly afraid of the dark. All the same, he preferred the lights. This was the third time the lights had gone out, and so far, they had kept coming back.

He decided to avoid another climb and see where this floor led him. Lots of cables in this hallway, and it got the engineer in him piqued. His path branched off to the left and into a room of buzzing generators. Fascinating to discover their versions of portable power units, how they were arranged. Not a lot of thought went into concealing cables, though the rest of the facility wasn't like that. Then he saw something and instinctively crouched near the wall. What was he looking at?

He realized he was looking at Helena, or at least what was left of her. "Good grief, you poor lass," he covered his nose from the smell of burnt flesh. Poor girl. She was hardly recognizable, and he looked long enough to be certain it was her.

He spun around at a sound behind him.

It was Dmitry, walking into the room, seemingly oblivious of what was in here. "Dublin?" he said finally.

"Aye, it's me. Good to see another face."

"You're alive?" Dmitry wiped his hands on his pants.

"Aye. But listen, before you come any closer…"

"Dublin, I'm sorry about before, it's not what you think," Dmitry pleaded.

"Lemme' stop you right there, it is what I think, and don't bother trying to protect him. Now look, I hate to be the one to tell you, it's poor Helena down here. I think the creature got her somehow."

Dmitry took a step forward and looked at her. "Oh my God, what happened to her?"

"Found her like this. Listen, Austin owes me a little explanation from before, but right now I want to know what happened to her. Who was with her?"

Dmitry seemed to think for a moment. "I never should have trusted him after what he did to you." He watched to see Dublin's reaction to that.

"Aye. Go on…"

Satisfied, he continued. "He just… we were all down here looking for a way out. That's when we heard the monster."

"Aye?"

Lies came too easily to Dmitry, as he wove his fictions and sold them. "I climbed up into that air shaft to hide. I reached my hand down for Helena, but Austin pushed her out of the way because he wanted to go first. Before I had time to help either one… the creature stormed in. Austin practically threw Helena at the monster to escape. I didn't see the rest because the lights went dark, and I stayed inside the air vent. I was too afraid to move… I'm sorry. I was just too afraid."

Dublin's face had turned a deep shade of red. When he finally spoke, it was dark and slow. "Aye, you did what you could… *Austin* is the one who should be sorry, the bastard sacrificed someone to save himself…again! Where is he now?"

"It was about fifteen minutes ago, so he can't be too far… what are you going to do to him?"

"Jus' never mind that. Is the kid still with him?"

"No. Austin wasn't even trying to find her… he seemed relieved that he didn't have to 'babysit'…his words. All he kept talking about was doing anything to get out of here," Dmitry added. That was probably the dumbest lie he ever told. Austin would never abandon Carolina. But Dublin was eating it up, and it made him giddy to watch it. Mostly because he thought he was going to have to fight Dublin, and that would be a tough fight. All this time, ha! Dublin thought it was Austin who trapped him in with that beast. Damnit if things just didn't have a way of working out for ol' Dmitry.

He impressed himself sometimes. Dublin was always headstrong and a little gullible. Hopefully, he killed Austin before they had a chance to discuss the truth. The fewer crew members that remained, the easier it would be to bring the creature home, and the easier it would be to explain any version of events he wanted. "Austin went crazy. I guess I can understand, people are quick to save themselves. You never really know someone," Dmitry said. He'd better slow down; he didn't want to oversell it.

Dublin's anger was redirected as something brushed against his leg. A small, parasitic snake was wriggling out of Helena's body, inching its way towards him. He smothered it with his boot and some unnecessary anger.

"I'll crush every one of these bloody things!"

"Let's just stick together and find a way out of here."

"Seems I have something to take care of first," he said, shaking off his boot. "And Dmitry, if you see Austin before I do… don't tell him I'm still alive."

"Okay. I won't."

"Dats' good. Be sure of that now."

CHAPTER 22

Forgiveness?

Nary a chance in hell.

Dublin left by himself and exited down the corridor into a large room full of alien billboards. It looked like a train station, very different than the exam rooms he'd encountered. It cut across to a new hallway, and he followed that one, looking for ways to track Austin. The first elevator he tried had no power, which meant Austin didn't go that way.

A promising stairway appeared on the right. He approached them, revealing wide and squat steps, unnatural for a man's stride. He could try the stairs, or he could keep on tracking these hallways. Which way, which way… Austin would have taken the stairs because they go up, and up means getting out of here. He crouched to sit on his heels as he peered to get a closer look at something on the wall. At that, he smiled a tiny smile. Carolina had doodled on this wall; he recognized the work of her marker pen. Bubbles, the kid drew bubbles. If she didn't need therapy before, she would after finding her dad's corpse. Regretful, but necessary at this point.

She had been here, that much was certain, and it was his best chance of running into Austin. Dmitry said they were split up, but things change.

He rose to his feet and then bounded up the stairs, taking wide strides. Not too fast, not too loud, he didn't want to announce himself, not with that monster roaming around.

When he reached the top of the stairs, he stopped to admire what he found.

The architect in him was in awe. Here was a spacious, decorated showroom with soft lighting, black walls, shiny gold elevators, and an aquarium that decorated the center. The aquarium diffused light in soft, peaceful blue tones, despite the dead creatures within it. This room wasn't like the rest; it wasn't stale and incomplete. There were gilded elevators that lined the wall opposite the aquarium. At the far end of it were a few crates and a gaping entrance to a new area, along with another cargo elevator. He couldn't say that Austin absolutely went that way, but a wide-open entrance like that was pretty inviting.

He crossed the room with haste, the light from the aquarium coloring him blue. He passed the crates through the doorway, just waiting to be shipped, even after all these years, and then found a small train-car and tunnel on the inside. An alien train platform, right here underground. Stretching to the left was an endless tunnel; just in front of him was a simple platform. This place continued to amaze him—there was a train? Here? It was white and oval-shaped, a commuter train just waiting, hovering actually. It had power. He wouldn't mind seeing where it went.

He boarded and stood. There were seats, but he was looking for a control panel of sorts, something he might need to press to make it 'go'. But as the train began to move, he decided it was best to sit. Automatic, apparently.

"Aye, alright then," he said as the train picked up speed. Uncertainty crept in, but trains had destinations; he just had to wait it out. He focused on what he would do to Austin when he found him. He hoped the coward would be alone; it wouldn't be great killing him in front of the others, especially not in front of Carolina. But, it wouldn't stop him either. A sharp hydraulic sound hissed, and he felt the train slowing.

He subconsciously looked for something to hold on to. The train floated, which was unnerving. He peered ahead as they neared the docking platform, and he smiled at the sight of daylight.

"Bless my feet," he remarked as the train came to a halt. A final hiss as the aged commuter fully stopped. Dublin had to wonder how long it had been since all of this was a thriving hive of activity. He had many questions, but at least they had one answer. They were not alone in the universe. This trip turned out to be the one that made them all rich and famous... except for Helena. She wouldn't get to enjoy it.

The fresh air was a welcome relief, coming in through a clear dome above him, letting in glorious daylight. The ceiling looked to be retractable, letting in daylight and more. A gap had formed at the top of the dome, with plants and vines dangling down, looking for somewhere to take root. He had to shield his eyes from the intensity of actual daylight. It was nice to have everything bask in the glow of their sun, even if it was a bit obstructed.

Off to the side were a dozen cubicles, lined along a wall that stretched the length of the room. The top of something smooth and round was peeking over the lip of the wall. The cubicles were sectioned off to the left, while the space beneath the dome was open and clear, like a helicopter pad. There were crates and drums precisely stacked, and he saw a handful of unusual tools organized on racks. The floor was wide and open-spaced.

He turned and found Austin, standing near the corner of a cubicle. He was waving at him to be silent, waving at him to hide with some urgency. He was gift-wrapped and ready.

The hand motions trailed off as Dublin ran at him. Time to collect on a tab long overdue.

Austin put his hands out and silently pleaded, but was tackled with all his force. They collapsed to the floor, rolling to the ground. A flurry of wild punches came down as Dublin decided to get this over with quickly.

To his surprise, he wasn't on top anymore. Austin had shuffled his hips or his feet and flipped Dublin to the side. He watched as Austin scrambled to his feet.

"You aren't getting away that easily!" he swore and wrapped his arms around Austin's legs. He tripped him into a row of barrels, knocking them over. One of the barrels cracked and oozed a fluid out onto the ground. It was abrasive and quickly burned the nostrils.

Dublin pounced after him, but Austin kept retreating, making it hard to land a good hit. The coward had decent footwork, and there was that little judo move he used earlier. Dublin had a sensible thought that tried to surface: he should fight smarter, refrain from all-out aggression. However, his anger made it difficult for him to remain calm and fight smart. Austin hadn't crumpled yet, which he hadn't expected this fight to last even this long. He'd underestimated his prey. To expand on that, the next thing Dublin knew, he was seeing double; a quick punch combo had rocked him.

"Stop fighting me!" Austin urged, his voice a harsh whisper. Dublin should have picked up on his attempt to be quiet, but he was too angry.

He finally had him back against the wall, with nowhere to evade. Dublin charged and picked him up, smashing him through a cubicle before they came to the ground. Austin had his legs wrapped around him, and Dublin just couldn't get the right angle to land his punches. For all the bar-fights he'd ended, Austin was a squirrely fellow. Again, he had to stop underestimating him.

The scalding smell was overpowering them. If he got the chance, he'd smear Austin's face in whatever toxic goop was leaking all over.

"Daddy!"

"Carolina, hide!" Austin ordered.

"Stop it!" she cried.

"Sorry, kid, but Daddy killed Helena, tried to kill me!"

Dublin's hands found their way to Austin's throat with big, gnarled fingers that squeezed, draining the life from him. Austin's face bulged, and his skin was turning color. Carolina grabbed Dublin by the hair to make him stop, so he pushed her away. In that moment, the anger that shot through, combined with the momentary distraction, let him rip those fingers away from his neck. With his hips and feet, he flipped him, but Dublin was strong, and they both scrambled to stand up.

"There's a bigger problem, you idiot!" he hissed at Dublin, still not raising his voice. Dublin should have picked up on that, too.

The leaked fuel ignited on the ground next to them. A small eruption and intense popping filled the room. Another small burst, the fuel ignited quickly and spread flames. Dublin was torn between fighting and getting away from the fire. A gush of flames rushed between them, roasting them both.

Backing away from the flames, Dublin bumped into something that felt different, something solid but not a cubicle wall. Now he realized why Austin had been shushing him. He'd been wrestling right next to an alien spacecraft, which was easily spotted if he'd taken a moment to look around. The flames were reaching it, which couldn't be good.

Then there was another sound, and it concerned him the most.

The creature stormed up to them, or rather to the ship, discovering it engulfed in flames. Dublin tried to move away, keeping out of its view.

The creature released a furious, deafening howl that shook the room.

CHAPTER 23

The fuel was a potent accelerant. Fire blanketed eagerly, and in a short time, it produced flames that licked the ceiling, searing at the roots coming in through the roof's dome. Austin grabbed Carolina by the shoulders, shielding her from the waves of heat. He felt his neck hairs shrivel from an intense blast.

They scrambled away from the cubicles towards the oval train platform.

The creature climbed to escape the heat or just for a better view. It effortlessly suspended itself from above the cubicles, using its various limbs with ease.

"Faster!" he ordered, all but carrying Carolina by the scruff of her neck. It took a moment to steal a glimpse, but it was enough to lend strength to his legs. They slipped across the empty space from the hangar bay, back towards the monorail.

Another explosion drowned the room in heat. He spared another glance behind and saw the creature stalking an unaware Dublin. Yelling would put the focus on him…

"Watch out, Dublin!" Austin cried, pointing. The puzzled look on Dublin's face was brief as he saw it, but he took the warning and hid through the maze of cubicles not yet on fire. That would at least give the Irishman a chance to get away, though his misplaced anger was something he'd need to deal with later.

The train was his best way out of there, but helping Dublin had drawn the creature's attention, and now they were vulnerable until the train departed. He had a split second to decide, and he didn't think there was time for them. Carolina could make it, but only if he gave her a head start. The creature swooped down from its perch and began running towards him.

Carolina boarded the train as that happened, pounding on the wheezing doors to move.

"I have to drag it away!" Austin yelled. Carolina planted her hands against the back window, eyes full of disbelief. She saw the creature coming and banged the glass for him to hurry.

"Get in, Daddy!"

"Find Athen!"

They locked their eyes for a moment, and he prayed it would not be the last time he saw them, hazel-brown and full of hope. He pivoted his run to lead away from the train.

The shuttle activated, and air hissed as the cabin door closed. Slowly, it picked up speed. Austin crossed the tracks, running so fast his feet barely touched the ground. The creature leapt up and grabbed the ceiling, climbing hand over hand with nothing to grab onto except the suction of its pod hands. They easily gripped the otherwise smooth ceiling.

He looked again, saw nothing, but then felt a crash in front.

A last-ditch effort sent him diving behind a pallet of barrels. The creature had landed in front of him; there wouldn't be anywhere to hide. He could practically smell its breath. The barrels were all he had for protection.

It was pissed. It planted its feet, four of its arms grabbed the pallet he was on, barrels and all, and the next thing he knew, he was tossed through the air. He careened in trajectory with those barrels, the upwards motion hurling him up into the air. In the midst of certain death, he grabbed onto the roots dangling from the ceiling dome. He clutched them as if his life depended on it because it did.

He swung from the inertia as the remaining barrels flew and bounced upon landing. A spot-check revealed the monorail was gone, thank god, and the creature was still throwing a tantrum. Austin, meanwhile, was dangling from roots of dubious tensile strength. The vines and roots were slick, something his adrenaline-fueled grip began to realize. Falling would be bad, but there was still a chance of going up. The creature searched among the barrels but didn't find him.

A hiss from beneath made him grimace, as the creature seemed to have found him. It slapped a barrel in frustration, and he watched it smash against the wall. He swung his leg up to attempt to hook a vine, but the motion threatened his grip to fail. He wrapped a gnarled tendril around his wrist and tried again.

Another hiss, but it was not the monster this time. Fire suppression was filling the room, which was great because he felt like a pig on a spike above the flames. With a better grip, he swung his leg again and hooked the vine. He was horizontal, trying to gain elevation, when a draft from the dome's gap swept through, swift and inviting. Another roar from the beast before he felt it land again. That sound was never good. Paphos' dirt floor was just above that gap, he knew it.

"Ah hell," he cursed. The creature was crawling up the wall like a spider, its six arms acting as legs. He looked up, which was a mistake as the natural daylight blinded him. He wanted to climb through and out, but it was hard enough just to hold on. *Teeth!* He needed any bit of friction he could get. He bit into the vine, the taste bitter as juice poured down his tongue, but he ignored it. He used the leverage to adjust his hands and then his feet. He climbed higher and could almost reach the dome's entrance. Sweet, fresh air was howling for him to make it. Unfortunately, something else was howling too, and it would soon be upon him.

He stared up at the rings of Paphos. The sky was glorious.

An explosion made the creature stumble, dragging it several meters down the side of the wall before catching itself. That gave him the chance he needed to wrestle his way out. He hooked his leg over the lip and shimmied himself free, not breathing, not resting until he was on hands and knees on Paphos' soil. If it mattered, he now had two entrances to the facility, one of which just saved his life.

He collapsed onto his back and shielded his eyes from the sky, taking in great lungfuls of air. He'd exerted so much effort between fighting, running, and climbing that his lips were numb from oxygen deprivation. The roots and vines that had just saved his life made a poor pillow, sticking into the wrong parts of his back, but he let them. He couldn't move from the exhaustion anyway.

The creature wailed in defeat beneath him, which was a little bit of a surprise. He'd seen it punch through walls; surely it could get up here, too. But now, even if it did, there was nothing Austin could do about it. He didn't have the strength. Was it afraid of daylight? He wondered about this as he continued to suck in air.

And from below the dome where Austin rested, below the surface of Paphos, Dublin was forced to contemplate much from his hiding spot. A spot he wouldn't be leaving anytime soon, especially now that the fire was under control. He wouldn't be leaving until the beast left first. Until then, he waited and thought.

He had seen much and therefore had much to think about. First, he'd been wandering right towards the beast until Austin warned him. That's why he was still alive, because Austin warned him, gave him a chance to hide, and it also put Austin right in the beast's crosshairs.

It was not a cowardly act.

Then, he sacrificed himself to make sure little Carolina got away safely.

That was no cowardly act, either.

It was only by some freak jungle-swinging that Austin wasn't a mangled pile of flesh. He'd managed to survive after risking his life for both him and Carolina.

And that didn't fit right, not with everything else he'd been stewing over for the last few hours. The man he saw in action just now would not have pushed Helena aside to save his own skin.

It just did not fit right.

CHAPTER 24

Carolina beat the window, but her father shrank out of view despite that. Tears forced her to her knees, where she sobbed as the cabin raced away, uncaring.

She chanted the word *daddy* in a delirium. She felt the transport stop and wiped her face with the back of her hand repeatedly, and hated how her nose was stuffy when she cried. The door slid open, yet she didn't get up.

There was nowhere to go.

She forced herself to stop seeing the last image of her dad, which made her think of it even more. She scolded herself when she considered grabbing her marker pen and drawing, a poor therapy for this level of distress. He couldn't be dead; in fact, she felt enough... something... that he could be alive. In fact, he'd gotten away... Carolina staggered. The clearer the thoughts came, the more disoriented she felt.

Clinging to hope was as painful as not; she knew why she wanted to believe that he was alive. It was called denial. She grew to her feet and stepped off the train. *Go find Athen,* those were his words to her. So that's what she would do.

She stepped off the train, her own feet blurry through the threatening wall of tears. Her legs carried her through the adjoining cargo door and along the aquarium wall without really looking at any of it; the gold frames of the elevator doors went by unimportantly. She'd hidden above that aquarium in an air vent, thanks to her dad's help. He was always trying to help her; it's all he ever did. Why didn't she ever give him a break? She just remembered always being mad at him, but didn't know what for. At least he tried; he had always tried. She balled her fists and vowed; she'd never be mad at him again.

The emotions propelled her legs into a run. She ran the way they had come, to the stairs, down them, and collapsed at the base of them when another crying fit took control. This time, it wasn't the word *daddy*, it was the word *why*.

Part of her knew she could stop crying; sometimes emotions could be controlled. But the only thing that helped right now was thinking that somehow he would be okay and that he would find her. She wanted to believe it anyway. Praying he was still alive was the only way she could keep moving. And so with that desperate wish, she stood and continued down the desolate hallway until she found an elevator. Dad told her to look for Athen, that's what he would do. She pressed a button and waited for the elevator doors to close. She didn't know if she had taken this elevator before; they all looked the same to her.

"Why won't you close?!" she screamed. Anger… it felt so much better than grief.

She steadied herself, calmed herself before having another fit. There's only so much you can cry before it loses its meaning. What was left was her, sitting in the elevator, staring down a lonely hallway, wishing the doors would close. Her eyes were blurry, but she blinked them clear and then examined the dark hallways. Just at that moment, she'd seen something move. She rubbed her eyes again and waited without motion. After several moments, she figured she was wrong, just a light flickering at the end of the hallway. Carolina pushed herself to her feet.

She tried the control panel on the elevator again. She had never seen how the adults had gotten it to work before. She looked at the buttons, shaped with markings and strange features. Subconsciously, she held her hand to her head, and then she pressed a button which opened a new menu. She toggled the menu, looking for the tabs she wanted, and then activated the elevator. It had been a long time since she was on the *Himark Kesh's* floor.

"What?" Carolina fell back as the elevator doors closed, trapping her. How did she know that? That was a clear, very specific memory, and she knew it wasn't hers. The floor jolted as the motors whined. When the doors opened again, they got stuck, making her remember the first elevator of this cursed place. This elevator had docked too early; she could see the floor line well above her eye level, and the doors were stuck halfway. If she could get up there, she'd wriggle through them easily enough, but it was getting up there that was the problem. There wasn't much to grab hold of. She should have kept to the stairs. She slapped the buttons a couple of times and felt the elevator attempt to correct itself, but it still seemed stuck.

What did she have that she could use? That's what her dad would be asking.

She examined the inventory available to her. Her belt was stitched into her pants, loose-fitting cargo pants that were expedition-worthy. She had her boots. She had her markerpen, she pulled it from her pocket and worked the tip into the door threshold which she could barely reach. It gave her some grip, maybe enough? She pulled down, the tip wedged deep, and bending under pressure. She tested her weight, but the marker slipped out. Carolina threw her hands in the air. There was that anger again, sweet and inviting.

She dug her hands into her pockets, making sure she missed nothing. She found a wrapper from a protein bar, which she ate. She balled the wrapper and tossed it in the corner, doubting it would be of any use. She wanted to cry again... she just needed to be tougher.

'Think outside the box,' her dad said at times. Were there any resources around her?

The floor was tiled and smooth, so she would not be able to pry anything up. The ceiling was... out of reach, so that didn't matter. Maybe if she sprang from the wall with her foot, she could latch on somehow. Carolina tried it, using the wall; she catapulted off the corner to get her elevation. She got her hands higher but missed anything to hold on to, and when she landed, the elevator croaked an inch.

"Whoa," she said, steadying her weight. The floor felt like it was about to pitch. "Bad idea, bad idea." She was steady, but the elevator shrieked as it dug down an inch. She yelped, arms out, praying the elevator didn't burst into a free-fall. The sudden drop must have loosened something, and the motors of the elevator started to moan. She watched the floor line come closer as her elevator moved before getting stuck again, but it put her just in reach.

Fingers dug into the threshold as she climbed. She managed to get her face and shoulders up and over, while the rest of her precariously dangled and threatened to drag her back down. There was a moment she was impressed at the lack of dust, a thought that was a little out of place, but it wasn't often she had her face this close to the floor. Using the door frame, she pushed off with her feet and finally found herself lying on her back, panting, but off the elevator. The hallway ceiling stared back at her with a flickering light. Two quick, one slow, two quick, one slow, a nice pulsing flicker of light.

"Heck yeah...woo..." she said. She did not want to move, but she knew she didn't have too long before the creature came this way. It was going to be mad about its ship, vengeful in fact. After all, it was *this* close to returning home to *Sregart.*

Carolina blinked. She was confused and disoriented. It took her too long to remember who she was this time, where she was. That was the strongest vision yet, and it made her forget herself. For the first time, she worried one of these visions would be so strong she might not come back.

CHAPTER 25

Athen now hated stairs, and she hated whoever had invented them; she pledged that if she ever held a public office, they would be outlawed. Stairs were obviously devices of torture sent from the pits of hell to punish mankind.

She had wrestled Orlean up these stairs with the help of a cot fashioned out of framing materials, and with her leg in the condition it was, she had nothing left by the time she made it to the top. Orlean wasn't well; his face was pale and covered in sweat, and he hadn't said anything in an hour. He was still breathing, though, albeit barely. How he was alive, she didn't want to know, but she was certain every damn one of those parasite worms was gone. They *really* didn't like electricity. But the holes they left had coagulated remarkably well and… and she didn't want to think about it.

Athen had kept from shutting down halfway up the stairs. The moment had come when she couldn't take another step, when she was ready to leave Orlean there and attempt to save herself. The harder her muscles ached, the louder that selfish voice was. But she just wouldn't listen to reason. That part of her didn't care about exhaustion; it only cared about right and wrong. And it would not be right.

Athen had rested for just a minute and genuinely wanted to rest longer, much longer. But she couldn't. Resting for five more minutes would not recharge her; it would only delay her. A stop now would just be stopping. She didn't know how to quit, and that's the stubbornness that had saved her life in the Kazakhstan Prefecture. If she made it home, which seemed impossible, she intended to treat herself to a month in the Lunar Spas.

Orlean made a sound at last, groaning as he struggled to lift his head. Clear plasma squeezed out of holes in his chest, soaking the already damp utility shirt.

"Water…," he pleaded. It was the first word since she moved him to the poorly made stretcher. "Water…"

"Easy, pal, try to stay still," Athen said, kneeling next to him and wiping hair from his forehead. "No water right now."

"Thirsty..." he said again, his eyes closed. Athen put a hand to his forehead and almost pulled it away from the heat. He was burning up. The water was long gone, and the ambient heat was making everything ten times worse.

"I'll get you water soon. We just have to keep moving," she said softly. If she could make it topside, it might be best to leave Orlean at the entrance, hobble back to camp, load the water, and hobble back. In fact, she considered doing as much right now, but leaving Orlean down here meant possibly never finding him again. It meant leaving him trapped helplessly inside this alien facility. She could at least get him topside, then she could feel safe about leaving to get supplies.

Orlean faded back to sleep, and Athen was glad he did. She couldn't stand to hear him in pain. She set the handles of the stretcher down for a moment and stopped. She wasn't supposed to stop, but she was too tired to keep going right now. Damn, she was tired. She looked at Orlean, considering him carefully. Leaving him to go topside, if she was honest with herself, was about more than just finding help. She was beyond exhausted and didn't know if she could do it—she could barely make it up these stairs with the rod in her leg. It was the despair, but she had thoughts that were not like her. Being honest with herself, it was the leaving part that made the most sense, but also made her feel guilty. She should go, now, without Orlean, and she hated herself for thinking about it.

Reality gnawed at her. How was she helping? Those wounds had to be fatal, so in a way, he was probably dead. She was wasting her strength trying to help him, trying to save him. It might be a tough choice, but she should consider it.

The stretcher rested on the floor. She took a few steps away from it. It didn't burn yet. She summoned a few deep breaths and took a few more steps. She was justified in leaving him there and hadn't felt a drop of guilt yet. Another step. She would not look behind her. A few more steps. She could do this; she could leave him there, alone, helpless, bound to a stretcher.

Her head drooped, and her shoulders fell. *Damn.* "Bastard, you owe me big time," she said before coming back to grab the handles. Guess she wasn't beaten yet. Close...but not yet. She grunted and groaned, cursing at Orlean as she tugged him down the hallway. Between curses, she missed something moving at the far end of the hallway, but her senses made her stop. A long pause ahead as her eyes took in everything they could. It felt like she was being watched. She gripped the handles on Orlean's stretcher with new intensity. "Come on, Orlean..." she whispered. "Come on... come on..."

She yanked Orlean down the hallway, dragging and sweating. She kept looking up, scanning the yellow and grey interior halls, dragging the stretcher as silently as possible. The shadows changed. She saw the outline of shoulders and gasped. Behind her were three doors, office rooms by any guess. She thrashed and pulled, gaining only inches at a time. She had already pushed herself beyond any depth. The creature's frame at the far end of the hallway came clearer into form.

It looked graceful for something so large. It lurked at the far end, just watching for something. This was the first good look she had at the thing, and it appeared not to have seen her yet. She remained motionless just outside the office door, praying for mercy, about thirty meters away. Maybe it would go back down the way it came. That and she didn't have the strength to run, though standing still was becoming worse. Her grip on the stretcher was weak, her forearms warned her she couldn't hold it forever, her muscles needed to adjust. Her back and neck ached on queue as her thoughts ran up and down.

The creature still waited, contented to be the gatekeeper at the end of the hall. Something came out of its shoulders, like a dozen writhing snakes, tasting the air around it. Suddenly, they slid back inside its body as the creature disappeared down the far stairs. She could hear its footsteps leading away. She exhaled, thanking any spirit that could hear her. Her hands were shaking from the weight of the stretcher. Athen propped her good leg under one of the handles to rest her grip. The motion shook Orlean, and he let out a long, soft groan.

"Uhnnn..."

Athen's breath froze in her chest, and her spirits sank when the footsteps stopped. She tugged on the stretcher, and Orlean tried to sit up. "No, no, no," she hushed. She was almost through the doorway, trying to angle the stretcher calmly. "Come on, damn you," she begged, pulling on the stretcher more. The creature emerged at the head of the stairs and was coming towards her. This time, it saw her, and she knew it. When its dozen eyes met hers, she suffered a fear deeper than any she had ever known. She lost the final shred of strength and did what she never thought she would. She left Orlean there.

She set him down softly and quickly, with the quick part taking precedence and causing another groan. With apologetic silence, she hid in an adjacent room, darting inside the gaping doorway and around boxes. Another way out would be best, but somewhere to hide would do. It was not betrayal. She'd done everything she could do. This was survival, but it still burned. She fell to the ground from pain, crawling and dragging her leg with her. Her leg had finally betrayed her; it could no longer be willed into cooperating.

Inside the room was a desk she might fit under, also a tall cabinet that looked sturdy, and some shorter filing cabinets she could almost hide behind. A monstrous hiss echoed throughout, a terrible vibration that shook off every wall. She limped to the tall cabinet and sealed herself inside its double doors.

This was worse. Her ears were ringing now, and she couldn't see anything. The sounds around her were amplified in her hiding place, sounds she struggled to comprehend. But there was nothing to do. This was her play. *Wait, and hope.*

The creature hissed again, and she heard a word she could almost articulate. She held her mouth closed to keep from crying, but it did nothing to slow her beating chest. Athen bit her hand, holding on to silence amidst fear. Suddenly, the cabinet she was in fell over, with Athen helplessly inside it. The room erupted all around her, thrashing boxes and upending cabinets.

After a few moments, the carnage stopped. That's when she wished she had not heard the next part, as Orlean's cot slid along the floor. He cried out, and Athen smashed her hands over her ears. This was too much. The sounds she heard… She waited there. She didn't even know how long she waited, but it was a while. She waited well after the sounds had stopped.

She couldn't hold it in any longer. She needed out. She wrestled the doors, but the frame had bent from the commotion, and they wouldn't budge. She wedged her knees against, despite the pain. She pushed and thrashed as panic worked itself up. With a burst of strength, the frame popped outwards, and she fell out of the cabinet. If the alien was out there, just kill her now. She couldn't take it anymore.

The room was destroyed. The creature had completely thrashed it. The desk was broken in half, and the cabinets were tipped over. It must be angry, that was all she could figure. It was some relief to have survived and be in this room alone. Yet she dreaded what came next… finding Orlean's body.

Guilt. She did not want to see him.

She placed her hand on a broken piece of the table, leaning heavily on it. The jagged edges would have hurt if she cared. She dragged her leg onward, throbbing and unbending. Her strength had returned for that burst, thankfully too, or she may have spent her last breaths in a misshapen cabinet. She struggled to move around boxes to reach the doorway; once there, she leaned against it to recover. She waited until she was ready to look.

She opened her eyes to the yellow and gray interior of the hallway. On the floor was the empty, misshapen, blood-soaked cot she had used to move him. But he was gone. Where the hell was he? The hallway ran bare, except for its long, uninterrupted grooves —a decorative facet of alien architecture —but no Orlean. Did the creature take him away? It's not like he escaped on his own; he couldn't even stand. All that was left was the blood-soaked cot on the floor. She'd feel better knowing he was dead if she saw his body. Now she would have to go find him…

No. She was naïve to even think it. She couldn't save him. Was she going to fight the creature, too? He was dead now, or may as well be.

"Lass?"

Athen spun at the familiar voice. "Dublin!" she cried, falling into him.

"There now, be good, it's alright," he said, soothing her. She'd never cried in front of him before, but the occasion was well warranted. He reeked of smoke, his hands stained black, his expedition pants charred. Black smudges marred his face. She wondered if he'd crawled through a chimney.

"An' where are the others?" he asked.

"I'm alone… I don't know about the others. But Orlean is…" she couldn't say it. She collapsed into Dublin's arms. She was only standing because he held her up.

"Tis' alright, you can rest now. Da' leg must be causin' some real grief," Dublin said. Effortlessly, he picked her up. She draped an arm across the back of his neck as he carried her down the hallway. It felt like true salvation to be the one being carried. He nudged open an exam room with his boot and set her down on a long table. He spent a second looking for something to cover her with, or at least to make her more comfortable. She did not need it.

"I can get up," she said.

"Nah, you rest. I'll watch over you."

That was all it took. She let herself rest as Dublin sat down next to her.

Dublin held his chest. Finding Athen was good, but he remained troubled… More than his pride was hurt as he grappled with the difficult truth; Austin was no coward. And in his revenge, he caused the fire, angered the creature, and split up the father and daughter. Dublin exhaled. He feared he'd made a mistake.

What was it that set him spiraling against Austin in the first place? He backtracked the events as he remembered them.

First, when he'd been trapped in the room with the creature, which he never actually saw, Austin did. He'd assumed it was him, but Dmitry was there too. Or the door just slammed shut out of the security response. Then, finding Helena's body, Dmitry told him all about what Austin had done to save himself.

Dmitry, again?

No, that was not possible. Dmitry wouldn't have done that, ever. He'd bet his life on it.

Except… Austin was no coward. He'd seen it for himself.

CHAPTER 26

Dublin stood guard as Athen fell asleep on the table. He looked over her leg. She was losing more blood than she should be; the coagulation gels could only do so much with all the walking she did. A bloody miracle she had done as much as she had. The fact that she was alive showed how tough she was. He always knew that about her; that's why they made such a good duo. No complaining from that one. He struggled to find Engineers who complained less than she did.

Seems the team had lost another, Orlean this time, or he assumed as much by her response. She could not even say his name. Now it was just him, Athen, Dmitry, Austin, and the daughter... He figured Austin was still alive, no thanks to him.

Dublin relaxed his shoulders, stretching out his neck. Hard to shake that feeling, hard to get past making a mistake like that. A simple 'sorry friend, I mistook you for someone needing to be put down' may not suffice.

He needed to burn off some of this feeling; moving about would help. He decided to explore his surroundings on this level. With Athen resting, he'd stay nearby. He was feeling more than a little protective of his fellow engineer. There may be a damsel-in-distress element as well, though he tried not to think of her as such, or it may simply be out of guilt. All the same, he needed to put some pace on these boots. He left the room but kept her well within sight and sound. He would not go too far.

There was always the 'what if' part, like what if that creature came back? Running and hiding have been their only options, but their odds of surviving diminished each time they encountered the monstrosity. In fact, they were lucky it hadn't been more determined and outright come after them. Thus far, at least.

When he'd found this floor, he stayed hidden while the sounds of commotion took place. When the sounds died down, he came forward, and that's how he ran into Athen. He had not seen much beyond that.

He walked down a way until finding the bloody stretcher, just outside the room, the creature had thrown a tizzy fit. Dublin would need a sledgehammer to cause this damage; the strength this beast possessed was humbling. The walls were shredded and full of holes, as if a construction robot had gotten its programming jumbled and gone off. Not a piece of furniture remained intact. With what little knowledge he possessed, between the parasite in its body and the way it slept in stasis, he figured it was not all evolution at work there.

And Dublin had set the creature's ship on fire, though accidentally. He's the one who pissed it off, who'd slung a rock at the hornet's nest. Well, at least it could not run home and bring back its friends… which was really a new thought he'd failed to consider yet. Dublin picked up a crumpled pencil sharpener, at least that's what it most closely resembled to him, and he thought about those scenarios. Now that his mind had wandered there, what would it have done if it had flown away? Would it just fly home and say, 'Honey, I'm home?' Did it have an Orbiter nearby and waiting, like theirs? Nothing on the scans, but that could be avoided, and they weren't really looking. Would it have insidiously followed them back, bringing an invasion to Earth? A sobering thought. They were just scientists, after all; nobody wanted to be responsible for starting an intergalactic invasion. The theoretical possibilities spun like a top.

Dublin had studied enough uninhabited planets to know Paphos was one of them, not enough here to sustain the kind of life forms they'd encountered. To get a species to evolve and build those structures, you'd need a foundation of so many other threats and readily available proteins to rely on; the plants here just didn't have them. Their monster must have come from another place, no different than Dublin. He wondered where that may be… Probably not anywhere nearby; their planet-detection scans found Paphos. It would have certainly found the alien planet if it were within a parsec.

Well, what's done is done. They had shrunk from fortune seekers to survivalists. Bringing it home was a bit of a fantasy now, having met the alien twice and seeing it push walls out of its way. It was strong, fast, and not some witless animal they could trap. What Dublin needed was a weapon, something that could level the playing field. Something he could make by hand, with the materials available, that gave him an advantage—talk about your engineering extra-credit. "Aye, Dublin, you've got a bit of a challenge here."

He ran a mental inventory of tools; there was his plasma torch, and he could do something with that. He turned and checked on Athen, who continued to sleep. His search for materials led to the table she was on; it had good legs that could help, but he was not about to disturb the girl. He found a similar table in an adjacent room and removed two of its table legs quietly. With some sharpening, they held an edge that was better for poking than for cutting. He hefted it up; good weight but a slippery grip. A handle wrap would settle things for now. All he had were his pants and his field jacket, and it was too hot down here anyway, so he ripped the jacket off and created some lengths of fabric. He wrapped the threads into a handle and tested the weight of the sharpened table leg again. He allowed a smile. He'd made an oversized prison shank.

"Aye, it'll have to do."

He checked on Athen again; she had stirred some but was still asleep. They'd have to be on the move soon. Dublin went to the hallway and inspected the wall indentations; a nice chunk of the wall would easily pry loose. Dublin grabbed his plasma torch and cut a heavy piece off. He could break it up and fashion a bolo… now that was just dumb. He could use the big piece for a hammer if he found something sturdy enough to make the handle. He didn't want to be that close; he would need to fashion it as a spear to give him a little range. So far, his machete was his best piece, which meant he would be in for quite a fight. He had to do better.

What Dublin really needed was supplies from the base camp, something he could use to fashion a trap, something high-explosive or chemical in nature… No point dreaming about what he didn't have. Dublin's thoughts floated as he continued to scout for more materials, waiting to hear Athen wake up, waiting to hear the creature come back. There was something urgent about scouting for weapon materials; he could sense his ancestors doing this in the ancient days before civility. He found a long metal pipe outside Athen's room, which was actually titanium if he had not known better, and used the torch to cut it free—finally, a handle for his hammer. By the time he had it free, Athen was sitting up and rubbing her eyes.

"What are you doing?" she asked.

"Tis' just a lil' walking stick, so I can shoo' the beastie with it."

"Walking stick?"

"Aye, until I'm properly equipped to deal with it."

"Dublin, we aren't going to fight it; we are getting the hell out of here. I need the med kit from base," Athen said.

"Aye, we're going back to base. Just a precautionary thing, as I said."

Athen held a questioning gaze. It was clear she didn't want anything to do with that creature, for obvious reasons. "What should we do about Orlean?"

"Nothin' at all, nothin' we can do."

"I know, but... damn it. We just need to get out of this place. And I mean like, yesterday," she urged.

Dublin worked with his back facing Athen. He drilled a hole in the piece of rubble and slid the titanium pole through it. He made a crosspiece that held the brick in place, and he fashioned two sharpened spikes to it. It was a spiked mace by the time he was done with it. He tested it in the air to make sure none of the pieces were loose. It was not beautiful, but it would do. Not something she could wield, but he could. The extra weight was needed against the big beast.

"Aye, let's get on with it then," Dublin said, wishing for better. If he landed one just right, he could probably brain the creature. That was assuming it had a brain he could get to. He scouted down across the hallway. He hadn't exactly formed a perfect map, but he knew which way he'd come, and he wasn't about to backtrack. "Able to walk, then?"

"I'm okay for now. Probably need help later."

"Grand."

Dublin led the way, slowly, for Athen to remain close. She kept a harder pace than she would have if she were alone. The dynamic between her and Dublin was always one that pushed, always made them earn each other's approval. He kept a pace that met her halfway; slow enough to help but fast enough she'd have to push to keep up, but she did keep up. They made it to the end of the hallway and found an elevator, plain and drab compared to the others. There were no doors or rooms this way either. Dublin kept a wary lookout as she caught up to him.

"Pretty sure the creature went this way," Athen panted.

"Aye." Dublin ran his hand along the side of the wall, and a panel illuminated as the elevator doors squeaked open. He could not decipher these icons any better than the previous ones; like a mouse in a maze, he just had to pick one. "Lass, have you noticed how many different symbols there are in this place?" Dublin asked as they entered the elevator. Small talk? From Dublin? And in all their time together, that was only the second time he'd called her 'lass'. She was stunned, and for a moment she forgot about the ache in her leg.

"It's all different to me, boss."

"Nay, I mean one elevator had a fixed button, this elevator has a touchless panel, I've counted three different doorway sizes, some of the tables are a meter high and others are almost half that… and while I can't read a single one of them, all the symbols look different too. I went to Canadian Pacifica once, and I learned *sortie* just by wandering around."

"Good point, I suppose. It makes sense if there are distinct species and dialects catered to here, they'd have to customize everything for each of those different species."

"Tis' exactly what I was thinking. So, where have they all gone now?"

"I don't know. I don't care. I just want out of here."

"An' come on now, think about the future, everything we see here will be pried from us when we get back. Every word studied, analyzed, and we'll have a lot to tell. They'll want us to detail everything we possibly can."

"I'm just thinking of the *near* future, Dublin," she sighed. "I'm not even sure we are getting off this rock." Her shoulders slumped at those words.

"Oh yes, we are, lass, we are getting off this rock. Had my fortune read once. I'm not meant to die here." Dublin and Athen rode the elevator down a level. *Down. Damn.* Athen held her tongue; she really didn't want to go down. Up, she only wanted up.

Third time he called me that.

CHAPTER 27

Not this floor, nobody was permitted to be here...

All that work getting herself out of the elevator, staring at the blinking hallway lights, and now she was even more stuck. Any floor was better than this one. This was off limits, forbidden, and the consequences were severe. Carolina knew this; she was so certain that it sent chills down her spine. She froze, still inside the elevator. She was not going to take one step, but she also didn't really know why.

This was not her knowledge, but she only knew that because it would not make sense for it to be her knowledge, as that would be impossible. Honestly, without a way to compare it logically, she couldn't differentiate lately. What knowledge was hers before and what knowledge was hers now... they didn't have a line between them anymore.

But she knew there were consequences for going any further, and until she knew why, she wasn't moving. This floor belonged to the *Himark Ambassador*. She didn't know who that was, but he was important. But he was not a person. Why did she know anything about him in the first place? Either way, it meant the elevator had gotten stuck on the worst floor possible.

Her head hurt, and her feet were tired. A steady flow of air blew through the elevator doors, which were waiting to close. Carolina relaxed against the frame and let the cool air brush over her. The air felt good, but it was impossible to rest as strange sounds echoed up through the elevator shaft, like the building dreaming in sound. It reminded her of putting a conch shell to her ear and hearing the ocean if you added some industrial groaning. She grew up near Lake Michigan, where they built shuttle parts; the constant hum of industrialization carried over late into the night. This was a bit like that, too.

She brought her hand up to her head. There was a trick to this floor. What was the trick? Her head was starting to hurt. What was the trick... She didn't want to shift between her memories and *its* memories, but she wasn't heading out until she knew. She stopped chewing on her nails and wished she had gum. Her memory was not improving. The hallway was, by previous comparisons, ornate. Red halftables decorated the walkway with a running carpet, adding depth. An extensive set of doors stared back from the end of the hallway, *the Ambassador's room*. He was gone… everyone was gone. But the security system was still alive; they learned that early. Athen nearly paid for that lesson early on.

The door… some memory was attempting to float to the surface. Something about the door… There had been an assassination attempt. She felt icky knowing these things, like an invasion of privacy. She had so many foreign memories, and suddenly she was disturbed to think the parasite didn't just give memories but took them as well. She shuddered. Now *that* was an invasion of privacy. She supposed her dad would be delighted by the scientific implications, but she was just a twelve-year-old; she didn't care about that sort of thing. She supposed she would care later in life, when it was time to study for her placement exams, if she ever made it home.

Carolina studied the large doors from where she stood. They were a death trap, a fatal response to trespassing. Maybe she didn't know more than that, or she meant it didn't know more than that. The other routes she'd tried had collapsed; this might be the only way through. Or scaling the elevator shaft.

She hated this place.

"I'm getting out of here," she vowed. That settled it, she'd have to climb up the shaft. Carolina dug her fingers into the overhang and pulled away ceiling tiles until she could see the cable holding the elevator. She was surprised she had the strength to hold herself there, given her small stature and current state. It made her fingers ache, but they weren't asking to quit. She looked up through the hole and saw the elevator cable dance above her from the slightest shift in weight. She pulled herself up through the elevator's ceiling. She was surprised she had it in her.

Crouched atop the elevator's box, she glimpsed a row of bolts going up the far side of the elevator shaft; it looked like a kind of ladder, and naturally, it was placed as far from her as possible. She carefully stepped across the elevator's boxed roof, hoping it did not cave in. She could reach it; she just had to repeat these steps slowly and steadily.

On the far side of the elevator shaft, she grabbed the bolts and studied her climb. Her boots were wide and thick at the toes, making them great for hiking but poor for climbing. She bent one leg back at the knee and pried a boot loose, letting it clatter down the hole in the ceiling of the elevator. She kicked the other boot off next. She didn't like being barefoot, but these bolts were too small otherwise.

She placed one foot on a bolt and rested her weight on it. The metal bit into her toes, but she had a good grip and good stability.

There was a pattern of small ridges running along the walls, extending through the diameter of the shaft, which she used for extra support. It was not enough to dangle from, but if she tried to hold on with her hands, it gave her a little support, and she liked having options. If someone could throw a ladder down for her, that would be ideal. Of course, she wasn't expecting that to happen. She felt tears coming... no, not tears. Laughter, she felt laughter coming. That's it—her mom would declare her insane.

She'd never climbed before, but she must have had a gift for it. A true natural. Her grip held; her feet were secure despite aching. Her confidence swelled until the bolts became sparse, and there did not look to be another step in the climb, as she dangled precariously high up the elevator shaft by this point.

The next floor was about ten meters higher up. Looking about, she had the cable dangling down the middle, slick with grease. There was also the way back down, which she wouldn't do. Luckily, but also a little frustrated at the timing, there just happened to be a service ladder on the far side of the shaft. The side she'd started out on, but the side across from her now. They couldn't have built the ladder all the way down now, could they! Carolina huffed.

"Here goes," she said before aiming and leaping for the rungs. She jumped as if in slow motion, eyes calculating distance and timing, and when the rungs were within range, she gripped them. The flow of time resumed to normal, and the rest of her slapped against the wall, her grip tested but holding.

She'd seen people do that in movies; somehow, it actually worked. Hitting the wall hurt, but the pain was kindly masked with adrenaline. Now it was just one rung after the other, much better than climbing bolts. Within a meter up the ladder, she realized how bad her toes hurt, as if she didn't need to shut out that pain anymore. They were throbbing and red, a small price to pay to make that climb, but still, she didn't feel their pain until just now. At least she was still moving up. *'Hiding the pain is an evolutionary gift,'* was something Dublin might say. Not that she wanted to think of him after he attacked her dad. She used to really like Dublin.

She brought herself up to the length of the door and smiled at her success. Now she just had to open them. She thought there was a release lever on the inside... a wave of dizziness came and went. She held her head and steadied herself. The dizziness had threatened to pounce, which she did not need right now.

"Okay, where was I? Oh yes, the door."

She wavered again; this time, she felt herself on the verge of passing out. *No, not now!* She held the ladder and felt her balance wavering with her vision. Despite her best efforts, her fingers were slipping as she tried to hold on. Thoughts and memories that were not hers flooded in sequence, and she was unable to keep from falling. She turned and jumped in desperation, grabbing onto the center cable, which sent her swinging.

Adrenaline snapped her back as she held on for dear life, trying not to pass out. The wave of exhaustion was sudden and unexpected, and now she dangled from the elevator cable. Her momentum bounced her against the wall and made her turn helplessly.

"Help me!" she screamed. She swung with the cable, but she could not let go without falling. "Help!" she screamed again. Spinning, she reached out with her leg, hoping to use the wall to steady herself. She aborted that attempt as the added exertion threatened what little grip she had. "Please!" she wailed. She heard the elevator doors slide open.

"Carolina?"

She looked up at one perplexed Dmitry, standing in the doorway above her. "Hold on!" he said, reaching out to steady the cable for her. She gladly felt the cable come under control, thankfully too, since her grip was moments from failing. Lucky for her, Dmitry had heard her cries and found her. He held the wall with one hand and steadied the cable with the other. He pulled the cable towards him until she rested against the wall with the service ladder. Carolina shook uncontrollably.

"You have to get onto the ladder and climb, Carolina."

"I can't," she panted, refusing to open her eyes.

"Slow your breathing. I can't reach you, so *you* have to climb."

"I can't!"

"Right now, little girl."

Carolina grunted. She never liked Dmitry, and she hated being called that. Her dizziness subsided, and she moved her hands to the rungs on the ladder. She climbed the ladder until Dmitry snatched her at the collar and hoisted her onto his level. She plopped to the ground, not very gently.

He gave her a few moments while she caught her breath; in that time, he sat against the open doors and looked over, studying where he had found her. He looked at her and then back down the elevator shaft. It seemed most unlikely she could have climbed up that. None of them could have. The girl was breathing steadily now.

"Carolina, where is your father?"

CHAPTER 28

Austin ignored the pebbles in the back of his skull as he rested against his dirt pillow, though he was aware of each granule. He watched the clouds as they oozed across the sky of Paphos from one horizon to the other. The sky without sun lent a rich flood of purple, plus all of its many hues, and his dirt pillow did nothing to alter its beauty. It could be morning or evening, sunrise or sunset, and neither mattered.

Eventually, he did look at his watch, which did not mean anything to local time. It was 03:14:02 Earth Central. He knew this because he never changed the time when he traveled. That somehow made him feel connected to home, a valuable tip for expeditioners like him. The breeze had a dry chill, reminding him how drenched in sweat he was. It was between the lazy gusts of wind that he could smell his own combination of fumes and charring. Being on the surface again was refueling his spirits, though he didn't yet know where he was. From here, it could be mistaken for a dry planet, but that wasn't the case at all. Paphos was mostly tropical. *Carolina...*

Austin rolled to his side. It was time to get up. The adrenaline dump had left him frail, a weak husk, but Carolina was alone down there. She wasn't safe without him, but he also desperately needed water. He needed to go back and find her; hopefully, water would be along the way. Regardless, he needed to get going. He looked up at the rings of this planet one more time, which hung sharply at a thirty-degree angle. He couldn't be far from the quadrohuts, though the term 'far' was subjective when on foot.

He was on his feet, feeling wobblier than he expected. He needed to get going; he had a daughter to protect, but his body protested. A few gentle slaps across the face helped.

He followed the gravel up and found himself looking across a pocketed desert of indents, some big and some you didn't want to fall into. He swore they resembled bomb craters. And beneath them, it was hard to imagine that facility, hidden and sprawling under the surface. It might be faster to go back the way he came, but who knew if he could get down. Not without rope, he figured. He needed supplies, and he had no way of knowing where Carolina would be now. Hopefully, her survival instincts were keeping her safe. He refused to think of anything else.

A minute was enough to show the sun was rising from the east, so it was morning. An eastern rise always made him a little less homesick, too. He tore open a glucose packet and downed it, the last one in his pocket. It'd been in that pocket so long he couldn't even read the expiration date, not that he cared. He didn't normally litter, but today was a day of firsts. Had it been a whole day since they first went inside? No, it was only a few hours, couldn't be more than that. Best not to think, his head didn't want him to.

The plan was simple: locate the quadrohuts, restock some supplies, get back in the facility, and find his daughter. First step was finding the huts. He wasn't exactly a human sextant, but the angle of the rings hadn't changed from his usual view, and he had a rough idea of how far he could have gone underground—though it was disorienting down there. Last, he vaguely remembered observing some dry patches to the Southeast when they were researching landing spots from orbit, so he pinged a direction to the Northwest. If he got close enough, it should look familiar, and from there he'd find the huts. He believed the train was just about underneath him as he tried picturing the layout of the tracks. Austin finally began his hike, kicking up dust that was carried away by the wind. The half-hearted gusts from before were building.

He felt the sugar in his blood already; that little glucose packet had a nice little boost in it. Ultimately, it was not enough to take away his exhaustion, just enough to keep him going. He would pace himself; pushing too fast now meant stopping too soon later. He wouldn't stop, he couldn't stop, not until Carolina was safe. He let his fears trail off because there was nothing he could do about them from here, fears of her being trapped with the creature, or even with Dublin. He didn't know what that was all about, but he had to be ready for more.

None of them carried a map; they never needed it when Orlean's prosthetic was connected to the Orbiter up above. He continued along the rim of bomb craters, though calling them that suggested a battle had occurred here. It didn't take long before he had no sense of relation to the facility beneath him, but that wouldn't matter if he found the quadrohuts. He shielded his eyes from the sand as another warning gust came. The clouds above were broiling with activity to the west. Guess the planet thought they needed a storm, too. Maybe it would pass by; the quadrohuts could handle wind up to about 65 kph.

He'd hiked for several minutes now, and nothing looked familiar yet. At what point would he need to head back and try again? He scanned the sky, but his head hurt to the point that it all looked the same. Soon, he'd recognize something. But just in case, he made mental notes in case he had to backtrack. It would help if he had any idea how far that train had shuttled them.

A large crunch stopped his thoughts and forced them down. He'd stepped on something brittle and lifeless, but it wasn't dirt or a branch. He brought his foot back and saw the print left in the dirt and bone. It had to be bone; there weren't vases on the ground out here. The wheels in his head whirred slowly. Next to his boot was a skull with a bowl-shaped cranium, short jagged teeth, eye sockets wide and deep, and a cluster of horns at its forehead. No human skull, no animal he recognized, which would be obvious given the circumstances. He'd been hiking and looking up at the sky and was otherwise lost in a swirling panic, and somehow he'd stumbled upon a den of bones. Hidden in overgrown brush, here was a veritable graveyard of alien bones. At first glance, there were at least three separate skull types. Bleached, brittle from the sun, and scattered by the dozen.

The intense sun cooked on the back of his head, reminding him how warm it was about to be if the clouds didn't get here first. He shielded his eyes from the light reflecting off the bleached earth. He had seen nothing more than dry brambles until this crunched under his boot. How did he miss this? To the left, he noticed something else, something mechanical. Maybe they really were bomb craters he was walking around.

Austin examined his discovery and recognized a wing partially submerged, charred, and misshapen. Similar in shape to the vessel he and Dmitry recently sabotaged. This was in pieces and scattered, indicative of a crash landing. The weight of importance rested on his soul; something big had happened here, either a battle or a flat-out massacre. And here he was stepping on the bones, ignorant of sacred ground.

He wavered with thirst. Maybe he could come back and re-examine all of this later; it demanded as much, but he had to keep moving. Austin looked around and had to re-center himself on where he'd been and where he was headed. He'd lost track of his path. "What the hell…" He scanned the surrounding area in all directions, and yet nothing looked familiar. Worse, he couldn't even find his own footprints, except for the skull he'd crushed. The shattered bones held a good impression, one solid print with the toes pointing a little to the left. One print was all he had to go on. One print would have to do. He placed his foot in the shape and positioned his body in the same direction.

It didn't look familiar, but then again, he had hiked in a daze until that crunch. He'd been tired, distracted, and made a mistake. He was about to lose the planet's rings, too, as dark clouds now covered half the sky.

He hoped this bootprint was correct and resumed his hike into the wind.

Charcoal clouds swirled in the upper stratosphere; the storm was headed towards him and would soon blot out the intense sun. Always a positive, always a negative, or always a silver lining, as they used to say. An hour of hiking went by; if he didn't find something familiar soon, it meant he had gone the wrong way.

The ground rose, and he had to climb up with it, even using his hands to help himself. He only had the strength to keep going, and nothing else. He was able to conserve some of his energy by closing his eyes for a minute, incremental but helpful. The wind was against him now as he came to the top again. At first, he cursed his luck; it felt as if even nature wanted him to fail. But when he gazed from his new position, he found the start of the sprawling forest. This was his forest, and he was able to spot some clear patches he'd seen from satellite maps. This was the right direction; he'd be there within the hour. That meant the train had taken them over ten kilometers, maybe more.

Confidence sprang within him. Previous doubts were now filled with resupply checklists, an internal debate on how much water, how much food, what kind of weapons. That was suddenly a thing; of course, they didn't have proper weapons, but he'd make do. A speck of rain touched him, and he sensed it was but the first of many more.

With determination, he descended towards the beckoning forest. Under the canopy of trees, it was now two shades darker, but the wind was no less, tossing leaves and forcing a dance of limbs. The snapping bend of wood echoed in the distance. *Haha*, he laughed. A tree falling on him now would just be a tragic-comedy. Let the storm come; nothing would stop him. Let the wind howl all it wanted to. He wasn't stopping now.

CHAPTER 29

She stared at his face, his eyes dark and serious, letting the silence creep in.

"I said, where is your father?" Dmitry demanded a second time.

Carolina would not answer that question.

"Well?"

He'd get nothing out of her. She did not trust Dmitry, even though he had just saved her life. He was dangerous. However, it was also dangerous to treat him as an enemy.

"Thank you for saving me," she said. He paused, his eyes taking her in, weighing her. She could see the wheels scheming behind those eyes. He was always a schemer, and she especially recognized it now. She would have to be careful in his presence.

"Okay, you don't know where your dad is," he began. "And I gather you haven't found a way out yet."

Carolina shook her head, a subtle gesture.

"Still not saying much?"

Carolina remained still, but she stopped looking him in the eye. Predators took eye contact as a sign of aggression.

"That's okay, I hate the small talk anyway."

Carolina caught herself glancing past him and tried to correct it. But it was too late; he'd noticed it. "Does something look familiar to you?" he asked, nursing his hunch.

It was familiar to her, like an old house she might have lived in. It was those memories again; she'd been careless, and he'd caught it. She said nothing, but her face gave it away. She was off to a bad start with being careful around him.

"Come on," Dmitry said and guided her down the hallway. It was darker than she liked, tall and narrow to the point of walking side by side with him. She felt him looking down at her, an eagle at a mouse, which made her ball her fists. She tried to walk faster, moving only to the sound of their footsteps until the hallway ended in a large room. Spacious like a gymnasium, the room was littered with tables and chairs, benches too, all tossed about from some great commotion.

Dmitry carried on casually. "I think this is near the first floor, if we're lucky, we're under the hospital rooms from the beginning," he said. They didn't feel like innocent observations; it felt like he was testing her. She kept her face still, wishing to conceal any sort of response. Yes, she knew things, and he'd been the first one to catch on.

He pointed at the large double freight doors on the far side of the room, beckoning her towards them. Blocking the doors was a barricade of tables and chairs, but that's not what she was worried about. It was the invisible security system that she knew was there.

"Come on," he urged.

Her feet stopped in place. "We can't…"

His smile was unwelcome. "Something you'd like to share?"

"It's blocked, that's all," she said, referring to the barricade, because how would she know about the security system?

"You are small enough. Climb through and get those doors unlocked," he demanded.

It was a test. Maybe now she could throw him off. She had to feign ignorance, or else she'd be the test-subject for every death trap. "Okay." She walked towards the barricade as if unaware of the deadly measures about to take place. When he realized she wouldn't stop, he snatched her at the last moment.

"Hey!" she yelled. An electric barrier arose just in front of where she was a moment before. A dazzling swirl of sparks and debris flew up into the air. Dmitry set her down; he'd obviously discovered them and was testing her. She hoped this failed hunch of his made him reconsider what he thought about her. She was especially glad he stopped her, because she knew it was there all along, and she was just about to stop. But he didn't need to know that.

She glared at him expectantly.

"That was a close one, eh? I saw the prongs of that nasty security at the last second," he said, trying to explain it away. The prongs were slightly visible, and his voice had changed. "Well, that was the entirety of my big plan. Now I'm stuck. With the elevator collapsed over there, this is probably still our best shot. Any ideas?"

"Why would I have any ideas? I'm just a kid," she said and walked away. She sensed him tense up; he didn't like being dismissed. But eventually he relaxed and went about gathering small objects and tossing them into the dazzling electric barrier, testing for any gaps. He tossed a small box at an inconspicuous spot near the wall. The force field arose and ate it, appearing from nowhere and disappearing as swiftly. He almost had a complete perimeter mapped out in flecks of white ash. She waited as he continued on, both of them pretending to ignore each other. Dmitry tossed a short metal tube, looking away as he predicted the electric arc to leap. This time, he saw something: a sensor in the wall. It was perfectly camouflaged, and he was surprised to see it, despite the fact that he was looking for it. Someone didn't want anything going through this door.

She watched as his mind unraveled this puzzle. Alien technology notwithstanding, it looked like a proximity sensor or a motion laser. He inspected it cautiously with his hands. Carolina remained quiet as he gave her a thin smile. He returned his focus to the wall. She had a sobering thought that while she didn't want to share her knowledge, it may be worse to feign total ignorance. If she wasn't useful, he had no reason to keep her around. Maybe she'd be better off showing something, just enough to remain invaluable. He was that kind of dangerous.

He seemed to have found something else in the wall, too small for her to spot, but he carefully traced it. She found some relief, not knowing what he had found, she'd known there was a trap here, but nothing more. The relief came from not being omnipotent, as if that were something to fear. It seemed she knew as much as that parasite knew and not any more than that.

He picked at it with his fingernails and pulled back gently, carefully so as not to disturb any circuitry behind it. Time had made the adhesive brittle, and a wide strip gave way. A very simple setup of wires hid inside, and he pulled them out altogether, ripping them apart. With the dangling end in one hand, they collectively sensed a hum of energy dissipating. To be certain, Dmitry grabbed a chair and tossed it into the perimeter of white ash, and it careened until bouncing helplessly off the wall. There was no dazzling display of electrical energy; the trap was disabled.

He turned to her. "It's safe, try the doors."

Her revelation lent a voice, *be useful, be valuable.* She ignored it. "You try them."

Dmitry smiled. He put his hand straight out, towards the ring of white ash, further and further until he was well inside the trap's perimeter.

It was down, he'd disabled it.

Carolina stood in front of the barricade with her shoulders slouched. She grabbed a tiny little piece of junk and hocked it behind her. See, she was useful. They both tossed articles behind them until they could get to the doors. Dmitry grabbed the handle and pulled, only to find it refusing to budge. His frustration grew; she saw it rising dangerously. *Be useful, be valuable...*

"There's a button," she said.

Dmitry looked at her, then over at where she was referring. Tucked behind a leaning cabinet was a button, recessed in the wall. She knew it was there all along, but to him it looked like she just had keen observations. Either way, he tipped the heavy cabinet out of his way and pressed the button.

With a mechanical *'shwoop'*, the double doors disappeared into the walls. Air gushed at them as the room exhaled. She hung her head, not wanting to see.

The room was smaller than he'd expected, as if this were a CCTV room or some security hub for observation. He spotted a giant window, and behind it, another room was also visible. Dmitry entered and gazed up at the arched ceiling, twice the height of a man. Once inside, he spotted a spiral staircase on his left, seemingly leading up and down. Dmitry inspected the entire room, but his gaze kept returning to the large window on the far wall. He recognized what he saw through that window; it was the receiving area from when they first entered the facility. It seemed visitors to this facility were observed in secret, from this very room.

He stepped around boxes that spilled from the table to the floor, having scattered themselves decades ago. They had the look of being sorted vigorously. On the opposite end of the table was a control panel, different from the previous ones, like a computer or a server. Holograms illuminated near it, cycling through a basic message, nothing to do with their presence. Dmitry stepped around the table to get another look and was startled when something touched him. He jumped back, tripping over his own feet. Whatever touched him fell too, clattering like dry kindling. He sprang up in embarrassment and found the remains of an alien skeleton. It had been in the chair that he bumped. There were large femurs, talons, several small ribs, and a skull dotted with horns. Hard to determine height, except by the size of the femurs, and it would be tall by that indication.

Carolina walked into the room. "He died alone."

Dmitry regained his composure. He should have noticed the skeleton right away, despite the poor light. His eyes were adjusted now, and with a quick search, he didn't see any other alien remains. "Obviously, he died alone," he said. "I'm wondering about those stairs over there," he added. "Maybe they lead somewhere." He was interested in any way out of here that didn't involve a shimmy down the elevator shaft. He stared at Carolina, waiting. He wanted her to volunteer to scout those stairs.

Sure, why not? She had to be useful, for her own sake. So she walked over to the spiral staircase, which went up to the right or down to the left. She climbed up and to the right, seeing where it led. It was a relief that nothing was familiar to her yet. Whatever this place had been, whatever its intended purpose, it was bad news for many unsuspecting specimens. She climbed up out of view, disappearing into a dark attic space.

"Stay where I can see you," he ordered, shining his light towards her. It was his idea that she scouted out the stairs, but now he didn't want her out of his sight. Dmitry followed up after her. When he arrived, he saw what she saw: an empty attic space. There was nothing here, no alternative route, just an attic.

"Want me to try down?" she asked.

His frustration threatened to boil over. "Quickly, and don't go far."

She pushed by him and went down the steps quickly, much faster than an adult felt comfortable doing. No handrails, but she didn't need them. Her feet were steady and swift, and the air was noticeably different heading down. Dmitry followed after her, though much slower than she was.

He arrived and turned on his personal light to get a better view. The walls were cave-like, having simply been carved out of the earth, much different than most of the facility. It was dirty and warm, and there were strange beehive holes in the walls. The holes were big enough that you could climb in them. And then something came out of one, so Carolina screamed.

CHAPTER 30

Athen collected herself as the elevator descended. When the elevator went down instead of up, she could have thrown a fit. But Dublin was there, and his presence always forced her to be her best. She couldn't handle going down again and hated these elevators for their random button assignments, but as always, she wasn't going to fail in front of him. So when it went down, she somehow didn't throw a fit.

The elevator doors opened to a blinking scene of indicator lights. She readied herself to try another button, but if they went down again, she really didn't know if she could handle it. She turned to ask Dublin what he thought, but the look on his face stopped her cold. He slowly brought a finger to his lips in the universal *shhh*.

Her adrenaline spiked as she turned her head, knowing only that something was wrong. Then a shadow moved, the creature's silhouette against the equipment and glowing indicator lights. Dublin looked at her and nodded, then he slowly reached over and pressed a different button. Any other floor would do. The elevator doors scraped shut, giving that audible grinding that made her wince. The last thing she saw before the doors sealed was the shadow raise its head, and then her elevator ascended.

Their relief at going up disintegrated as something crashed under them, so hard the elevator pitched. Athen fell into the wall. Next, a corner of the floor disappeared into loose, falling pieces, with tentacles climbing up them.

"Damn thing is holding on!" Dublin cursed. He steadied himself over the hole in the floor and swung at the tentacles with his hammer. The elevator stuttered as a cable threatened to break. "It's gonna' bloody drop us!"

"Dublin!"

The elevator continued to rise, although much more slowly. He spun to see another part of the floor gone, with a thick tentacle snared around Athen's middle. He dropped the hammer and retrieved one of his machetes, cutting into the base of it. Thick orange splattered as Dublin hacked repeatedly, forcing the limb to sever. Athen braced herself against the wall, trying to keep from being pulled in as another tentacle came to take its place. Dublin pinned that tentacle with one hand and hacked at it with the other.

The elevator stopped, and the doors scraped open as Athen tumbled out, with Dublin behind her. The wounded limb chased after her and found her boot, latching on and threatening to pull her back in.

"Help!"

Dublin impaled the sharp end of his machete into the creature's flesh. Athen's boot ripped free as the tentacle retreated away. Athen was on her feet as Dublin cupped an arm around her, ready to hoist her over his shoulder. Before he had time, they heard a *snap!* as the elevator cable gave way to the creature's weight. They heard it plummet, dragging the monster with it until it crashed several floors below. The slam echoed throughout the building. As they waited, the air became very quiet, except for their own breathing.

"Never thought I'd be happy to crash another elevator," she panted.

"Any chance that you got it?"

"I hope so. Hell, I'm not going to hold my breath though."

Dublin looked down at his makeshift machete. "Lookin', my hammer was in that elevator."

"Did you even hurt that thing?"

"Got a lil' orange blood on me, not much," he admitted, inspecting his blade. His machete was decorated with oily bits of flesh, bright and slimy. For as much chopping as he'd produced, he should have hurt it much more. In fact, his forearm was aching from the way he hacked at it. He could have cut a tree down with all that effort, but he'd barely cut through a tentacle as thick as his wrist. "Aye, I stung it, at least a little." He looked over at Athen, who was examining her missing boot.

"Guess it's better to go barefoot," she said, removing the other one. She was not about to struggle her way out of here with one boot on. Luckily, she still wore her sock liners, although one of them was caked in dried blood. "Ugh," she moaned before ripping her socks off, too. The bad leg was more challenging, but she was barefoot in no time. Now she was looking at her unladylike blisters. *Never a break!*

"You've got my respect, lamb, you're tougher than any man I know."

Athen's mouth was stuck. Did Dublin just give her a compliment? That didn't happen, and they both felt the weirdness. He cleared his throat and stepped forward, surveying this floor. That was possibly the nicest thing he ever said to her;

he never gave compliments. Must have been the bevy of near-death experiences at work.

"Gimme a moment to scout," he said and walked down the hallway, hoping to find something promising. He came back a moment later with a very blank face.

She closed her eyes before she spoke; she wanted to remember their victory before things got worse. "So, what's the good news?" she asked.

"Tis' a dead end, this is an oversized utility closet, best as I can summarize," Dublin said.

"Can we cut through a wall?"

"Aye, just go fetch me' kit from the *quads*, I'll get us through in an hour or so."

"Okay, I'll grab us a beer on the way," she joked. But it was short-lived; she understood what he meant. They were *stuck*. She hadn't seen this floor yet, and it was more or less a utility room by the looks of it. The defunct elevator was the only way in or out. Dublin went over and peered down the elevator shaft, resting his arm against the open door.

Athen forced herself to follow until she looked down the gaping shaft as well. She could make out the outlines of the former elevator cabin, but its condition and any remaining pieces were shrouded in darkness. Looking up, the nearest cable was further than she could reach, and besides, there was no rope-climbing with that leg of hers. She forced the despair down, yet again. She would get out of here.

She gave a look at Dublin, a look that he returned. No comfort or false hope; they were headed down, and neither of them wanted it. If the light could just penetrate to the bottom, it would at least give her some relief.

He seemed to be thinking her thoughts too. "If it's still breathing, then we'd better get going before it wakes up. It's a dead-end here, and tickling it with this poker won't help much." He sounded beaten talking about his machete, all things considered. Athen wondered how disappointed he was at the performance of his makeshift weapons. They were both craftsmen, so she understood how hard it was not to consider it a personal failure. "Leavin' us to figure out your first-class elevator, lamb."

Athen loosened the tourniquet from around her leg, the belt that had kept her from bleeding out until the coags did their job. She readjusted her pants and formed a loop with her belt, ready to figure out some rappelling. It was a bit shorter than she needed, which he noticed. They were masters at communicating in silence after years of working together, and Dublin removed his belt too, handing it to her. She had a way to rappel now, but what she wouldn't give for a karabiner. Those near-death experiences were also bringing out some new nicknames; he didn't usually call her "*lamb*."

She glanced back down the elevator shaft, this time just to feel the slightly cooler air that flowed up. She'd need some water soon, but it was best not to think on that. She used one of her remaining tools, an impact screwdriver, as a handle and tied the end of her belt to it. Dublin watched her work. When she was finished, he climbed in, using the doors for support as he slipped his feet over. He said nothing about Athen's repel design, for which she was grateful.

"This is gonna work, just so you know, old *two-tooth*," she said.

"Aye, I haven't a doubt."

Was he just going to ignore her brilliant return-nickname?

Apparently so. He climbed down with ease despite the minimal surfaces available. He moved like a man without fear. "And *two-tooth* is mostly used in England, *lamb*."

"I knew that, *tup*," she argued, trying a new one.

"That one's Scotland. I'm from Ireland."

"Same difference," she said with a wide smile. He ignored that one with a cautious laugh, as those were fighting words.

Athen was stalling; she wasn't feeling confident about this climb, which, like anything else, she wasn't about to let Dublin see. Leaning over the edge, she slipped her rappel cable around the back side of a tiny pipe running up the elevator shaft. She wound the other end through her cargo pants' belt loop and tied it, holding the screwdriver handle as a brake. If she slipped she would have this to hold her, assuming the pipe was strong enough. Given the age of this place, she had her doubts. It would be best if she didn't test it. Next came the part where she was supposed to shimmy over the side, but that part was taking a bit of time. This wasn't going to be pretty.

"I need more line, this won't work," she said with one leg hanging over the ledge.

"Aye, but you'll have to make do."

She knew he would say that. Screw it, she wasn't going to sit here anymore. She threw a few curses at her leg and spun herself over the ledge, hanging on with fatigued hands.

"An' I hope you don't plan on making me catch you. I can't after the Scotland thing."

"Wouldn't dream of it," she grunted, holding the screwdriver and trying to land her bare toes onto any ledge. A connecting piece securing the pipe to the wall gave her something to stand on, but it also cut into the ridge of her foot. She steadied herself before loosening the strap and retying it near her hips. With that back in place, she readied to repeat the process all the way to the lower level. "Dublin?"

"Aye?"

She bit down on any insecurities that were about to follow. "Never mind." She pushed the fear aside, reading herself to do this. She held the pipe and lowered her legs again. They traveled this way for about a meter until her hands were barely holding on. She was putting a lot of weight and trust in the rappel line. At the next pipe support she was struggling to get her toes into a proper foothold.

"Easy now, steady yourself," he said.

"I am steady!" she snapped back. He smirked and didn't reply, which was just as well. Then she swore he muttered something akin to *'that's better, lamb'*. Criticism filled her with strength as her toes found the connecting joint, and this time she barely noticed the way it cut into her skin. She huffed and lowered herself another meter, hand-over-hand until needing to re-fasten her line again. She looked up and saw herself somewhere between the floor she was on and the floor they were headed to. She was in it now, no turning back, and that felt a little suffocating. It was all mental, but still. The only way out was through.

Dublin moved much faster than her. She was only halfway by the time he reached the next floor down, still a ways above the crashed elevator, but a good ten meters lower than where they'd started. He was working the doors open, kicking and wrenching them free. At last he looked up with a grin of Irish triumph. "I've got us reservations, love."

"Oh that's so sweet dear," she grunted.

"Seem' I'm always taking care of you, aye?" It was a joke, and it only burned a little.

"You could get me a ladder."

"Nay, left it in my other pants. You're not stuck, are ye?"

"Well, yes…" she admitted. She'd been failing to get her feet onto the next ledge, she was struggling with this part. If only her repel line was a bit longer.

"Hurry now, we don't want to lose our table," his voice carried up to her. He was only a few steps inside, but not seeing him put an unexpected anxiety in her. A few deep breaths and she'd get there, she just needed to refasten her rappel line. Using her arms she steadied herself and lowered her good leg as far down as it could go while her bad leg dangled. The rappel line slipped free, stinging as the screwdriver flung at her and whipped loose before falling to the floor. So much for the repel line.

"Damn!"

"Alright dear?"

"*Aye*," she mimicked in his voice.

"Nay, it's *aye*."

"That's what I said."

"*Nay* it's not. And don't scare me again."

The lighthearted jokes helped to a point, but her hands were sweating, and the reduced grip was adding heavily to her anxiety. She needed to be on solid ground. Without the safety of her rappel line she extended her leg all the way down until her foot was firmly planted on the connecting joint beneath her. Holding on with one hand and the other gripping a bolt she lowered herself, as she did that, a definite sound clanked beneath her.

"Quit dropping things."

"Wasn't me that time time… Dublin?"

"Shush now," he said in a whisper. She held the pipe with ailing strength as Dublin squinted down at shapes too murky to recognize. But the shapes moved, so he looked up at her with a calm face. "Ya' better hurry, lass," he said, softly.

The debris stirred, slow and rousing. Of course they weren't lucky enough for that thing to have died from the fall. Athen reached frantically for the next bolt as a somber tentacle climbed up along the wall. The limb slapped and stuck to the wall, using the leverage. The debris gave way as the creature steadily pulled itself out from under the elevator pinning it. She was staring at it so hard she forgot where her priorities lay. Right on cue, her foot slipped. One tiny slip because she was distracted was all it took. She was falling, briefly, because then Dublin's big arm snatched her in midair.

He fell back with a wince, tumbling her on top of him. He'd caught her, he'd miraculously grabbed her midair. He stood to his feet and winced as he tested his arm, but he wasn't waiting for anything. He drew her over his shoulders into a fireman's carry and forced himself into a run. She dangled over his back and heard the scraping of elevator doors as they cycled closed, muffling the sounds of the stirring rubble.

Dublin made good speed considering the extra carry, and she took a brief note at his impressive strength. This floor was wide with several paths branching in different directions, which meant there was a chance they could lose their pursuer. Her thoughts stopped mid-beat when the doors behind them smashed open. Fear gave his run added speed. She watched the machete bouncing on his leg, wishing she wasn't what was slowing him down. They didn't have a prayer of outrunning the creature, and by the last encounter, that machete had limited value.

She looked behind them as the beast emerged through the elevator doors. Their options were dwindlind as Dublin kicked the nearest door open and plopped her down inside. The creature was far away right now, but that would change quickly.

"Dublin!" she cried, warning him.

"I know," he said, slamming the door shut. He was looking for a hasty barricade.

"It won't help!"

"Right," he paused before reaching for his machete.

They had seconds left.

Their room was split into quarters like office cubicles. On the walls were gaping holes similar to laundry chutes or dumbwaiters, they could be promising. Before they could inspect them the door burst open, ripped from its hinges. Dublin turned to face it, wielding his machete, a look of embraced certainty.

"Jump!" Athen ordered, pointing at the holes. Dublin knew what she was thinking.

The creature hurled a huge desk between them. She hobbled and tumbled into one of the holes, and Dublin quickly had to pick a different one. He trust-jumped into one, not expecting to live, but knowing he wouldn't if the creature got him first.

Only he didn't fall, instead he went weightlessly up.

CHAPTER 31

Carolina shrieked but only for a moment. She hadn't been expecting Dublin to appear out of one of those beehive holes, wielding a machete no less, and it gave her a momentary startle.

Dmitry ran up to him. "Dublin? How the hell…"

Dublin was disoriented, not surprisingly, since he had virtually floated up and out of a hole in the wall.

"Athen? Where is she?" he said, holding his head. He shot a glance behind himself. "Am I dead?"

"Not yet. I don't understand, were you hiding down here?"

"Dmitry, dat' you? Where is Athen?" he demanded, stumbling to his feet. Dmitry grabbed him by the shoulder.

"Easy does it, you aren't making sense."

Dublin shook his head and blinked a couple times. "I jumped in a hole to get away, but I went up, not down," Dublin said. He looked over his shoulder at the wall again. "Am' not really sure of the details, it was all very *Erin go Bragh*."

"Jumped?"

"Aye, the wall had a hole just like this, but I went up," Dublin reaffirmed. A look moved across Dublin's face as he was talking to their team leader, one that Carolina wasn't sure she actually noticed. He looked angry.

Dmitry poked his head over and felt only an air draft. Carolina had seen him arrive, but Dmitry didn't, so he was trying to make sense of it all. It was really quite simple, Dublin fell up and out of the wall.

Carolina remained at a distance, visions of her father fresh in her mind. Dublin noticed her tenseness, but said nothing.

"Relax, Carolina, it's just Dublin, nothing to fear." Dmitry's words fell flat, and the wheels in his head started turning again at what he was observing. Dublin had an edge about him, and he couldn't tell which of them it was for. "We are stronger together, and we've all been split up. It's good to find another friendly face."

"Aye," Dublin said, though his voice lacked optimism. Carolina broke eye contact before Dublin tried to make any sort of conversation. If he felt guilty, well, he should. She returned her attention to the walls, wondering why she knew so little about them.

"Tis' much to go over, when there's time," Dublin said. Something about the way he said it got Dmitry's attention as the Irishman crossed his arms. But if something was on his mind, he dismissed it when he turned to address the beehive-like holes. "Damn anti-grav system here, or something," he said. "Athen went in one, I went in another. And here I am, so we need to find her."

"She's down there?"

"Aye, or somewhere. I jumped into it and it led me here… no elevator, no power, no rope, just *swoosh*. Felt like falling, but I went up. An' I'm not leaving Athen again, I'm going to find her."

"We will," Dmitry said, observing the holes closely. "So this must be some kind of transport system, hidden in the walls? With everything we've seen, why would they do that?"

"Every species has bloody secrets to keep, most likely," he said. Again, Dmitry's eyes sharpened at the choice of words. Dublin continued. "Which one did I come out of?" he demanded, struggling to think back. The process had left him disoriented, but he felt compelled to do something. He'd jump in all of them, one at a time, if it brought him to Athen.

"I didn't see it," Dmitry replied. "Carolina?"

She shook her head. She wouldn't help him.

Dublin looked into one, and then into another hole in the wall, looking for anything that might give him clues or direction. It all looked like dirt and shadow to him. He reached his hand out, feeling nothing. No glow or activation, no indication it had ever even happened in the first place. "Lookin' a big gamble trying it this way. I'd end up anywhere. But damnit, I can't leave the girl," Dublin cursed, his fists ready.

"We will find her," Dmitry said.

Dublin pulled out a glucose packet from his cargo pocket and tore it open. He downed it and tossed the wrapper into the catacomb hole he thought he came out of. It didn't fall, and at first it didn't rise. Then, like an ocean current, it was whipped up and out of sight.

"Fascinating," Dmitry muttered. Dmitry turned to Carolina, wondering if she might have an explanation. "Do you have anything to add?"

Carolina shook her head no, one quick jitter.

"Bloody hell, I'd spend all day getting lost in these trying to find her!"

"If she made it this far, she'll make it until we find her. She's tough."

"Aye, jumped into a tube like this one," Dublin said, looking around. "S'how far does this place go?"

"We don't know, we just found it," Dmitry said. "Was Austin with you?" He watched Dublin this time instead of Carolina. Dublin shook his head *no*. His face was hard to read. She knew the reason for that.

"Orlean?"

Dublin didn't answer at first. He inclined his head softly, as if sparing Carolina's delicate ears, and shook his head *no* again. Carolina could have spat, which wasn't a very kid-like thing to think. Why not just spell it out in single letters, thinking that would elude her? Worse, Dmitry almost seemed relieved that the team had shrunk. She held out hope for her dad; she had to.

Dmitry remained quiet long enough to finish his train of thought in silence. No doubt he weighed each of them in his mind, probably discounting Orlean the moment his prosthetic lab went missing. She knew her dad was an electrical engineer or something, so that was likely important. Dmitry didn't act as if he cared about any of them. She wanted to crack that head open and know more… which was also a strange thing for her to think.

"What do you keep looking at?" Dmitry finally asked, having noticed the Irishman checking over his shoulder repeatedly.

"Jus' that when we jumped in the holes, it was because the creature was chasing us, I'm half-expected it to show up, too."

Again, Dmitry folded his arms. Again, Carolina watched as his mind calculated these facts; she pictured him selecting the ways it would help him. The man was such a rat.

"One of these mystery tunnels must go topside…" Dmitry said, as if that's what he'd been thinking about.

"That'd be lovely, but which one? The holes are as random as buckshot, not a single marking."

"Maybe we can figure it out," Dmitry said, reaching for an answer. Dmitry ran his fingers inside one of the tunnel entrances, wondering what could be so discreet and yet capable of transporting matter so easily. Upon closer inspection, his fingers probed the dirt and found a few small, copper-colored, metallic nubs. They must have something to do with how these tunnels worked; he'd love to get a proper scan of them.

"We erased all of the markings to trap them inside…"

Dmitry's smug little face told her she said something. She'd said that? Yes, that was her. She was the one who said that. She crossed her arms and turned, stunned and awash in confusion. She didn't remember anything about this room, and it came out of her mouth, but she wasn't the one talking. What was happening to her? She trembled, her breath shortening, tears at the ready.

The Irishman carefully approached one of the catacomb holes, raising his small flashlight for a better look at the circumference. He could see the remnants of old markings now, too old and scratched out to be of much use. Dmitry followed, squinting at the faint markings that had been scratched away.

"Anything else?" Dmitry asked. "Well, there has to be a map or something."

Dublin's head was cocked. "Ya' hear that?"

They stood still to listen; there were always hollow sounds in this place if you listened. It was picking up the important ones that kept you alive, tuning out the strange industrial clicks and nameless echoes, yet capturing the footsteps and dragging sounds.

Dmitry turned to Carolina with that nasty, smug grin of his. She wished her body were different, bigger, so she could remove that look from his face. "We can't go back the way we came, not with that thing going around chasing people," he smiled. "It looks like we'll have to pick one of these little *swoosh* tunnels and hope it takes us somewhere better. Dublin, are they safe?"

Dublin seemed reluctant to answer the question. "Safe enough, it scared the hell out of me. No idea how far I went."

"We will just have to make an educated guess," Dmitry voted, giving another look in Carolina's direction. He chose one of the larger holes, wondering if the diameter had anything to do with importance. "This one?" he asked. She gave no reaction. Dmitry drummed his index finger on his pant leg. "Carolina, you will go first." Dmitry walked over to her. "Is this the one we should take?"

"How would I know?"

"Because you do. No more games. You knew how to get inside, you knew about the traps, and you kept making comments about things you shouldn't know anything about. And while I don't know exactly how such insights came to you, I do know I can use them. So, which one is it?"

"Give the lass a break. She's gone through enough."

"Oh, she knows." Dmitry took a step closer to her, towering over her. "I'm not playing any more games. Which one is it?"

"I don't know."

"Which one?"

"Dmitry, I said back off…"

"Speak up, little girl, or I'll pick for you."

Carolina couldn't stop herself from shaking.

"That one…" she said, pointing at a different hole.

"You're sure?"

Carolina nodded yes.

"Well, in that case…" Dmitry grabbed Carolina by her arm and pulled her towards the hole.

"Let me go! Get your hands off me!" she cried.

But Dmitry wasn't listening. He scooped her up and tossed her headfirst into the hole she had picked. Then, he watched in amazement as she zipped up and out of sight, her screams fading away in a mere second.

"Do you think she was telling the truth?" he asked Dublin with a grin.

The Irishman had a deadly glare. "You're mad, Dmitry, gone and lost it. We're having a lil' chat about things, you and me, and soon," Dublin said, pushing him out of the way. He jumped in after Carolina.

Dmitry stood in the room alone. "You keep your opinions to yourself, Irishman!" he said, though Dublin could not hear him. "I'm still the Commander of this team!" he shouted to no one.

Mad? Hardly. This was history in the making. His discovery here, his actions here, would be famous for all time. "Time to see if the little brat was telling the truth….. Hello?" Dmitry hollered, calling into the opening. "Well then."

He placed his hands on the outer rim, which felt a little like clay. He slowly pulled himself inside the entry until, and it was just like Dublin said, he fell upwards.

CHAPTER 32

Athen's chest pounded from the warp in reality. She had jumped into a hole in the wall, and from what happened next, she thought she was seeing things. She had somehow fallen without falling, guided through a complex pathway hidden behind walls and beneath floors, a tunnel system that defied physics. It pulled her like a toy boat down a river; she simply followed the current, traversing a maze behind the seen. Her path was illuminated from vents at times, dark at others. Then she was spit out on the ground, disoriented from the sudden appearance of gravity. She landed on a grated floor, cold and sharp and unwelcome. She didn't know up from down at first, but her anti-grav training helped her get her bearings. Still, it took a minute to recover.

She had yet to get to her feet, largely from the pain, but not entirely. Every step of the way today, she'd been proud of herself for not crying, and this day easily fell into the category of worst day ever. But then she made a mistake; she looked at her feet. She looked down at her dirty, bare, and blistered feet. That's when something inside her had had enough. Like the little girl she'd forgotten, Athen cried. She bawled. She let the tears roll because once started, she couldn't stop. Sure, her leg hurt like hell, the pain was crippling at times and worse at others. And she was tired, hungry, and especially thirsty. But when she looked at the layers of dirt pushed into the lines around her toenails, it was just enough to push her over the edge.

She cried awhile, she let it happen until she was done, and she embraced the doubt that Dublin was behind her, just about to arrive. It all happened so fast, but if he wasn't here by now, then he was probably somewhere else, assuming he made it out of there. As long as he was safe, that's all that mattered. The worst was not knowing.

A questioning doubt of the tunnels arose in her thoughts, as if they had been a hallucination. That fed into a greater daydream; that somehow all of this was a hallucination. The fantasy became that she was really back on Earth and in a hospital, as if she'd simply hit her head or something. That would be nice in the sense that she wasn't really stuck here on Paphos, but she knew better. She couldn't indulge in hoping it was all a dream. The tunnel flight was real; it was some impossible technology, and beyond that, she put it to rest. She wouldn't be waking up out of this. It was all very real.

The air felt different; her senses told her that before she was done wiping her eyes. She was on a grated walkway elevated by stairs hung above a main floor, and there were blinking lights next to her. A row of squat control panels was hung along the stairs. Athen dragged herself to her feet, using everything her hands could grab so she could get herself upright. Her leg was again deciding that going anywhere was not an option, and those negotiations were final. She looked down at the ten steps she would eventually take to get to the floor beneath her and decided to wait another minute before attempting them.

She'd go step-by-step, slowly and safely. It was time. Gripping the handrail with a death grip, she carefully pressed her weight into it and slid her bad leg down. Crying out in pain, she recovered and waited. One step down, but she'd really appreciate more pain meds, please. She groaned. She had a strategy in place, nothing now except to get it done. One step and then another, she carefully made her way down. A fear of tumbling grew as she became lightheaded with shaky hands, until fifteen minutes later, when she finally reached the bottom of the stairs.

The room seemed unfinished, like so much of this place. After a short reprieve, she hobbled towards an open doorway; the flat floor was so much nicer to move across. It made all the difference in the world right now. Light came from a thick blue window, casting a line in sapphire. The floor was still gritty at times and dug into her bare feet. She began charting a path that avoided the grated sections. "Damn aliens knew I'd be here one day, and they knew I'd be barefoot, and they put this here just to piss me off," she cursed. Another moment came for curse or cry, she didn't need to cry again.

She made it to the open doorway. It was a small room with a table, a pile of bones beside it, and a thickly tinted window. To the left of that window, she noticed a spiral staircase going both up and down. But it was the window that captivated her. Through it, she saw the room from the beginning, the reception area they'd called it. Tables, chairs, large markings; she recognized it as the first room, the one after the decline that almost killed her. Her heart leapt; this was the top floor! This was where the façade began, before it turned into the abyss of experiments and whatever else. This was where the building ferried in different species, made them feel comfortable, and then took them below. She didn't hold back her smile. She was getting out of here.

Eager to see real daylight again but blocked from her destination by this thick window, Athen looked for a way to get herself from here to there. So far, she has come up short. No doors seemed to lead to that room; it was as if only the window connected them. She pounded on the window, a simple test to see if it would budge. It did not. It was thick, at least as thick as the wall. In fact, she didn't remember seeing this window from the other side; she was sure she would have noticed it when they first entered. It was seemingly camouflaged on that end, like a one-way mirror you didn't know was there. Unless, and she prayed this to be wrong, it was a completely different room.

No, couldn't be. She recognized everything beyond this window the longer she gazed. She'd been in that exact room, the one just beyond this cursed window.

Athen grabbed a chair and hurled it into the window, but any hope for it to be that easy quickly faded. She rebounded her efforts before the chair finished bouncing. She was getting out of here, damnit.

"You will break!" she yelled. "And then I'm getting out of here because I'm taking a hot shower tonight!"

Athen faced the window with a willpower so strong it might have shattered of its own accord. She wondered if she could pry it free. She made another vow before digging into her pouch for a screwdriver. She wedged the sharp end into the corner and wiggled it into the windowpane. An explosion would be helpful, but all she had for materials was her flashlight, and it wouldn't be much. The flashlight was often a critical device down here, but it'd be worth it to get topside. She unscrewed the battery and performed actions with the wires that contradicted the safety warnings before taping it to the same corner as the screwdriver. It wasn't protocol, and she'd have to avoid breathing its fumes. She ducked down and covered her ears.

Nothing? She rose to check on it just as the battery exploded. Bigger than a firecracker but hardly anything close to demolition level, she was hit in the face with a shower of sparks and smoke. *Great timing, Athen.* She pushed on the window and saw that it moved almost a millimeter, which was much less than she needed. But there was a bit of movement now, so she wrestled the screwdriver in and out. It wasn't much. It wasn't enough.

She tried not to breathe in the fumes, but she worked on it anyway. She wiped soot from the window and found a crack had occurred in the glass, somewhere near twenty centimeters across and at least five deep. "Now we're talking." She took the screwdriver and ran its point into the crack, then she grabbed one of the bones off the floor and started hammering the back of the screwdriver into the glass until it shattered.

Sweet air gushed at her from the other room as a chunk of glass fell, almost removing her toes, but thankfully missing. The window's age had helped, as it shattered like big chunks of ice for her to push aside. The air had a taste, like sweet freedom. She climbed through the window pane, ignoring her leg's protests. It was a good meter down to the table beneath her, and she sent herself flying to it before any fear might stop her.

With a thud, she landed and cried out, her body paralyzed from the fall. Of course, adrenaline was pumping now, and then came a fear that she wasn't alone. But look as she might, there was no sign of the creature. She looked at the drab interior, checking every corner and shadow, until she heard the wind howling outside.

The wind. Just outside. When she heard that, she found the ability to drag her crippled self off the desk and hobble towards the incline, the way out. A trail of blood followed her; she'd need to get patched real soon. Landing on the table probably undid all the coags in her leg.

This was absolutely the area where the parasite had attacked them; the same furniture was strewn about in the same way, and everything was the same. She saw their own boot prints, fresh from the dirt above, confirming everything. Caution was ignored as she barreled forward; she could almost feel the sunshine. With guilt, she suddenly stopped and turned her head. Her teammates were down there, but what was she going to do? Hobble down and save them? Not in this condition.

Her body was shaking; she hadn't noticed it until now. She was likely in shock. No, she was in no position to help anyone. She needed to return to patch up at the quadrohuts, or at least bandage her wound. She needed more pain meds, too, and water. If she could make it out with this leg, they could make it out too. She had to trust in their ability. Or she had to trust in their survival until she could help. That was the best she could do.

Athen stood at the incline, staring up the ramp at true daylight. The sky above the trees was dark and cloudy, but she still had to shield her eyes. The wind howled up above like the most beautiful of freedom songs. She wished she could share this with her teammates. *Soon*, she promised them as she forced her way up and out.

The incline was longer than she remembered, but nothing stopped her until wind gusts rippled her suit. At last, she stood victoriously in the forest, exhausted but smiling at the trees like a madwoman.

Thirst. Her victory would have to be celebrated later; she needed water. She suppressed a groan as she realized the quadrohuts were still a good kilometer away. Her leg was stiff and unyielding, but her spirits were high as she forced herself onwards. Trees became crutches, bushes became helpers as she grabbed everything she needed to pull herself forward. It started to pinprick with rain, guess she'd made it in time for a storm. She scoffed. Rain? Bring it! She opened her mouth to the sky, taking in the free droplets.

Tiny roots and pebbles dug into bare feet. She ignored them and pressed harder, filled with a strength that bordered on madness. She recognized a peculiar bush, gnarled and with orange leaves that had a purple streak through the tips, and she knew she was on the right path. She passed a familiar boulder with striated green moss. Finally, the clearing emerged, the white of her *quadrohuts* appeared in all their glory. At the end of the clearing was also their return shuttle, raindrops sparkling off its glorious polished hood. Everything was here as it should be. She had never felt so glad to be home.

The *quadrohuts* waited beneath the gray sky, its white glare mottled by the coming clouds. It felt like midday. The frames of the *quadrohuts* shook from a gust of wind; the storm was quickly spoiling her daylight. Athen traversed the unsteady ground all the way to the sealed door of the quadrohuts, trying not to slip in mud as it formed from rain. She waited an agonizing three seconds for it to recognize her and open. Surrounded by man-made things, she barreled inside with a fierce smile and headed straight to the mess hall. She collapsed at the sink and slurped water from the faucet. She had made it!

As she quenched her thirst, she admitted a little guilt, which she couldn't help. She had to at least partially plan her return trip while trying to relax and recover. She would need to get herself bandaged up, pack food and water, more tools, and more medicine, as well as shoes if they had extras… *soon*, she promised. She deserved this victory. She deserved to sit on the cold floor and look around at her human-built dwelling, to gaze down the lightless hallway shaped for a human being, lined with doors that were all perfectly her size. Actually, it was largely assembled by robotic units, but those robots were manmade, probably. She shook her head clear and then lay herself flat on her back before looking up at the cable-lined ceiling. She was tired, too tired to find her bunk. But when she wiggled her toes and felt the dirt between them, she found the strength to take a shower. "Okay, girly…," a word she hated, "…time to get cleaned up."

Athen climbed into the shower fully dressed. She blasted warm jets of water down her face and neck, her clothes suddenly weighing double. She embraced how good this felt and watched the water swirl in brown as it drained out the bottom. She grabbed the soap and scrubbed what she could reach, taking joy in washing away dirt. She wiggled her toes and frowned; they were blistered and encrusted with stubborn dirt, and her leg hurt too much to really get down there. Despite that, the intense pleasure of hot water covering her body was religious. She carefully stripped down in the shower, leaving a wet mess where she tossed her clothes. When the pain in her leg took over, she leaned against the wall. It was a long while before she stepped out of the shower naked. She had soaked up every ounce of satisfaction before turning it off.

Naked, she hobbled over to the medical bay. She couldn't have imagined doing this before getting clean, but now it was time. She struggled to get a proper angle at the narrow steel rod, still trickling with lines of red. Whatever Dmitry gave her was a miracle drug for being able to numb that, and by looking at it, she knew the meds were still doing something. She needed that taken care of, soon, but she couldn't remove it. She dug into the med cabinet, looking for painkillers she might recognize. Athen found a small vial and took it without delay, dropping the torn package for the server bots to clean later. She hoped it was the same one Dmitry had given her. Then she dug around and found some spray-on skin and emptied the cannister over her wounds, then she wrapped a bandage for added security. She took a step back and almost fell onto the exam table. How much did she take?

Still naked, besides her leg bandage, Athen stumbled over to the mess hall to fill a coffee mug with hot water. She looked for a packet of instant and suppressed her guilt once more. It was selfish to sit here and enjoy a cup of coffee, even though every bit of her deserved it. She needed to get back to her teammates.

Her face turned at the sound of the main door opening. The wind howled before it was shut out again. A man had entered, staggering and ominous, and she gripped her coffee cup in wait. The sudden cold made her body shiver, amplified by the shower droplets still covering her.

It was Austin, standing in the hallway, the definition of exhausted. There were no tentacles or worms coming out of him; he just looked like a man dragged through hell. She dropped the mug.

"Austin!" she cried and ran to him, grabbing and holding on.

Austin hugged her back, with a grip that ignored all fatigue, a silent grip filled with a dozen words. On any other day, it would have been an awkward moment.

CHAPTER 33

After that moment passed, the awkwardness of nudity did settle, and Athen went to dress. Austin sat and rested before gathering supplies. As he felt better, the storm continued to worsen. The walls of the quadrohuts shook with punishing gusts. Huge raindrops drummed above him.

He'd just seen Athen naked, held her tightly too, which would have been a bigger event on most days. Her emotions, and he had to admit his as well, were so pure and sincere that modesty wasn't an issue for the first several seconds. Then a laugh and 'I suppose I should get dressed.' It ranked low on special things today, all things considered.

He was relieved someone else had gotten out of there, and he had plenty of questions for later, but right now, he only had thoughts of heading back. She was getting dressed, but could be ready before she was done buttoning. And if he waited for her, she'd slow him down with that steel in her leg. With Carolina needing him, he couldn't wait for Athen. He needed to fill a canteen, stock up on some glucose packs, and grab something heavy he could swing with.

Fully dressed, she limped her way back to the mess hall where he was filling a canteen. She actually laughed at the pipe he'd grabbed. "Sorry, it won't do anything to the creature."

"It's for something else," he assured her before turning to the main doors. The wind was practically shouting for him to wait, then he felt her grab him by the arm.

Austin looked over his shoulder, and she let go of his bicep. "I'm leaving. I'll be back."

"If you patch me up a little, I can help you save the others," she said.

"I'm not worried about the others," he replied bluntly. She appeared a little confused, and he didn't blame her. She probably didn't know about Dublin attacking him or the way Dmitry had ditched them all. But his only real concern was Carolina, and she needed him. Still, Athen looked pale. She'd taken some medication, he could tell, but she'd lost a lot of blood. She really did need his help.

In two minutes, he could patch her up—two minutes, not a second more.

"Wait here."

He grabbed a blanket from the supply shelf and wrapped Athen in it before leading her to medical. He was no medic, but he knew enough, and he moved with a certainty that Athen needed right now.

"Go light on the painkillers, I helped myself a little while ago," she said.

She'd already cleaned and wrapped her wound, and he wouldn't be performing any removal surgery, but it was plasma she needed. He found an emergency kit in the First Aid box and injected her with a pouch of synthetic blood and plasma. Then he gave her another. He brought her a pillow, a fresh pair of boots, and then looked around at whatever he might be missing. Athen closed her eyes and lay her head back. She was exhausted, and his being there allowed her to close her eyes.

"You saved my life," she said with her eyes still closed.

Austin dismissed it, his face hardening. This was taking too long.

"I mean it. You saved my life."

He offered a weak smile. "You needed two blood packs. I'm amazed you could still walk. I'm amazed you survived."

"I'm tough."

"You are. I have to go now," he said and left for the doorway. Whatever she said and whatever she needed didn't matter anymore; she was taken care of. The doors slid open, and the wind screamed at him; rain pelted a line at his feet, warning him not to cross. He looked out across the puddles forming as the storm gushed. If the wind gets any worse, the quadrohuts might tip over. It was a good thing Dublin had reinforced them after landing… Dublin. They better not cross paths. This place was making everyone crazy.

Athen said something too soft to hear as he stepped outside, letting the doors close behind him. The day had turned dark, with charcoal swirls blocking out all evidence of the sun. To move forward, he had to lean into the gusts, cutting a line with his body and using gravity to help. The wind improved somewhat at the forest line, though it grew in volume as it whistled through the trees. He moved slower than he wanted to as the ground was quickly becoming muddy and slick. He grabbed a trunk and used it to get up a small incline just as a branch snapped above him. He did not enjoy being in a forest during a windstorm. He didn't make it this far only to get crushed by a falling tree.

He wouldn't get crushed. If a tree fell, he'd dodge it. And if a flood came, he'd swim it. Nothing would stop him from getting to his daughter. Nothing would happen to her on his watch.

At about halfway, he was crossing small rivers formed from the downpour, which concealed many of the giant tree roots he needed to avoid. It also camouflaged the trail, and that could be disastrous. Hearty cracks of wood echoed above him as trunks bent against the wind. After several minutes of uncertainty, he found a recognizable boulder, which helped. Austin put his foot down in a newly formed puddle and fell when the ground wasn't there, falling chest deep and splashing his face. If it was this bad in the forest, he wondered how the facility was faring.

Austin reached the top of the ridge where he had expected to see the wall, but when he looked around, all he saw were trees bending to the wind. Another massive snap erupted in the air, and he heard a tree fall in the distance.

"Oh hell," he snarled. He looked around, studying the area, begging not to be lost. He turned back, but the rain was making it all but impossible to see. The storm was making every trail look different. He closed his eyes and thought back to his path, and in a moment of clarity, was able to pinpoint where he may have overshot. He backtracked carefully and found another path, the correct path, as it had a distinct gnarled branch that he remembered. When he rounded the top of this ridge, he sank to his knees before the obsidian wall, which lurked impervious to the rain and wind.

To think, this was where it all began. This was the long, cursed wall, hidden from their satellites, discovered by his little girl, and his nightmare light-years from home.

Carolina was still inside.

He ran over to where the wall had been opened and stood above the decline, his feet coated with mud. It was still open, funneling a torrent of water from outside. An ankle-high pond had formed at the base and was eagerly growing. He wasted no time and went down the slope, mindful of the security system that should still be disabled. *Should.* The storm's volume lowered like a dial as he descended into the first room. He recognized this one, where Carolina was... It's when he first discovered she was infected.

After a moment or two, his ears adjusted to the sounds of trickling water leaking its way inside. He strode through the center of the room where they had first met the parasite, the vision of it plopping out of Carolina's mouth. That was this morning... or was it last night? He didn't really know.

The way led through a short hall before reopening into the reception lobby, which featured tables and relatively friendly signage. The warm and soft decor was so different from the lurking experiments below. There were three hallways to choose from. Austin tried to remember which way they went the first time around. It felt very different now; the optimism they shared the first time was all gone. Knowing what lurked below also altered the way he perceived the soft blue alien signs. This place was a lie, a trap to the poor species it had lured here. *The middle path, it was illuminated red,* he remembered. He was pretty sure. He took the middle again, and again the floor degraded abruptly, with water marks that stained the walls; he remembered all of this. At the end of the hallway, he found the broken elevator doors trying to close and occasionally shooting sparks. He approached without hesitation and gazed down the shaft, the one where they'd all fallen down. It was the elevator that had condemned them below; it was still down there, hiding in the shadows. That was where Athen had hurt her leg. He forced the memories to stop.

He sat and dangled his feet in the emptiness. The shaft was dark, but he could see light coming in from the level below. He remembered it vaguely.

He reached out and grabbed hold of the center pulley cable, carefully transferring his weight to it and preparing to shimmy with the flow of gravity. At halfway down, he could see the entry where the elevator had decided to fall, where Orlean had lost his prosthetic limb, and where it still remained, just blinking and waiting to be retrieved. Orlean was lucky it was only his arm. Imagine being halfway out when it happened... no, best not to imagine that. Austin couldn't dangle from this cable all day; he had to finish the climb.

At least this part of his plan was working. He lowered himself until he was level with the entrance, where the prosthetic arm blinked in standby mode. A soft, single yellow light rose and fell, rhythmically, waiting to be re-attached. Austin gave a moment of reflection before he swung, pushed off the wall, and snatched it. It was a careful dance of holding on with one arm and tucking the prosthetic down his pants with the other, but once there, he carefully climbed back up to the first floor. The sooner this part was over, the better; he couldn't climb like this forever, and going up was predictably harder. With strong hands, he pulled himself up to the floor above. Then, with another swing and another counter push, he propelled himself back to the floor and climbed his body through. He came to a seated position once more, with his feet again dangling over the abyss. It was a lot of work getting back to the exact same spot, but he needed that prosthetic.

It felt a little strange having an arm down his pants, so he retrieved it. He wiped the illuminated display on the forearm clean and began accessing the menu. He worked his way through 'Settings' and then 'System Functions', where a password prompted him. Austin didn't have a perfect memory or anything, but for some reason, he could always remember this one: *b81590c*. He remembered saying, *'Bring 81,590 caramels, please,'* and it stuck. He followed the menu into a section that controlled power management and made some adjustments that were unwise. He had worked on Orlean's prosthetic once before. It had malfunctioned a few years ago after it was hit with a radiation burst in deep space. It had partially fried itself, and he was the best with the software engineering. That was a while ago; Carolina was eight. Seven? Her mom wasn't diagnosed yet, so it was around that time. He thought it was strange how he had to compare dates with events to remember them.

According to the power readings, this thing was good for another seventy-five years, but that wasn't going to be the case. The battery on a device like this was virtually endless, unless you did something moronic with it. Then you could generate quite a bit of energy and use the power all at once. He then used another menu option to get each finger-digit to unlatch, one by one. Austin removed them, contemplating their value back on Earth. Quality prosthetic replacements were a lucrative business, he had heard. Oh well, he chucked them into the darkness of the elevator shaft.

The limb was now volatile and fingerless, with steel prongs where fingers used to be. They were sharp and exposed, and he attached what he'd made to that pipe he'd brought. Now he had a bolt of lightning ready to pop, and if he was really lucky, the battery might be good for two bolts of lightning. He finished wrapping a wire and buttoned it down to the handle. When he pressed it, a circuit would complete, and whatever was touching those finger prongs would be annihilated.

Now he was ready to find Carolina.

CHAPTER 34

Carolina emerged from the tunnel system in the ceiling, in a junction of ventilation ducts. She knew little about the tunnels; in fact, *she* knew nothing about them.

Her head was throbbing, and it wasn't just from traveling through those tunnels. She struggled to think clearly, and she'd felt this sensation before. She felt it every time they'd been near that creature, and that's what this felt like now. So when she heard its deep and throaty exhale, a long huff that shook the walls, she swirled in her own head. It was too nauseating to think; just escape, nothing else. She crawled through the ducts, grateful to be the size of a kid in these tight spaces. As she moved, she sensed it beneath her; somehow, it had beaten them here.

The ventilation duct imploded, smashed by large tentacles that retreated. Carolina scooted back a meter when the creature struck again, rocking the ceiling and sending terror through her. If she was planning to jump back into the anti-grav tunnels, that plan was gone; the ceiling between her and there was now crushed. But she couldn't stay here, either.

She scooted further back, though moving risked giving away her position. The duct she was on buckled under her weight; she felt it wanting to break loose from the ceiling. The creature had made the whole path unstable, with aged ceiling rods threatening to give way. She couldn't see the floor beneath her and decided upon stillness. Footsteps stalked underneath, and another throaty exhale that reverberated through the air. Carolina shrieked as another section erupted in debris and electricity. The creature's swath of devastation had stripped power cables, which now dangled and showered the floor with sparks. It did not know where she was, yet she hoped. She tried to recall the layout of the room beneath her and crawled quietly again. She just trusted that the carnage beneath her would mask the sounds of her moving.

The ventilation shaft became a three-way split, and she picked the middle one. The creature had become unusually quiet, so much so that it unnerved her. She quit moving long enough to take a few breaths, waiting to know more. Then she heard something else.

Something down the ventilation shaft, coming closer. She wasn't relieved when she saw it was Dmitry, crawling towards her, barely fitting in the ducts. His added weight made the floor buckle. "Stop!" she hissed.

The panel between her and Dmitry imploded. Then another as it smashed further down. The suspension rods shook and then snapped, tilting them. They tumbled out of the ducts, and she reached out desperately, but there was nothing to grab hold of. She landed on the floor in pain, frozen from impact. Her lungs wouldn't even breathe, as if her muscles had frozen from impact.

The ceiling was lit up with sparks, and she found herself shielding her eyes. But she hadn't fallen in the room; the ducts had dropped her in the hallway outside. Dmitry was back on his feet, having landed better than her, and she felt him pick her up off the ground. She was being carried, quickly, while the creature demolished something else she couldn't see. Dmitry hauled her into an office and took cover behind a row of squat chairs. She winced as he practically dropped her. Part of her was grateful he'd bothered to grab her. Though knowing him, it wasn't for her own benefit.

Crackles of electricity burst, and smoke blanketed above them now that the air-channels were disrupted. She felt her lungs and chest relax enough to move again; having the wind knocked out of her had been extremely unpleasant. Dmitry raised a finger to his lips, ordering her silence. Behind him, the smoke twirled in the ceiling. It was quickly getting worse. She nodded and followed as he checked to see that the hallway was clear, then they scrambled quietly down. They stopped at a barricade, and they'd been this way before, but the barricade was new. Seems the creature was blocking their escape. It would take time to clear this, and it wouldn't take the creature more than two seconds to stop them once it knew.

In a rare moment, Dmitry hesitated, worried that this might be a fool's attempt to escape, but Carolina wasted no time. She climbed up and pulled a piece loose. She dug furiously into the wall, thankfully quick but unfortunately loud. Going all in, Dmitry joined her.

"This better work," Dmitry said, calm but urgent.

"What about Dublin?"

"He can handle himself. Nice tunnel choice by the way, did that work out like you wanted?" he sneered as he removed a plank in the rubble. The barricade was halfway dismantled, and she went for an opening at the top. With time running out, Dmitry went after her, climbing over what remained for leverage. She slipped through, but Dmitry was twice her size. The corner of a chair had wedged into his ribs and wouldn't let him slip past. With his feet dangling out the other side, he forced himself through the small opening, ignoring what may have become a broken rib, and tumbling down after her. By the time he came to a stop, she was ahead of him, splashing water with every footstep. Water?

Wondering why water flooded the receiving lobby would have to wait. He made it five splashes when the creature howled, followed by the sounds of thrashing metal. It was removing the barricade to get to them. Carolina wobbled on her feet, holding her head to keep it from spinning, and then hid in a nearby room. Dmitry picked the room closest to him, too.

The doors burst from their frames, and the creature came bounding through, galloping on its spidery arms. It looked around for them and picked the room Carolina hid inside of, as if it knew. She had no doubts it did.

Carolina could hear its breathing as if it were right next to her, amplified by the connection that ruined her senses. She held still, as still as she could. She endured the drum beating in her chest, wanting it out of her head so badly.

Water had made it into this room, a trickle around her hands and knees. Then it stepped inside the room, and she knew because she heard something crunch. Maybe she could run for it... no. Her only chance was to sit there and hope and pray. Her hands began to shake. She stifled a cry and closed her eyes, knowing it was about to find her. She froze, waiting for whatever was about to happen. She couldn't think about it. She was aware of something, a distraction, though she couldn't say what. Simultaneously, the creature also turned its head, seemingly alert and listening. She took the opportunity to move, but instead she tripped, sending papers flying. *Get up!*

The creature rounded on her; in two steps, it crossed the room and smashed the cabinet away, decimating it. Carolina jumped back, slamming into the locker behind her as she tried to stay on her feet for what it was worth. *This is it...* She was going to die, right here in this cursed room. Carolina shut her eyes as hard as they could. It was going to kill her, because it didn't like having competition. Competition?

Then a voice she knew but didn't believe yelled something.

In her panic, she was hallucinating her father's voice. With trepidation, she opened her eyes and saw him. It shouted against reality, especially since he was running at the creature.

With a lack of common sense, he charged, leaping into the air and impaling it with something like an oversized spear, which landed square into the neck. Whatever her father had expected to happen seemingly didn't; he furiously pressed a button on his little spear until he was struck by a row of tentacle arms that flew him across the room. Her father crashed through an office window like a brick. She wanted to run after him, but the creature still blocked her path.

CHAPTER 35

Austin shook the cobwebs from his blurry vision. He couldn't lose now. His little girl was in there.

But why didn't his lightning work? *The menu screen!* It was sheer luck that he still wielded the spear; the impact made him clench so hard that he propelled it with him. He quickly navigated the options screen so the changes would update. Idiot, none of his changes were viable until he reset the unit... which might now take a minute to reload. He'd need to buy some time for himself and for Carolina, so he ran out of the office, splashing with every step. He glanced down at the spear in his hand as the prosthetic powered down. The creature howled and stomped towards him, crawling on its six arms like a spider.

"Daddy!" Carolina screamed. There was a command in that word... he instinctively ducked as a huge tentacle whipped above him, one that would have removed his head from the rest of his body. The creature shot another arm at him; this time, he slipped to the side, barely. The tentacle cracked the floor tile and regressed into its arm. Water now saturated the bare wires of his device, water that might sabotage its circuitry.

"Oh come on!" he cursed, trying to power it back on. He didn't expect the water to be such an issue, or he would have waterproofed it first. Another mistake, another mess-up that threatened their lives. He had to do better! The creature was almost on him. Austin dodged behind a table, pinning it between them. The beast was large and confident. It wasn't going to play table games; instead, it simply hammered the table, splitting it in half. A green light illuminated on the prosthetic as it loaded its BIOS. Then it would cycle through operating system, default functions ... *hurry, damn it!*

The creature closed the distance to him in one step and then swung again. Austin blocked with his spear; the force of it picked him up off the ground. This time, he landed on all fours before tumbling, the spear sliding away and out of his grasp.

"Run, daddy!" Carolina shrieked. She couldn't watch him die again, but she couldn't look away either. "Hide!"

The spear lay flat on the ground a few meters away. He bounded for it but stopped as a tentacle tried to smash him. The air swooshed at his face, and without wasting another moment, he slid, rolling and snatching the spear. When he spun, spear first at the beast, he felt a wire that needed to be put back to complete the circuit. The creature jumped into the air and grabbed the ceiling, clinging to it. Austin took cover underneath a table as he adjusted the wire. The table barely held as it crashed on top, toying with him. He wouldn't get another chance.

A long, thick tentacle extended down underneath the table and grabbed him by the arm, pulling him up until face-to-face with it. The pain was immediate as he waited to be ripped in half. He couldn't check to see if the battery was ready or not. In another moment, it wouldn't matter. So he impaled the short metal finger-prongs into the tentacle holding him, as far from his own body as he could reach, and pressed the button again.

White fire arched from the creature's tentacle to its chest, and Austin fell. The creature staggered in pain as smoke billowed from its arm and torso. It left a terrible halo of smoke as the creature's tentacle fell limp, the one that had been zapped. The other arms swung defensively as the creature stumbled back. Austin ducked the wild flailing, though wild or not, it still left a bowl-shaped impact in the wall by his head.

His weapon had fired, but the creature still lived. He looked at the spear; the tips were blackened, but the prosthetic was still online, its graphical interface struggling to reform. He might have another charge left, and it was now or never. So he gripped the spear with added determination and jumped onto the table before drilling the prongs into its terrible face. This time, the battery spat and popped with flames. There was a jolt, but no flash of light. Still, the creature collapsed against the wall and slumped in a heap on itself. Like a switch being flipped, the creature just shut down.

"Daddy!" Carolina came running, arms open and fast.

"Are you okay?" he asked, panicking, looking her over. He picked her up off the ground with ease, giving an internal thanks to his guardian angels. She squeezed him back harder than ever.

"I thought you were dead," she cried. Her tiny arms were strong, and her cries in his ear made him awash with guilt. But she was okay, she was right here, and she was okay. "I didn't want to believe it!" she said, squeezing him tighter. He almost couldn't breathe.

"I won't ever leave you. I *promise*," he swore, wondering how she was so strong but ignoring it for the sake of the moment. It was an intense hug between father and daughter under the most difficult of circumstances, at least it was until Dmitry stepped out from his hiding spot.

Austin's stomach tightened. The last time he'd seen Dmitry, the man was running to save his own skin. Part of him had hoped he'd never see him again. No one was safe around a man like that.

"Come on, Carolina, let's go back to camp." Austin then turned to address Dmitry. "Athen is at the huts, resting. She'll need you to perform surgery soon."

"Wait… was that Orlean's prosthetic?" Dmitry asked as he cautiously approached the creature, stunned by the organic details he could see up close.

"We're leaving, it's time to prep for an early departure," Austin said.

"Negative. I am in command, especially now. You've neutralized it. Our company would expect us to bring this creature back with us." Dmitry crossed his arms, gazing upon his treasure.

Austin set Carolina down. He didn't like to argue, which was why he usually avoided it. He couldn't wrestle the finer points or choose the best words, and besides, he didn't always have the stomach for it. "Have fun carrying it, because I won't. You can report me. Come on, kid, we're getting the hell out of here." Austin turned, holding Carolina by the hand.

"I will not tolerate insubordination!"

"Insubordination? How about some common sense!"

Dmitry grabbed him by the shoulder, and Austin spun and pushed him back. Whatever else might have happened stopped when they both heard the creature inhale and then exhale, relaxed as if sleeping. But it wasn't sleeping. It was looking at them, with its speckled eyes and rows of bare teeth. The creature winced as it climbed to its feet, using its hands to pull itself up. The creature stood but leaned on a chair for support, wobbling on its feet. It wasn't at full strength.

Dmitry picked up the spear, though Austin knew it was a paperweight at this point. But Dmitry didn't know that, and apparently neither did the creature. It took one look at the spear, and he shoved the chair at them before stumbling straight for the incline to the outside. Austin backed away to give it plenty of room. The creature disappeared from the first chamber and was gone.

Dmitry was about to say something more when they both heard something else. Startled, they spun to see Dublin, oblivious, arriving seconds after the commotion, unsure as to what had just happened, wielding a machete.

"Dublin?" Dmitry asked unnecessarily. It certainly was him.

He sized them up and down. "Needin' to know right now—were you there when Helena was attacked?" Dublin asked.

Austin wondered why Dmitry wouldn't answer until he realized he wasn't the one being asked. *Me?* "I haven't seen Helena since the three of us broke away at the elevator," he said, giving a quizzical glance to Dmitry. "And I'm also not the reason you were in that room with the creature. I tried to get you out of there."

"Aye, was starting to figure that," the Irishman said, leveling his gaze on Dmitry. "Well, fearless leader, starting to think you lied your ass off to me."

Dmitry's lips were thin and tight, but Austin was distracted by Carolina tugging at his hand.

"It wants our ship; it still needs off this planet," she said.

It was loud enough for the three of them to hear. The Irishman looked at Dmitry from behind his barrel chest. "Important matters to attend to first. Suppose'n we can settle up after."

"Daddy, we can't let it leave the planet."

"Aye, maybe we should listen to the girl. I don't want to lose our pony home."

Austin looked the Irishman up and down; the hostility that was there was different. He had a heavy weight around his shoulders, of guilt and also anger, different than before. He was in a blind rage last time, and Austin still didn't know why. But now he suspected it had something to do with Helena. Dublin's anger seemed focused on Dmitry instead. *Good.*

"Athen is alone at the quadrohuts."

CHAPTER 36

The team that once operated with such precision now trekked disjointedly out of the facility, up the ramp, and against the current of water, which had become a trickle. The wind howled from the top, but it felt like less, Austin was glad to note. The trees had cast down many branches, but he saw blue sky beyond them as he neared the top.

He led the way in front of Dublin and Dmitry, though he would have preferred not having those two men behind him. He could only hope that after everything that happened, they'd put aside their problem with him and the radio. Hadn't this proven his point exactly? They should have radioed for help like he said in the beginning.

As they traveled the forest from the place Carolina had discovered, a thought he kept pushing aside refused to be ignored, and it weighed more than his clay-saturated boots. How did Carolina know things?

The question was harder to put aside than it had been. Something was off with her, and he'd have to address it at some point. She knew things that she simply should not.

Any fear he had of Dmitry re-conspiring with Dublin seemed abated. The fearless leader was well behind the Irishman, who was well behind him and Carolina.

Carolina was difficult to keep up with. In fact, his neck still hurt from where she had squeezed him. The raw emotion of finding your father alive must have given her incredible strength, but still. She shouldn't be that strong.

"What time is it?" she asked, charging forward and barely slowing.

"Almost lunch. The entire night has passed, and it doesn't feel real," Austin said. She'd tuned him out somewhere along the way, he could tell. Why did she want to know? She had to be hungry, tired, but it didn't feel like any of those. She had a determination to get back, and it was stronger than theirs. She was also shielding her eyes from the natural light, which wasn't that bright.

The storm had left the air feeling crisp, and some rain still fell, soft and mist-like. The heavier the storm, the quicker they often faded, though it was a bit of a shock to enter the building with a powerful system and leave with it breaking clouds and glimmering daylight. The forestry was dense enough that more storms could be looming; he wouldn't know until they reached clearer grounds. Usually, the Orbiter would inform them of such things, but not since the radio was sabotaged.

Dublin cursed as he slipped to a knee, grabbing a branch and snapping it on his way down. The rain had turned their walkway into clay, slick and unpredictable.

Carolina exhaled.

"What is it?" he asked, hoping not to sound too paranoid.

"Nothing. Tired."

He didn't believe it was just tired, even though he wanted to. He felt paranoid. True, he had plenty to be paranoid about. They all did. He knew she needed rest, of course, she did; they all did. And being younger, she probably needed it the most. He pushed bright leaves out of the way as he hurried ahead. As tired as she looked, she did not slow down. The sharp spots of purple and the orange on the leaves sparkled, refreshed by the rain, as if their colors were awakened. But the trail was often steep and narrow, slowing them down. His stragglers refused to get any closer to each other. "Wait up, kid, we can't go much faster."

"You don't understand!"

"I know, it's headed for our ship. But it wouldn't know how to fly it, and we're going about as fast as we can go. The clay makes it harder. I can't risk breaking an ankle," but she was barely listening. *Geez, we can call another shuttle from the Orbiter...After I fix the radio. If I can fix the radio, it was in pretty bad shape. If I can't fix it...* He may not be able to fix it. He dug through the cargo pocket of his pants and grabbed a glucose pack, handing her one also. Neither of them liked the taste, but it was easy to consume without slowing down.

"Thank you," she said, stopping. "We really should have a plan for when we get there. We can't take it head-on." It felt good to stop, even for just a moment, but this wasn't a conversation he expected from her—definitely Dmitry or Dublin, but not his twelve-year-old.

"I'm all ears," he replied.

"First thing is not letting it know we're there."

"Okay. Second thing?"

Carolina shot him an irritated look. "I'm working on that."

Austin let her go back to planning. He'd rather not take orders from Dmitry, but this was still some kind of shock, with Carolina in the lead. The whole day was a shock, but it made the problem he'd been ignoring weigh even more. At least they were almost there. The trail was well recognized. From here, it was a decline and then patches of flat grass, which were hopefully not ponds by now, and then they'd crest above where they could see the quadrohuts. Making a plan now was good because they'd be in the thick of it soon. The creature may be wounded, but it is still likely to outmatch them. So they'd better figure something out, even if it was just another weapon, something better than Dublin's machete.

Dmitry finally passed the Irishman and caught up to Austin. Something about that was decidedly suspicious, though everything Dmitry did was now under his scrutiny. This was the crest overlooking the quadrohuts, where Austin stopped, and now they would all catch up. Crouching behind the line, they spotted the quadrohuts about fifty meters away.

"It's there," Dmitry pointed. He didn't need to point; they all spotted the creature standing outside the west end of the huts, near the generators. Those generators were not designed with security in mind, considering all planets had been devoid of sentient life to date. It would be easy to do something bad to them.

"That can't be good," Austin groaned.

"Athen is down there?" Dublin asked.

"Yes, waiting for us. The creature may not know about her, and hopefully it stays that way."

Dublin held the machete with white knuckles. "Aye, then I'm going down there."

"You will stay here!" Dmitry ordered. But Dublin gave him a snarl instead, followed by a push that sent Dmitry to the ground. That constituted assault of a superior officer, but Dublin wasn't interested in the debate. He was already moving along the bushes towards the quadrohuts, machete at the ready. The look on Dmitry's face was enough that Austin took a step away, shielding Carolina.

"Austin, go and stop him," he demanded.

"Sorry, boss, I don't think so. Sounds like he has a bone to pick with you."

Dmitry turned his vile glare towards him. "You will both regret defying me," he vowed.

"I'll regret it after I know what that thing wants with our generators." Austin felt Carolina's tiny hand squeeze his. He looked down and saw Dublin sneaking his way inside the quadrohuts. "He made it. Why don't we just go help him?" Austin asked, ignoring Dmitry's order, while leaving him a small way to be part of their team effort.

Just when he moved, Carolina tugged his arm, telling him to be still. It's then that the creature ripped a cable from the generators, causing a loud snap and flash of light. The creature suddenly turned and scanned the hills where they were hiding. They instinctively ducked down, except Carolina, who held her head in pain. What was going on with her? He was afraid to lift his head and get spotted, but the lack of sound was too much. There was nothing beyond the rustle of the grass and leaves in the wind. Slowly, he poked his head up to get a look.

"Where did it go?" *And why did it do that,* he wondered.

"It doesn't matter, we wait here," Dmitry ordered.

"Have fun with that," Austin said, moving from his location along the bushes the way Dublin had. But Carolina didn't want to. "They need our help," he said, urging her. She waited before giving a nod of admittance, seemingly fighting nausea. "Come on," he said as she followed behind him. He wasn't about to leave her in the care of that man.

Dmitry cursed something, but he ignored it. None of this would matter. Only surviving mattered right now. As Austin got closer, he found the creature, spotting it through the bushes. It had left the disabled generators and climbed onto the roof of the huts, and it was definitely limping, one of its arms dragging and useless. Anyone inside could easily hear it above them, so they would have taken cover. But still, what the hell was it doing? The huts weren't designed for a siege; the creature would easily break inside if it wanted to, wounded or not. But even that wouldn't be necessary, because the doors were wide open. *Of course!* In a power failure, the doors to the quadrohuts stayed open as a safety measure. Could it have known that? He prayed Athen and Dublin were hidden, that it was only on the roof for a better view.

Dmitry planted a hand on Austin. "I ordered you to stop!"

"Get that hand off me," Austin warned, but Dmitry held him firm. He didn't have the time, and he didn't have the patience for Dmitry any longer. That creature was the threat, the team was in danger, but his captain wanted to go down with the ship and die. He wouldn't take it. He spun and punched Dmitry in the lip, cocking his head back and almost dropping him. Austin had a follow-up glare ready. "That's a warning shot. Back off."

Austin turned and went for the quadrohuts. He traveled three steps when Dmitry tackled him from behind. He fell to the ground in disbelief, rolling to get control of Dmitry's grip. He spun to his back as punches came, hard and fast, to his face. Austin caught one that made his vision go, instinctively turtling and holding on. He bucked his hips and pulled Dmitry to the side with a wrestling move he used in college, sending them both scrambling for top position.

From their fighting, they both saw Dublin emerge from the quadrohuts. The Irishman gave them a distant look and then continued on. Even in the midst of fighting, with the taste of blood in his mouth, Austin had to wonder why Dublin was walking across the field, completely exposed.

Long organic lines flowed in and out of Dublin, writhing with ease through the flesh of his body, protruding from one of the creature's hands, guiding him like a dog on a leash, like a puppet. "The ship!" Austin cried, blood dripping from his nose. Dmitry pushed away and sat up. They both watched as the puppet led the creature over to their shuttle. Dublin paused for a moment in front of the control panel, swaying on his feet. The organic worms stiffened, and he began activating keys, programming the ramp to lower for boarding.

"Dmitry…"

"This is your fault!"

"Do something!" Austin demanded and looked around for Carolina, but she was nowhere to be seen. For now, that was possibly best. "What are we going to do?" The ramp protruded and fully lowered, and the rain that had accumulated now spilled from the grooved edges. With the ramp finally settled, Dublin went up it, staggering in a daze, still under the creature's control, blood pooling in spots where the organic veins pulsed in and out of. As the creature approached the ramp, the vessel tilted slightly from its weight. It disappeared inside the shuttle with Dublin.

Dmitry was on his feet but unmoving, as if none of this was possible.

Austin still didn't know where Carolina was hiding, but he made a sprint for the quadrohuts. He bolted, swiftly and silently, faster than the slick ground should let him, threatening him if he slowed down even a little. He made it to the main entry of the quadrohuts and burst inside. The moment he did, he slipped to the ground, slamming into the wall. It was dark except for the light coming in, also a result of the damaged generator. A smear of clay went along the ground to his boots, but it was Athen's state that pulled him out of the moment. It was her that he saw in the dark, strung delicately to the wall, like a cocoon. The last thing he expected to see was Athen hovering off the ground by organic webbing.

"Athen?" he said, a whimper as much as a word.

She didn't seem hurt, and she had a pulse. He snatched a scalpel from the med kit, cutting into the organic material. She was breathing, but seemed confused and unable to use her voice. The more webbing he severed, the more coherent she became, until it could no longer hold her and she collapsed into Austin's arms.

"We're getting out of here," he said.

"I'm dizzy, I can't…"

"Now, Athen, we have to go now." And for the second time, her eyes said what words could not. Austin carried her over his shoulder out of the quadrohuts. He stole a look at the ship and saw that there was no sign of Dublin or the creature, but he did notice that the departure ramp was raised and the engines were burning.

Athen wasn't heavy, but he still struggled to carry her over the slick mud. He carried her fireman-style to the tree line, where Dmitry waited. The Pegasus engines swelled in volume. It was preparing for liftoff.

CHAPTER 37

"Where's Carolina?" Austin demanded, finding her nowhere in sight. She couldn't have gone too far, but he'd feel better as soon as he knew that for certain. He set Athen down delicately, with Dmitry ignoring them. He seemed consumed with anger as the ship neared takeoff.

"Help me stop them," Dmitry ordered, snapping his finger.

Austin turned, ready to break that finger.

"I'll watch out for Carolina," Athen said, trying to be of some help. They definitely needed to do something, but Dmitry needed a lesson, too. Austin followed, but not because of the finger snap. If there was a plan to stop the ship from leaving, he'd help.

The hum from the Pegasus engines turned into a roar as they filled with power, causing leaves and grass to fly around them. Austin followed Dmitry quickly into the quadrohut's open door; their shared knowledge meant there were about two minutes before it departed. They could roll around on the ground, punching each other, after they stopped it from taking off.

"I need a wireless transmitter, something I can connect to the ship with," Dmitry ordered.

Austin grimaced. That wasn't a great-sounding plan. "You're going to try and override it? There's not enough time."

"I can do it," Dmitry replied, icy cool as he fished out a field manual full of technical data and launch codes. Full of doubt, Austin went into the com room and grabbed an array of wireless gear, cables, and any other units that looked promising. Dmitry was adequate with com, and he would know what he was looking for. Of course, the main radio was down, which would have been the one to use. He returned with everything collected and dumped it on the exam table. Dmitry stood over the table and looked for something he could use, tossing pieces to the ground until the table was almost barren. After a tense moment of staring, he pounded the table in frustration.

"This isn't working," Austin bemoaned, rubbing his face in frustration. There had to be something they could do, but they were running out of time. If the creature fled in their vessel, they would be trapped without another way off the planet. They'd probably get discovered eventually, or get a distress beacon out eventually, but still, a year at least. Austin pictured spending that time, stranded and low on food... they'd be cooking plants, hoping for the best at some point. But alive, at least. But then he also imagined a hostile alien species -possessing an Earth-based vessel, equipped with star charts and satellite data, an enemy with exact coordinates to Earth. There could be a much deeper threat here than his own survival; this could doom Earth. And that simply could not happen.

While Dmitry remained scheming over a pile of useless com equipment, Austin went and grabbed a flare gun from the storage closet. Next, he went to the electrical closet and removed an emergency battery unit. Tweaking things to explode had become his new pastime.

"What are you doing?"

Austin ignored him.

"Austin, you can't possibly be that stupid," Dmitry said.

"Sure, I can," he replied while hastily removing protective caps from the battery cell. "Our ship has a lot of delicate information, a lot of coordinates, especially those going back to Earth, not to mention space ports along the way, trade routes, satellite coordinates," he looked Dmitry in the eye as he spoke. "We can't let a hostile enemy gain that information."

"I'm going to use *this* transmitter to override the ship. Do you hear me?" Dmitry said, wielding his chosen device. But Austin wasn't listening; he grabbed his makeshift explosive and left. Dmitry's face warned him not to leave.

Standing outside, he prepped the flare gun with his modest explosive. The battery he'd chosen could power the shuttle thrusters out of orbit, so it had a lot of juice. He heard the doors of the huts open behind him, expecting Dmitry. "This has to be done," Austin said, but when Dmitry didn't reply, he casually looked over. Had he waited a moment longer, his skull would have been split open.

A wrench swung over his head as Austin ducked, quick reflexes saving him in that moment. Dmitry's eyes demanded blood, and he came at him fast, tackling him to the ground. He could only do so much in this slick mud, diminishing his ability to wrestle. It was all he could do to block the wrench from crushing his skull. This wasn't a fight; this was combat. He needed to survive.

"What are you doing?" he yelled and wrapped his arms around Dmitry to keep him from swinging that wrench, slick with mud and trails of red from somewhere. If not for an engine blast, he'd have almost forgotten all about the impending liftoff. "We have bigger problems!"

Dmitry landed the wrench against his skull with a glancing crack. He didn't actually feel it, but his vision blurred, so he knew he had taken a hit. Dmitry arched back for another strike, but Austin slipped and bucked to his hands and knees. He pushed himself free and scrambled to his feet.

The ship now hovered inches off the ground, stabilizers reaching their checkpoints. Austin reached over for the flare gun submerged in mud and tried to aim, but was tackled again. The flare gun went flying out of his hands as he went face-first into the mud. Dmitry was apparently beyond reason; if he couldn't end this soon, they were all doomed.

Dmitry smothered his head into the mud with one hand and landed punches with the other. His wrestling was fading as the blows were adding up, but he managed to roll and get to his back. The mud was in his nose and mouth, and it was all he could do to breathe as another punch rocked the back of his head. He felt himself barely holding to consciousness. Dmitry, sensing a wounded foe, reared again to finish him off. Austin sprang, bucking his legs and shoving him off with surprising dexterity.

The madman was on his feet but stopped. Austin took longer getting upright, having exhausted what little strength he had and spitting blood. He raised his hands slowly to fight as the jet blasts pushed the ship higher off the ground.

"Great timing, boss, you just couldn't have done this later, could you?" Austin said.

"Dublin is a terrible pilot, I still have time," he said and retrieved the transmitter from his cargo pocket. He plugged it into a tablet and began uttering voice commands. Company codes, passwords, and the things the Orbiter would use to dock wirelessly with a ship.

Austin barely held himself up with his hands on his knees as blood trickled from his forehead, nose, and mouth. The flare gun was nowhere, or it was in half a foot of mud. He dug through the mud where he'd last seen it as the shuttle raised several meters into the air. Lord, he was exhausted. Had Dmitry at least come back to his senses? Did one of them have to die for this to end? He couldn't lose; he had more to worry about than just himself.

Dmitry grew frantic; the further the shuttle went, the harder it would be to connect with it. He knew the override codes and continued the process, praying Dublin's weak piloting kept him in range long enough to override and bring it back.

Austin finally saw Carolina. She was looking up at the ship, the flare gun in her right hand at her side. She stood adjacent to Dmitry and Austin and removed the safety cap and cocked it back, aiming high. She squeezed the trigger and watched the battery payload shoot up in a blinding hot arc, landing on the wing. The ship continued to rise and pull away as sharp flashes of light burst from the wing. Higher up the ship went, as a visible blaze flickered, growing in size, molten and hot. A deafening pop rocked the ship as the modified battery ruptured.

Dmitry shook with anger.

The ship struggled to ascend briefly and then began its rocky course to the ground, like a boat in choppy waters. A trail of smoke stained its course as the wing continued to blaze, down and down until disappearing from view behind the trees. Then a sickening boom.

"You little bitch…" Dmitry snarled. He crushed the radio in his hand, staring at the plume of smoke about two kilometers away.

"Was Dublin…?" Athen cried, limping her way towards them.

"That was our only way home," Dmitry snarled, dropping the crumpled pieces at his feet. He picked up a fist-sized rock and turned to Carolina. "You wanted to test me, is that it? You wanted to see what would happen if you all disobeyed me, right?"

"She's just a kid," Athen protested.

"Shut up, or you're next."

Carolina backed away towards her father, who had taken a knee to keep from falling. He'd exhausted too much effort and was low on oxygen.

Athen staggered in front of Dmitry, using herself as a shield. "Stop it!" she begged.

Dmitry swung and hit her in the head, knocking her unconscious.

"Come on," Austin said, summoning his will. He wasn't going to win a fight right now, he'd taken too much of a beating already, and he could barely stand. He started towards the tree line, holding Carolina by the hand. It would buy him time, and it would drag him away from Athen.

"Oh yes! Run from me! I can chase you all day! I've got nothing else to do!" Dmitry screamed, his voice going hoarse. He stalked them towards the woods. At the base of the trail, Austin stopped to catch his breath as Dmitry neared. He tried to walk up the trail, but it was so slick he couldn't get even a step in. He clenched his fists in agony. He'd never outrun Dmitry; he couldn't even get up this trail with it being so muddy and slick. With his daughter at risk, if he couldn't get into those trees, then he'd have to fight here, and he'd have to win.

"Get up there, kiddo."

A smile crossed Dmitry's face. "So many interruptions before, but I don't think anything is going to save you now."

Austin pulled himself into the tree line, his foot slipping but making strides through sheer force of will. He gave whatever speed he could and barreled into the trees. "I'm right behind you, go!" he ordered his daughter. She went ahead of him, moving much faster than he. With optimism, maybe he could get her far away, too, for her own safety.

"Keep going! I'm right behind you!"

CHAPTER 38

Blood drew two lines down the side of Austin's face and neck. He wasn't sure which hit had caused it, but thankfully, it trickled around his eyes instead of into them. Being blind would give an advantage to Dmitry, who still held his rock. Not that he needed it; the rock or the advantage. Austin was so spent he couldn't fight, let alone stand upright. Between not being able to breathe with his face in the mud and the exhaustion of wrestling, he was worn out completely.

Yet he somehow ran, hollering ahead to his daughter that he was right behind her. Dmitry was gaining on him effortlessly.

"Not much in you, I see," Dmitry taunted, cresting the slick hill with ease compared to him.

He ignored the taunts and kept on, getting whatever distance he could. If he stopped, she'd stop, and he wanted her safe.

"Dad!" she cried, fifty meters ahead, and realized how far back he was.

"Get to the wall! I have a plan. Go!" he ordered. She waited, doubtful. "I swear, I will meet you there."

He'd kept so many promises already that she must have wished it so, because she believed him. She disappeared out of view, just as Dmitry sauntered closer.

"Well, that leaves me in a pickle, doesn't it? I mean, do I chase you? Or do I chase her? Truth is," he said, catching up to Austin, who was found leaning on a tree for air. "The truth is, you're a lot easier to catch." He smiled a sickening grin that didn't touch his eyes. At some point, he'd abandoned the rock, which was a relief of sorts.

Austin's headache was of the worst kind, but he didn't show the pain on his face. He wiped blood from his nose, followed by acute throbbing, meaning it was probably broken, too. He couldn't take much more punishment. He already needed a doctor, and not the one standing before him. His body could only endure so much. Dmitry had abandoned all the safeguards of a healthy society; the man was homicidal. And he was stronger, faster, and more vicious than Austin could manage in this state. No way out of it, though. Once the fight started, he'd be losing quickly unless he landed a swift knockout blow, something that he could muster and drop Dmitry with.

Even the mud was against him. The storm had dumped so much water that there were parts of the trail that had slid away, with baby waterfalls trickling into newly formed ponds down below.

"Not still mad about the radio, are you?" Austin asked half-heartedly.

"I never liked this team much anyway."

"So you're just going to kill us all? Because we don't agree with you?"

"There's only one punishment for mutiny."

"It's not mutiny! We're scientists, not military!"

Dmitry stretched his neck to his left shoulder and then to his right shoulder. "I'm looking forward to the silence, if I can be honest. Your opinion has always grated on me." Dmitry brandished a pairing knife, small but deadly sharp.

Great. Austin readied himself for whatever may come. He remained slouched and exhausted, a ruse to lure his enemy in closer. It wasn't much of a ruse; he was all those things. When Dmitry was in range, he moved, hurling mud up into Dmitry's eyes to blind him. Then, in the moment of distraction he'd created for this, he launched his right fist with a haymaker punch, which landed on the jaw. But the mud made him slip, and it didn't hit with all the force it should have. It didn't hit with all the force needed to put him to sleep. Dmitry staggered back briefly and then attacked. Austin dodged away as best he could as the knife started slashing at him. He was cut on the cheek, then he was cut on the palms, trying to defend. *Defensive wounds,* something in his logical brain noted. This wouldn't last long.

Dmitry grinned and inverted his grip on the knife. Austin dove for a tackle as Dmitry swung at a downward angle, skewering his shoulder instead of his head. The knife was for small kitchen work, small but razor sharp. He didn't even feel it, but his body did. He fell to a knee. If he didn't do something quickly, his promise would be forever broken. Dmitry looked like he was enjoying himself as he wiped the mud from his eyes.

"You'll need more than that," Dmitry said.

Austin rose and took a step back, raising his hands, though a setting gloom was telling him there was no way out of this. He'd try the knockout punch again, because if Dmitry wrestled him down, he'd be unable to do anything about it. Or at least he was going to when the ground slipped out from under him and he suddenly fell.

The roaring of earth and mud followed him down the slope, as water-logged dirt gave way to an avalanche. The fight had carried him to a ledge, and his added weight forced the landslide. The earth fell, dragging him down like a log in a river, which he desperately tried to fight. Austin slid down, steep and fast; he was completely unable to control the fall. He flattened out, still sliding, hands digging into the mud to try to stop himself. He reached for anything: bushes, branches, but it wasn't until he splashed into water that he stopped, and a blanket of mud slid on top of him. The storm had left massive pools, and now he was struggling neck-deep in the mud. He looked up to see Dmitry at the top, but he couldn't worry about that right now. He was about to drown.

He knew he was in trouble when his feet didn't touch the ground, and there was no staying afloat in mud like this. Like quicksand, it slowly submerged him, and it wasn't stopping. "Help!" Austin yelled in panic, struggling to keep his head above, yet every movement sank him deeper into the mud. His hand groped for a strand of roots, but pulling on them simply ripped them out of the earth. "Help!" he yelled, desperation taking over, sinking deeper. He searched for something that might save him, all the while sinking dispassionately. He flailed his arms for what it was worth, despite the stab wounds in his shoulder. The taste of earth and chai invaded his mouth. His muscles ached from the futility. The heavy, wet soil invaded his clothes, chilling his torso, armpits, neck, and now the top of his head. He kicked his feet, getting his mouth above the mud-line for one final breath. A warbled mush filled his ears and then covered his face.

He could no longer kick; his strength had drained away. His arms were next; the muscles had fought their hardest and had nothing left to give. A fleeting hope; he probed the floor with his toes, hoping to use solid ground and kick himself back up. But his toes found only darkness. Little by little, his body quit moving, and sorrow flooded him. It was dark, and he was being swallowed into this cursed planet. He would rot in the mud, never to see his daughter again. She used to be so small that he could hold her in one arm like a football. His life wasn't what he wanted it to be. He shouldn't be dying here. In this calm, he listened to his beating heart, waiting for it to stop. Being so calm, he felt something along his inner wrist, and he pulled at it, studied it, realizing it was a tree root. In the black tomb of oblivion, he wrapped his hand firmly with the slippery root and gently tugged. He felt his body edge slightly forward. An ember of hope blazed in him.

Don't snap it! Don't yank it! Just tug, gently, gently, and please don't break!

He pulled on the root harder than he should, but only because he didn't have long and his lungs were screaming. If the roots failed, then it was over, but it was going to be over anyway. He at least had to try. He felt the root as it twisted and strained, the pull bringing him slowly through the mud, the experience in complete blackness. His lungs were dying as he took in the new slack and pulled himself forward again. He felt the water line at his head, and he strained up for a breath. He had to be calm; he could just as easily inhale mud and choke to death.

He gasped in a breath of sweet air and, in his excitement, tugged on the root a little too hard. The root went slack, and he went back under.

He kept his eyes closed and pulled on the root, taking it in, begging it to become taught again. *Calm, calm,* he focused, knowing that panic would only kill him quicker. Austin kept pulling, even as his hope faded. So when the root was finally taught again, he vowed to tug slowly and cautiously, as much as his desperate soul would allow him to. He felt the mud giving way gently as he inched forward; the edge of the pond had to be getting closer. Two more tugs and his foot brushed the ground. He stood on it and climbed forward until he crested the mudline once more. This time, he took a huge breath. He could do it again. The earth was too soft here, so he sank into place, but he had bought a little time. He pulled himself onward, closer to solid ground. He edged nearer until both feet were on something solid and the bank reluctantly shared itself. There was madness in his determination, and he didn't quit until he was half in and half out of the pond. His face and chest rested on solid ground, wheezing, choking, but breathing.

"Thank you… thank you…" He whispered, lips kissing dirt.

There were many moments following where he did not move. He may have even passed out, briefly. He certainly couldn't have climbed out of there, not until his blood composed critical nutrients and oxygen. He'd give a million dollars to rinse his mouth with a water bottle right now. Eventually, he rolled to his back, shimmying a few centimeters, and then waited again. For ten minutes it went that way, until all of him rested on the bank, shivering, face up, staring at the trees and sky. "Thank you…" He cried to whatever nameless spirit was listening. "Thank you…"

The shivering ceased, the mud had been draining his body temperature, but the weather was actually getting nice and warm. When he had the ability to move, Austin carefully stood to his feet. He didn't have much, but he could stand. He angled his head up at the hills where he had come from.

He didn't see Dmitry, which was good news for him. He must have assumed he died in the mud. Either way, now it was all about Carolina. She would be on the run, and Dmitry was likely hunting her. She blew up their shuttle, and Dmitry would not forgive something like that.

"No way in hell… okay… get going, you bastard… get going!" Austin scolded, stoking the embers inside him. Function had trickled back to his limbs, enough to stay on his feet and carefully hike forward. The closest tree was gnarled and brittle, the orange and purple bark crumbled easily under his grip. He fixed his posture, summoning mind over matter. He had learned about that from his old wrestling coach. Back in school, he always told Austin to keep his head up between wrestling matches. Sure, you were dead tired, but you kept your head up as if you weren't. First, because it made your opponent afraid. And second, he was convinced that being tired was always mental. Austin figured it was just coach talk, but he was embracing it now. He thought about his daughter, about Dmitry's crazed eyes hunting her. Yes, he could do this.

The gash in his hand and shoulder had something to say, lest they be forgotten. It was hard to believe things had come to this. Dmitry had really tried to kill him. Austin had been cut and stabbed fighting for his life… not to mention the swollen lumps from all those punches. He smiled with gallows humor. At the beginning of this voyage, if someone had told him he would be fighting another scientist for his life, he would have laughed. It was ridiculous, then. But now, a world away, it was reality.

If nothing else, he wasn't easy to kill. He'd found that out well enough.

He started the long path climbing back up, which already wasn't off to a great start. His feet slipped the moment he tried to climb; he could only get the leverage he needed by grabbing bushes and branches along the way. He ascended about three meters and looked around, wondering how to maneuver the next part. He might need to find a longer way around, but that'd be assuming the trail worked its way up without him getting lost. But the last thing he needed was to go sliding back down. He decided to circle and find a more manageable way up. He climbed across, keeping his eye on the muddy pools dotted beneath him. The thought of falling back in one… "No, you don't," he swore, taking a route that wouldn't drop him back in. He was lucky to survive once; he could not fall in again. He pushed a thick, prickly bush out of his way and cursed when one of the barbs sank into the cut on his hand.

Nursing his hand, he realized it would be easier to climb if he bandaged up a little first. He pulled some gauze from his cargo pocket, which he'd selected for anyone but himself, yet the need was here. He tied it around the palm of his hand. What he really desired were stitches, but at least making a barrier would help until then. Plus, infection wouldn't be a problem, not with the kind of antibodies they all had in their blood. He finished the hand wraps, and next, he tested his shoulder. It did not want to move sideways, but up was okay. At least he could punch, if not wrestle. There were many muscles in the shoulder, enough that he could manage for now. He found a cut on his forearm that he didn't know about; he must have blocked the knife there, too. It was hard to imagine he wouldn't remember that one, but with adrenaline and everything, the whole fight was blurry. He wrapped gauze around that too, coming to the end of the roll faster than he wanted. The rest of him would just have to stop bleeding. He reached into his cargo pocket and grabbed another glucose pack. *Good for what ails me,* he smirked.

Ready to continue, he circled around the death pool along the base of the slope, careful not to stand on anything that looked less than sturdy. The storm did a good job creating swamps; it seemed half a dozen mud-slides had avalanched. As he crawled and observed this, to his great misfortune, it started to rain. Heavy drops, though nothing like the freak hurricane from before. He needed to finish getting up the slope before any more landslides took him back down again. But he found himself not wanting to move. At the halfway point, Austin was arguing with himself about whether exhaustion was really a mental state. He thought of his old coach again, and then he heard him talking. Then, somehow, his coach was unexpectedly there, but he wasn't. He was hallucinating.

"What are you doing, superstar?" the coach asked.

He hated that nickname. "Nothing, coach." No one was there; he was daydreaming. Or hallucinating, Austin couldn't really tell. But somehow, he was having a conversation with his old coach.

"Looks like you're taking a break, superstar. You must be done for the day."

He hated disappointing the coach even more than he hated that nickname. "No coach," Austin said.

"What's that?"

"Not tired, coach!" Austin barked.

"Well, that's better. Except you gotta' prove it, son."

"Proving it now, coach!"

"Then quit sucking wind and move!"

"Yes, coach!" he barked again, this time at the bush in front of him. He wasn't going to let his coach down. He snatched a loose dangling vine and pulled himself up a little more. If his feet slid, he'd just try again. If his hands gave up, he'd just use his teeth. If he fell back down, he'd climb back up. Nothing was going to stop him from reaching the top. Nothing.

CHAPTER 39

Carolina had gone too far before realizing something wasn't right.

She stopped when the obsidian wall came into view, the dark eye hiding in the earth, and she searched for her father to re-emerge. He'd been much slower, but he'd urged her to go on ahead, so she went. He was still coming, though, right?

Her anxiety grew the longer he didn't appear, and she made the choice to go back for him. He may be in trouble. He may need her help.

A minute later, she saw a head bobbing in the forest and stopped just short of crying out for him. A good thing too, because it wasn't her father. It was Dmitry. When she saw him, she took cover.

"Come out, little dove, come out, chiclet, come out, come out, wherever you are," Dmitry taunted. His arms dangled freely, his gate relaxed. He could be taking a stroll in the forest by the calmness of his jaunt, but his eyes said otherwise.

He was so confident, so at ease, she instantly feared for her father. But he said he had a plan, so she had to trust him. He wouldn't leave her... but still, where was he? Why would Dmitry be this way?

Dmitry walked up the path as she crept behind a tree, quiet as she could, taking her out of sight but also letting him closer. Truth of it was, she was no more than a stone's toss away from him. Also, it was hard to stay silent when her heart pounded so.

Dmitry continued on and made it to the top, where the ominous wall loomed, but then he stopped and looked around. She'd been careless, expecting him to just continue on. Now she ducked down, but made noise doing so. Possibly. Time would tell... but what would she do if he came after her?

"Come on, little girl, I won't hurt you. Come *awn'* out," Dmitry said, slowly creeping through the bushes in her direction. "*Caroooo-lie-na.*"

She stole a look and regretted it instantly. He was close, very close. He must not have seen her, or he'd be on the charge, but he'd likely heard her sound. His senses were leading him right to her, off the path, and in her direction. It couldn't be a coincidence.

"Where *aaaaare* you?" he sang. His body was turned away from her, and she might be able to sweep around quietly enough to reach the safety of the wall. His face was still looking away, and she had a chance.

She started crawling with his back to her.

"There you are," he smiled, turning around. He'd tricked her into coming out.

She bolted up the hill, and he cut the path to block her off.

"Ha!" he yelled, reaching out for her but just barely missing. Her little legs pounded up the hill, and she made it to the wall before he could intercept again.

Dmitry yelled, giving chase. He sprinted after her, but she found herself to be faster. Yet with her speed, she made a mistake, she didn't slow down atop the ramp, and she went sliding uncontrollably down. She didn't stop until the wall at the bottom stopped her, sliding into it with considerable force.

"Hahaha, *ahh* that's good… hey, I think you hit something," Dmitry laughed from the top of the entrance. She fumbled to her feet as he stood at the top, looking down at her.

They made eye contact, and for the briefest of moments, he looked surprised. Was he expecting her to cry or something? She hobbled towards the adjoining room, hoping to get her wind back, hoping to get hidden and fast. The impact from the wall still hurts. Dmitry slid halfway and jogged the other half, legs apart like a surfboard, hands out for balance, feet pedaling to stay under him; the slope took care of the rest. The momentum forced his small trot to continue when he reached the bottom. His smile was gone now. "Hey kid, it's not safe in here without an adult."

"Leave me alone!" she screamed, ducking out of view. She didn't have long to get a hiding spot; he'd be there in a matter of seconds.

He strolled inside the first interior chamber. All the tables were still tipped over and scattered. The dim walls and alien signs waited, like a puzzle wanting to play again. She saw him holding a knife, and it made her tense up. He twirled it in his fingers, balancing it mid-spin on the tip of his thumb. She hid behind a table, working her way towards the hallways leading inside. Dmitry stopped to get a closer look at his knife, as if it had some blood on it that fascinated him.

"Ha!" he cried, gleeful. Dmitry stared mesmerized at it, and then he licked the knife. She recoiled, unsure of why someone would do that. From the look on his face, he didn't know either. He disregarded the knife's fascination and went back on the prowl to find her. "Alright, enough games, where did you go?"

She listened to the nameless ambience that surrounded them, feeling compelled in a certain direction. She needed to get out of here, fast. But her father? He'd need a way to track her, a way to find her, so she brandished her companion in boredom; the markerpen. She drew a face with a long nose, a circle, and an arrow; if you looked, something that could be perceived as a doodle, but really was a breadcrumb that he needed to find.

There were two doors on her right, a shelving cabinet lying on its side in a few centimeters of remaining water. The splashing made it impossible for her to run quietly, plus the debris was everywhere. She could probably sprint down to the three hallways by sneaking away on the left side of the room. One of those hallways led to the elevator that had first crashed on them. This wasn't going to be easy, and she also had a compelling urge to try the left hallway, if she could reach it.

Dmitry entered the hall and stopped to look down at the water, rippling evenly and weaving reflections of light. She moved slowly at first. The way light shimmered and reflected on the ceiling and walls was actually very pretty, but the water proved impossible to remain silent.

"There you are!"

She was sprinting now, but yet again, he could not catch her. It was confusing to both of them; surely adults were faster? Adrenaline, fight or flight, that must be what gave her such speed. Around the corner and out of view, she stopped long enough to plot another little breadcrumb, hastening a prayer to the universe that only her father would find it.

"You're delaying the inevitable. I'll hunt you as long as it takes!" his words haunted her. Then came his footsteps, splashing closer. She went down the left hallway towards the barricaded room, coincidentally where she'd helped Dmitry get to safety. She crossed through the rubble easily and looked for a new place to hide on the other side, following nothing but instinct. The lights were dim, not quite dark, with sporadic flickerings of a circuit trying again and again. This was the hallway where the monster had barricaded them in; on the other side of the wall was the hidden CCTV room, the one-way view that had been shattered. Not that she could reach it anyway, but it was a good hiding place. She heard him on the other side of the barricade, stumbling his way up. The hole was larger since the creature had gone through it, and he wouldn't get stuck this time. Again, she took to hiding; again, she struggled to form a better plan.

What am I doing inside this room? It's a dead-end! She didn't risk looking out into the greater hall, relying on her ears instead and staying out of view. His footsteps were difficult to place, either from the echo or from a deliberate softness in his step. Perhaps his confidence was fading somewhat, as he realized it was not so easy to catch her. That didn't lessen his threat any; she could only run for her life so many times before it quit working. And her instincts had led her to a room without an exit.

"Ha!" he shouted, picking a room but not hers. She stole a look through the doorway and found him; he'd entered to kick around a few things and ensure she wasn't inside. He'd get to her room eventually.

Looking around, she agonized over her choice to come here, and her hiding options were slim. There was a desk, but it was not a proper hiding spot. All he'd have to do is bend down and look. There was a cabinet, but nothing she could get inside of. It was only by luck that he hadn't chosen this room yet. Why did she pick this room?

"Hiding, eh? Don't worry, I'm good at this game. I'll find you. Eenie meenie, I just might know…"

Dmitry pounced in the room between them, only one more to check before he'd find her. She held her head; it was swimming with that sensation she hated. There was a reason she hid in this room. It wasn't random… There was a reason…

She opened her eyes. *The tunnels.*

One of the tunnels went into this room, and she almost threw up as the *memory* surfaced in her brain. But she mustered herself, knowing she didn't have long. She found the concealed entrance, hidden behind the shelving cabinet, appearing exactly as a wall, except it was no more than a hologram. She found it through the 'companion' hiding in her thoughts, the one that she hated but needed so often. But how would her father find this? He wouldn't. So she retrieved her markerpen again and drew on the wall just beneath it, small and casual, something she hoped only her father would find. Then she climbed into the wall, through the hologram pretending to be a wall, behind where one of the tunnel entrances waited, perfectly concealed.

The experience was expected this time. She curved around a corner through darkness, weightless, yet this was far less disorienting than before. Up and around, with no sense of direction left, lights from ventilation slits peppered her vision. The trip was ultimately brief as she landed on the grated floors. The first thing she noticed was how warm it was, which meant she was several floors down. She groaned at the sickening knowledge that she led herself here; she did not simply flee out of desperation. She'd been traveling towards something, but only her 'companion' knew it until now. The passenger that she hated but needed. She tried to let it go because she knew she had other things to be upset about right now. She exhaled and released the fists she'd made. So, where was this?

She recognized it, the real Carolina that is. This was the ornate and finished depot, the one with all the trains and cargo bays, the one with the long blue aquarium where she'd hidden with her father once. A train waited on the other side of one of those bays, the train leading to the other ship.

She didn't know it, but fortune played a trick on her. Many floors above, Dmitry eventually checked the room she'd been in, and he did not see her breadcrumb. Yet, to her impending dismay, it didn't stop him. Between the cabinet being crooked from the wall and a noted subtle change in the air, Dmitry also knew about the tunnels, and it was not long before he had the same discovery as she.

Somehow, when he landed on the grated floors, it startled her, and she screamed.

Dmitry's balance was still flimsy, but he leapt after her, his unsteady feet galloping like a drunkard. She turned to jump, and in a moment's hesitation, Dmitry's hand gripped her firmly by the neck. He tackled her back until slamming into the wall, pinned at the neck by his hands. She tried to look away, but he wouldn't let her. He brought his face low to hers until she looked him in the eyes. "I told you I'd find you," he whispered.

Her tears started and wouldn't stop. She couldn't breathe, though she pulled at his grip, hoping to loosen it.

"There's knowledge in that head of yours, and I want it. But how do I get it from you?"

Whatever he meant by that, she didn't like the sound of it.

"I don't suppose you'd just tell me?" he mused.

She'd better say something good, she knew that much. "There's another shuttle; we can reach the Orbiter with it. But there's something else too, something you'll want to see, a special radio," Carolina said, barely able to speak.

"That's rich. I should just kill you now," he said, though he loosened his grip enough to let the pressure alleviate in her face.

She gasped for a few breaths before speaking. "It's not a lie. You don't want to go back empty-handed, do you?"

CHAPTER 40

If someone had told Athen before this job that she would watch her friends die and be stoned in the head by her team leader, she would have waited for the laughter to start. But damn, somehow it'd come to that, and it hurt. Painkillers helped; she could only imagine her discomfort without them. When the fog of being concussed subsided, she worked on getting to her feet. Then, as soon as she struggled, the pain started again. No one was around, so crying and cursing at the top of her lungs wasn't something she needed to restrain.

With effort, she could stand. She was still fresh on her modest cocktail of pain relievers, mixed with anti-inflammatory helpers. So while walking wasn't the best thing to do, she could still do it. It's not like she could go to sleep, not with the very tender spot on her skull reminding her she'd been knocked unconscious. Somehow, it didn't help knowing her leg wasn't her biggest injury anymore. Inspecting her leg, she admitted that the job done by Austin, the bandage couldn't have been better. That was good, one small piece of good news in a storm of bad.

The sun was beaming through intermittent rain clouds. It was easy to track the crash by the line of smoke billowing up, easier to track than to get there. But get there she must, because she couldn't ever leave here without knowing Dublin's fate. He was her work friend and also a true friend, a mentor, partner, and, without ever being romantic, it was a powerful bond. She was closer to him than anyone, and there would always be doubt if she didn't know. So, she had to know. Towards the smoke trail she went.

She pictured him fatally wounded and in pain, she pictured him building a shelter perfectly unscathed, she pictured many things. Most of what she pictured was either something she needed to know or something he'd need her help with.

The black trail of smoke from the crash showed no signs of softening, even as the wind pushed it across the sky about as far as it could. Athen hiked and checked for her smoke beacon. It couldn't be more than a kilometer or possibly two, and the ground was kindly level in this direction. Though without a better viewpoint, she could only guess for how long. As the trees swallowed her and the trail wound in coils, it became harder to keep track of her beacon. A thick tangle of vegetation blocked the sky. Climbing a tree was out of the question. With her multi-tool, she could fell one easily enough. When it was needed, she'd keep it in mind. For now, there was just enough gap in the web of tangled branches, and she spotted the smoke trail, then delineated its source. She continued her hike.

Each time she saw the black plumes, her stomach turned with thoughts of finding his smoldering remains, but even if that was her reality, she still needed to know. She focused on her hike, forgot about her leg, and nearly rolled her ankle over an ambitious root. It was a challenge to find steady ground without constantly watching the dirt. The terrain was changing from earthy clay to complete rock, and trees were becoming sparse because of it. At least she wasn't barefoot; she was wearing the boots Austin had set out for her. The rocks were hard to navigate, but it made spotting the smoke column easier.

Wispy bushes now were all that managed to survive this rocky terrain; the trees had quit. Grass reached up in tufts; she still didn't have a visual from the rocks that swelled high and low. She did everything she could to avoid climbing one. As she lumbered around a boulder, she detected her first note of machinery, the smell of heat and metal, and she paused. This close, she had doubts about herself. She may not be ready for finding him, torn asunder, dead or dying. She gathered her resolve and went up and around the boulder, careful with her leg, more careful not to fall on her head. The ground on the other side rolled upwards, and when she reached the top, she surveyed the field ahead.

She could see the shuttle itself, and were she blind, she could easily smell it. Flames casually digested the wings, which were still attached to a bent main cabin. Something down there was moving amidst the wreckage.

Athen held her breath when she saw a tentacle arm flap out of the back of the ship. A moment later, some fresh fuel popped and ignited, channeling eager black smoke. The heat swelled with it for a brief few seconds. The creature squealed and desperately tried to gain distance from the ship, crawling and unable to stand. It looked wounded, dying even. Athen's chest tightened. Was this the proof she needed? She stayed hidden; it was for the best if she did not have to run. This wasn't proof. This didn't confirm anything, except that the creature lived.

Long, drooping tentacles pulled the creature away from the ship, as smoke continued to stain the air above. Then, propping itself up on one good arm, it opened its mouth and wretched. Athen covered her mouth at the sight of it, but still caught the image of the jellyfish parasite exiting its host. If anything was in her stomach, she would have expelled it. The moment the parasite was free, it scurried away, flopping in fear like a helpless doe, desperately away from the heat. It must have been too hot inside the ship to safely exit its host, and with soft transparent flesh, the parasite was likely not able to withstand extreme temperatures. It likely couldn't withstand direct sunlight. If she could feel the heat up here, it had to be much worse down there. A puddle of gooey matter followed out of the host's mouth; the once terrifying creature was now simply *off*, shut down like a flipped switch.

The jellyfish didn't know of her presence, but she also couldn't swear it would stay that way. She grabbed a frail stick, a dried-up branch that was within reach. If that thing came after her, she would at least be able to hit it, though a better stick would be appreciated. She closed her eyes and took a deep breath. If she had to go down there to know for sure, then that's what she would do. Looking at the wreckage... she didn't know. Maybe. The hull was mostly intact. He could be alive, and in pain, burning to death. All she needed to know was that he was dead, and she could leave. Otherwise, she would help him... whatever that meant. She would drag him back to the quadrohuts if she had to, or if it was only a matter of time and pain, she would be there to ease his suffering. Either way, she would help him. She'd never euthanized anyone before, but she would do it for him.

When Athen was ready, she stood, her joints were stiff, and she didn't want to move. She was exhausted, and the sooner all of this was over, the better. She stepped carefully down the lava rock towards the ship. There was no way to stay hidden at this point, and she carried the stick in her hand for protection. She had to cover her nose and mouth from the fumes. The air was abrasive, the fuel burning from the ship was part chemical and part radioactive. She couldn't stay here long.

Athen tried to keep her eyes on the jellyfish, but it had disappeared easily among the porous rocks. One minute it was there, the next minute it was not. That was enough to make her want to wait, but her sense of duty kept her. She knew if this situation were reversed, that he would absolutely be there for her, for whatever she needed. She maintained a healthy distance from ship debris and large rocks, anything the parasite might use for hiding. She made certain to scout diligently, in case Dublin had tried to crawl away. The heat this close to the burning ship was close to unbearable. It must have been lethal ten minutes ago. There was no way she was going to get inside to look.

She was closer to the shell of the creature now. It slouched as a husk, an exosuit. It was so out of place, dropped on the ground, disjointed like a suit of armor, waiting to be picked up. Where it once was so terrifying, now it was just a prop. An awesome, nightmare-inducing prop. Genetically speaking, much to study here. Bulging muscles, armor skin, but without its own brain, its own sentience. It had to have been bioengineered. Athen wasn't a geneticist, but with the way the creature turned off… it reminded her of a weapon. The parasite was a hermit crab, and the creature was the shell. The sounds of moaning shook her from the train of thought.

"Dublin!"

Athen gasped and ran towards the sound. She came around the other side of the ship and saw Dublin lying on his back, struggling to sit up. "Wait!" She ran to him, carefully cupping his neck and shoulders to help him. "Dublin, don't move, you're… hurt…" she said, her voice stalling on the word *hurt*. He wasn't just hurt, there was a gaping hole in him, revealing bone and organ and meat that was charred and black. How was this not final? How was he moaning and trying to sit up? Where was all the blood?

"Oh no…"

Dublin's head flopped over at her; his eyes were gray and unfocused, lifeless, though his head was looking at her, trying to move.

Athen shrieked. She tried to retreat, but Dublin sat up and grabbed her by the shirt.

She cried out, pulling herself free. She stumbled back as Dublin then grabbed her ankle, and she fell in pain, unable to balance herself. His grip was devastating, and with his hand on her ankle, he pulled her closer. He wasn't in control; he was dead. He was the shell now. She sat up and cracked the stick across his face. It shattered in her grip without fazing him. He pulled her closer, and she punched him in the face, but he wouldn't let go. She swung three times, each time like hitting a mannequin, his expression plastic and unchanging. Her hand hurt.

She kicked with her free leg, landing him in the mouth and popping his head back. She was freed and backpedaled, unable to take a real breath from the heat and fumes. Dublin found his way up to his feet, moving with an unsteady waver.

"I have my answer."

It was time to leave. She turned to run, knowing by the way he moved, he couldn't give much chase. But after two steps, she had to stop and fulfill her duty. Looking at Dublin, who still struggled to come towards her, she studied those dull gray eyes for any sign that he might be in there. And if so, was he suffering?

If yes, if at all it was possible, then she hadn't helped him yet. Not until his torment was over. Tears were streaming down her face. How was she supposed to help him like this? In this pause of agony, she wished the roles were reversed. Dublin would finish her off. But how? A gun would work, but she didn't have one. She picked up a rock, large enough to break a skull, and readied herself. But when she stared at Dublin, even hoping he was dead, *knowing* he was dead, she fumbled for the resolve to do it. He'd tell her something about *no point in wishing*. She closed her eyes and hurled the rock. By the sound it made, she didn't miss.

Athen cried there, against the wall of heat, surrounded by fumes and desolation, flesh and destruction. She wept for her friend, stomach-churning the sound the rock had made. After a few good cries, she couldn't tolerate the heat and fumes anymore, so she wiped her eyes and turned to go. She took several steps, leaving the flames and heat behind her, letting it become a memory she'd continue to push away. After a dozen paces, the heat had become much more bearable. But in her thoughts and agony, she was distracted and didn't hear something fleshy crawling towards her. She was unaware of her stalker until it wrapped itself around her ankles.

Athen shrieked at the sight of tiny limbs climbing up her and around her neck. They constricted as she tried to pull them away, struggling to keep them from her. She screamed and wished she had not. Limbs crawled inside her mouth. Athen bit down hard as she could, her mouth filled with rancid tastes, but it only made the parasite constrict harder. She felt the sliding inside her mouth and down, and there was a swiftness and a grace that she completely did not expect.

CHAPTER 41

Carolina led Dmitry down the hall, walking close along the interior for drawing a line to follow. Leaving a trail of breadcrumbs for her father to find, leaving it under Dmitry's nose, was a high-risk game.

Dmitry was asking her something; most of his words were lost on her. But she heard, "I really hope you didn't lie to me about that."

She stopped at a crossway, studying each direction. She knew which way led to the *radio*, which was a gross simplification for lacking a better word. "Hmmm," she said, drawing an arrow as discreetly as she could, as he peered ahead with her. "I think it's... hmmm," she stalled.

"What are you doing?" he asked, the markerpen concealed behind her.

"I'm thinking. Wait, it's this way."

Looking across the hall towards the room, she paused. A memory flooded over her, more real than any before it. She remembered the *I'ilshiks* that had built these tunnels, they worked for *Ambassador Himark* but had staged a secret revolt. The parasite had played both sides... They'd stormed this floor, about to overthrow the *Ambassador*, but then something went wrong. Carolina could see their long bodies, their one leg when standing, and three arms that crawled when moving. The guards were ready for them... Carolina blinked. She was on the floor, being kicked in the ribs by Dmitry. He was about to kick her again.

"I said get up!" he ordered.

She climbed to her feet, nursing her ribs.

"What was that?"

"It's nothing! I had to remember where to go. It's this way," she answered, leading him across the hall towards the room. The visions had disappeared; they were so powerful, she didn't remember falling or Dmitry kicking her. Now she just had incredible pain in her sides, evidence that it had happened. She reached into her pocket and stuck her fingers in ink. The markerpen was leaking, damaged from Dmitry's kicks. Carolina moved to her left to give him space, lingering near the wall as she contrived how to leave the next breadcrumb while she still could.

She leaned on the wall with one hand and drew a hasty line with what ink remained in the markerpen. She couldn't lose her father in the hallway here.

"There," she pointed at the one on the left.

"You first," Dmitry said. Carolina stalled a moment and went ahead. After a long, winding hallway, the room expanded to a golden door. She stood in front of it.

She had to do something to open the door first, which she attempted without trying to summon any memory of how. She placed her hand out, triggering a web of lasers that scanned her, producing her copy on the screen opposite her by the door. Then the door slid open with a deeper, heavier whoosh than the other doors. Indeed, the door itself would have been impossible to move, even for the creature, a symbol of what it protected.

Sparkles of light reflected all around her, as the focal point of the room, the *Lens*, hovered in the middle. Dark, floating in a pool of radiant nothing. She stood there, in awe.

"Well, it's certainly very pretty," Dmitry said, entering the room. Neither of them could take their eyes off the *Lens*, its hypnotic dance of murky photons. It shimmered with reflective black, hovering in an orb suspended by energy weaves that blinked in and out of existence. It took up the center of the room, and she knew it was a very important piece of this facility. Carolina knew that with the *Lens*, she had a near limitless view of the universe, and that it was linked to other locations with a *Lens*. Carolina shook her head. She didn't know which memories were hers anymore. This certainly couldn't be one of them. *Hurry, daddy!* she prayed.

"This is the radio you mentioned? At least you weren't lying," Dmitry said, staring at the *Lens*. By the look on his face, he found it quite remarkable. "So, what did you say just now?"

Did she hear him? Carolina shuddered. She didn't mean to say that out loud. "Nothing," she said.

"No, I think you said, *hurry daddy*," he said. Dmitry sighed and smiled. "Well, I have my doubts that he'll find you this time, Carolina. For one thing, he's dead." Dmitry waited for her response.

It was a lie; he wouldn't leave her. But Dmitry went on, "…and even if he's not dead, he'll never see that cute, tiny line you drew on the wall."

Carolina's eyes widened.

"That marker pen of yours wipes off so easily, one of the drawbacks of wet ink…" he said, smiling. "Oh, you thought I didn't notice them? Tsk tsk."

At last, he was satisfied, having gotten the reaction he wanted out of her. He walked past her, letting her wallow. All she could do was picture her dad getting to that intersection of halls and looking for the next clue…

"Show me how this thing works," Dmitry said, pulling her attention back. Carolina stood up, but she couldn't think. Her thoughts were fading with her hopes. If she ran fast enough, she might be able to escape. Dmitry must have been reading her mind, because he stepped in front of her.

"Don't even think about it."

CHAPTER 42

Austin approached the entrance to the facility, abandoning the bush he used for cover while he scouted for his enemy. Tracking Dmitry would be a blend of haste and caution.

He was badly hurt. His hand wouldn't stop bleeding, and his shoulder was swelling. It was worsening to the point that he could barely use his right arm. He knew he would be outmatched when he caught up to Dmitry; it was simple. He was physically weaker than before, Dmitry was likely no worse off, and he probably still had the knife. The knife… crossed off any curiosity of getting stabbed from his bucket list, if ever it was there. The memory of that metal through his skin and the suddenness of it, he closed his eyes and shuddered. He did not want to experience that again. He was in poor condition for a fight; he would have to change the equation in order to beat Dmitry. If his daughter wasn't down there, he'd never go chasing another encounter with that knife.

A weapon to even the odds, that's what he needed. Hopefully, one would present itself along the way. At least he was able to wash most of the mud off his face. The light rain removed some of the mud, and he took a moment here to contemplate how to track his daughter. He just had to know where she'd head to… though that presumed she wasn't just headed anywhere trying to escape Dmitry. He closed his eyes, withstanding the crushing thoughts. He'd find her. He had to.

The emotions threatened to capsize him, and he needed the help of rational thoughts. Finding her wouldn't be enough if Dmitry were there. Maybe he could sneak up and take him by surprise; it would all depend on how it happened. A little luck would go a long way here.

Water still poured in, bubbling down the sloped entrance from the rain. Austin was still crumbling away mud as he controlled his slide down to the hall. The water at the bottom was not receding; the intense downpour must have overloaded the drainage. It would be hard to track her without knowing anything. In fact, she might not even be inside; that itself was a gamble. Maybe she was still ducking around trees in the forest. Well, he'd told her to head for the wall. It was the last thing he said to her, so she'd probably have at least waited near the entry. If she were outside, she would have seen him approach and reached him that way, so no, she definitely went inside. But in hindsight, he wished he'd suggested something else. The facility was sprawling, massive, and dangerous. They could be in the next room, or a kilometer below ground. His daughter didn't have forever to be found, and he had a promise to keep.

He went from here to the first main room, which echoed from the remaining water, bouncing the smallest of sounds all around him. The room had been upheaved; no single desk or chair was upright. He wasn't interested in reciting every memory that bounced by; he'd been a day without sleep and would benefit nothing. Focus and deduction would help him find her, not reminiscing. There were three hallways, and Austin felt like she'd take the one in the middle… but that led to the elevator that crashed. If she went that way, she couldn't have gone on. Carolina was smart and organized; she would have remembered that. So now it was the hallway on the left, or the one on the right. Fifty-fifty odds were not the worst, but he wasn't about to risk everything on a coin toss. The water had not entered this room, and the slightest evidence of footprints remained, fading quickly to the hallway on his left. He listened for her, or for Dmitry. He'd rather not stumble upon them; he'd rather not announce his arrival. He'd need the element of surprise. The muddle of echoes was all that he heard.

Austin went down the left hallway, following footsteps that were already faded halfway down. The invisible suffocation of time spurred him into a run, caution of silence be damned. He ran, dried mud crumbling off him in bits. He ignored the office doors on his right and on his left. At the end of the hallway was a mound of junk, a barricade, with a gaping hole he could climb through at the top. Would she go this way?

He rubbed his hands through his hair to help himself think, and then chose to climb over the mound of rubble. It was the most direct path, so he'd stick with it. He climbed up and over, wondering in passing the nature of this barricade, but giving it no more thought than that. On the other side, he discovered more tables and chairs, and saw what looked like a broken window a bit out of his reach. There were also several rooms, and otherwise, this seemed to lead nowhere. In dismay, he entered each of the rooms, his heart sinking the more she wasn't inside one of them. The last room gave him the slightest of flickers of hope, for the cabinet had been dragged from the wall. He gave it a look to ensure she wasn't hiding behind it, and of course, she was not. It was a fool's wish.

But there was something drawn on the wall, he recognized it as Carolina's doodle pen, no, her marker pen. Well, she doodled with it, constantly, even here apparently. When would she have had the time to draw something here? This was a strange place to find one of her doodles. The parent in him made a note to correct this behavior of hers.

His hope was slipping away; he had nothing to go on. He was choosing blindly. He would have to backtrack and try the hallway on the right. Maybe those wet footprints had been Dmitry's, maybe she'd given him the slip, and he was aimlessly searching too. That would be a good thing, actually.

Austin began his backtracking, approaching the barricade he'd already climbed over once. He felt time slipping endlessly away. His mind wandered, a combination of stress, exhaustion, and how worried he was for Carolina. He thought about that doodle, wondering when she would have made it, and stopped with his leg ready to hoist him upwards. He concentrated and spun to face that particular room. It wasn't possible.

There shouldn't be a doodle there; she couldn't have drawn it early on because they didn't come this way originally. He supposed she could have made it when they'd been separated earlier, or else it meant she'd made it just now, and she'd have done that because she knew he'd be looking for her. It could be, couldn't it? Could he be wrong about this? She may have left it knowing he was trying to find her. His heart was pounding way ahead of him, as he sensed he was on to something. Was it really possible?

He went back to the room. It still didn't make sense, even if she did. He stared at the wall, trying to keep his world from collapsing. It was just a wall. There was nothing important about it. He uttered the start of several protests, clutching his hair. Why would she draw this here, behind a cabinet no less, if it wasn't a clue of some sort? The pressure was becoming too much.

He studied what looked like a cartoon head with a pointed hat, although it also looked like an arrow pointing conspicuously up the wall. Why here? Why behind a cabinet? Nothing about it was hinting towards an answer.

He had one inclination; the ink took time to dry. If Carolina had just drawn this, then the ink would still be wet. Austin rubbed the tip of his pointer finger against the doodle, and he was so terrified to see that he shut his eyes. He held his pointer finger not a foot from his face, but he struggled to find the courage to look.

His hope rested on this ink being wet. If his fingertip was clean, then the doodles were long dried and they weren't clues… they were just doodles.

Black ink stained the grooves of his fingertip.

With renewed vigor, he examined everything again. He toppled the cabinet, hoping for a trap door beneath it. He pushed away tears and looked at the crude, simple drawing. Was the drawing a location, a symbol to jog his memory? If it was, he was still missing it. It was just a circle for a head and a pointed hat. What was he missing? Maybe nothing, because maybe this was where Dmitry caught her.

If Dmitry caught her in this spot, then there'd be nothing else. He leaned against the wall as his hope died, and his hand fell. His hand fell *into* the wall.

Austin recoiled, a quick test of his senses. He believed himself sane, not hallucinating. So then, what the hell just happened? He put his hand out again, shaking with the unexpected, testing to see why his arm went through the wall. The hologram shimmered as his hand went in, a perfect image and undetectable. It was just enough for him to see that this part of the wall was an illusion. There was something behind this! And seeing it now, the arrow definitely pointed to this spot, to the fake wall. It was only luck that he unraveled this clue.

The trail was fresh, though he had no idea what to expect. He reached in with his hands, then his head, and looked at the inside of a strange tunnel. *Okay,* he figured, hidden tunnels, naturally. It should surprise him, but it was a week of firsts. She was in here? No point waiting, he climbed in, but then things changed quickly.

He fell. No, he flew. Wait, he was falling, but not down; he was falling through the tunnel, sideways at times, down at others, banking as if on a slide he couldn't touch. What was this? Austin reached out to grab hold of something, but the way he moved felt like he was being carried. After a brief panic, he realized that this was supposed to happen. Carolina led him here; he reminded himself of that, so he could relax because this was the correct way. This *tunnel* was carrying him effortlessly somewhere. He trusted her, but also hoped to be prepared for whatever may come. After about ten seconds, he was even able to open his eyes without disorienting nausea. Then it shot him out.

Austin didn't land on his feet. He launched out of the wall about a meter high and fell on a grated floor, which couldn't have been worse on his shoulder. Amidst the wave of pain, he tried to decipher where this was. He remained disoriented, feeling like the kid who jumped off the *merry-go-round* at the wrong time. He wobbled to his feet while his senses gathered. "Carolina?" he called, still grimacing. No answer, and it was deadly silent beyond the ever-present hum of ambient sound.

How the tunnel worked was beyond him, involving physics unknown. It would be a mystery to ponder on the way home, one of many, if he made it.

Which way now? He followed ahead until the way branched again. Carolina had led him here, so there must be another clue as to where to go. He was specifically on the hunt for more drawings. He inspected a hallway and the wall near it. He inspected the one next to that. He inspected everywhere his little light would shine; nothing had any marks from Carolina's marker pen. The walls were bare. Everywhere was bare… he rested and shut his eyes. Another wave of feeling like he'd never find her. Another wave of her slipping away, and there was nothing he could do about it. He should at least pick a path and hope for the best. Would fate bless him so kindly as to let him pick the right one? Why couldn't Carolina leave another clue?

His eyes focused on a smudge. He'd been looking for a doodle, but a smudge was equally out of place; it was pure luck that he even spotted it. Not a drawing, just a smudge, but it looked like the same ink. Austin got closer to it, shining his suit light against it, exposing every pore in the wall. Not a drawing, but definitely ink. He had seen the shape before, on a card she'd made some Father's Day ago, part of a little girl's handprint. It wasn't a doodle, it wasn't even a smudge; the ink on her fingers had left a print. She'd been here; it was closest to the left hallway.

He went down the hall, longer and longer until it stretched into a lobby, and on the other side, a gaping doorway. Light shimmered from inside. As he neared, he wondered about the colors and shadows that moved curiously, wondered what was casting them so. Standing in the doorway, he spotted something dazzling and murky, something brilliant and beautiful, the source of the light, hovering in the middle of the room. Hypnotic, majestic, and unbeknownst to him, it linked to a dozen other points in the universe.

"Daddy!"

She was here. The look on his daughter's face would be stamped in his memory for all time, because she looked saved. Any relief he felt faded just as quickly because the last person in the world he wanted to see was next to her. The look on Dmitry's face would also be in his memory for all time, the pure and utter disbelief.

This wasn't good. He'd lost twice to Dmitry, though none of those times was a fair fight by any means. It didn't change what he had left in him, or the fact that he'd been wounded. But the look on her face… he couldn't let her down.

"No! How many times do I have to kill you?" Dmitry groaned. "Remember this?" he said, brandishing the knife. The pain in his hands and shoulder gave no illusions about how much he regarded that sharpened steel. Austin retreated towards a ramp to the side, leading up, looking for something he could use as a weapon, since he had yet to encounter one. No tools, no pipes, not even a tissue box to throw. The equation had not changed.

"Just let us go," Austin pleaded.

Dmitry pretended to contemplate for a moment. "Nah."

He stalked forward as Austin retreated back and up, taking him to the upper level. They were now above the hypnotic light source, on an elevated platform decorated with control panels. Retreating so readily emboldened his adversary. Yet until he had an opening, he couldn't just run towards his end. He may lose, but he'd take his fighting chances at their best.

"I'm surprised, I really am, Austin. I underestimated you, though not by much. A change of location, that's all your hard work has gained you. Your lifeless corpse will rot down here, instead of up there. Because I am never really wrong," Dmitry said. "Wouldn't mind if you begged for your life, though. Come now, go ahead."

He let the invitation linger in silence as he stalked forward. "No? Pity."

His words burned and ignited, something primal that existed in any man, something that was ready to die for glory or honor. Austin was tempted to cast his hesitations aside and charge, but he managed to stay calm. He would wait for his opening, and it all depended on Dmitry's feet and the timing of his steps. Once he started a step, the longer he talked, the greater the opening. He circled around a desk, one with blinking controls covering it, and looked down at Carolina, who waited on the floor below, worry in her eyes.

Dmitry opened his mouth to further his taunts, stepping casually, his face turned to the side, making certain Carolina remained privy to his diatribe. He was just as close and just as distracted as he'd ever be. Austin made his move.

Dmitry stepped forward, the start of a new taunt about to flow, and Austin blitzed. He feinted up high with his hands, quick and sudden, and Dmitry slashed up in defense, bringing his attention up high and his body off balance. Austin set it up to get him worried up there and then dropped low. Like a train, he slammed into Dmitry's gut, hands wrapping around, picking him up in a tackle. It was so fast and so hard, he heard the knife clatter as Dmitry failed to hold it.

It was the setup for a single-leg takedown, except he modified it for knocking the wind out of someone and dropping them over a railing. His coach wouldn't have approved in most circumstances. Ignoring the protests on his shoulder, he heaved and launched Dmitry over the side, plummeting him. He stood and watched from above, holding the railing for support from the pain in his shoulder.

Dmitry fell and crashed unnaturally, smashing the control panel on the bottom floor in a shower of sparks. The reaction caused an electrical surge, making the floating orb in the room vibrate and then turn black, colorless, becoming a shiny obsidian like the wall outside.

"Damn you! I'll kill you!" Dmitry screamed. He tried to get up but instead growled in pain, clutching his back and launching a number of curses.

Smaller arms were hugging him. He reached down and picked up Carolina, ignoring the gash in his hand. She squeezed him with strength unbecoming.

"I told you I'd find you. I promised," he said.

"He told me you were dead, but I knew he was lying!"

Almost not a lie, but damnit, I'm here now. "I don't think I have what it takes to kill a defenseless man. Let's get out of here before he makes me," Austin said as he set her down. He led her down the platform towards the doors as Dmitry flailed.

"I'll kill you! I'll kill both of you!"

He stood in the doorway long enough to see that Dmitry was struggling to stand; it was difficult for him, but he wasn't paralyzed. Austin clenched his fists. Now would be the best time to finish him off. Neutralize the threat… but he just wasn't the type. Fight only for defense, yet the man before him was no threat. He couldn't bring himself to do it.

"Let's go."

"Not that way, Daddy, follow me," she said, letting go of his hand and running.

"Carolina! Wait!" He ran after her. They went down a hallway towards a tall, gold door that opened as Carolina approached. It was another cursed elevator; he hadn't had great luck with these, but he followed her inside. "Do you know where we're going?"

"We're going to the other ship, the one from when Dublin… you know. That one."

The doors closed, and he felt the elevator drop.

He didn't feel Dmitry's thoughts, or he might have had the strength to finish him off just then.

Dmitry didn't carry the burden of morale qualms. He burned a vow of revenge into his soul, watching them both leave. He'd rolled away from the jagged edge of a control panel that was in his back, and his muscles were at last relaxing. He'd likely be in a wheelchair tomorrow, but pure hatred fueled him today. With his muscles unclenching, he was starting to move again. He heard Carolina just before those elevator doors closed. *Follow me…* she said. The little bitch apparently had a plan.

The flowing black orb, the *Lens* or whatever it was called, was no longer black. It was now murky and gray, devoid of the energy and sparkle it boasted earlier. He wondered what it really was, or if even *she* knew the answer. She certainly didn't show concern for it being broken. Maybe it was nothing, something she did to stall, to distract him so that her precious *daddy* could find her.

And it worked. They would live to regret that.

Dmitry climbed to his feet and traced the path he last saw them going. He found the gold elevator doors and waited for them to return. When it opened, he stepped inside, seeing drops of blood from Austin's cut hand. He gave a deep smile. Sure, he had a broken rib now, and he likely wouldn't be able to walk without a cane tomorrow. But his drive was greater. Wherever they went, he would follow.

CHAPTER 43

Austin held his hand against his stomach, applying pressure to the gash in his palm. He wasn't succeeding. By the time the elevator docked again, the floor was a red fingerpaint. It was a sinister color to complement his muddy white expedition outfit. While his appearance may have been the handiwork of repeated life-and-death struggles, Carolina seemed not to notice how he looked. In fact, she hardly seemed herself since getting on this elevator. The warmth, the elation at finding each other again, was somehow gone. She was gone, or it felt that way. Her thoughts were firmly on whatever it was ahead of them.

When the doors opened, Austin immediately recognized the room. It was hard to forget the aquarium wall, especially after the encounter he had with the creature up close. They had taken the stairs to get here the first time. He remembered scooting Carolina up on top of that aquarium wall, and the memory of her eyes when he couldn't follow. Her face when she realized it was a heartbreaking image he hoped to never relive.

Carolina stepped off the elevator and set a brisk pace, showing little interest in the familiarity of her surroundings as she headed directly to the big loading bay doors. Austin wished for a moment that she was following him and not the other way around, because that would mean that things were normal. Somehow, she knew with certainty where she was going, and that was a problem he had no way of facing. He stared at her, one of a dozen uncertain looks he'd given her, each of them leaving him more unsettled than before.

He couldn't hold his silence any longer.

"Kid, are you okay?"

"Of course I am."

He groaned. "Why do we want to go back to the alien ship?" he asked. He was probing, unsure.

"I destroyed our return shuttle. We need a craft that can take us to the Orbiter."

"The alien ship was destroyed too, during the fight with Dublin. We barely got away."

"The alien vessel is designed to withstand fire."

"How do you know that?" Austin asked.

Carolina looked at him, with an expressionless face, like a doll, and it stopped him midstride. "I just do."

"Then why did it come for *our* ship?" He hated every part of this conversation because each answer made it impossible to ignore the change in her. The knowledge she had came from the parasite; he had to accept it. But if she knew the ship was okay, then the parasite knew it too. He hadn't even gotten to the part where he wouldn't leave without Athen. This was a dangerous conversation for him, because this was his little girl.

"Because of me. Because I saw the fires and the explosion, and I believed it was destroyed… I don't know how to explain this. Since I thought it was destroyed, it has my thoughts just like I have its thoughts…"

She looked down at the admission.

"Hey, it's okay. We're way past that now," he said to be supportive. But in reality, this was crushing him. He just wouldn't let her see it.

"I was afraid of it taking our shuttle, so it decided to do it. It might have done it just to toy with us… I'm really not sure."

She held her head and then resumed the demanding pace.

"Hey, it's okay, whatever it is. It's okay," he said, hoping to lend some comfort. Still, he ached with worry. Here he was, following his daughter towards an alien ship that no human could pilot, and he suspected that she was going to do exactly that. His little girl wouldn't know such things. This was a problem, and it had no solution. How would he deal with this, except to do nothing? It was his daughter, after all.

Carolina found the small white train and entered, Austin not far behind. She traced a pattern across the control panel, and the glowing light display blinked green and blue. He stood by, pretending this was all totally normal. From now on, he just had to accept it. This was real; she was different, but it changed nothing. He was her dad, and he would protect her.

Maybe this wasn't so bad, maybe he was looking at it all wrong. It's not like he couldn't use the outside help, seeing as how they were utterly stranded on Paphos. If Carolina knew things that would help them off the planet, then maybe this was a good thing. Without Carolina's unique insight, weren't they worse off? Those thoughts did little to help the weight in his chest.

The white cabin doors opened on the monorail, and Carolina boarded without a word, followed by Austin. He watched her, but the whole time, Carolina looked out the window as the system engaged. Finally, he had to say it.

"Are you okay, kiddo?"

She blinked. "Of course, Daddy," she said and smiled. Austin smiled back, and the monorail sped them both away. Austin nodded his head, trying to accept her answer, wanting to accept it. But he knew she wasn't okay. He couldn't avoid this out of fear, even though he wanted to.

"Hey, look at me," he said after a moment. Carolina's big brown eyes took him in. "Who are you?" he asked.

He was not staring into the eyes of his daughter. Austin gulped, forcing himself to be calm, waiting for the answer she seemed to be contemplating. He wished he had never asked, because now he was terrified. He was terrified of getting an answer, an answer that never came. The monorail slowed down and docked. Carolina looked away and prepared to disembark. Truthfully, Austin was glad she didn't answer. In a cowardly way, he needed to go back to pretending for a minute that nothing was wrong.

He adjusted the bandage wrap on his hand, trying not to move his shoulder to do it. Between the cuts, the broken nose, and the rib, Austin wondered how much more he could take.

"We're gonna' get out of here, I promise," he said. It's just a thing to say, and he was saying it. Carolina stepped off the train, and Austin followed. The hangar dome was smoky, and the air was stiff. Austin looked up at the gap in the dome top where he had escaped, amazed at how he managed to get tangled in that foliage, amazed he was able to climb out. It was another miracle he survived that encounter. Looking around, he saw that most of the hangar was untouched by the blaze, which was hard to believe considering how quickly it spread. Perhaps the facility had some sort of sprinkler system to put out fires, one that he didn't get a chance to witness.

Carolina stopped suddenly.

"What is it?" Austin asked.

She glared across the hangar section, beneath the dome. Over the dividing walls, they both saw the purple top of the alien ship. Just then, something clattered, and Austin found himself seeking cover, while Carolina did not.

"Hide!" he ordered, waving her over. With a blank look, she turned her head to him and then forward again. Something was over there, but Carolina wasn't moving. When he took a look for himself, he found Athen. She was pushing a crate towards the ship on a mechanized dolly.

"Athen?" he called. "How did you get here?"

"She already knows we are here."

He looked at Carolina, as if the silence might elaborate what she meant. Her words made the hair on his neck bristle. It didn't help that Athen wasn't limping.

Carolina started shaking, convulsing.

"What is it? Carolina?" he begged, coming to her side.

Athen also cried out in pain, collapsing to her knees, stealing his attention back in time to see her open her mouth. Wispy tentacles stretched out of her mouth and then recessed back in.

"We can't do that!" Carolina yelled, gripping her hair, eyes shut. Austin didn't even know who she was yelling at.

"Can't do what?!"

"Run!" Carolina shrieked.

Too late. Athen leapt for them, covering the distance in a single move. By the time Austin responded, she tackled him. They rolled to the floor, and he managed to spin and grab her by the throat. Her neck was incredibly warm, feverish even. Athen was freakishly strong; she easily knocked his hand away. She leaned forward and opened her mouth again, revealing a pair of yellow eyes deep in her throat.

Sheer terror gave him a burst of strength. He pushed and scooted his hips back, creating enough space to kick Athen off of him. He forced himself to his feet. She stood too, but she didn't give chase this time. Instead, she held her stomach and doubled over, retching and choking for air. Austin stood still. Carolina was well away from both of them, though she wasn't holding her head in pain anymore. Athen's coughing became more violent.

"Oh God," he moaned, totally disgusted. The tendrils reached out of Athen's mouth. Next came the jellyfish parasite, wriggling out of her body with fleshy goo and mucus. Athen was on her hands and knees when it plopped on the floor in front of her. Austin had actually seen this once before, when the parasite had left Carolina. It was no easier to watch the second time.

Strong, slender tentacles came out of the parasite's mass, and it stood upright. It looked at Austin and then at Carolina, with yellow eyes that formed at will. It was trying to choose one of them. *Like hell,* he said, ripping the lid off one of the fuel crates. He knew first-hand how toxic the fumes were. He was ending this.

"Hey!" Austin roared, wielding the crate lid like a shield. The creature raised itself up, quizzically as tall as Austin, which he was not expecting. He readied to swing, but something wrapped around his ankle.

"Daddy!"

The parasite had slid a tentacle low; rising up was just a distraction before it made a move. Hell, he'd just done the same trick to Dmitry. The parasite squeezed, forcing him to the ground in pain. It then lunged, but the lid of the fuel crate blocked its considerable force, and it fell back. No doubt the contact with fumes against its soft flesh helped, which he intended to take full advantage of.

He rose and slammed the lid flat-end over the jellyfish. He felt it splatter beneath the blow. His determination soaring, he raised the lid over his head again. The limbs of the parasite retreated to its body, curling in pain. The only mercy he would show was a swift death.

The parasite was futilely trying to scoot away. No compassion stayed his efforts as he slammed it again. Flesh splattered in chunks as he swung up and down. He pummeled the creature without words, smashing it with the crate lid over and over until chunks and liquids were beyond any recognition. The parasite's body was not durable; it easily dismembered from the crushing blows. It wasn't until Austin could barely hold the weapon in his aching hands that he stopped beating the lifeless flesh.

Sweat dripped off his face, landing on the globs that remained of the parasite. He turned to face the others, finding Athen crouched on all fours as Carolina tended to her.

"It's over," he said and dropped the lid with a worthless clank. Carolina wouldn't look at him. Actually, she looked angry and hurt. He wondered why at first, except that maybe part of her was in mourning, the part that was connected to the creature. Or perhaps it was because she was a young, innocent girl, and she wasn't accustomed to the brutality he'd just exhibited.

Athen was clutching her stomach in pain.

"Are you better?" he asked.

"Yeah… I just… I…," she stuttered. Athen held her head as nausea took her in and out of consciousness. She held her forehead, blinking away the dizzy spell that had threatened her.

"Thank you, I think I'm okay now," she said to Carolina. "I remember everything. It's strange, but I remember it better than any other memory I have. I was fixing its ship… or it was, but through me," another wave of nausea came over her, and she stopped, forced to hold her head until it went away. "I don't ever want to feel that again," she finally said.

Carolina stared at the floor in shame.

Athen's face did little to hide the turmoil of being possessed by the parasite. And seeing it on her, he could only imagine what this had been like for Carolina. How was his little girl so strong that she could have gone through the same thing? His guilt was worse now than it had been before. How would he make this up to her? Therapy? He feared that it would fall tragically short of what she needed. Would he ever be able to get her help?

"How much of the ship is functional?" Carolina asked.

Athen blinked and wiped her eyes clear. She brushed her hair aside and thought for a moment. "Well… uhm," she stuttered, struggling to speak. Austin recognized what he was seeing; she was sifting through the creature's memories. "The fire wasn't as bad as we thought," she looked at Carolina with questioning eyes, the moment she said *we*.

"Go on," Carolina said.

Athen nodded reluctantly. "It's ready to fly. I—I remember adding fuel because the flight home, I mean, not Earth, but…*it's*… home was such a long journey," Athen said. It took her many pauses to get through that.

"So there's plenty of fuel right now to get us to the Orbiter," Austin added, taking some pressure off Athen. "So, now what?"

"We fly the ship to the Orbiter, and then we go home," Carolina said. Austin wished she had said *Earth*. He hated that he wanted to clarify.

CHAPTER 44

The three of them stood before the alien ship. A burnt air lingered in the hangar; the ship and everything around it were covered in black soot, evidence of the blaze prior. The intense fire had spread quickly, but then disappeared before causing much damage. Carolina turned her attention away from the vessel; she looked as though she were concentrating, but on what Austin didn't know, or didn't want to know. He knew what they were about to do, but he had yet to come to terms with it. At last, Carolina approached the alien ship, her image reflected in those few unmarred spots. She walked around it, studying its smooth, featureless shape. It looked like a massive, sideways, purple teardrop, resting on three pegs. Carolina reached up to its belly, then a button panel suddenly started glowing. She pressed it, and on the side of the ship, a door smoothly appeared. It morphed down into a ramp silently, effortlessly.

He groaned. Yes, he was witnessing technology far superior to anything on Earth, but he was increasingly uneasy about this. When it finished, Carolina walked up the ramp and disappeared inside the alien vessel. Athen followed behind her with a limp; the sight of its return had brought him some tiny comfort. She stopped midway up the ramp, feeling a little unsure of the idea.

"You're worried? What could we possibly have to worry about?" he chided.

He never saw it coming. Something bashed him over the back of the head, and he fell in an unconscious heap.

"There won't be room for you," Dmitry snarled. He stepped over Austin's dazed body, and a weighty pipe that he dropped clanked on the floor.

"Austin!" Athen cried.

"Daddy?"

"*Daddy. Daddy,*" Dmitry mocked. "I'm so sick of hearing it," he said, mixing both sarcasm and hate. He was far more disheveled than the last time she saw him, and he moved under clear discomfort.

Athen's face was ghostly. She stood between Dmitry and Carolina, shielding the child with her body for what it was worth. "Please," she managed to say. But there was something in his eyes that couldn't be negotiated with.

"Sorry, ma'am, your ticket has expired," Dmitry said, grabbing Athen by the hair. He yanked her neck at an angle, pulling sharply, and launched her off the ship's ramp. She fell almost a meter and landed poorly. She cried out in pain, clutching her wounded leg, unable to stand. Dmitry was also in pain; the effort seemed to hurt him, but he recovered as he gazed up the alien ramp.

Carolina appeared in the doorway.

He considered her posture. "You aren't planning to cower in fear, are you?"

"My dad comes with us," she declared.

"So full of surprises, you are. I was certain you would say something else entirely. No matter," he spat. His warped mind wasn't asking any questions as to why.

Carolina let him approach, and the nerve of her nearly sent him over the edge. If he could refrain from killing her, he would, because he needed her to fly them to the Orbiter. It was a big if. Just looking at her made his blood boil. Dmitry grabbed her by the hair and forced her inside the ship. The cabin lights came on when they boarded, glowing hazy colors of green against the dark purple walls. The control panels lit up blue and orange, illuminating in unison along what was presumably the cockpit.

Austin opened his eyes, coming to just as Dmitry disappeared inside the ship. His head ached fiercely, but judging by the pipe lying on the ground next to him, Dmitry was weakened, well below full strength. Otherwise, he shouldn't have been able to wake up.

He touched a wet spot on his skull and sat up, trying to make sense of what was happening. He spotted Athen in pain, on the floor near the ramp. The ship was still here; he could still do something.

He braced his hands and managed to climb to his wobbly feet. Carolina was in trouble. He had to get to her before something happened to his little girl. Austin staggered up the vessel's loading ramp.

Austin made it to the top and clutched the porthole for support. Inside, the cabin was spacious, with dark purple walls bathed in green light. He found Carolina. Dmitry had her by the hair. She spun and bit Dmitry's hand.

He screamed in pain, furious, and backhanded her. She collapsed from the strike.

Austin clenched his fists and prepared to kill this bastard once and for all. "Don't you touch her!" he screamed. Rage guided his unsteady feet as he charged.

Dmitry lunged at Carolina as she lay there, unconscious, unmoving. Austin was too far away to do anything about it.

"Stop!" he screamed, his soul coming through in the desperation only a helpless father knows. 7

Dmitry lunged, ready to stomp on her, defenseless.

Austin charged but never got within reach before Dmitry froze. Or rather, something stopped him. Dmitry's muscles twitched, his hands extended. He stumbled on his feet.

Something had happened, and Austin was still trying to figure out what. He covered his mouth in disbelief. "Oh no, please no," he begged.

Carolina's eyes were closed, but something was sticking out of her mouth. There was a long, organic limb that had shot out and impaled him in the chest. Blood dripped down it along the course of gravity, impaled directly in his heart. He was gasping at the red, quickly spreading across his white shirt. He was unable to do more than look; he could not even scream, though he tried. Then the tentacle ripped free of his chest and disappeared back inside her throat. Dmitry's knees gave out, and he fell, dead.

Her eyes remained closed. She looked just like a sleeping girl again.

Austin saw it, knowing he'd failed her. His girl was infected; she had something inside her. When they returned, she'd be gone forever, and he would be forced to explain it to her mother. Carolina would be quarantined, studied, ripped away from him, and endlessly examined. He knew the scientific community, and he knew he would never see her again if they ever found out. *Athen!*

She didn't see it, she couldn't find out.

Austin grabbed Dmitry and dragged his body as Athen stumbled up the ramp.

"What happened?" Athen asked. Blood painted the floor as he dragged Dmitry; the hole in his chest was the size of a thumb.

"I killed him," Austin said. How could he explain this? He needed to think, and fast.

"You killed him?"

"Yes, he was trying to hurt Carolina, so I killed him," he said curtly, dragging Dmitry around her. He positioned the lifeless body at the top and pushed it off. "Let's get going," he said. Athen watched Dmitry collapse on the floor outside the ship, nursing her leg to stand.

"How did you kill him?" she asked, studying the trail of blood.

"What?"

"I said, How did you kill him?"

"I… stabbed him. Hurry and get on board."

She seemed to accept his answer. Why not? Carolina was asleep as far as she knew. The girl couldn't possibly have done anything; it would be ridiculous unless you were the one who saw it. Athen carefully stepped over the blood and chose a seat, more from exhaustion than by choice. Her leg stuck out, unable to bend.

"Hey, kiddo, time to wake up," he said, kneeling next to Carolina. He couldn't help but be wary of her mouth as he tried to coach her awake. He moved slowly and announced himself, hoping to lend all certainty that he was not a threat. Whatever was protecting her had acted to stop the threat, to stop Dmitry. He carefully lifted her head and called her name again. "Wake up, kiddo, hey, wake up," he kept trying. Finally, she opened her eyes.

"Daddy?" she asked. He brushed her hair back and fought against the fear of being close to her. Her eyes were innocent.

"I'm here," he said, pulling her close to his chest. He held her there, feeling unsafe. Dmitry was dead because Carolina defended herself. Rather, *it* defended her. This changed everything, but only Austin knew it. What was he going to do?

She hugged him back.

How was he going to tell her?

He wouldn't.

Could he still get her home, like this?

That one, he still didn't know. But he would find a way; he would smuggle her in his luggage if he had to. As he thought that, he knew it wouldn't work. There were protocols and long debriefing sessions that his sponsoring company would put them through, and that was on a normal expedition. This expedition was anything but normal, and by the time he uttered the words *life form*, the debriefing session would become exponentially longer.

"What happened? Where's Dmitry?" Carolina asked.

He was quiet for too long. He hated lying to his daughter. "You don't have to be afraid of Dmitry; he's gone now."

"Thank you, Daddy," she said.

Austin said nothing. He didn't save her; she saved herself. His anxiety fluttered, knowing she could open her mouth and that thing could kill him at any moment. But she wouldn't if she were in control, but that begged the question, was she in control? The sudden vision of that *thing* shooting out of her mouth made him shiver.

"What's wrong?" she asked.

"Nothing. Nothing. I'm just glad you are okay," he said. Austin had to pull himself together. He had to think. Carolina didn't know what was in her, and Athen didn't know either, yet. Athen herself was likely contaminated, because the same parasite had entered her, too. Right now, only Austin knew this truth.

He would keep it that way, to protect her. That was his job. He was a good dad, and he would prove it. He would find a way to keep this secret.

Athen must have sensed the tension; she was studying him from her seat before he noticed.

"I'm feeling better now, thank you. But if we aren't waiting for anyone else, we should get going," Carolina said.

"What of Helena?" Austin asked.

"Dead," Carolina answered.

He didn't need to know how. "And Orlean?"

By the look on Athen's face, he was dead too.

"That leaves… well," Austin sighed, "…no one. Everyone is accounted for." He didn't name Dublin; the fiery crash was still emblazoned in his mind. And of course, Dmitry, but there was obviously no need to name him either. They were all that remained of the crew.

Carolina stood and walked over to the pilot's chair perched in front of a large curved windshield. She climbed into the oddly shaped seat, which was wide and poorly angled for a human, especially a twelve-year-old.

Austin sat across from Athen, who was fading in and out of pain. He couldn't imagine what she must be feeling, but he also couldn't help but wonder if it was more than just exhaustion. The parasite had entered her as well, if ever so briefly. Would Athen have a similar transformation? Would he soon be outnumbered? Austin shook his head. First things first, they needed to get off this planet. He would have time to think after that.

"You were right, Austin, you were right all along. We should have contacted Command immediately, maybe none of this would have happened," Athen said. "Once we get to the Orbiter, I'll radio in and tell them what happened."

"Yeah, that's protocol," he said, staring at the floor. But he couldn't let her do that, protocol or otherwise. It would expose Carolina. But exactly how he was going to stop it, he wasn't sure.

The ramp raised and morphed back into the wall of the ship. Carolina placed her hand on a sphere in the center of the dashboard, and lights surrounded her hand as instruments gave readings in alien script. He accepted what he was seeing, but he still hated it. Suddenly, the engines activated, and he felt a wave of uncertainty as the vessel moved. With the door closed and engines on, there was no turning back. Not that he would give up now. He braced a hand against the panel for liftoff.

Flight was a much different feeling; if it weren't for the images outside the cockpit, he never would have known they were flying. The dome above them retracted, and a heavy groaning of shifting earth followed. Pebbles and rock splattered the top of the vessel, popping and scraping in a hollow shower of dirt. The earth fell easily away from the cockpit, and he watched as the ground level came and went. Austin saw the barren rock he had marched across shrink slowly as they rose higher and higher. His stomach was begging to abort, and more than once, he watched Carolina for any sign of worry, of concern. He held on to her confidence as they were soon a hundred meters above ground and climbing. In actuality, he had never had a smoother liftoff, but still, he wished the pilot's windshield were not so large. The entire horizon could be seen. Now the ship moved faster. They had to be five hundred meters now and climbing. When they entered a cloud, Austin had to close his eyes the rest of the way. He knew how high up they had to go, and he had never felt so alone or helpless on any flight before. When he felt Paphos' natural gravity disappear, he knew they had left the atmosphere.

He was floating. He opened his eyes; the worst part was over. The first thing he saw was stars.

"Ahhh, that feels bad," Athen said as her leg adjusted to weightlessness.

"The Orbiter is coming around soon. I've charted a course that will dock us in three minutes," Carolina said.

"I only have a faint idea of how you know all these things, kid, but I'm damn glad you do," Athen said, grimacing as the pain in her leg settled.

In about three minutes, they'd all be on board the Orbiter. Three minutes, that was how long Austin had to figure out how to keep Athen from contacting command. She was only following procedure; he couldn't blame her for that.

He looked down at his hands. He'd let Dmitry live, even when he knew better, and it'd come back to bite him, hard. There was at least one way to keep her from contacting command, but it was the last thing he wanted. It meant he'd have to kill Athen.

No. No way. He'd find something else. She just couldn't be allowed to send the transmission.

Austin took a farewell look at Paphos as they orbited above it, at the rings softly circling without end. It seemed to be looking right back at him. He felt nothing as he stared at its blue and purple hues. The further he was from this cursed planet, the better.

"There it is," Carolina said, pointing at the Orbiter. It was only a speck in a sea of black at this distance. Athen smiled and floated over to Carolina, grimacing in pain as she did.

He could choke her to death. That would be painless, quick.

"I still can't believe you're flying this. God, this is amazing. This changes everything," Athen said. Her spirits had never been higher, between being saved and changing the course of humanity forever, despite everything that had happened.

Elation was something Austin couldn't entertain under these circumstances. They were two minutes away from docking inside the Orbiter. He couldn't hide the fact that they encountered an alien species if they came home with the alien vessel docked in the Orbiter. After killing Athen, he'd have to jettison the alien ship. They'd never know it was there; they'd pretend their own shuttle was lost, by some equipment failure in the loading bays. It'd be a tragedy of scientific loss that, again, only he would know anything about. Undoubtedly, the company would return to Paphos, at least to follow up on all of the claims. But during that time, he could disappear, and she with him. So at least, she'd still be safe. He was not equipped for these decisions. He at least needed more time to prepare for what he was about to do.

The Orbiter's features were visible now; it was long and round like a summer squash, purposely built to be unable to enter an atmosphere. Orbiters were built in space and would forever remain there. The belly opened wide as they neared, with Carolina guiding the ship to land. Austin smiled when he saw big, bright *CAUTION* signs. He didn't realize how homesick he felt until seeing a sign he could actually understand.

The craft docked through the gaping entrance and parked with a sliding platform. Big loading bay doors slid closed with a resounding *whoom*, and they waited as air flooded in. Once the room was pressurized, the signal lights came on, and then the Orbiter's artificial gravity re-engaged. As it did, they clanked the distance to the ground with a hearty lurch.

"Sorry!" Carolina said, suddenly, a nervous kid again. Austin looked around; they were jolted but otherwise in good shape. He saw the yellow signal lights outside become bright green, and it was safe to disembark the craft.

This time, the faux gravity wasn't so strange, probably because they had only been weightless for a little while. But noticing that was simply a distraction, an occupation in his mind since he was avoiding what he needed to do now. So far, Austin had not devised a better solution to his problem.

"Next time, we put her in charge!" Athen joked, patting Carolina on the shoulder. "We're here! I can't believe it," she added, her face becoming a little more serious as she looked at Austin. "It feels good, Austin, salvaging this alien ship to bring home. It means that after everything, no one died in vain," she said. They both knew there was much more to the story than that.

Austin stood at the exit and waited for the alien ramp to lower. When it finally opened, he watched it descend completely, taking in his first sights of the Orbiter's receiving dock. The sterile smells, devoid of all that pollen. The loading bay was a tall grey cubicle with a set of stairs and two control panels. Dublin's bag, the bag he had cursed himself for forgetting, lay on the bottom stairwell just as Dublin had said. Looking at that bag was another reminder of loss.

"We made it," Athen said, probing to cheer him up. After he wouldn't acknowledge her, she nudged him in the arm. "What's wrong?"

"Nothing," he said. He felt Carolina's arms squeeze him around the waist.

"We did it, Dad," she said.

He was quiet.

"Alright, let's radio in already," Athen said.

"Wait. I'm the ranking member of the crew; the Company would want me to do it," Austin said.

"At this point, Austin, who cares?" Athen replied.

They disembarked, and he let her walk in front.

She approached the control panel at the base of the loading bay stairs. She could use any control panel to send a message to Command; the Orbiter's computer was accessible all over. Austin went down the ramp and approached Athen with a heavy heart. He placed his hand over hers, stopping her from logging in.

She looked up to him. "Are you okay?"

He couldn't answer; he could barely look her in the eye.

"Austin?"

"Daddy, what's the matter?" Carolina asked.

"Nothing, kiddo."

"Austin, what's wrong?"

"Athen," he said and then swallowed. "Listen to me, listen carefully. We can't tell them what happened. We can't tell them any of it."

She blinked. "Why not?" she said, followed by a nervous laugh.

"Because we can't," he simply replied. She knew him well enough to know that he was deadly serious.

"You were the one who said we needed to follow protocol, let's just do it already," she urged.

She wasn't getting it. She just didn't see what he was trying to say. That was her answer; he had to accept it. He'd given her a chance, at least. What he was about to do next was for the good of his child. He knew in his heart that he had given Athen a chance. Now he needed to kill her, because if he didn't, his daughter would not be safe. As ugly a truth as it was, killing Athen was the only way to keep his daughter a secret.

"Okay. We will radio in. But like I said, I'll do it," Austin said, pushing her hand away.

"Have it your way," she replied, a little hurt and confused.

He opened the radio frequency. She'd been given a chance, though she didn't know it at the time. This was hard for Austin; he really liked her, and he lacked the stomach for murder. But the situation with Dmitry had taught him everything. It wasn't fair to her, but fair didn't matter. He just couldn't see any way around it. Letting Athen live meant losing Carolina. His daughter would be hurt, experimented on, and a prisoner for the rest of her life.

"Voice message, prepare to send… This is what remains of the Orbiter crew, the crew returning from Paphos Station One…" He was about to report that after a serious malfunction during the return voyage, there were only two survivors: Carolina and himself.

Athen stood in his space, close enough to kiss him.

"Wait," she said. She placed her hand on his wrist. "You are right. Of course you are," she said, staring into his eyes. She pointed to Carolina. "If they find out, if they ever found out…" she added.

Austin prayed she said the right words.

"You're her father, and… she knows things, things she shouldn't know. You're afraid they might hurt her, that they might take her away from you," Athen said.

"You have no idea," he replied, his voice so soft and pained it sounded like a whisper. He held back the flood waiting at the gate. "What are you telling me, right now?"

Athen never took her eyes from his. "We jettison the alien ship. The others died in a tragic accident; we can figure out the details later. Nobody knows what we went through, because I understand now. I know what's at risk for her," she said, choosing her words carefully. "We die with this secret."

"You better swear—"

"No one will find out!" she said.

The tears couldn't be stopped. "Thank you," he managed to say. Austin's breaking point had arrived. Every pain he had endured, every stress he had absorbed, every fear suppressed was now released. He didn't realize that Athen had activated the radio until he heard her speaking into it.

"After an incident that nearly ruined the entire mission, only three of us have survived, and we lost the landing craft as well. Some of the experiments and their data were salvaged. The survivors are preparing to embark home, finally," Athen said. She held eye contact with Austin the entire time.

"They'll want to come back to retrieve the bodies, the experiments, and then the insurance claims. They'll come here," he said.

"It buys us time. We can volunteer to return, be the ones to clean up."

He hadn't thought of that.

"We're in this together. All the way."

She said everything he needed to hear, and they shared a vow at this point. All they had to do now was explain four deaths and a missing shuttle. All they had to do now was bury the greatest scientific discovery of their lives and go home empty-handed.

They had a secret to keep.

The solution Austin had been desperately seeking had presented itself, and it was just in time, too. A moment later, and it would have been too late. It was one big problem down, a dozen little ones to go. But he could handle little problems.

His thoughts plagued him as they went about being normal for the next several minutes. What would become of Carolina's condition? Was Athen destined to have a similar transformation? Would their hypersleep monitoring trigger some alarm?

He was looking in the other direction, so he didn't see Carolina and Athen. They held eye contact with each other for several seconds, expressionless the entire time. Then Carolina nodded, and Athen resumed preparations for the return home.

Austin collapsed into his chair. The return voyage had begun. The answers to all of those questions had solutions, and he'd solve them one by one.

Nothing would stop him, no matter the stakes. Whatever did or didn't happen, he still had a job to do. He would protect his daughter.

The End

HISTRIA BOOKS

HISTRIA SciFi & Fantasy

Other fine books available from Histria SciFi & Fantasy:

For these and many other great books visit
HistriaBooks.com